VICTORS!

With the steady *clank-clank* of shifting actuators, a towering shadow emerged from the open door, a ten-meter shape more humanlike, and more menacing than the ugly little *UrbanMech*. Alex recognized that heavy-shouldered, roundheaded silhouette immediately and wondered where in all possible hells Wilmarth could have found hardware like that.

The *Victor,* eighty tons of armor and death, creaked and whined clear of the open 'Mech bay doors. Close behind the first came a second *Victor,* its head turning as it surveyed the battle wreckage of the courtyard.

Victors! I had been all Alex could do to take down that single, lightweight *UrbanMech.* Two *Victors* . . . stopping them was not something a pair of lightly armed humans could even attempt.

"I think, lad, we'd best get the hell oot' here," McCall said.

"Couldn't have put it better myself, Major. Let's move!"

But the *Victors* were crashing toward the barbican as fast as their massive legs could carry them.

Escape was impossible. . . .

BATTLETECH®

TACTICS OF DUTY

William H. Keith, Jr.

A ROC BOOK

ROC
Published by the Penguin Group
Penguin Books USA Inc., 375 Hudson Street,
New York, New York 10014, U.S.A.
Penguin Books Ltd, 27 Wrights Lane,
London W8 5TZ, England
Penguin Books Australia Ltd, Ringwood,
Victoria, Australia
Penguin Books Canada Ltd, 10 Alcorn Avenue,
Toronto, Ontario, Canada M4V 3B2
Penguin Books (N.Z.) Ltd, 182–190 Wairau Road,
Auckland 10, New Zealand

Penguin Books Ltd, Registered Offices:
Harmondsworth, Middlesex, England

First published by Roc, an imprint of Dutton Signet,
a division of Penguin Books USA Inc.

First Printing, August, 1995
10 9 8 7 6 5 4 3 2 1

Series Editor: Donna Ippolito
Cover: Romas Kukalis
Mechanical Drawings: Duane Loose and FASA art staff

Roc REGISTERED TRADEMARK-MARCA REGISTRADA

BATTLETECH, FASA, and the distinctive BATTLETECH and FASA logos are trademarks of the FASA Corporation, 1100 W. Cermak, Suite B305, Chicago, IL 60608.

Printed in the United States of America

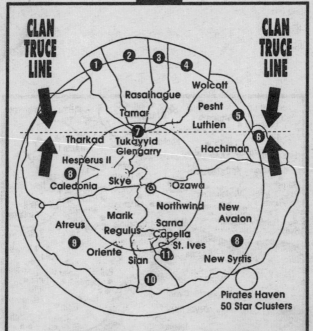

MAP OF THE INNER SPHERE

1 • Jade Falcon/Steel Viper, 2 • Wolf Clan, 3 • Ghost Bear,
4 • Smoke Jaguars - Nova Cats, 5 • Draconis Combine,
6 • Outworlds Alliance, 7 • Free Rasalhague Republic,
8 • Federated Commonwealth, 9 • Free Worlds League,
10 • Capellan Confederation, 11 • St. Ives Compact

Map Compiled by COMSTAR.
From information provided by the COMSTAR EXPLORER SERVICE
and the STAR LEAGUE ARCHIVES on Terra.

© 3056 COMSTAR CARTOGRAPHIC CORPS.

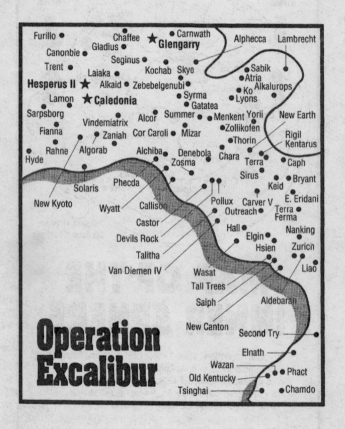

Operation Excalibur

Prologue

Ryco Pass
Glengarry, Skye March
Federated Commonwealth
0952 Hours, 17 April 3056

Laser fire flashed, a dazzling strobe of ruby brilliance searing through the swirl of smoke and dust. *Close!*

Alexander Carlyle's ARC-4M *Archer*, seventy tons of towering, twin-fisted, steel-edged destruction, lurched across soft and uneven ground, each step a test of uncertain footing. Ryco Pass was an arroyo through the arid, near-desert terrain southeast of the Glengarry town of Halidon, a wide, steep-sided gully with a floor that was silt-soft layers of powdery, bone-dry sediments and sand washed down from the distant Teragorma Hills by snow melt and flash floods. Firmly packed beneath, the upper layers were soft enough to shift and give beneath each of the *Archer*'s ponderous steps, threatening to pitch the lumbering, heavy 'Mech to the ground.

Alex, his neurohelmet relaying the feedback of impulses necessary to let him keep his twelve-meter-tall combat machine balanced with each swing of a leg or arm, countered the uneven ground without having to think about it. His full attention was locked on four steadily advancing blips scattered across the gully less than two hundred meters ahead. He couldn't see them yet, not with his naked eyes, anyway—his "Mark I eyeballs" as old Davis McCall might say.

The battle had been raging off and on, a broken and disjointed running engagement, for the past twenty minutes now, and smoke hung in the still air like white, filmy curtains. But a 'Mech's other electronic senses could see what human eyes could not. The enemy was just ahead now, screened by battle smoke, their four-'Mech vanguard well in the lead of the main body.

"Gold One! Gold One!" crackled over Alex's tactical channel. "Lad, what the blazes are ye doin'?"

That thick Caledonian burr was Davis McCall, the big, blunt, heavily muscled veteran who was Alex's number two in the Command Lance.

"Gold Two, this is Gold One," Alex called back. "You've got the unit, Davis."

As if Davis McCall hadn't been running things all along, him and the other old hands from the Gray Death Legion.

"Negative, lad! Ye dinnae need t' do this!"

Alex didn't answer, save to increase the lumbering speed of his *Archer* down the broad, steep-sided gully. He *did* need to do this. There was no other way.

For hours now, the Gray Death Legion, under Alex's temporary command, had been battling for its life. Rebel forces—his warbook program had them pegged as elements of the Fourth Skye Guards under the command of General Kommandant von Bulow—had caught the Legion at daybreak in Halidon, mauling them severely. Somehow they'd managed to break contact and retreat, but von Bulow had shown an uncharacteristic zeal, doggedly pursuing what was left of the Legion without stopping to rearm or resupply. The General was obviously convinced he had the Legion forces on Glengarry right where he wanted them, and he wasn't about to open his fist and let them slip away.

But Alex was determined that the Gray Death Legion would escape; its secret base in the Glencoe Highlands lay just a few tens of klicks further to the southeast. If they could reach that sanctuary, if they could find just a few precious hours to repair the worst of the damage suffered in the trap at Halidon . . .

Alex could see only one way to slow von Bulow's relentless advance. The Skye rebel forces must be nearly as spent as the Legion was right now . . . they *must* be! The pursuing MechWarriors would be tired—and they'd be cautious, despite von Bulow's urgings to press forward and run the Legion's survivors down. All Alex had to do was give them a hard, hard push right where they weren't expecting it.

Long-range missiles howled overhead, scrawling white contrails down the Glengarry sky. Explosions thundered in the distance as the Legion rear guard continued trying to break contact. Alex ignored the missiles, ignored the continuing flash and pulse of 'Mech lasers.

One hundred meters, and closing. Any moment now . . .

There! Movement, highlighted by the targeting crosshairs projected onto Alex's HUD by his *Archer*'s Instatrac Mark XII targeting computer. Data cascaded down the right-hand side of the HUD, repeating columns of text flickering across the secondary monitor. The pursuers were light and medium 'Mechs, probably an ad hoc pursuit unit thrown together from the remnants of the enemy's recon and medium lances. A VND-3L *Vindicator* and a *Commando,* those two alone massing as much as Alex Carlyle's *Archer.* And spread out to left and right were a thirty-five-ton WLF-2 *Wolfhound* and a forty-ton *Assassin,* armored monsters confidently closing in for an easy kill.

With his *Archer* out-massed more than two to one, Alex's lone hope was that those four had already suffered combat damage, either in the melee as the Legion rear guard had opened up on them just moments before, or hours ago, at Halidon. Zooming in with his *Archer*'s long-range optics, he scanned the approaching enemy for signs of damage and was rewarded by the sight of torn and cratered armor. *Yes!* There was *still* a chance!

The problem was, Alex was already low on LRMs, with just twenty-eight rounds left in his *Archer*'s tubes, and one more reload of twelve in reserve. When those were gone, he would have to rely on his lasers . . . and on the brute-force slugging power of his already battered *Archer.*

Range and targeting data scrolled down the border of his HUD. Alex pivoted his *Archer*'s torso left while maintaining its dead run toward the enemy. Reacting more by instinct than by any certain knowledge of target acquisition, he punched the firing key, triggering a spread of Doombud long-range missiles. A dozen contrails scratched curving white lines across the intervening space, the missiles' white-hot motors showing briefly as a cascade of dazzling stars before they slammed home against the *Vindicator*'s upper works.

Alex was already shifting targets before his first missile struck; as orange bursts of flame and hurtling bits of scrapped armor exploded from the VND-3's chest and right arm, a second barrage was already shrieking toward the COM-5S *Commando* standing close beside its heavier consort. Doombuds blossomed, their ghastly orange petals unfolding faster than the eye could follow, slamming the *Commando* back with a jack-hammering salvo of blasts high on its chest.

For a deadly instant, the battlefield was wreathed in an impenetrable fog of boiling smoke and showering dust. Alex heard the dull chunk of a Doombud magazine slamming home in his *Archer*'s right torso launcher, and the wink of red-glowing discretes told him he'd just loaded his last twelve LRMs.

No matter. Alex Carlyle was caught now in battlefield madness, a wild and unreasoning berserker's lust that drove him on, unthinking, heedless of the enemy's greater numbers or his own 'Mech's weakness. He heard a full-throated scream of pure, raw fury sounding over his neurohelmet's com receivers, and it was seconds before he recognized the shriek as his own war cry. Continuing his wild charge, he crashed at full speed into the battered *Commando* with a mighty clash of steel on ringing steel.

The *Commando,* outweighed almost three to one by the Legion *Archer,* hit the ground flat on its back with a jolting crash, its fall throwing up a pall of roiling dust. Alex paused, triggering a third missile barrage, clearing the last of his right-side tubes with a point-blank volley into the *Assassin* advancing from the right, before slamming one huge, armored foot down onto the *Commando*'s torso.

Flame spurted from ruptured seams as short-ranged missiles stored within the 'Mech's hull detonated, the first blast of a rippling chain-reaction of flashing, thundering detonations that threatened to knock Alex down as well. He spun sharply right, recovering his balance on expertly flexing knees, unloading a pair of laser bursts into the *Assassin* as he moved. The *Assassin,* its right arm already badly damaged, seemed to crumple in that withering salvo of coherent light. Its right arm, the one mounting a Magna 400P medium pulse laser, was torn wide open from elbow to shoulder. Internal wiring and power feeds sparked and flashed in a cascade of short circuits as the arm went dead, dangling uselessly by the 'Mech's side as the target damage readout on Alex's primary monitor showed compete power failure to its actuators.

Laser fire struck the *Archer* from behind, but Alex ignored the attack, loosing another barrage into the *Assassin* already in his sights. The *Assassin* went into a crouch, and Alex's readouts showed a sudden build-up of power; the *Assassin* pilot was readying for a jump. Lumbering forward, Alex triggered a final volley of lasers at point-blank range, slashing through the *Assassin*'s already mangled armor. Closing in to touching distance, his *Archer*'s steel fist rising high overhead, he brought the arm down in a hammerblow that connected with the *Assassin*'s back and armored left shoulder with an ear-tearing shriek of tortured metal. The *Assassin* tried to respond with a left-armed swing of his own, clumsy and badly timed. Alex blocked it, then smashed his right fist into the other 'Mech's torso. Stricken, the *Assassin* dropped to hands and knees as though in submission before the blind and battle-maddened fury of the rampaging *Archer*.

But before Alex could finish the job, more laser bolts slammed into the *Archer* from the rear. Others narrowly missed his 'Mech and burned away bits of the stricken *Assassin* instead, so closely were the two 'Mechs engaged. Alex pivoted hard, pushing away from the fallen *Assassin*. The *Wolfhound* was fifty meters away, the large Cyclops XII laser in its right arm loosing a dazzling beam that slashed high across the *Archer*'s chest.

Alex's heat levels, already high after his long run to meet the rebel vanguard, soared at the raw caress of the laser. Ignoring the warning discrete flashing across his instrumentation, he triggered his last twelve missiles, hurling them in a close-packed swarm straight into the *Wolfhound*'s center of mass. Explosions flared, white-hot flashes of vaporized metal and hurtling bits of shrapnel. Alex followed up with a salvo of laser fire, snapping off shot after shot after shot, before turning once more, this time to deal with the rebel *Vindicator*.

The last of Alex's luck—like the effects of surprise won by his suicidal dash into the enemy formation—was very nearly used up. At forty-five tons, the *Vindie* was the heaviest of his four opponents and arguably the most dangerous. He'd hoped to knock it down a notch or two earlier on, but the lighter rebel 'Mechs had blocked him, and now the *Vin-*

dicator was raising its massive Warrior particle projection cannon.

It was extremely close range for a PPC—possibly too close. Alex lunged to the side, hoping to sidestep the deadly weapon's aim, but the *Archer* was too big, too slow, too battered by earlier damage. A searing blue-white bolt of ball lightning burned into his empty left missile rack, vaporizing the hatch, shredding electronics and circuit relays like tissue. The blast sent an electromagnetic pulse surging through the *Archer*'s primary feeds and power couplings; blue sparks curled and twisted off his instrumentation, as outside, the excess charge grounded itself in jaggedly forked bolts of lightning.

"Warning! Warning!" a computer's voice sounded in the cockpit. *"Major damage to primary coils and power feed. Major damage to relay circuits. Shutdown imminent. Shutdown—"*

Reflexively, savagely, Alex slapped the shutdown override and manually engaged his backup relay net, buying himself . . . how much time? Seconds? As much as a minute? The damage was bad, the heat build-up deadly. Words written in flame-red LED alphanumerics scrolled across his HUD, recommending that he eject.

He loosed four laser bolts in rapid-fire succession squarely into the *Vindicator* at close range, took two unsteady steps forward, and triggered four blasts more. Clumsily, the *Vindie* tried to swivel its head, bringing its single medium laser to bear, but Alex circled right, sidestepping, forcing the *Vindicator* to rotate its torso, then its entire body, in an attempt to track the *Archer,* and all the while Alex was slamming bolt after bolt of coherent light home, ripping away whole slabs of armor, smashing the exposed cylinder of the laser mounted on the side of the helmet-like head, bearing down on scabbed and heat-blackened strips and plates on the enemy 'Mech's side and legs where it had taken hits earlier and must already be weakened.

The *Wolfhound*'s lasers fired from behind and Alex's right knee buckled, sending his combat machine crashing full-length to the ground. The jolt slammed Alex so hard that his vision went red for an instant and the concussion nearly knocked him senseless, despite the padded harness anchoring him in his cockpit seat. Rolling, he tried to raise the

'Mech, but both the *Wolfhound* and the *Vindicator* were closing in now, confident of a kill. . . .

Missiles streaked in from the left, exploding against the *Vindicator*'s leg and torso armor. For the briefest of instants, Alex thought that one of his foes had accidentally fired on a comrade; "friendly fire" was always a deadly and terrifying possibility in a close-in dust-up like this one. Swinging his torso left as he levered into a sitting position, he was startled to see the billowing dust cloud and flaring plasma jets of a *Shadow Hawk*—one of *his Shadow Hawk*s, which meant it was either Sergeant Propst or—

"Alex!" a familiar voice, young and adrenaline-edged, called over the Legion's tactical channel. "Alex, what in the name of Blake are you doing?"

"Get clear, Davis!" Alex yelled as the *Shadow Hawk* grounded, its legs flexing deeply to absorb the impact. As the enemy 'Mechs turned to face this new and unexpected threat, he brought the *Archer* upright and at the same time pivoted the torso about until his targeting cross hairs slipped across the image of the battered *Vindicator,* turned now to expose its profile and rear. Laser light flared; armor on the *Vindicator*'s side and shoulder exploded in a white haze of metallic vapor. "Damn it!" Alex yelled again. "Davis! Get out of there!"

But Davis Carlyle Clay was not so easily or casually dismissed. Straightening, the *Shadow Hawk* turned to the left, the long, heavy muzzle of the Imperator Ultra-5 autocannon mounted over the 'Mech's left shoulder dropping into line with the *Vindicator*. With a thunderous *slam-slam-slam* of high-velocity, high-explosive shells, Clay's autocannon barrage walked across the *Vindicator*'s chest and legs, smashing and twisting already damaged armor, tearing, gouging, ripping man-sized chunks free and hurling them through the smoke-clotted air.

Davis Carlyle Clay was Alex Carlyle's number four in the Legion's First Battalion, First Company Command Lance . . . and his best friend. Young, impulsive, a born warrior if you could overlook his recklessness, Davis was the son of one of the original MechWarriors recruited into the Gray Death Legion. His name reflected the interweavings of friendship and camaraderie within the Legion; he'd been named for Major Davis McCall, another of the Legion's old hands, and for Grayson Carlyle, the Legion's founder.

Alex's father.

And now Davis was squared off almost toe-to-toe with the *Vindicator* and the *Wolfhound,* trading shot for shot for shot in a furious exchange of sizzling laser bolts. Clay's *Shadow Hawk,* Alex knew, was already bone-dry for long-range missiles. That salvo a moment ago had probably emptied the last of his SRMs, and he must be running low on autocannon mag reloads by now as well. When his last high-explosive round was expended, he'd have nothing left but the laser mounted on his right forearm. His 'Mech had been badly worked over at Halidon, too, and there were great, blackened craters and scars pocking the machine's torso and upper works. Under the deadly, concentrated fire from the two Fourth Skye Guard 'Mechs, Clay's *Shadow Hawk* appeared wreathed in a coruscating aura of red and gold light as the dust scuffed into the air mingled with smoke, growing thicker and more opaque. In the shifting, uncertain light and haze, the *Hawk* appeared to be bleeding ... as steaming, dark green coolant gushed from a half-dozen rents in its armor. Davis Clay's 'Mech must be on the verge of going into heat shutdown as well.

But the two rebel 'Mechs had made a critical mistake. They'd seen Alex's 'Mech go down, then turned their backs on him to hammer at the newcomer, believing him out of the fight for good.

With the *Archer* on its feet once more, Alex guided it forward, moving in behind the *Vindicator,* bringing his 'Mech's huge fists together and swinging them, hard, the blow connecting with the back of the *Vindie*'s head and flame-blasted shoulders.

Metal shrieked protest and gave. The shock of the impact nearly dropped Alex's 'Mech a second time, but somehow he kept his feet as the *Vindicator* lurched forward, the back of its head smashed in, sparks leaping from severed power leads like swarming fireflies. Its pilot was probably dead before the big machine crashed face-down in the dust.

The *Shadow Hawk* slammed a last handful of explosive rounds into the WLF-2; a spent magazine cassette spun clear of the autocannon's breach, and the heavy weapon fell silent. Still standing in a literal hail of fire, Clay continued to loose bolt after bolt of laser energy into his remaining opponent. But he was badly outmatched in weaponry now. The *Hawk* outmassed the *Wolfhound* by twenty tons, but the

WLF-2 mounted three Defiance B3M medium lasers in its chest, and the Cyclops XII large laser in its arm alone outmatched Clay's single operational weapon.

With the *Vindicator* down, Alex pivoted toward the *Wolfhound,* his targeting cross hairs centering on the machine's back where its armor was weakest. As he triggered a barrage, the WLF's rear-mounted Defiance laser opened up in reply, striking the *Archer*'s right arm.

Alex's heat monitor showed his 'Mech's heat off the scale, and his computer was once again advising him to eject. Ignoring the computer's voice and alphanumerics, he kept firing, aiming for the ball-and-socket-mounted barrel of the WLF's rear laser, and then, as the weapon vanished in a white-hot flare of vaporizing metal, he walked the fire up the enemy 'Mech's back.

"Alex!" came Davis Clay's cry over the tactical link. "Alex! I'm burning!"

"Punch out!" Alex yelled back. The *Wolfhound* was trying to turn to bring its full battery of front-mounted laser weaponry to bear on the *Archer,* but Alex kept the ARC-4M moving, circling the damaged WLF as quickly as it could turn. An explosion tore access panels from the *Wolfhound*'s side, sending them dancing and spinning across the wreckage-littered floor of the arroyo.

"Alex! Help me!"

But Alex was too far gone in the blood-lust of battle. The *Wolfhound* filled his vision, his mind, its flame-wreathed form shimmering beneath the lash of his lasers as he moved closer. Slowly, reluctantly, the other 'Mech collapsed, dropping to its knees. Smoke was curling from seams and openings as sparks jittered and flashed in the shadowy, wire-packed recesses revealed by the blown panels. Abruptly, a curved sheath of armor slid back on the machine's sloping head; there was a flash, and then the *Wolfhound*'s pilot was rocketing clear of the open cockpit, his seat trailing a column of yellow-white flame. The WLF-2 balanced there for a moment; then, as the pilot's chute opened, another internal explosion pitched it to the ground with a ragged crash.

Only then did Alex turn to check on Davis. . . .

The *Shadow Hawk* was on fire, with black, oily smoke spilling from a crater in the 'Mech's chest just below the cockpit spaces, and orange flames licking about the machine's upper torso. *"Davis!"*

He started toward his friend's *Shadow Hawk* just as a fireball blossomed from the 'Mech's interior, and the right arm spun clear, trailing smoke from its half-molten stump. The fire spread. Alex couldn't be sure what was burning; possibly the *Hawk*'s power plant had ruptured and ignited the tungsten-steel struts and internal bracings. Even steel will burn when the temperature is high enough. . . .

"Davis!" he yelled. "Punch out! Punch out, damn it! Punch out!"

The only reply was a shrill scream of raw agony, ragged in his neurohelmet headset.

In seconds, Alex reached the *Hawk,* which stood immobile now, burning furiously. His own heat was still high, and this close to that inferno it would go higher still, but he ignored it, trying to figure out some way to stifle the flames, to rescue his friend.

"Davis!"

The screaming stopped. There was a long and death-still silence, punctuated by the roar of flames, the hum of Alex's instruments, the shrill *ping* of overheated metal.

"Davis! Do you read me? Come in!"

Or, rather, the *outward* screams, the screams coming to Alex over his taclink, had stopped.

But he could hear them still in his mind, going on and on and on. . . .

1

The Residence, Dunkeld
Glengarry, Skye March
Federated Commonwealth
0275 Hours, 10 March 3057

With a shout to rival the screams echoing in his mind, Alexander Carlyle came full awake. He was sitting upright in bed . . . in *his* bed, in his quarters within the Residence, the ancient, hilltop structure that the Legion had converted to a planetary defense facility and home base fortress. His sheets were soaked, his naked body coated with a clammy sheen of sweat. Trembling, he slumped back onto his pillow, eyes wide and staring up into the darkness. Sleep, he knew from past experience, would not return to him anytime soon, nor did he relish the thought of the dreams that were certain to return.

"Computer!" he called into the darkness. "Lights!"

Obediently, the wallscreen displays came up, illuminating the room. Decorated in Glengarry's early colonial period, the bare, ferrocrete walls were covered over with thin vidscreen panels that could show real-time imagery from high atop the castle ramparts, or any desired recvid in the base archives. At the moment, they played a simple, mindless light show of interpenetrating shapes and colors, a design in greens and blues by Tomo, the twenty-fifth century New Edinburgh master, that was intended to be restful.

To Alex, it felt as though he were trapped underwater, that

at any moment he would drown. "Computer," he said. "Normal lighting."

The Tomo designs faded away to a soft, warm light, balanced to match the normal daytime illumination of Glengarry's orange sun. Swinging his legs out of the bed, Alex rose and padded barefoot across the room to the master terminal. "Computer, voice connect, MedTech Jamison," he said, sliding into the chair. "Negative vid."

A window opened in the portion of the vidscreen above the terminal, but it remained blank save for the word "Connecting" flashing on and off. The flashing went on for some time, longer than Alex had expected, before the word was replaced with a new legend. "Connection established. Negative vid."

"What is it?" came a woman's voice over the room's speaker system. Her tone was brusque and not a little annoyed.

"Ellen?" Alex asked. "Alex. Did I wake you?"

There was a moment's pause. "It's oh-two-seventy local and you ask me if you woke me up?"

"Sorry. I . . . I thought you had the duty tonight."

"Watson's on tonight." The annoyance faded somewhat, swallowed in the sound of a yawn. "What's the matter? The dream again?"

"I can't sleep, Ellen." Slowly, almost unwillingly, Alex looked down at his hands. They were still shaking, a faint, barely perceptible trembling that was completely beyond his control. "I'm having trouble sleeping," he finished, unhappy with his lame response.

"I'll be right down."

"No, listen. Patch me through to Watson. I'm really sorry I woke you up."

"I'm up. I'm up. Ten minutes to get some clothes on."

The screen's legend shifted to "Transmission ended."

Rising from the chair, Alex glanced down at himself. One year after Halidon, four months after the savage and desperate guerrilla campaign that had followed, and his torso was still so lean and stringy that he could count his ribs.

He decided he'd better put something on as well. Being a MedTech, Ellen Jamison wasn't prudish about male nudity, but Alex didn't want her to think he'd rousted her out of bed in the middle of the night for anything more than a chemical sedative. A word to the computer unfolded his closet access, and a few moments later he was wearing a jumpsuit, dark gray and short-sleeved, with the gray-on-red skull emblem of the Gray Death Legion.

The dream . . .

Again . . .

The Glengarry campaign had begun over a year ago, with the revolt of Skye separatists against the Federated Commonwealth. Colonel Grayson Death Carlyle, Alex's celebrated father, had passed temporary command of the Gray Death Legion to his son, with orders to keep the peace on the FedCom world of Glengarry.

Command? Yeah, right. With old-time 'Mech vets like Davis McCall, Hassan Ali Khaled, and Charles Bear in the unit, his stint as regimental commander had been more of a training simulation, with a whole company of instructors to grade his performance.

Unlike those of a simulation, though, the battles, the suffering, and the deaths had been all too real. At Halidon, the Legion had suffered a sharp and bitter defeat. Alex's charge against the vanguard of the rebel pursuers at Ryco Pass was credited with saving the Legion, but at a terrible personal price for Alex. And after that, seven long months of guerrilla warfare, of hit-and-run strikes against the rebel forces who'd occupied Glengarry's population centers. In particular, there'd been a bitter campaign against the enemy's supply lines, concentrating on Glengarry's maglev network.

But where the rebels had access to the factories and machine shops and other high-tech privileges of power, each loss the Legion suffered was irretrievable. Fresh recruits had dwindled to a trickle as the rebel government had tightened its grip on Glengarry's civilian population. New 'Mechs and the parts to keep the old ones running were scavenged from battlefields . . . or the Legion had done without. It had been the most bitter and unrelenting of all types of warfare, a guerrilla conflict that the rebels would win if they could bring the Legion to bay, just once forcing a stand-up fight. . . .

It had been, from start to finish, an assignment seemingly calculated to test the young Carlyle's performance under pressure and his ability to accept the responsibility that went with command.

"You have a responsibility to your people, to the men and women who look to you for leadership." So spoke the nor-

mally taciturn Charles Bear, just before Killiecrankie Pass, and the concluding action of the long Glengarry campaign. Bear, a legend within the mercenary community, was a third-generation MechWarrior from Tau Ceti II who, like McCall and Khaled, had been among the first to join Alex's father almost thirty years ago, when the Gray Death Legion was first being organized. He'd been in secluded retirement on Glengarry, until he'd heard about the desperate straits the Legion was in. His appearance at Killiecrankie, and in particular the morale boost generated simply through his unexpected arrival, just might have been what turned the tide at last in the Legion's favor.

Responsibility.

Yeah, it had been Alex's responsibility that Davis Clay had died horribly, trapped in the cockpit of his burning *Shadow Hawk* at Halidon. It had been his responsibility that Hassan Ali Khaled had been badly wounded at the fight in Lochabar Forest, six months later.

Hell, it had been his responsibility, from first to last, that the Gray Death Legion had suffered over sixty percent casualties on Glengarry by the time his father had finally arrived to lift the siege and rescue him.

Sixty percent casualties . . .

It was a grim and bloody statistic, and not one that spoke well of his handling of the campaign. It was all the worse, in Alex's opinion, that somehow or other he'd been painted as a hero, the man who'd held the Legion together and kept the Fourth Skye Guard rebels off balance until the relief force could arrive. Truthfully, the rebels had been in nearly as bad a shape as the Gray Death by the time the balance of the Legion's "Old Guard" and the famous Northwind Highlanders had arrived. Alex's campaign against the maglev lines had been remarkably successful.

But at what a horrible, at what a *damnable* cost. Alex knew well what the people who called him the "Hero of Glengarry" did not—that Bear and Khaled and the other old-timers of the Legion had propped him up in his command and covered his mistakes, that he was not ready for the pressures of that command and probably never would be.

A chime sounded.

"Enter."

Ellen Jamison was a tough, attractive brunette, a skilled MedTech, one of the recruits who'd joined Alex's fugitive forces during the rebellion. She'd started out visiting Alex's men at their hideout in the heavily forested Glencoe Highlands, bringing antibiotics and bandages, and treating the more serious injuries with a portable medkit. After rebels had killed her husband and eight-year-old son and burned her home, she'd signed on with the Legion permanently.

One section of the vidscreen wall slid open and she walked through. In one hand she carried a slender circlet of black plastic, the kind designed to be worn around the head, with a hand-controller attached by wires. "So. Restless night?"

"I guess so." Alex nodded toward the device in her hand. "What's that?"

"Electronic sedative." She held it up for his inspection. "Modulates your alpha waves and passes the neural messages that lower adrenaline production, ease muscular tension, and generally help you relax."

He frowned. "I was hoping for something a little stronger."

"What, pills? You know my feelings about that."

Ellen was notorious for her dislike of any chemical cure even remotely addictive, physically or psychologically. "Well—"

"Or sex? I can't help you there, I'm afraid."

"I didn't mean—"

"Oh, it's not that you're unattractive," she continued in a matter-of-fact tone as she unwrapped the wiring to the headset. She gestured for him to lie back on his bed. "Quite the contrary, in fact. But it wouldn't do to flaunt a relationship like that in front of the men and women of your command."

"I'm *not* interested in sex, MedTech," Alex said bluntly. "I just want to get some sleep."

"This is the ticket, then." Standing by his bed, she slipped the circlet over his head and made some adjustments to the fittings. "Though I wonder . . . How's Caitlin these days?"

"Caitlin? What does she have to do with it?"

"You said you weren't interested in sex. I was wondering whether that was a symptom of your depression or if you'd had a fight with Caitlin."

"Depression?" He shook his head. Conversations with Ellen Jamison tended to be jerky, confused exchanges. The lady had a lightning-quick mind that could jump and veer unpredictably. "What depression?"

She was closely studying the readouts on the hand controller and making subtle adjustments to a rheostat knob. Alex could feel the tingle of a current flowing through contacts in the circlet. "A thousand years ago," she told him, "you likely would have been diagnosed as suffering from shell shock or combat fatigue. 'Post Traumatic Stress Disorder,' or 'PTSD,' was the clinical term for the condition. It means you've seen too much, suffered too much, and your mind is telling you to curl up in a tight little ball and let the universe go to hell."

"I thought that was cowardice." Alex was surprised at how bitter the words sounded in his own ears.

"That too. Combat does terrible things to a person. Especially if he lets himself *feel* too much. It can turn a strong man into an emotional cripple. It can knock every prop of decency and social protocol out from under you and leave you unable to trust or believe in anyone, not even those closest to you. It can make you withdraw so completely from reality that everybody else thinks you're a coward . . . or catatonic. Modern-day warfare, especially—in spite of all the conventions and the courtly formalities—will chew up a man's soul in no time at all. I think that's because it pits frail, unprotected human beings against twelve-meter BattleMechs. Man against killer machine, you know? Only the man doesn't have a prayer of survival, not unless he's part machine himself."

The circlet was humming softly now, though Alex found himself unable to concentrate on the sound. He was feeling more relaxed, yet sleep was the last thing on his mind.

Sleep was where the nightmares awaited him, and he couldn't face that. Not yet.

"You're saying I should be more like a machine? Lose my emotions? My feelings?"

"Of course not. But you might have to do some hard self-evaluation about whether or not you're cut out to be a MechWarrior. Even heroes have to retire sometime."

"Heroes." The single, sharp word was almost a curse, an indictment of the events that had placed him where he was.

"You're the Hero of Glengarry. Or had you forgotten?"

"No. I remember. All too well. I'm finding it kind of hard to live up to the role."

"Nothing surprising there."

"It wasn't me that held the Legion together during the campaign, Ellen. You know that. You were there."

"Seems to me you did all right."

"Seems to me I was being propped up by Major McCall and most of the other old-timers in the regiment. Half the time I never even knew what I was doing."

"I'm not a military person, Alex. I wouldn't know a flank march from a flank steak, well done. But it seems to me that any good military commander is going to rely on his more experienced subordinates for advice . . . and maybe even to jerk his tail out of the fire once in a while. You held the Legion together until the relief force arrived."

"Until my *father* arrived, you mean." Storming out of the sky at Inverurie . . . DropShips laden with fresh 'Mechs. And how the survivors of the Legion had gone wild at the sight, knowing that *the* Carlyle had returned!

"Do I detect some bitterness at that? Or is it jealousy?"

"Jealous? Of my father? I don't think so."

"Bitter, then. About having him come and rescue you, as you put it."

"Maybe. Maybe that's it." He sighed. "I think, Ellen, that I'm just very, very tired. I'm tired of trying to live up to the image expected of the son of the great Grayson Carlyle. I'm tired of living in his shadow, tired of trying to live up to the standards of tactical brilliance and leadership he set years before I was even born, tired of being compared to him, tired of never, never being quite good enough. . . ."

"There is another explanation, of course."

"Oh? And what is that?"

"That you're feeling sorry for yourself."

"Maybe that too." It was too much trouble to refute the charge. Besides, it didn't matter much, one way or the other. Nothing seemed to matter much, anymore.

"You thought about chucking it? About giving the whole thing up?"

Alex turned his head, trying to focus on Ellen. Somehow, in the past few moments, the room's decor had been returned to the blue-green movements of the Tomo abstract. Had he ordered that? He couldn't remember. Still, it wasn't unpleasant anymore. It was almost . . . restful . . .

"What . . . do you mean?"

"Just wondering." She was continuing to study the readout pad in her hand. "I mean, if you're not happy piloting a 'Mech, what else would you want to do?" When he didn't answer right away, she pushed ahead. "After all, Alex, it's not as though you have to live up to your father's ideals, your father's plans for your future, is it?"

"He didn't *make* me become a MechWarrior," he replied. But was that strictly true? The son of Grayson Death Carlyle and Lori Kalmar could hardly help but soak up the mythos, the language, the very atmosphere of what it meant to be a mercenary MechWarrior. Surely, there'd been the unspoken assumption all along that Alexander Carlyle would pilot a 'Mech someday. He could remember playing in 'Mech simulators when he was six years old and sitting around in the regiment's barracks lounge listening to the vets' war stories. He'd wanted to be a MechWarrior for as long as he could remember, not so much out of any thirst for glory or love of danger, but because he quite simply knew nothing else.

For several months, though, ever since the end of the Glengarry campaign, he'd been wondering if it might not be better to strike out on his own, to get away from the Legion—away from his parents, away from the men like Major McCall who'd been his mentors and his role models almost since he'd learned to walk. He'd thought about that a lot. He had some money—probably enough to buy passage to Galatea or one of the other big, mercenary hiring centers . . . maybe even Outreach. Forget about all that officer stuff and the responsibility of command. He'd hire out as an enlisted MechWarrior in some other merc unit, or even sign with a House unit.

Of course, he'd have to change his name. . . .

Damn it, could he *ever* escape his past, escape who and what he was?

It was possible. The three-dimensional volume of space known as the Inner Sphere was enormous beyond human comprehension. With a thousand worlds or more to choose from, he ought to be able to find a place for himself, a place where he was *not* known as the Hero of Glengarry . . . or as Grayson Carlyle's son.

More worrisome by far, though, were the conflicting thoughts raised by Ellen's question about what he would do if he were no longer a MechWarrior. On the one hand, he knew nothing else, could *imagine* doing and being nothing else. On the other, though, was the secret dread—one rarely examined and then never at all closely—that the seven months' campaign on Glengarry had crippled him emotionally. What had Ellen called it? PTSD? "Combat fatigue" sounded more to the point.

He felt, quite frankly, like he'd lost that vital warrior's edge, the keenness of mind and reflexes and senses that alone allowed a man to pilot a 'Mech in combat and survive. Recent training runs in the Legion's simulators had not been encouraging at all. The readouts indicated that he'd slowed by nearly twenty-five percent, that he tended to think about things now instead of reacting by training and battle-honed instinct. A skilled 'Mech pilot acted as though his Battle-Mech was his own body. *"Don't think so much!"* Vernon Artman, the regimental weapons master, had told him time after time. *"You've got to be one with your 'Mech!"*

One with his 'Mech? For months now, Alex had been *driving* his huge machine rather than becoming the perfect fusion of organic brain and steel-armored machine that was expected of any good MechWarrior.

What he had not dared to mention to anyone—especially Anders—was that every time he'd climbed into a simulator in the past four months, he once again heard Davis Clay's dying screams.

He never noticed when Ellen Jamison removed the circlet and left the room; he slept soundly for a time.

In fact, the dream didn't wake him again until it was very nearly light.

2

"*T*ha' bluidy wee Sasunnachs!..."

Davis McCall slumped back in his chair, his normally ruddy complexion gone so pale that the thick mottling of freckles and age spots across his face seemed a dark, sharp-edged brown by comparison. He reached up with one meaty hand and ran his fingers through his brush of red beard and hair, hair that long ago had begun shading to silver at the temples and around the ears.

He was in the lounge of the Legion's recreation area, a broad, low-ceilinged room with a sunken gaming area in the middle and numerous partly enclosed telecom stations around the periphery. At his back, a small group of Legion-naires was engaged in a vigorous exchange of good-natured insults and wagering as two of their number guided holo-graphic images of a pair of BattleMechs in electronic combat with one another.

They seemed to be paying no heed to the big Caledonian with his considerable bulk squeezed into one of the communications cubicles.

Good. McCall continued staring at the legend glowing on the large vidscreen in front of him.

END HPG TRANSMISSION
CHARGE CB 932
THANK YOU FOR USING COMSTAR

"Angus, Angus, y' wee scoundrel," he whispered softly. "Wha' kind a' dragh hae ye gotten y'sel' intae noo?"

Major Davis McCall rarely lapsed into the Gaelic-laced dialect of his native Caledonia, reserving the luxury of such displays for times of great stress. In particular, he disliked the comment he got when he referred to any unpleasant person as *Sasunnach*—literally, an "Englishman," a verbal relic of peoples and feuds buried more than a hundred light years distant in space, and a thousand years distant in time.

Almost guiltily, he glanced around. Satisfied that no one else in the room had heard his quiet outburst, he tapped out a command on the keyboard in front of him.

REPLAY TRANSMISSION
ACCESS: 3937

The screen blanked for a moment and was replaced seconds later by a repeat of the ComStar logo and a new message.

HPG TRANSMISSION
10 MAR 3057
ONE WAY, NON-PRIORITY
CALEDONIA TO GLENGARRY,
VIA GLADIUS RELAY 3
5

The "5" on the screen was replaced by a "4," and at one-second intervals the numerals continued to count down to "1." The screen dissolved once more, then reformed into the creased and age-worn face of an old woman.

"Son," she said. "It's your mathair. I'm sorry to gi' ye th' charges a' this call, but it's a matter most urgent, y'ken, an' ah hae nae C-bills for th' charges."

Clara Stuart McCall was eighty-one years old. Her silver-blue hair, once flame-red, was so thin now that Davis could see the freckled skin of her scalp beneath it. Once, centuries ago perhaps, during the golden age of the fallen Star League, genetic regenerative techniques and advanced medical therapies had extended the human life span to perhaps twice or even three times its ancient Biblical three score and ten. That, like so very much else, had been lost or deliberately sequestered in the past three centuries of unremitting and unrelenting warfare. There might be some few people within the Inner Sphere—the rich and powerful able to command luxuries denied to common folk—who might live 150 years while still looking and acting 50. On Caledonia, however, 81 was *old*. . . .

"Is tha' damned contraption recordin'?" she asked suddenly, looking to the right. Caledonia was fairly backward in technical areas, with only minimal electronics in most homes, and even computers were rarely found in ordinary households. Davis McCall's mother had never trusted such devices, and had apparently not changed one iota in the nearly ten years since he'd seen her last.

Someone out of the pick-up range must have assured her that she was, indeed, on. Turning to face the camera once more, she nodded and said, "Och, aye. I'm sorry tae hae t' tell ye this noo, son, especially after all that's passed afore, but there's been trouble here, vurra bad trouble. Your brother Angus has been taken by the Blackjackets. Ah vurra much fear tha' the governor here means tae execute him, along wi' all th' others."

"All the others," McCall repeated thoughtfully. "Now wha' the divil does she mean by tha'?"

"There's nae we can do. Ben an' Robert both hae been tae th' Citadel tae plead wi' the governor, but he threatened tae hae them up on charges as weel. There's tae be a trial, all according tae FC law, fit an' proper, but we all ken tha' tae be a sham. Wilmarth, tha' bastard, is nae—"

And with a cold suddenness, like a punch to the gut, Clara McCall's face vanished from the screen. After a moment, the "Transmission terminated" screen came up, as unhelpful as before.

END HPG TRANSMISSION
CHARGE CB 932
THANK YOU FOR USING COMSTAR

Caledonia was twenty parsecs from Glengarry—over sixty-five light-years—but in an instant McCall's mind was there once more, looking down on the sun-sparkling Firth of Lorn from the weathered hills above Mull, with the two Caledon moons riding low in the western sky, huge and silvery Stirling, small and golden Bannochburn. McCall's family had lived for generations in Dundee, an agricultural community on the outskirts of New Edinburgh, Caledonia's rather rustic and isolated planetary capital. The Citadel his mother had referred to was an old Star League fortress, once the housing for the charged particle weaponry banks of planetary-defense batteries looming from the cliff tops of Mount Alba, now the Governor's residence.

McCall rarely let himself think about his family anymore. He'd left Caledonia decades before, and the parting with them had not been a pleasant one. Davis McCall was a second son, and by long and old tradition, the family landholdings were to pass to the oldest son and heir.

In the case of Davis McCall, those old laws of primogeniture, transplanted from Terra to Caledonia, had served to spawn another soldier, as they had so often in the past. "Ah dinnae ken how ah can stomach bein' naught but a wee showpiece," he'd told his brother in that final confrontation over thirty years before. "I'd rather be a *real* warrior than a toy soldier in't pretty uniform."

Angus, his older brother, would have taken fine care of him, of course. Davis would no doubt have been given the position of Master of the Guard and remained a valued part of the McCall household.

But Davis McCall had always detested the idea of being *kept* . . . of depending on someone else for room and board. He'd elected instead to become a mercenary warrior—and for that his family had never forgiven him.

It was a situation that had been played out endlessly throughout history. Second sons had abandoned ancient Scotland, on ancient Earth, for the promise of riches, lands, and a future across the sea in the New World. Later, second sons had carried old Scotia's culture and ideals across another kind of sea, colonizing worlds like Glengarry and Caledonia that still, centuries later, bore the place names and the musical Celtic cant of Scotland.

McCall, for all the pain arising from his split with his family, was still fiercely proud of his Scot's heritage. He'd remained a Jacobite—a member of that radical and far-flung

Scottish political party that drew many of its ideas from the ancient Libertarians of Terra while somehow managing to mingle them with notions of a revived constitutional monarchy and a royal succession. He'd remained a Jacobite, in fact, even after becoming disillusioned with the power politics the current leaders had been indulging in for the past few decades; the bickering and in-fighting within the party had been almost as much the reason he'd decided to leave Caledonia as the trouble with his family. Angus, of course, had been a Jacobite as well, an ardent supporter of the current party leadership.

The real problem, though, had been young Davis's determination to strike out on his own and become a mercenary. Caledonia had suffered in the past in raids mounted by merc units, and the McCall family had lost several members, including McCall's grandfather on his mother's side, in the defense of New Edinburgh. It was a kind of treason for him to leave his family and seek the money-for-blood life of a merc.

When Davis had left Caledon, he'd been on speaking terms with few indeed of his relations.

But McCall was stubborn too. He'd received his baptism of fire and blood with a mercenary unit on Furillo, and finally ended up, broke and out of work, at the merc clearing house on Galatea. That had been where he'd first met the young Grayson Carlyle.

Year upon year had passed. McCall was actually the second person Carlyle had recruited; only Lori Kalmar had been with the Gray Death Legion longer. Together, the three of them had forged the new mercenary unit into a company, then a battalion, and finally a regiment. In thirty years, McCall had been back to Caledonia exactly twice—most recently in 3048, to attend the funeral of Katherine, his sister ... the only member of the clan who had still been on speaking terms with him.

The rest, including even his mother, had few words for him then, save for the curt and coldly austere formalities demanded by ceremony and the situation. A stiff-necked, stubborn, neomule-headed bunch, the lot of them. For his mother to bend so far as to ask his help now, after all these years ...

Damn! What kind of trouble had old Angus managed to get himself into this time?

True, his mother hadn't precisely *asked* him for his help,

but what other reason could she have had for calling him? The fact that her transmission had been abruptly cut off suggested that someone at the other end had been exercising a measure of censorship. She'd referred to Caledonia's governor as a "bastard," and an instant later McCall had been staring at an empty screen. She must have been about to ask him for help but been cut off before she could do so.

He needed more information. He'd tried to keep up with news of his homeworld for years now, not always successfully. He did know that the governor there for the past five years had been someone named Wilmarth. What was this character like, anyway?

With a sigh, McCall cleared the ComStar Logo from the screen and accessed the com center's newsfeed. Once he was into the net, he entered the key words for a subject search: "Caledonia," "New Edinburgh," and, just on a hunch, "Jacobite," limiting the search parameters to the past three standard months. As an afterthought, then, he directed that the download be presented as text and vid, rather than by voice. He didn't want the others in the room to hear what he was about.

He frankly doubted that the search would turn anything up. Several private news agencies provided interstellar news feeds through arrangement with ComStar, though human-occupied space was so vast, with so many worlds and a population numbering so many hundreds of billions, that no news service could record and disseminate all that happened everywhere.

Still, what he was looking for was news of an incident that had happened recently on a world twenty parsecs distant, a system, like Glengarry, that was part of the Federated Commonwealth's Skye March. If he'd been looking for news from some backwater world in remote Luthien space, say, or from the no-man's land of the Periphery beyond the boundaries of the Inner Sphere, there would have been no chance at all. But as it was—

Yes! One, and only one news entry included all three key words. Indeed, as he expanded the search to related articles, the short column of text proved to be the only story involving Caledonia in the entire past year. A grainy, digitized vid accompanied the text, which scrolled down the left side of the screen as the images spread across the right.

2 MAR 3057 (Std)
THOUSANDS ARRESTED IN LOCAL UNREST

Caledonia, Skye March (FC)—A peaceful religious demonstration turned violent yesterday as thousands of people
rioted in the streets of New Edinburgh, forcing Governor
Wilmarth to call out the Planetary Guard. "Martial law is
regrettable but necessary," Wilmarth said in a telecast
from his press room in the Citadel this morning. "The
good and law-abiding people of Caledonia can thank this
handful of religious nuts, political radicals, and street rabble for the inconvenience. I assure you all that the martial
law directive will be rescinded just as soon as order is restored and decent people can venture into their streets
once again."

There was no word on casualties, though eyewitnesses
report that the Planetary Guard's 'Mechs did open fire at
one point on a large crowd of protestors. "It was horrible!" one woman, who declined to identify herself, said
afterward. "We were trying to leave the square, but there
were too many people, and those big black machines
were just sitting there, blocking the exits and firing into
the crowd. I've never seen anything like it!"

The demonstration was called jointly by leaders of the
resident Jacobite Party and by the Chief Proclaimer of
the Word of Jihad movement, calling for civil disobedi-
ence against the planetary government. Reportedly, members of both groups are now in hiding and could not be
reached for comment.

"Malcontents, fanatics, and heretics, all of them,"
Group Leader Terrance Grant of the Planetary Defense
Force said after the incident. "Decent people should have
nothing to do with rabble like that."

The Governor's office announced late yesterday that
the general martial law order had been extended until at
least next week, but that citizens should remain calm and
cooperate with the government authorities. "The situation
is now well in hand," a spokesperson for the Governor
said. "The worst of the crisis is behind us now, and I
know all of us want to work together with Governor
Wilmarth to see law, order, and peace restored to our
world."

McCall scanned down the lines of text twice, then requested a replay of the images that accompanied the words. It was hard to distinguish much. Most of the shots were of a large crowd filling the elliptical stadium that was New Edinburgh's Malcom Plaza. He estimated that there might be as many as five or six thousand people there—a fairly sizable turnout when you remembered that New Edinburgh was small for a planetary capital, with a population of only eighty or ninety thousand. Some close-ups showed women and children, and none of the people visible, not even the young men, appeared to be armed. A variety of placards, banners, and signs were in evidence, however. "The Day Is At Hand" was one popular slogan, as was the rather cryptic equation, "Machines = Death." There'd always been a strong Luddite strain to Caledonian demonstrations. "Freedom of Thought; Freedom of Spirit" was another frequent message, a Jacobite slogan old when McCall had been an active member of the movement.

It appeared the report that the demonstration had been essentially peaceful was accurate. The crowd seemed orderly and well-behaved, if noisy. But then the crowd scenes were replaced by ominous long-ranged views of armored vehicles, including several BattleMechs, moving through the familiar gray streets of New Edinburgh. The crowds began scattering the moment the 'Mechs appeared, but the press of the mob was so large that the plaza couldn't be emptied immediately. McCall wished there were sound with the images. Had the authorities demanded dispersal? Surrender? Or had they simply arrived and opened fire?

He couldn't tell from the news broadcast, and he suspected that the content had been censored by the government authorities on Caledonia before transmission, for there were no scenes of any actual gunfire or civilian deaths.

Almost none, at any rate. Some scenes had evidently slipped past the censors, for there were a couple of shots, brief and almost furtive, of bodies lying in a deserted street.

One small drama, though, arrested McCall's attention. The shot was wavering, as if from a hand-held camera shooting through a telephoto lens at considerable distance, so very little detail could be made out. McCall could see, though, that the 'Mech in the scene was an ancient and much-patched *Wasp*, painted black with bright yellow stripes, but with several panels and armor plates missing and a limp that suggested to McCall's mind a faulty hip actuator assembly. As it advanced with slow, almost mincing steps into Malcom Plaza, it was momentarily stopped by a lone man in a white tunic and dark trousers, who stood in its path.

The confrontation was so brief that McCall almost missed it, and perhaps that was why it had slipped through past the censors. As it was, he had to replay the clip several times, using the comm system's enhancement controls to get a better view.

As near as he could tell, the man momentarily blocked the *Wasp*'s advance, shaking his fist up at the ten-meter giant before him. Most of the crowd had fled by that time, but this one man seemed determined to face down the government militia armor. Perhaps he wanted to force a confrontation for the benefit of cameras he knew were watching; possibly he was simply lost in fury and blood-lust. For perhaps three seconds he stood there, an unarmed and unarmored man facing down twenty tons of steel and ceraplast.

Suddenly, the man stooped, plucking something—a rock, McCall thought—from the pavement, then leaned back and let fly, hurling the object as hard as he could. The transmission was too blurry for McCall to see whether or not the missile struck home.

The *Wasp* paused only a moment, as though considering how best to go around this defiant mite before it. Then, almost casually, it lifted its left foot and set it down once more. McCall winced and briefly turned his head. "Och, laddie," he said quietly. "Tha's nae way tae take oot a 'Mech!"

As the machine strode on into the center of the plaza, little remained of the defiant man but a red and white smear on the pavement. The censors had, apparently, missed that pathetic bit of gore.

Or maybe they'd left it in as a warning of some sort, while excising shots of mass murder that might invite outside interference in Caledonian affairs. As always, the bureaucratic mind was a total mystery to Davis McCall.

Angry now, he blanked the screen once more and was about to sign off the newsnet when a flashing logo in the screen's upper right corner caught his attention. There was, it seemed, a second news story on the net that included at least one of his key words. What was it?

When he typed in the Accept command, McCall felt a jolt

unlike any he'd felt before, worse by far than the kick-in-the-ass ignition of a dying 'Mech's ejection seat.

The article, it seemed, wasn't from the newsnet at all. It was a feature in one of the local Glengarry broadcasts. The date stamp on the image was seven days old. Damn! Why hadn't he heard about this?

". . . and the rumor mill is going full out tonight, for you members of the Legion," the pretty blond announcer said with a sexy pout to her lips, though with the audio suppressed, her words appeared only as scrolling sentences across the bottom of the screen. "The word around Dunkeld is that you may be on your way to Caledonia soon, as part of a Federated Commonwealth peacekeeper force! These reports are unconfirmed but come from the usual 'very highly placed sources,' and it's rumored that a sizable retainer has already been paid for the Gray Death's services. At least we can all be glad that the Caledonians speak the same language we do!"

There was nothing else of substance in the report, which evidently had been a light bit of fluff rounding out an evening broadcast on a slow news day. What shocked McCall the most was the fact that he'd not heard word one of that particular rumor. Like any military man since the time of Sargon the Great, Major Davis McCall depended on rumor as the primary means of finding out what was really going on in the unit. And if the rumor had to do with the Legion being transferred to his own homeworld . . .

He bit off a particularly vehement Gaelic curse. Likely as not, he'd been excluded from the rumor circuit precisely because he *was* from Caledonia, either to spare his feelings or because it was assumed he already knew what was happening there. A peacekeeper force to his own homeworld? That was often something of a nightmare for mercenary warriors. What happened when you moved in to break up a riot or an outright rebellion, only to find yourself looking down from a 'Mech's cockpit at your own friends and family?

For some it didn't matter, of course. The pilot of that black and yellow *Wasp* was probably a native of Caledonia, and that hadn't stopped him from turning one of his fellows into a grim red smear on the street. But for McCall, the thought of having to face his own clan in battle . . .

That, no doubt, explained why the rumor had never made it to his ears, might even explain the looks he'd been getting lately and the silences that had fallen a time or two when he'd entered a room. For the first time since he'd joined the Legion, Davis McCall felt isolated, an outsider, and that hurt more than anything else.

The Legion? Going to Caledon? Did that have anything to do with Wilmarth and the popular unrest there? McCall rose to his feet, glanced uncertainly back toward the gaming pit, where two recruits were gleefully shooting one another's holographic BattleMechs into glittering fragments.

"I think," McCall told himself, with a growl like the quiet rumble of a distant, gathering storm, "that I'd better go and see the Old Man about this."

If there was one person on this whole planet he could talk to about anything, it was Colonel Grayson Carlyle.

= 3 =

The Residence, Dunkeld
Glengarry, Skye March
Federated Commonwealth
1060 Hours, 10 March 3057

Colonel Grayson Carlyle leaned back in his seat, rubbing his eyes with his hands, then stretched wide and high, trying to get the kinks out. His computer monitor glared at him balefully, as though indicting him for even a moment's pause from his work. He'd been wrestling with this probe for what seemed like ages now, and there was still no resolution, nor even the promise that a resolution was possible.

"How in the *cosmos*," he groaned, "anyone could get one set of records so drekked up . . ."

Timekeeping. He was a MechWarrior, damn it, not a damn timekeeper and not a damn computer programmer. He really didn't need this, just now. . . .

The keeping of time and dates had been a problem ever since humans had first left their homeworld and ventured into space. Since the beginning of the interstellar era at least, starfarers had retained what was known as "Terran Standard" time or, more simply and more commonly, as "Standard" for all timekeeping routines. Based on the natural cycles of Terra, they assumed twenty-four 60-minute hours in a day, an unwieldy 365.25 days to the year, and two intermediate units of time, the "week" and the "month," that seemed to have no basis in logic at all.

The system worked fine, however, for ships in transit between the stars. For time out of mind it had been the responsibility of ComStar to keep the necessary standards of time measurement and to broadcast them through the medium of the hyperpulse generators that formed the communications net linking the great states of the Inner Sphere worlds together. Since ComStar had always been headquartered on Terra, this made perfect sense. But ever since the once powerful organization had lost much of its old authority, it was feared that timekeeping, like so much else, would soon be the responsibility of individual systems or governments.

And that would, of course, mean chaos, for the myriad worlds of the Inner Sphere could, quite simply, never agree on *anything,* not even what day of the week it happened to be.

There was chaos enough, Carlyle thought with dark humor, every time starfaring people ended up living on one particular world for very long. No Terra-based system could easily adapt itself to the day-night or days-per-year cycle of any other world, and Glengarry was a case in point. Circling a K1-class star cooler and smaller than Terra's Sol, Glengarry orbited its primary at a pleasantly cool .577 of an astronomical unit—the "A.U." which was itself a relic of Terra, the distance between Terra and its sun. Glengarry's year, then, was just less than half of Terra's year in length . . . 179 Terran days long.

That much wouldn't have been so bad. It was easy enough to make a simple conversion from standard to Glengarry years. But things got more complicated with the fact that local days had nothing to do with Terra's days of twenty-four hours. Closer to its sun and subjected to stronger tidal forces as a consequence, Glengarry rotated on its axis once in thirty-two hours, fourteen minutes, twelve seconds, for a year that was only 133.28 *local* days long. By a system going all the way back to Glengarry's first colonists late in the twenty-third century, the local year was divided into nineteen 7-day weeks, which in turn were grouped into six 3-week "months." The left-over week at the end of the year was an intercalary festival period, with the last, year-end day given an extra nine hours to bring the calendar up to date with the planet's year. The months, in keeping with Glengarry's Gaelic heritage, were named after figures out of ancient Celtic mythology: Nemain, Myrddin, Mab, and others.

Today—Grayson had to check his wrist computer to be sure—was the sixteenth of Dana and late in Glengarry's autumn. By standard dating, though, it was early spring, March 10.

The point was, the two calendar systems didn't mesh. They *couldn't* mesh, and sane people didn't even try to make them work together. In practice, units like the Gray Death Legion adapted to the local time system as necessary for work that demanded it, and maintained their own Terra-based calendar and timekeeping system for everything else. For most day-to-day activities, the eighty-minute Glengarry "hours" worked fine on a standard twenty-four-hour clock, plus a middle-of-the-night quarter-hour add-on to make things come out even.

Carlyle sighed as he checked the time display on his wristcomp. Eighty-minute hours did make for long, long mornings. Harder, though, was the fact that humans weren't designed to handle thirty-two-hour days. Most people ended up working eight- or ten-hour shifts, which meant their sleep periods alternated with day and night. Others, like Carlyle, preferred to put in longer days of twelve or sixteen hours, followed by an equally long downtime. Unfortunately, when there was as much work to do as was inherent in running a mercenary BattleMech regiment, the work still managed to spill over into the supposed downtime, making for very long and tedious days indeed.

Especially in cases like this.

A new recruit, a young woman from Dunkeld who'd signed up with the Legion late the previous year, had been assigned to the logistics office at Legion Headquarters after completion of basic training. Two months ago she'd begun entering Form 1290s into the regimental data base, each a description of a particular item of equipment, food, or other expendable purchased in bulk on a regular schedule from the local community. Once entered into the data base, these forms triggered the automatic purchase from various suppliers of such routinely necessary goods as cooking supplies, frozen sides of *crogh*—the principal source of meat in the Dunkeld area—boots, weatherproof ponchos, and office supplies. The regimental commissary officer could, for example, expect the arrival of four hundred sides of frozen crogh once each month.

Once each *standard* month.

The first time four hundred frozen crogh carcasses had arrived a week early, Lieutenant Dobbs, the Commissary Supply Officer, had assumed there'd been some minor and one-time mistake and let it slide. The second time it happened, three weeks later and two weeks before scheduled delivery, he'd begun to suspect something major was wrong. He was running out of storage space in the mess-area freezer.

And then the bills from the local producers had begun to arrive in Disbursing.

In effect, the regiment's operating expenses were suddenly twenty-five percent higher than they should be, because that much more in the way of expendable goods was being delivered each month, and the bills were coming due faster. The Gray Death Legion was successful as mercenary units went, but like any such unit, it lived or died by the cash flow. That unexpected deficit in the monthly books could very quickly wipe out the Legion's monetary reserves. Even worse, it might mean they wouldn't be able to afford other supplies such as short-range missiles, that long-awaited replacement power plant for Margo Shaeffer's ailing *Enforcer,* or a refit on that new lieutenant's aging *Zeus.* What was his name again? Walter Dupré, that was it.

And all because that programmer newbie had forgotten—or perhaps she'd never realized in the first place—that the regiment operated on the *standard* calendar as opposed to the one used by civilian Glengarrians. As nearly as Grayson could tell, some two hundred request forms, supply/logistic, local procurement 1290s had been filled out with future autopurchase dates, but counting in three-week Glengarry months instead of four-week standard months.

Grayson rubbed absently at his beard, once brown, but now gone a bushy gray-white. He'd been up much of the night—and all of yesterday as well—trying to sort out the mess, which had been brought to his attention two days ago. He had a small army of programmers both in Disbursing and in Supply working on it as well, of course, but someone needed to coordinate their separate approaches to the problem, and someone needed to make sure that the confusion wasn't made worse by new mistakes added to the mix along the way. Neither Lieutenant Dobbs nor his boss, Captain Levinson, the regimental supply officer, was as experienced as Carlyle would have liked, and he wanted to maintain close control over the entire operation.

Normally this sort of thing would have been the work of the regiment's Executive Officer, but Lori Kalmar Carlyle was offworld at the moment, attending a conference on Tharkad, and wouldn't be back until the seventeenth. Her last HPG transmission had promised him a surprise when she returned. Knowing Lori, there was no telling what *that* might be. She could be as unpredictable as she was—still, after all these years—beautiful.

He ruefully wished the surprise could be a vacation—about six months or so, *standard* months, not these misbegotten tenth-liter Glengarry months, on some tropical paradise of a world that had not even seen a BattleMech or a DropShip in the last five centuries . . .

The depressing part of it all was the knowledge that once this crisis was resolved, there would inevitably be another. And another. And yet another after that. Damn it, he was fast becoming a glorified clerk with a colonel's rank, and that distressed him more than the physical act of wading through these confusing and irreconcilable numbers.

His office door chimed.

He felt something akin to relief. An interruption, any interruption just now, was more than welcome. "Come."

A door at the far end of the room slid open, and the Legion's weapons master walked in. WM Vernon Artman was a muscular, pugnacious-looking black man who'd joined the Legion twenty-five years ago at Galatea, signing on as an ammo handler and working his way up to being the man in charge not only of the regiment's munitions, but of all combat training. Even though Weapons Master was a specialist command rank in its own right, somewhat akin to the warrant officers of ancient, planet-bound militaries, he still preferred to be called "Sarge." He had the hard-edged look of a drill master—understandable, since training recruits was one of his duties; from the impeccably neat, trim black mustache to the crease in his uniform trousers, there was not a speck of dirt, not a hair out of place, and he carried himself with the confident and precise bearing of the long-time military vet.

"Got a minute, Colonel?"

"For you, Sarge, always. Whatcha got?"

"Same as usual, Colonel. Trouble."

"Grab yourself a chair. Talk to me."

Artman gestured to the computer screen, which still showed the avalanche of screenwork. "It looks like I've come at a bad time."

"One of your recent recruits," Grayson said. "A small matter of using local dates instead of standard."

"That would be Callaway, sir?"

"Yes. Julia Callaway. How'd you know?"

Artman gave the tiniest of shrugs. "I know. She never could get the hang of converting to standard in her head." He hesitated a moment, as though gauging Grayson's mood. "It's your son. Sir."

Grayson had assumed that to be the case. Somehow, he'd known. . . .

"What's he done now?"

"Oh, he's not in any trouble. At least, not yet. But I thought it was time you had a look at these."

Reaching across the desk, Artman held out a slim, plastic memory card. Grayson took it and slipped it into a reader on his desk. A window opened, overlaying the 1290 work. It was a set of simulator scores, listing reaction times, kill ratios, and instructor's "grudges," the outright mistakes made by the trainee in a simulated combat encounter.

"Overall reactions are down eight point five percent in the past week alone," Artman said in the clipped and efficient tones of a human computer. "That's twenty-four point two percent since we began the training/testing regimen, four months ago. He's been making mistakes in simcombat. Grudges are up ten percent, but the kicker is that those pilot errors have been stupid, rookie mistakes."

"Such as?"

"Yesterday, he was simming in a *Shadow Hawk,* squared off against an *Assassin.* Should've been an easy kill for the boy. He's got talent, a real feel for operating a 'Mech, for becoming almost one with it. But then—here. Look." Leaning over the desk, Artman pointed to the engagement on the screen, an interweaving of colored lines on a graph that carried the story for those trained to read it. "There. Twelve seconds into the encounter, the *Assassin* started moving to his left, turning away from him as it did so. Practically an invitation: 'Hey! Come get me!' Your son's proper response would've been to move in, pivot hard left, and drop onto the 'Sassy's tail. But he turned *right* instead." Artman's brown finger traced along the rise and fall of colored lines, up to a point where all the lines came together, then dropped sharply to the floor of the graph. "The *'Sassy,* with its greater speed, seized the initiative and got onto the *Hawk*'s tail instead. Six seconds later . . ."

Grayson felt a cold pricking at the base of his neck. It wasn't easy looking at the electronic record of his son's death in combat . . . even when that death was a simulated one.

"In my opinion, sir," Artman continued, straightening upright again, "Alex hasn't recovered from what happened to him during the campaign last year. In fact, judging from test scores like these, I'd say he's rapidly growing worse."

Grayson studied the computer display for a long moment before allowing himself to reply. He'd already read a memo posted to his terminal that morning by Ellen Jamison, a gentle and worried note to the effect that Alex had been having trouble sleeping, had been suffering from recurring nightmares in which he relived various of the Glengarry campaign battles. Her diagnosis was PTSD; her recommendation, that he be taken off of combat duty.

"So. What do you recommend, Sarge?" Grayson asked slowly.

"Get him out of 'Mechs, that's certain," Artman replied without hesitation. "I won't tell you to drop him from active duty, but the idea probably warrants some consideration. More than anything else, young Alex needs time to heal."

"You know," Grayson said, "there's an old piece of advice about getting back on the horse after you fall off."

Artman raised an eyebrow. "Sir? What's a horse?"

"A riding animal, native to Terra originally. Quadruped, pretty fair-sized. It was taken along to quite a few other worlds during the first big interstellar outleap, though its biological needs restricted it to planets a lot like Terra. The point is, learning to ride one took some patience and, I gather, a few spills before you learned how to stay in the saddle. They used to say that if you got thrown, it was best to climb back in the saddle right away, before you lost your nerve."

"There's some truth in that, sir, certainly. But there's a danger, too."

"What danger?"

"That you'll push your son too hard, too fast. Or maybe

I should say, that you'll let him push *himself* too hard and fast, trying to live up to your standards."

"I see. You've seen evidence of this?"

"I know he calls up your simulator profiles and pores over them before he climbs into the sim cockpit himself."

"I didn't know that."

"I think he sees the Glengarry campaign as a personal failure. His unit took sixty percent casualties before you came along to bail him out, then rescued him, in front of his command." Artman shook his head. "That's not easy for any man to live with. It's a lot harder when your old man is Grayson Carlyle. Sir."

"I appreciate your frankness."

Artman spread his hands. "That's what you pay me the big C-bills for, Colonel. You knew I wasn't a damned hard-wired yes-man when you assigned me to the training cadre."

"I'll let you know what I decide. Thanks for coming."

"Not at all, Colonel." Artman snapped to a crisp and precisely military attention and saluted. "Good day, sir."

"You too."

Grayson remained thoughtful for a long time after Artman had left. He didn't have an enormous number of options here, and almost anything he did could be the wrong thing . . . or at least could be perceived as wrong.

The Glengarry campaign had been a grueling, seven-month hell, one that had very nearly destroyed the Gray Death Legion as a fighting unit. Four months after the conclusion of that campaign and the defeat of the Skye rebellion, the Legion was still seriously understrength. It wasn't for any lack of newbies—Glengarrians had been flocking to the Legion recruiting centers across the planet—but just that it would take time and seasoning to make them Legionnaires.

The administrative problem Grayson Carlyle was facing here lay partly in the simple fact that *everyone* who'd been on Glengarry under Alex's command had suffered in that campaign. If Grayson were to release every Legionnaire who was still having nightmares, or who'd lost friends, or whose reflexes might have suffered as a result, he might lose half his active duty roster.

Nor could he be seen to be giving his son special treatment. That had always been a major disadvantage of having members of his own family under his command in the Gray

Death. If there was even a hint of favoritism in his conduct or in his orders, the morale of the entire unit could collapse overnight. He had to be perceived as being fair; it helped, even, if he was seen to be harder on Alex and Lori than on anyone else in the regiment. Finally, and as a father, he couldn't simply step in and redirect his son's life. Alex Carlyle was twenty standard years old, for Blake's sake, old enough to decide for himself what he wanted to do with his life.

Hell, had he pushed Alex into a BattleMech cockpit? He didn't think he had; certainly, that had never been his intent. Even now, Grayson knew he could accept it if Alex didn't want to be a MechWarrior. In a lot of ways, that decision would make life easier for Grayson, who hated the necessity of giving the orders that might well result in Alex's death—a *real* death, not a simulator's readout.

But the important thing was ... what did *Alex* want?

He needed to find an assignment for Alex that would give him time to recover from the campaign—and to make up his mind about what he wanted to do with the rest of his life.

Just as he was settling back into his chair and trying once more to concentrate on the confused tangle of forms and dates on his monitor, the door chimed again. "Come."

Major Davis McCall walked through the door as it slid open, clad in his finest regimental dress grays, the medals and ribbons he'd won over the years forming an impressive display of metal and color over his left breast. From the expression on the big Caledonian's face, this conversation was going to be no more pleasant than the last one.

"Hello, Mac," Grayson said. "What's up?"

"Ah dinnae ken quite how t' begin, Colonel." McCall rubbed the brush of his red beard, looking as uncomfortable as Grayson had ever known him to be.

"It's the rumor about our getting a contract for Caledonia, isn't it?" Grayson said bluntly. The expression on McCall's face, a mixture of surprise and dismay, told Grayson he'd hit the mark. "I should have told you sooner," he continued, "but there wasn't anything definite. Hell, there *still* isn't. I didn't want to worry you unnecessarily."

"Then, sir, the rumor's nae true?"

"Not yet, anyway," Grayson replied. He sighed. "We did have an inquiry from ComSquared a few weeks back, and I imagine that's how the rumor got started. But it was *only* an inquiry, checking on our readiness in case we needed to go on what they called a peacekeeper deployment."

"An' . . . an' what did y' tell them, sir? If I may ask?"

"That right now we weren't in any shape to take on any kind of deployment. Third Batt was still out at the time. And you know what kind of condition the First and Second are in right now."

"Aye. Aye, I do that."

"I've been considering—*considering,* mind you—deploying Third Batt if we need to. I most certainly would not order you in against your own people."

"I appreciate that, Colonel," McCall said. "I really do. But is it not likely tha' th' boys would see that as just a wee bit a' favoritism, noo?'

"They know—as you should know too, Mac—that it is not my policy to force my people to engage in combat against their own families and countrymen. That's asking rather too much of them, don't you think?"

McCall looked concerned, his head cocking to one side. "Aye, but is Third Batt ready for deployment again, sir?"

It was characteristic of the man, Grayson thought, that he would still think about the rest of the men and women of the unit, even though he was obviously preoccupied with problems of his own.

"They're ready enough." On phosphor, at any rate, the Legion now mustered three battalions. The Third Battalion, under the command of Major Jonathan Frye, had been organized immediately after the Glengarry campaign primarily as a moneymaker, a unit of thirty-some 'Mechs that could be hired out for small jobs on a regular basis to provide a steady income for the Legion.

But the Third had returned to Glengarry with their roster badly thinned. They'd been fighting incursions by the Draconis Combine on the border for months and had ended the campaign with a clash with Clan raiders. Casualties had been heavy, and it would be a long while before the losses could be made up from the Legion's training cadre.

"Garrison duty would be a vacation after what they've been through," Grayson continued. "The point is, Major, that if we take a contract on Caledonia, you won't have to go. We would deploy Major Frye and, if the situation warranted, Major Houk. You would stay here in Glengarry with First Battalion."

"An' have the lads think I'd wriggled oot? I dinnae think so, Colonel."

"Damn it, Davis, it's not 'wriggling oot.' The First wouldn't be in line for this next job, even if it was on Tharkad. Someone's got to stay behind and guard the fort. It's going to be you."

"Och, weel, Ah appreciate the consairn you're showin' me, Colonel," McCall said, his burr and Gaelic rolled Rs especially heavy. "Ah truly do. Bu' there's aye a wee bit more of complications t' the contract. Sir . . . this is nae a spur a' th' moment decision. I've been giving this a good deal of thought."

Grayson could hear it coming and steeled himself. Davis McCall was one of his oldest and most trusted comrades in the Legion—and besides Lori, his best and oldest friend. "Yes?"

"Sir, it pains me deeply, but I'm afraid I must tender my resignation from th' Gray Death."

4

The Residence, Dunkeld
Glengarry, Skye March
Federated Commonwealth
1115 Hours, 10 March 3057

"**S**it down, Davis," Grayson said, indicating a chair on the other side of his desk.

"Sir, I—"

"Sit down, man, and quit towering over me like your damned *Highlander*." He waited while McCall took a seat, the medals on his chest clinking with the movement, then pressed ahead. "I can't accept your resignation, Major," Grayson continued in a hard and level voice. "Damn it, man, we need you. *I* need you!"

"I'm sorry, Colonel. I truly am. But there are personal reasons. . . ."

"Your family? On Caledonia?"

McCall nodded.

"I thought you weren't on speaking terms with them."

"Well, I've had a message from home." McCall hesitated, as though trying to decide how to say what he had to say. "Sir, it's my brother, Angus. He's been placed under arrest by the Caledonian government and there's been some kind of uprising. I don't know what th' whole story might be, but I've got t' go there, an' quickly."

Grayson shook his head. "I don't understand. What can you do?"

"I dinna ken, not yet. But y' must understand, Colonel. Wi' Angus gone, I am *the* McCall now. They'll be needin' me at Glen Aire."

"Glen Aire?"

"My family's wee estate ootside a' Dundee."

"An estate, huh? I had no idea you were so well off, Davis. Maybe I should talk to you about the Gray Death's financial situation."

"Och, weel, I'm not, sir, not really. But there is some money in th' family, aye. The McCalls were First Family, sir, back in the early colonizing days. Put up part of the capital for the colony ship tha' brought them oot from Terra. A number of McCalls ha' been governor of th' place."

Grayson leaned back in his chair, steepling his fingers as he stared appraisingly at the big Scot. There was an opportunity here. . . .

"Your brother—"

"Angus Charles McCall, aye, sir."

"I gather he's not governor. Who is?"

"A man named Wilmarth, sir."

"The word 'governor' suggests that Caledonia is being run from someplace else. But it's not a Steiner term. . . ."

"Och, aye. Tha' title dates back to three centuries ago, noo, when the Kuritas conquered themselves a good part a' the Lyran Commonwealth."

"The Battles for Hesperus II."

"Aye. And the Fourth Royal Guards held oot on Caledonia for seven long years against th' worst old Hugai an' the Draconis Combine could throw at them. They lost in the end, though, and the Kuritas damn near scorched the whole bluidy world. Wee Caledon was a long time in recovering, and during the next century or two, she was ruled from offworld, first from Hesperus II, right next door, and then, when the Lyran Commonwealth was back on its feet, from the Commonwealth capital at Tharkad. The governor was appointed by the Steiners and approved by a vote of th' Caledonian High Council. Usually, he or she was a native Caledonian, whose name was submitted by the Council in the first place. The appointment became a mere formality, don't y' see?"

"I take it this . . . Wilmarth, you said? I take it from your tone of voice that he's not a Caledonian."

"I don't know much aboot him, noo," McCall said, shaking his head. "Th' word is, though, he was a toady to the Davions an' got his appointment as some sort of reward, back a few years."

Grayson considered this. This whole damned political situation was made a hell of a lot worse by the fact that he, himself, had been named Baron of Glengarry by the highest-ranking Davion of all—Prince Victor Ian Steiner-Davion. Grayson Carlyle owed his own position as ruler of this world to a similar reward from the Davions, and every day he was feeling more and more backed into an extremely uncomfortable corner.

As though reading his thoughts, McCall caught himself, eyes opening wide. "Ah dinnae mean, Colonel—"

"It's all right, Davis. I know you weren't calling me a Davion toady. But it's a damned tight spot, no matter how you look at it."

"Aye, sir, it's all a' that."

Throughout the three hundred years known as the Succession Wars, the Lyran Commonwealth, ruled by House Steiner, and the Federated Suns of House Davion had been two separate states, each encompassing hundreds of star systems from the neighborhood of Terra clear out to the Periphery, albeit in opposite directions. Sometimes they'd fought; more often they'd been allies, particularly in their ongoing border struggles with House Kurita and House Liao.

In all those years of war none of the five great Successor States had been able to win the upper hand over the others, but that all changed when Prince Hanse Davion and Melissa Steiner had married in 3022, allying their two powerful states and tipping the balance once and for all in favor of the newly created—and formidable—Federated Commonwealth.

If the political marriage of Hanse and Katrina was an amicable one, however, the marriage of the two states was not. There'd been strains on that alliance from the beginning; the Second Skye Rebellion that had engulfed Glengarry, among other worlds, just a year ago had been an attempt by pro-Steiner separatists to break the old Skye March away from a political superstate that was becoming increasingly monolithic and remote from the needs of its citizens. The defeat of the separatists did not mean that the discontent was any less.

Quite the contrary, in fact . . .

The appointment of Caledonia's outsider of a governor

was scarcely an isolated instance. Many high government offices once held by people loyal to the Steiners had been awarded to pro-Davion individuals after 3022, and resentment had been running high in those circles for years now, especially as Prince Victor had begun working behind the scenes to consolidate his own power after Hanse Davion's death. Duke Ryan Steiner, the longtime leader of the Free Skye Movement had been conveniently assassinated after the rebellion had been put down last year. Then Prince Victor had replaced Ryan's number two man with the strongly pro-Davion David Sandoval as both Duke and Marshal of the March. This mingling of the military with the civil authority felt like the imposition of military rule to most of the citizens of the March; Grayson could understand why they were growing restless.

Unfortunately, these political entanglements—and the unraveling of the old Steiner–Davion alliance—promised to make plenty of trouble for units like the Gray Death Legion, and for men like Grayson Carlyle. Technically, Grayson Carlyle owed his primary liege responsibility first to David Sandoval, the Duke of Skye, and then to Victor, who'd named Carlyle Baron of Glengarry in the first place. The Gray Death Legion's original mercenary contract, however, was with the Steiners, and extended clear back to the days before the Federated Commonwealth had been formed. FedComMilCom—the Federated Commonwealth Military Command, or "ComSquared," as most military professionals called it for short, was the current legal executor of the contract.

Personally, however, and emotionally, Grayson's loyalty still resided with House Steiner.

It was a curious thing, he thought, this concept of *loyalty* in a mercenary unit. By definition and by popular supposition, mercenaries were supposed to be loyal only to their paychecks ... and a better offer could turn this week's enemy into next week's employer.

In fact, though, things were rarely that simple. While some mercs jumped from employer to employer, the best professionals—and the ones that commanded the highest prices on the military market—were those who'd demonstrated they could be relied upon over the long haul. Few employers were willing to risk their C-bills on a merc unit with a reputation for jumping contracts.

There was much to be said, too, for the fraternity among combat veterans. When you fought side by side with someone, sharing the dirt and the danger, the triumph and the grief, it was hard to think of him as an enemy after that. There'd been a number of incidents throughout history of mercenary units that once had been comrades meeting as enemies in battle . . . and refusing to fight.

The history of the Gray Death was inextricably bound up with the recent history of the old Lyran Commonwealth. While the Legion had served other employers—notably House Marik, for a time—they'd always come back to the Steiners, fighting first the Draconis Combine in that never-ending trade of blow and counterblow up and down the Commonwealth-Combine border, and then the Clans, when those high-tech descendants of an ancient Star League-era exodus had come swarming in from beyond the dark Periphery from the direction of the galactic core.

And now, the political cords that bound the Federated Commonwealth together were rapidly fraying. Many people of the Lyran sector of the Federated Commonwealth felt neglected by the preference Victor was giving to things Davion. Added to that, the Lyrans had suffered severely in the war with the Clans while the Davion half of the alliance had not been touched. It was a quandary for Grayson Carlyle. His personal sympathies were with the people and with House Steiner, while his legal authority and his money came from Victor Davion.

And sooner or later, he knew, that web of conflicting loyalties was going to trap him and the Gray Death Legion as well.

"Sir?"

Grayson looked up at McCall, aware that his mind had wandered. "Sorry, Davis. What was that?"

"I said, Colonel, that if th' Gray Death is sent t' Caledon, it'll aye put us under th' bastard Wilmarth's command. Wi' all due respect, I dinnae think I can stomach that. Th' man sent BattleMechs in against a civilian demonstration. I saw it wi' me own eyes on a newscast downloaded from th' HPG net."

Grayson winced. "And you wouldn't care to be in a 'Mech on Caledonia following his orders. I understand that."

"Aye, but it's more than that. I must go an' see if I can help my family, my *brother*. Do y' see, sir? It would place you an' me against one another, an' if I remained under your command, it would force me t' choose, like, between you an' my family."

Such decisions, Grayson realized with a small, cold shock, had been the tragedy of civil wars since the beginning of human history. "I understand that."

"I wish there were another way. . . ."

"Tell me, Davis. Does this trouble on Caledonia have anything to do with your Jacobite friends?"

"Oh, aye." McCall gave a wry smile. "When there's aye trouble on Caledon, like as not the Jakes are in on't." The smile froze in place, then vanished. "Sir, you'll not be wantin' names of—"

"Good god, no," Grayson said, holding up a hand. "What do you take me for, man?"

"Sorry, sir," McCall said, relaxing slightly. "But if the Legion goes to put down—"

"It's a damned big if, Davis. What I want right now is to understand the situation. If the Legion *does* get dragged into this mess, I want to know the score. But I don't want you to name friends or kin who might be involved, and you don't have to tell me a damned thing if you don't want to."

"Thank you, sir." McCall looked relieved, but it was obvious he was trapped between conflicting loyalties.

Like Grayson himself.

"Th' Jacobites," McCall continued after a moment's thought, "are like a political party in some ways, like a brotherhood or secret lodge in others. They pride themselves on a lineage they claim goes clear back to ancient Scotland, on Terra, but there's no way they could prove such a claim. They want t' restore an ancient monarchy as ruler over Caledon, though tha' is as much for pride's sake as for any reasonable legal claim. Their politics, though, call for a constitution tha' limits the size an' power of any government. It's as though they were sayin', if their neighbor cannae run his own house an' finances, why should he be given power to run my house an' finances as weel?"

"A reasonable enough question."

"Governments tend to dislike such groups," McCall said with a flash of dark humor, "though I cannae understand why."

"And this demonstration Wilmarth put down with 'Mechs . . . it was the Jacobites?"

"T' tell the truth, sir, I'm not sure. They were involved, aye, but the accounts mentioned another group as weel. A religious group called the Word of Jihad."

"That's all we need. To mix religion with politics." Grayson frowned. "Word of Jihad? I've never heard of it."

"Aye, sir, nor I either." McCall looked thoughtful. "Judging from the slogans on some of the banners in the demonstration, however, I'd have t' say tha' the Jihad is some kind of anti-tech movement. It would figure, of course. The Jacobites ha' neer been too happy wi' the machines an' all, especially wi' the Kurita 'Mechs stompin' to and fro across their grain fields an' villages for years on end. A neo-Luddite movement might well find fertile ground there on Caledon."

"Neoludds, eh?"

McCall nodded, and Grayson crossed his arms, sitting back in his chair. The original Luddites had been a loose political group back on Terra in the nineteenth century—laborers, mostly, who'd feared losing their jobs to the machines of the industrial revolution and who'd sought to fight back by acts of sabotage. In the twelve centuries since that time, new groups with Luddite philosophies and fears had risen time after time, and on world after world. With the BattleMech as the visible manifestation of *all* machines, it was particularly easy nowadays to point to technology as the evil threatening to tear civilization apart and ultimately to destroy humanity.

Grayson had little patience with such arguments. If technology threatened humanity through weapons, it also offered civilization its one real hope for ending the age-old cycle of want, ignorance, and warfare.

"I know how you feel aboot the antitechnology sorts," McCall said. "Still, they're not so much evil as misguided."

"Agreed. And if they find themselves armed with rocks against BattleMechs, they're likely to find out just how misguided they've been."

McCall's eyes closed, as if at some remembered pain. "Aye," he said softly. "Tha's true enough."

Grayson turned to his computer monitor, cleared it of report forms and orders, and called up the Legion's library net. Part of the same planetary data system that McCall had accessed for word about Caledonia, it was a continuously updated encyclopedia of worlds, personalities, events, and groups across the Inner Sphere, assembled on the theory that what was happening on a neighboring world might one day be part of a political or a tactical problem facing the Legion's battle staff.

"Word of Jihad," Grayson said, addressing the computer. "Screen only."

As text flickered across the screen he felt a stab of disappointment. The data base offered painfully little information on the group, which in any case must have appeared quite recently. It had apparently begun as an heretical offshoot of the Unfinished Book Movement, a quasi-religious order founded a century before in the Federated Suns, and dedicated to the unification of the various great faiths.

The "Unfinished Book" referred to the fact that there was still much spiritual truth to be discovered. The Word of Jihad had evidently decided to write a chapter or two on its own, for the only mentions of the new movement appeared in reports of rioting and insurrection on Federated Commonwealth worlds from Rigel Kent and New Earth to Carstairs. So far, at least, it appeared to be confined to the Skye March, but the movement's spread was being discussed in Tharkad and in New Avalon, the twin capitals of the Federated Commonwealth. There was a growing concern that the Word of Jihad—which, as McCall had suggested, taught that machines were evil—would spread beyond the Skye March to other areas of FedCom space.

"Interesting," Grayson commented aloud as he read the little that was known about the Jihad movement. "It says here the Word of Jihad thinks the end of the universe is about to take place."

"Indeed, sir?"

"Mmm. They claim that there's to be a great tribulation, a time of blood and unceasing warfare, lasting three hundred years, followed by a time of cleansing when everyone uncontaminated by the demonic spirit of machines will be empowered by God to destroy all machines and put an end, once and for all, to war." Grayson cocked an eyebrow at McCall. "Three centuries of tribulation? That could be the Succession Wars, I suppose, measured from the death of First Lord Simon Cameron."

"Tha' was . . . what, Colonel? 2750, or '51, thereabouts? They're a wee bit past their time if they think that. Unless we're in their time of cleansing right now."

"Apocalyptic religions aren't always logical about their dating systems. That three centuries could be measured from the Amaris coup, too. That pretty much started the collapse of the Star League. And that was 2766."

"Either way, I can see how th' idea would excite them," McCall said. "After three long, bluidy centuries a' one House knocking another into wrack an' ruin, they see a time comin' soon wi' no 'Mechs, no damned invadin' armies, no war. . . ."

"Paradise. But I'm afraid I don't see that happening."

"Nor I, Colonel. Not tha' that'll stop 'em from tryin' t' take on BattleMechs wi' stones. Th' damned poor fools."

Grayson blanked the screen, then turned to face his officer. "Major," he said bluntly, "I cannot accept your resignation."

McCall's face first fell, then hardened into a stubborn and recalcitrant glower. "Sir, I'm vurra sorry t' hear y' say tha'. . . ."

"Shut up, Davis. Before you commit an act of mutiny."

"Sir, I—"

"I said shut up! Not another word!"

McCall's jaw clamped firmly shut, though his eyes continued to smolder.

Grayson touched a key on the console pad of his desk. "Sandy?"

A man's voice replied from the outer office. "Yes, Colonel."

"Track down Captain Carlyle, please. I want him here in my office immediately. Sooner if possible."

"Yes, sir."

Looking again at McCall, Grayson waved his hand. "For God's sake, stop glowering at me, Mac!" He indicated the far wall of the office, where a small but well-stocked bar resided behind a sliding panel. "Go fix yourself a drink. I think there's still some of that Glenlivet you like so much."

Caught between stubbornness and an automatic obedience, McCall started to rise, hesitated, then did as Grayson had commanded. "Sir," he said after a moment, while pouring three fingers of golden liquid into a glass filled with ice. "May I speak?"

"Of course," Grayson said. "I didn't mean to be abrupt. In here, with just you and me, you can call me whatever you damn well please."

McCall broke a wry grin. "Well, noo, I was nae aboot to call y' names, sir. But I did wonder wha' had crossed your mind. I must return to my family, do y' see that, sir? I must, if I have to desert t' do it! Your orders leave me vurra little choice. . . ."

"You'd desert the Legion, Mac?" Grayson's voice was as soft as velvet.

McCall did not answer right away. "I would not like t' be put in the position where I would have t' choose."

"We may all have to choose before long, old friend." Grayson hesitated, then grinned. "Mac, there's no reason at all for you to resign your commission. Not when I'm just about to assign you to detached duty."

McCall's eyes widened slightly, and the golden liquid in the glass he held sloshed a bit. "Detached duty. Sir . . . you're nae thinkin' a' sendin' me to—"

"Caledonia, Mac. You're going home . . . and I want you to take my son with you. What do you think of that?"

"I think, sir," McCall said, choosing each word deliberately, "tha' th' Colonel has lost his bluidy mind. Sir."

5

Glencoe Highlands, Near Dunkeld
Glengarry. Skye March
Federated Commonwealth
1218 Hours, 10 March 3057

"**O**h, drek, *no!*"

The shrill chirrup of Alex Carlyle's comm unit shattered the peaceful quiet of the hillside and set a flock of bugbirds to raucous flight.

"Drek," Alex said again, for emphasis. "I don't drekkin' *believe* this!"

Caitlin DeVries moved beneath him, and her eyes opened. Her dark hair was tangled and wild. "Mmm," she said as the comm unit continued to chirp, two shorts followed by a long, repeated over and over. "Shouldn't you get that? It's the base code."

He sighed. "I suppose I'd better." Bending his head forward again, he kissed her long and lovingly. "Be right back, Cait. Don't go away."

Rolling off of her, Alex moved to the edge of the blanket they'd spread out on the grassy slope and began rummaging through the pile of their discarded clothing. "You would think," he said as he extracted the communicator from beneath his trousers, "that we could have a couple of hours' lunch break to ourselves." He flipped the receive switch and held the headset against his ear. "Carlyle!" he snapped. "What is it?"

"Alex? This is Sandy Gunnarson. Better get back here on the double. Your father's looking for you."

Alex groaned. "I'm off the base."

"I know. We've been scanning for you here, but when your ID tag didn't show on the locator, I decided to try the comm. Where are you, anyway?"

"Oh, up in the Glencoes," Alex said with only the least bit of evasiveness. Standing rules required Legion personnel on duty to remain within five kilometers of Castle Hill, and while the Glencoe Highlands technically began their erratic series of step-upon-step rises to the eight-thousand-meter mark just outside of Dunkeld, Alex had, in fact, brought Caitlin considerably farther than that for their picnic and lovemaking tryst. From here, the fortress lay about twenty klicks to the southwest, and perhaps half that again if one measured the mileage of the dirt road winding down those treacherous slopes.

"Well, you'd better hotfoot it back here. The Colonel wants to see you, and his word to me was 'immediately—sooner if possible.' "

"Make it an hour."

"You want to tell him that yourself?"

Alex muttered something unpleasant beneath his breath. Turning, he saw Caitlin standing on the other side of the blanket, pulling on her underwear. "Wait," he said. "What are you doing?"

"I, ah, didn't copy that, Alex," Gunnarson's voice said.

"Someone wants you back," Caitlin said, reaching for her top. "Am I right?"

"Okay, okay," he said into the comm. "I'll try to make it in thirty minutes."

"I could send a hopper for you. Give me your coords."

"Ah, negative on that. I've got my cycle. Look, tell the Colonel I'll be there fast as I can."

"Okay, but make it snappy. His next move might be to send a 'Mech out to pick you up." There was a roguish pause on the channel. "And tell Caitlin I said hello. Gunnarson out."

Alex tossed the communicator onto the blanket, disgusted. "Sandy says hello," he said.

Nearly dressed, Caitlin was sitting down now on the blanket as she pulled on her boots. "God. That means the whole Legion knows I was up here with you."

"Well, it's no secret that we've got something serious going, you and I." Alex had been attracted to her ever since she'd joined his lance as a rookie MechWarrior more than a year before.

"That's doesn't exactly make things easy for me, you know. Being the Colonel's kid's woman. So, who wants you back?"

"My father."

"Figures. You'd better get dressed . . . or are you going back to town like that?"

"Huh? Oh, yeah." Alex began pulling on his uniform. "I'm sorry about the interruption."

"It happens. We really shouldn't have come this far up."

"Hey, I'm the Colonel's son, right? What's the good of that if I can't bend the rules a little?"

He'd meant it as a joke, but she gave him a hard, quizzical look. "Are you serious? If there's one thing the troops idolize Grayson Carlyle for, it's the fact that he doesn't play favorites!" She produced a comb from her belt pouch and began working at the tangles in her hair. "You know," she continued, "I wonder sometimes why you're not more like him."

That stung. "Should I be?"

"You used to be. I think that's why I was so attracted to you. Lately though, I don't know. You've been . . . different. Colder, more distant, maybe. I know things have been rough for you ever since—"

"Maybe you'd rather be with my father," Alex snapped, angry now. "Of course, he's married, so that makes it harder for you, I guess. What am I, the next best thing?"

"Oh, I didn't mean it that way, Alex, and you know it! Don't be so defensive!"

A moment before he'd been about to suggest that they do something special that evening to make up for the interruption to their tryst, possibly dinner and a late, moonlight walk to a deserted part of the beach above the Firth of Moray, but the mood was broken now. It would be a while before he asked *her* out again! In a hostile silence, they finished with buckles, snaps, and belts, gathered up the blanket and the knapsack that had carried lunch, and stowed them in the cargo compartment of his cycle.

The machine was a low, gleaming Defiance Bluestreak, a powerful, gyro-stabilized monocycle powered by hydrogen converter cells. Alex strapped on his helmet, swung his leg over the top, and settled into the machine's saddle just ahead of the central bulge of the wheel well. He spent a moment checking the instrumentation as Caitlin squeezed in behind him and put her arms around his waist. Then he cut on the power and engaged the gyro, while the high-pitched whine of the flywheel rose to its peak telling him he could now easily balance the long, sleek machine on its single wide, deeply tracked tire by leaning against the gyro's firm push.

"Okay?" he called over his shoulder, and Caitlin squeezed twice. "Okay," she said. He cut in the throttle, kicked the accelerator pedal past its detents, and the Bluestreak howled, spitting gravel. With a single tire, steering was almost entirely a matter of leaning to left or right, though the control stick gave him some extra cornering when he needed it by shifting the flywheel from side to side. The road descended the hillside in a series of steep, sharp switchbacks; Alex took each turn with a reckless bravado that threatened to set them airborne with each swing.

Even driving far faster than was safe on that road, it was almost twenty minutes before the dirt track leveled off and finally joined a paved highway straight-lining toward the spires and domes of Dunkeld. Alex kicked in full power, the cycle shrieking beneath the two riders, the wind tearing at their clothing as they roared down the road. Before long they could see the grim gray turrets of the Castle Hill fortress rising from the cliffs above the town.

They were forced to stop at the Legion checkpoint on the outskirts of Dunkeld. There, an armored trooper checked their IDs in his hand-held scanner while a hulking *Vindicator* covered him from behind the base perimeter.

Glancing up, Alex recognized the *Vindie,* a much-patched survivor of the Glengarry campaign called *Tassone's Terror*.

"Afternoon, Captain," an amplified female voice boomed from the eleven-meter machine. "And Caitlin! What've you two been up to all morning?"

MechWarrior Veronica Tassone was a brassy redhead who loved to indulge in juicy bits of gossip, true or not. There was also, Alex was aware, some bad blood between her and Caitlin, a smoldering hostility that he'd long wondered about. It was flattering to think that the women might have fought over him. . . .

He didn't respond to Veronica's banter, however, beyond

tossing her an offhand salute. Then he accepted the IDs from the trooper, gunned the cycle, and tooled into the twistings of Dunkeld's streets. Five minutes later, they showed IDs again at the front gate of the fortress, before being admitted to the castle's lower-level motor pool area.

Almost the instant he pulled into his numbered parking area, Caitlin sprang off the machine and whipped off her helmet. "What the devil was *that* all about?" she demanded.

"What, Ronnie Tassone? She's just jealous of—"

"No, you egotist. I mean your damned wild driving down off that mountain! What's with you anyway?"

"Well, maybe you'd rather not do it again!" he flared.

"You've got *that* right, mister!" She was furious now, her dark eyes flaming, the usually pale and lightly freckled skin of her face flushed. She stood in front of him, fists on hips, chin jutting forward defiantly. "For a long time now I've been making some damned big allowances for you, Alex Carlyle, because of what happened to Davis Clay and everything, but this is just too damned much! You've been moody, testy, and unpredictable! You treat me like your personal property, like you have some kind of a right to *use* me whenever you feel like it, without regard to my schedule or my feelings in the matter, and when you can't have your own way, you rage off like a madman and nearly kill us both on this expensive toy of yours! One minute you're boasting about being the Colonel's son, the next you're so sullen no one can reach you! Well here's a class-A priority for you, Captain Carlyle. I've had it with your moods and I've had it with you. Next time you want to go AWOL for your fun, talk to your friend Ronnie!"

She shoved her helmet hard into Alex's gut, then whirled about and stormed off. "Wonderful," Alex said, turning the helmet in his hands. "Just drekkin' *wonderful*. . . ."

His thirty minutes were already up and then some, so he didn't stop at the officers' quarters to change his uniform. Instead, he rode a lift all the way up to Level 10, where he was waved through security by a bored trooper and into the Legion's Administrative Center. Captain Sandy Gunnarson waved him past the outer office and into the *sanctum sanctorum* . . . the Colonel's office.

Major Davis McCall was there, wearing full dress instead of his usual fatigues or grease-stained jumpsuit. The gold, silver, and polychrome glory of the medals on his chest snagged the eye with color and reflected light, contrasting with the deep gray of his tunic.

"At last!" the elder Carlyle said, looking up from the computer display on his desk. "The prodigal returns!"

"Sorry I'm late, sir," Alex said.

"An' is that any way t' appear before th' Colonel, lad?" McCall said with a disapproving glower. "Y' hae nae comit back from a battle, I'm thinkin', an' there're precious few other excuses for the condition of that uniform."

"Let it be, Mac," Grayson said gently. "Where were you, son?"

"I was taking some time off for lunch," Alex replied, a hint of sullenness creeping into his voice. "Took a ride in the hills above Dunkeld."

"I don't care about the condition of your uniform," Grayson said, "especially since my orders were to get you back at once. But you will stay within easy call while you're on duty. Am I clear?"

"Yes, sir."

"Very well. That's all we'll say about it, son. Meanwhile, what do you know about the Word of Jihad?"

Alex furrowed his brow. He'd heard something recently. . . .

"Isn't that a fanatic anti-'Mech religious cult of some kind? I remember seeing a download not long ago, something about a riot on New Earth."

"Aye, that's the one, lad," McCall said, nodding. "Not only anti-'Mech, but anti-*tech*. They'd have us back in the Stone Age if they could, an' even then they might be protestin' our chippin' flints an' making fire t' aye keepit warm."

"They'd have a rough time on Glengarry." Glengarry's climate, though on the cool side, was mild through most of its year, but the winters tended to be long and harsh, particularly in the northern latitudes.

"Maybe so," Grayson said. "But they seem to be making new trouble now. On Caledonia."

Alex glanced at McCall, but the big Caledonian's face was an impassive mask. "We're being contracted for Caledonia?"

"Not yet," Grayson said. "But there is a chance." He, too, looked at McCall. "Mac? You want to tell him?"

"No, sir. You go ahead. I still think th' idea's daft."

"That's what I like to hear in my people, Mac," Grayson

said with a half-smile. "Complete and absolute confidence in their commanding officer. All right, Alex, this is the situation." And he began filling his son in on recent events on Caledonia, including the arrest of McCall's brother Angus.

"I can well understand Major McCall's reluctance to go into a situation where he might end up fighting against his own family," Grayson concluded. "I can also understand why he wouldn't want to remain behind while his people were dying . . . quite possibly because of our intervention in their affairs. What I'm proposing to do is almost the worst of both possibilities, but it offers him an alternative and the Gray Death a better chance if we get sent in as peace-keepers. I'm putting him on detached duty and sending him back to Caledonia. I want you to go with him."

"Sir, for all ye ken, y' could arrive in Dundee in a month or two an' find me leading a rebel army against tha' wee bastard of a governor."

"Actually, Mac, I'm stacking the deck in the Legion's favor. The political situation sounds confused enough that the Legion desperately needs some eyes on the ground in advance of their deployment. When we land, *if* we land, we'll need to know who our friends are, who our enemies are, what their respective strengths and weaknesses might be, and we'll need to have all of that information immediately, without having to gather it for ourselves. You know as well as I do that the official mission briefings are likely to be slanted."

"Well, aye, there's that. An' to tell the truth, sir, I would nae trust this Wilmarth character oot a' SRM range."

"This won't be a combat assignment, Mac. It won't even necessarily be covert. You can go in as yourself, help your family, see about getting your brother's release. But you'll be keeping your Mark I Mod I sensors on full the whole time."

"Aye. Y' know, Colonel. It almost makes a crazy sort of sense a' that."

"But why send me?" Alex blurted out.

Grayson nailed him with a hard stare. "Is there any reason why I shouldn't?"

Plenty of reasons, Alex wanted to shout, but he clamped his mouth shut and said nothing. He was sure that Ellen Jamison must have been keeping his father apprised of his restless nights; that was, after all, one of her duties as a regimental MedTech. And his father would know about the trouble he'd been having in the simulators lately, too. It was Artman's duty to inform him of *that*.

He was confused, unable to order a whirlwind of conflicting thoughts. His self-confidence had been shaken to the point that he wondered if he would ever be able to function as a 'Mech pilot again, but there was still the question of what he would do, what he *could* do instead.

And he desperately needed to get away—away from the regiment, away from the other people. The other Legionnaires had been comrades once, but now more and more they were strangers. Alex could sense that the change was not in them, but in him, in the way he reacted to them. Caitlin had as much as told him that just a few moments ago.

"Well, Alex?" his father prompted. "I won't order you to go. It's volunteers only. But if you refuse, you and I are going to take up this matter of your simulator scores. I'm wondering if some extra duty might not improve your concentration. What do you say?"

"How aboot it, Alex? Are y' game?"

"I'll ... go."

"That's the spirit, young Alex!" McCall said, grinning. "To tell the truth, I think your father wants t' send you wi' me as watchdog. He cannae trust me on m' own wi' the Jacobites, an' he needs you t' keep an eye on me."

"That's not true and you know it, Mac. But I do want you to have some back-up, just in case. And Alex needs the experience."

"But what am I supposed to do?" Alex asked. He was feeling increasingly out of his depth.

"You'll watch Major McCall's back and you'll do what he tells you," Grayson replied.

"Aye," McCall added. "We'll let this battle plan write itself, Alex. Colonel? How soon can we leave?"

Grayson consulted his desktop computer. "Well, it wouldn't make sense to send regimental assets, of course. Too obvious. There's a passenger run schedule for next week. JumpShip *Altair*."

"The *Altair*! That's the one Lori's comin' in on, noo?"

Grayson smiled. "Yup. With her 'surprise,' whatever that is."

" 'Twould be a shame t' miss her. Two ships passin' in the night, as it were."

"Can't be helped. Unless you want to wait a month for the next scheduled passenger run. Or take a military Jump-Ship."

"No, that makes no sense at all. The *Altair* it is, if you'll gi' m' best wishes to your bonnie lassie when she grounds."

"That I will, Mac." Grayson glanced at Alex. "I'm sorry you'll miss your mother, son. She'll likely skin me alive for this."

Alex managed a small grin. "I'm sorry too. But JumpShip skippers aren't known for their patience, are they?"

"I'm afraid not."

JumpShips linked star system with star system. Their transit times were essentially instantaneous, but it took days—eight days, in the case of the Glengarry system—for them to recharge their drives between on jump and the next. Unable to operate deep within the local star's gravity well, Jump-Ships remained always in deep space, usually at the system's zenith or nadir jump points, and at a distance determined by the star's mass. DropShips provided transport between waiting JumpShips and the system's worlds; for Glengarry, transit time at 1G between world and jump point was about five days.

The JumpShip *Altair,* adhering to a tight schedule, would arrive in-system tomorrow—on the eleventh—and depart eight days later, on the nineteenth. Lori's DropShip, undocking from the *Altair* shortly after arriving in-system, would arrive at the Dunkeld spaceport on the sixteenth, but Alex and McCall would have left Glengarry two days earlier in order to reach the *Altair* in time for the jump. The two DropShips would, literally, pass one another in the night of space, one inbound, the other out.

Grayson continued to study his computer display. "How much of a hurry are you in to get to Caledonia, Major?"

"Well, noo, it would be nice t' be there for tea tomorrow," he said. "But tha' would be bendin' the laws of physics."

"Just a bit. The *Altair* is scheduled for two stops along the way, at Gladius and Laiaka."

McCall frowned. "An' wi' seven or eight days at each for recharge—"

"You wouldn't reach Caledonia until the middle of next month. But there's another way."

"Aye? A handoff express?"

Grayson worked at his keypad for a moment. "You could transfer to a FedCom military JumpShip at Gladius," Grayson said. "The *Neptune*. That would cut your delay at Gladius to three days. Then at Laiaka, we transfer you to another civilian job, an independent trader called the *Shoshone*."

"Independents won't be as certain of their schedules," McCall pointed out.

"True, but if you can cut a deal, you won't have to wait at Laiaka for more than two or three days. You could be on Caledon by the thirtieth of March. If you miss the *Shoshone*, you could still be there by April fifth."

"That sounds good," McCall said. "Better than I'd hoped by a damned sight."

"April," Alex said, looking up. "We won't be here for the ceremonies."

The first day of April was a special day for the Legion, the annual Day of Heroes, when fallen comrades were remembered.

Heroes like Davis Clay. Alex had been looking forward to *this* Day of Heroes for almost a year now, with both anticipation and dread.

"Can't be helped, lad," McCall said. "Perhaps we can have our own celebration, on Caledon."

"You all right, Alex?" his father asked.

"Huh? Yes. Yes, sir. I was just ... thinking."

McCall was looking thoughtful, tugging at his beard. "I'm wondering, though, Colonel. How much leeway do we have wi' equipment on this deployment?"

"Well, considering the fact that you two will be going back in an unofficial capacity, private citizens, as it were, I doubt very much that the local government will let you smuggle in a couple of 'Mechs."

"Aye. I was nae thinkin' of 'Mechs. Two BattleMechs against a planet is nae my idea of a fair fight."

"We should be able to arrange almost anything else, though. Personal arms, certainly. I'll want you to take a small commo base station with you, as well as personal communicators. We can disguise all of that as freight easily enough."

"Aye. I was wonderin', Colonel, if you could see your

way clear t' allowin' us to take along a couple of the new wee bairns, as well."

Alex looked shocked. "Is that a good idea?"

Grayson smiled. "I think we could probably arrange that, Major. And heaven help anyone who gets in your way!"

6

"So," Lori Kalmar Carlyle said, pressing up close inside the circle of Grayson's arms. "What do you think of my surprise?"

"As Mac might say," Grayson replied with a chuckle, "I'm just a wee bit thunderstruck." Releasing Lori, he turned to the short, compact, gray-haired and -bearded man beside Lori and grinned. "You don't know how long I've wanted to meet you, Commander!"

"Actually," Lori put in, "it approaches hero worship sometimes. Embarrassing!"

"The same with me, Colonel," the man replied, laughing. "Though I admit I'm delighted we could arrange the meeting like this, and not out on the field somewhere, 'Mech to 'Mech."

Jaime Wolf, supreme Commander of Wolf's Dragoons, was arguably the most celebrated—and notorious—mercenary inside the Inner Sphere or beyond it. Word had it that he no longer commanded in the field, that he had, in fact, retired at last after almost fifty years of active duty. The death of his son two years before had been a grave blow, and a rebellion by members of his own unit at his moment of weakness had very nearly finished him. But he'd fought his way back to win that one, final, critical victory, then returned to his world of Outreach to begin shaping the Dragoons for their new role as an independent power within the Inner Sphere.

Early yesterday, Lori had returned from Tharkad aboard the JumpShip *Altair*, bringing with her Jaime Wolf and several members of his staff. She'd encountered the celebrated mercenary on Tharkad, she'd explained, and persuaded him to return to Outreach by way of Glengarry. Wolf, expressing an interest in meeting Grayson Carlyle of the famous Gray Death Legion, had readily agreed. One of his JumpShips would be arriving at Glengarry soon to pick him up, summoned there by an HPG transmission from Tharkad.

"It's probably better this way at that, Commander Wolf," Grayson said. "Your *Archer* against my *Victor*, well, it just wouldn't be fair!"

"Please," the other man said with a grin. "Call me Jaime!"

"Jaime. If you call me Grayson."

"Grayson it is! Not fair for whom?"

"I'd outmass you by ten tons."

"Ten tons isn't that much in the way of armor, but it might make a difference with maneuverability. You might find I have a few surprises in this old carcass of mine!"

The light bantering felt good. Last evening, the Legion had hosted a formal banquet in Jaime Wolf's honor, but the formalities hadn't allowed Grayson much opportunity to really talk with Wolf. And, truth be known, he'd had other things on his mind than his famous guest last night. After all, he hadn't seen Lori in nearly six weeks, and they'd needed a long time together alone, after the party.

So he'd only just begun to really get to know Jaime Wolf, but so far, he liked the man a lot. He was intelligent, sharp, and quick on the uptake. The good-natured bravado of MechWarrior vets fit them both much more naturally than did their full-dress uniforms . . . or the stuffy formality of the banquet.

"Enough, you two armchair warriors, enough!" Lori said, laughing as she stepped between them and hooked their arms with hers. "That's why we've organized this show here today, so you two can show off to your hearts' content without strewing expensive 'Mech innards across half the landscape!"

"You still think this scheme will help the Legion pay off

its debts?" Grayson asked as she steered them down a corridor and toward an enormous set of sliding doors at the far end.

"And then some," she said, flashing her confident smile. "You two might not realize it, but you gentlemen are currently the hottest thing on Glengarry three-vee right now, and it looks like we're going to have a chance to sell the rights to Interstar Entertainment, too."

"We should have thought of this years ago, Grayson," Jaime added. "It's cheaper than fighting and not nearly as wasteful as the Solaris games!"

Carlyle laughed. The gladiator-style combats on Solaris had long been a sore point with him. Senseless, set-piece engagements where MechWarriors—usually the desperate ones hard-up for C-bills or recognition—and BattleMechs were ground up for the amusement of the populace and the enrichment of gamblers. Computer sims offered just as much realism and just as much a testing of skill, experience, and guts, but no one was actually hurt or killed.

Lori released their arms when they reached the door. "Well, you two, here's your public debut as stars of three-vee! Good luck, both of you!"

"Aren't you coming in?" Grayson asked.

"This is your moment. I'll be watching, though!"

The tall doors slid open, giving entrance to the heart of Dunkeld's Civic Arena, a vast, domed-over amphitheater ringed by circle upon rising circle of seats. As the two men entered, resplendent in full military dress, the crowd packed into the bleachers rose as one, venting a thunderous roar that filled the dome and echoed from every side. Side by side, Grayson Carlyle and Jaime Wolf faced the crowd, arms raised, turning slightly from side to side. After a moment, they shook hands with one another and, as the crowd continued to cheer, each walked to his assigned station at opposite ends of an enormous holographic projection table.

That table, measuring some fifty meters by thirty meters, was currently displaying in accurate 1/200 scale a rolling green landscape dominated by patches of dark woods, open, cultivated fields, and a web of dusty-looking dirt roads radiating out from a cluster of archaic-looking buildings near the table's center. Two long, parallel ridges extended south from that town, separated by a broad, open valley almost a meter wide on the projection; hills, some thickly wooded, some bald-topped and strewn with boulders. Much of the ground, especially in the east and in the south, was broken and difficult, with such thickly wooded areas that even BattleMechs would have trouble passing through them.

Grayson slipped down into the open, egg-shaped cockpit of his station positioned on the west edge of the map. Several display monitors above and to his left and right lit up as he took his seat. Numbers winked into view on his primary screen, detailing lists of units, conditions, and coordinates of BattleMechs.

"Gentlemen! Are you ready to begin?" a disembodied voice asked from somewhere overhead.

"Ready," Grayson replied.

"All set," Wolf's voice echoed, sounding as close as if the leader of Wolf's Dragoons had been seated at Grayson's side, instead of thirty meters away at the opposite side of the table.

"Very well, Colonel, Commander," the voice continued. "We're ready here. Stand by. Five ... four ... three ... two ..."

Somewhere, music crashed, martial and insistent.

"Ladies and gentlemen," another voice said, addressing the entire vast audience. "Welcome back to Glengarry Broadcasting's Sports Extravaganza: The Wolf and the Death's Head, the holographic battle of the year!"

As the music continued, Grayson adjusted a throat mike, then opened a private channel to Wolf. "I swear to God," he said, "I had no idea they were going to hype this thing this much!"

"No problem, Grayson," Jaime Wolf replied, voice just audible beneath the opening music. "If I were you, I'd be worrying more about what might happen if you lose here today! Sounds like you have some fans out there who might get a bit upset with me!"

Grayson could hear the chanting, a deep, rhythmic repetition of "Gray Death! Gray Death! Gray Death!" accompanied by the stamp of hundreds of feet.

"*If* you win," Grayson replied lightly, giving the first word all the stress he could, "I'm sure we'll be able to slip you out the back!"

"Sure. And next time, we do this back on Outreach, where I can pack the audience with *my* fans!"

"Deal."

The music was winding down, the announcer's voice giving a summary of the strategic situation chosen for the day's contest. With a brief, buzzing whine, the holographic images of Grayson's 'Mechs materialized along the northwest edge of the terrain, tiny, perfect representations of BattleMechs, each just five centimeters tall.

The Battle of Gettysburg, July 1, 2, and 3, 1863, refought with 'Mechs.

The game of BattleTech, in its myriad incarnations, had been an intensely popular entertainment for centuries, appearing in countless forms on every inhabited world throughout the Inner Sphere. Most common and popular were the two- to eight-player cockpit versions that pitted half-meter holographic images of 'Mechs against one another at close range, with computers to tally and record damage. They were, in fact, smaller civilian versions of the big simulators military units used for training.

Less common and more difficult to play were the strategic setups, whole, sprawling campaigns fought with hundreds or even thousands of separate holographic pieces projected by the computer onto an accurately scaled and detailed image of a given historical battlefield. Where the smaller sims tested a MechWarrior's tactical skill at handling one or a very few BattleMechs, the strategic battlefield simulators tested a would-be general's ability to command an entire army, struggling against not only the enemy, but such complications as terrain, breakdowns, and logistics.

For this highly publicized engagement between two well-known mercenary commanders, Jaime Wolf would play the part of General George Gordon Meade leading the Union forces, while Grayson took the persona of Robert E. Lee commanding the Confederates.

The mix of BattleMechs at each man's command had been balanced by the computer to roughly parallel the sorts of troops that had been engaged in the actual battle. Grayson could look up at any of the display monitors above him and actually see the battlefield as though he were observing it from the cockpit of one of the 'Mechs, right down to the ponderous, side-to-side lurch as the machine ambled along the road; the moderating computer could calculate all possible angles of view from any point on that enormous terrain map and create the appropriate image on the screen. From what he could see, the battle was now underway in earnest.

The first of Grayson's troops, representing the shoe-hunting infantry of a general named Heth, consisted of one company of light and medium 'Mechs. They began the contest by deploying in open formation along a dirt road leading southeast into the village. Waiting for them at the top of a low ridge, however, was Wolf's cavalry . . . in this case, a dozen light armored hovercraft, his high-speed scouts, supported by the long-range muscle of a single *Archer*.

An *Archer*. That was Wolf's usual 'Mech in the field, Grayson knew. In this simulation, it was possible at any time for the player to "enter" any one 'Mech and control it directly; the other player could never know for sure which 'Mech was the personal 'Mech of his opponent, but there was a point penalty if a player lost a 'Mech while he was running it. It was tempting to assume that the *Archer* up there on McPherson's Ridge was piloted personally by Jaime Wolf; destroying it would win Grayson some points.

On the other hand, that could well be precisely what Wolf was counting on. That *Archer* outmassed Grayson's heaviest 'Mech, a *Centurion*, by twenty tons. It would take time to hammer the *Archer* down with a concerted attack, and that might well be time enough for Wolf's reinforcements to come up.

A volley of simulated rockets streaked from the *Archer*, tiny pinpoints of flame descending on the advancing 'Mechs like hail. Grayson tapped out a command . . . then another. His four heavier 'Mechs pressed forward, taking hits but pinning the enemy's attention with a stinging, lashing barrage, while the eight lighter 'Mechs fell back, shifted to the right, and began circling around through McPherson's Woods.

The Second Battle of Gettysburg had begun.

Two men watched the contest with considerable interest from a media gallery high above the rows of bleachers and the crowd. The gallery was one of a number of enclosed balconies ringing the stadium, designed to provide comfortable surroundings for media commentators and members of the electronic press. The bodies of its previous occupants, a man and a woman, lay on the floor near one wall in twin puddles of slowly pooling blood.

From this elevated vantage point, the two men were positioned nearly eighty meters from Grayson Carlyle's station.

It was difficult to see the mercenary from here directly, though large vid monitors on the room's console gave close-ups of either Wolf or Carlyle on command, as well as any part of the battlefield. Both of the contestants appeared deeply engrossed as they manipulated their armies, which, for the convenience of the spectators thronging that hall, were displayed in blue or gray.

The two watchers, however, were less interested in the simulated troop deployments than they were in Carlyle.

"I could take him now," the first man said, his voice a low growl. "Easy."

"Not yet, Pardo," the other, a leaner, darker man said. He still held the snub-nosed needler pistol that he'd used on the two reporters. "We have to take down both targets at once. If we pop Carlyle now, we might not get a shot at the other one."

"Damn, boss, I hate this waiting."

"It won't be long now. There'll be a break soon. Maybe then."

An hour passed . . . and then another. The first day's fight, interestingly enough, actually paralleled the historical fight at Gettysburg on July 1 fairly closely, except, of course, that the simulated 'Mechs under Grayson's and Wolf's respective commands were considerably faster and more maneuverable than closely packed regiments of men or horse-drawn artillery pieces. With few of the forces on either side on the field as yet, the initial meeting engagement northwest of Gettysburg had rapidly evolved into a series of lightning-fast thrusts and slashes among the open, rolling hills and cornfields, with heavy casualties on both sides. The hover tanks and the lone *Archer* on the ridgetop had held, then slowly pulled back toward the town. Grayson's thrust through McPherson's Woods had run into tougher terrain than he'd been expecting, and by the time his *Locust*s and *Stinger*s broke through into the open, the heavier Union 'Mechs of Jaime Wolf's I Corps had arrived from the south, forcing Grayson to make a hasty retreat to avoid being cut off and surrounded or pinned against the woods and smashed in detail.

But Confederate reinforcements were arriving on the field too, timed to parallel the troop arrivals of the original battle, but in swifter succession. Soon, Wolf's Union forces were finding themselves trapped between swiftly growing numbers of Confederates streaming piecemeal onto the battlefield from both the west and the north. His XI Corps, still brittle after their rout at Chancellorsville two months earlier, broke suddenly as a handful of Grayson's 'Mechs flanked them to the east; soon, the entire Union force was in full retreat through the town.

Unfortunately, Grayson wasn't able to follow through on his initial tactical advantage before darkness ended the contest. His orders to one of his divisions to seize Culp's Hill southeast of the town—a position that would have placed him squarely behind the enemy's northern flank—had been ignored, presumably on the electronic whim of the moderating computer that periodically threw such glitches into the game in order to simulate the fog of war.

And then the battlefield faded into darkness, as a voice overhead announced, "Gentlemen. Time for recess. The first day's battle is concluded."

Blinking, Grayson leaned back in his seat, suddenly aware of the ache in his shoulders as the overhead lights came up once more. He caught Wolf's eye across that broad, hill-rippled table top and grinned; Wolf replied with a wry, two-fingered salute.

"The first day goes to you on points and position both, I'd say," his voice said in Grayson's earpiece. "The second day, though, will be different."

"The first day was a virtual repeat of the real battle," Grayson replied. "Right down to the troop positions at nightfall." Standing, he studied the darkened terrain, where simulated campfires winked and flickered, marking huge camps of armed men. "I would have expected *some* tactical digression!"

"We were simply feeling each other out" was Wolf's response. "Wait until the second day!"

"You know," Grayson said conversationally, "I find it interesting that terrain is playing as big a part in our version of Gettysburg as it did in the original. From the look of those campfires you have on Cemetery Hill and Cemetery Ridge, we're going to be fighting over the same ground on Day Two."

"It's been my experience," Jaime replied, "that terrain is always the deciding tactical factor, whether you're fighting on foot or in BattleMechs."

"You've certainly got the good ground on this go-round," Grayson said.

"Are you going to come take it away from me?" Wolf's tone was bantering, a joking dare.

Grayson was about to reply, but he stopped himself, frowning in concentration. He felt an odd, prickling sensation at the back of his neck . . . the same prickling he often felt in battle.

Danger . . .

Few combat veterans doubt that sixth sense that warns a man of danger. Grayson had felt this warning often before; he felt it strongly now, the sensation of being watched by hostile eyes. Turning sharply, he scanned the banks of seated spectators behind and around him. Their numbers had thinned somewhat with the intermission, but there were still hundreds of faces looking back at him, some intently, some with disinterest.

He saw nothing alarming, nothing suspicious.

"Is there a problem, Grayson?" Wolf's voice asked.

"Sorry," Grayson replied. "I was distracted for a moment there. Stage fright, I guess."

"It *is* quite a crowd."

Dismissing the nagging sense that he was being watched by hostiles, he turned back to his controls and brought up a small, well-lighted version of the terrain map on his main screen.

As had happened in history, the second day's battle would be fought on the hills, ridges, and farmland south of the town of Gettysburg.

Good ground . . .

Grayson had long before identified the key terrain features in that area. Historically, the arrangement of hills and ridges south of the town had been known as "the fishhook." Wooded Culp's Hill occupied the hook's point, joined to Cemetery Hill by a low, curving saddle. The fishhook's shaft was the eastern of the two long ridges, Cemetery Ridge running due south from Cemetery Hill for a distance of over two kilometers. South of that was Little Round Top, heavily wooded on its eastern and southern flanks, nakedly exposed to the west and capped by a tangle of immense boulders. South from there, rising even higher above the surrounding fields and woods and completely covered by trees, was the fishhook's eye—Big Round Top.

During the actual battle, Union forces under Meade had occupied the fishhook in a two-day defensive action, after retreating from the first day's field in defeat. Their opponents had occupied a larger, outer fishhook, from the woods east of Culp's Hill, up and around through the town itself, then down the length of the western, wooded height known as Seminary Ridge, after the Lutheran seminary at its northern end. The second day, Grayson knew, had been largely inconclusive, a series of sharp, hard fights precipitated by a staggered Confederate advance against the Union left. Mistakes on both sides, with a generous mix for both of good luck and bad, had resulted in some of the fiercest fighting of the American Civil War, and place names forever engraved in the memories of fighting men: Peach Orchard, Wheatfield, Devil's Den, Little Round Top. Most military historians counted the second day at Gettysburg as a draw.

Grayson was determined not to repeat the historical unfolding of the battle a second time. By the third and last day, his opponent would have all of his reserves up and would outnumber Grayson's army by a substantial margin. There was a way for the Confederates to win this fight ... and Grayson set out to find it.

The light on the big map was coming up again, revealing rank upon rank of silently waiting BattleMechs, tanks, and tiny images of men, each less than half a centimeter tall. Music came up, and an unseen voice made the expected announcement. "Commander, Colonel, if you're both ready, please. Five ... four ... three ... two ... Ladies and gentlemen, the Battle of Gettysburg, the second day. Brought to you live, here on Glengarry Broadcasting!"

Rapidly, Grayson typed in commands. Historically, Lee had failed on the second day partly because one of his subordinates had delayed in launching the attack. Aware that he was fighting now against time, against the slowly moving sun in the artificial sky above, Grayson urged his holographic army into motion.

"The two sides are still fairly evenly matched," the announcer's voice was saying over his headset. Grayson had elected to open the channel and hear what they were saying; the computer monitoring that channel would blank out any information they let slip on the positioning of Wolf's forces. "Wolf's Union 'Mechs may have a slight advantage in numbers and firepower, and they certainly hold the higher, stronger ground ... that fishhook of hills and ridges extending south from the town. It will be interesting to see whether Wolf repeats the historical Union strategy of sitting tight and letting Colonel Carlyle come to him across open ground, or whether he'll come down off that hill and launch a spoiling attack, maybe in hopes of upsetting the Colonel's timing."

"That's right, Rob," a woman's voice added. "And I might add, by the way, that we've just had word that both the Nagelring on Tharkad and the Sanglamore on Skye have signed onto the HPG net this afternoon in order to watch this epic contest between two master tacticians. . . ."

Grayson suppressed a snort at that. The Nagelring was arguably the best war college within Steiner space, with the Sanglamore a close second. Live HPG transmission time was frightfully expensive. Surely those institutions must have better things to do with their time and money than to watch two old soldiers play war games?

"Well, Linda," the man's voice said, "it looks as though Colonel Carlyle is making his move. . . ."

That part of the commentary, fortunately, would have been edited out by the computer, assuming that Wolf was listening to the chatter at all. What Grayson was attempting to do depended completely on the fact that Wolf would be as blind to what was happening from his side of the battlefield as Grayson was from his. Grayson's vantage point gave him numerous views of the battlefield, but all were limited to areas where his troops were positioned, and from ground level only, since there'd been no aerial reconnaissance in the original battle. The simulation restricted each side's views of the battlefield, limiting them to recreate the effects of distance, of intervening hills or trees, and of drifting clouds of smoke.

Seminary Ridge was thickly lined with trees along its entire length, and Grayson was counting on the fact that Wolf wouldn't be able to see through them and into the valley to their west, any more than he could make out what was happening east of that low rise called Cemetery Ridge.

Of course, were their positions reversed, Grayson knew he would almost certainly send out recon units to try to pinpoint the location of the enemy's main body. He would have to assume that Wolf would reason the same way, which suggested that the enemy's cavalry would soon be put into play.

Secrecy and timing both would be essential for Grayson to pull this off. . . .

In the press box, eighty meters away, the man called Pardo carefully picked up the attaché case resting by his feet, positioned it on his lap, and opened it. Inside, nestled snugly into formcut foam padding, a weapon gleamed in five separate parts: stock, receiver, magazine, electronic sight, and screw-in barrel with integral sound-suppresser.

The other man pressed a button that lowered one of the window panes in front of them, giving them a clear and unobstructed line of sight to their primary target. "Let's do it," he said.

Pardo grunted assent and began to assemble the weapon with swift, sure movements. . . .

7

Approaching Zenith Jump Point
Glengarry System, Skye March
Federated Commonwealth
1300 hours, 18 March 3057

For the past day and a half, the civilian DropShip *Skye Song* had been decelerating, backing down against the blast of her fusion torch as she slowed at a steady 1G thrust. "Below" her—in so far as terms like "below" had any meaning in space—was the system's zenith jump point, a nondescript point in space far "above" the north pole of Glengarry's orange sun. In another twenty hours they would be docking with the *Altair,* still invisible at a range of several million kilometers.

Alex and McCall had found seats for themselves in the ship's small passenger lounge—no small feat considering the fact that there were fewer seats there than passengers by half, and *everybody* aboard, it seemed, wanted to watch the Death's Head versus the Wolf match, which was being transmitted live from Glengarry—or as live as was possible with a speed-of-light time delay of nearly twenty-seven minutes.

At the moment, the 2D view screen covering one of the lounge's bulkheads was occupied by two commentators who were discussing the strategy in the contest so far, a scene transmitted almost half an hour before. Naturally, the strategy employed by the two was the topic of most of the conversation in the lounge as well.

"He'll be making a flank march, I'm thinking," McCall said confidently. "Pull back, swing t' the right, an' put himself across old Jaime Wolf's supply lines to the south."

"Would you like to make a small wager on that?" a florid-faced man in a loud shirt seated to McCall's right said. "The Colonel knows Wolf's troops are still disorganized after that drubbing he gave him. He'll head right up the center. Pow! Go for the throat! Like he did on Glengarry last year!"

"Och, an' I should take your money a' that, lad, just t' teach you not to gamble on the likes o' Grayson Carlyle!"

"A hundred C-bills says Carlyle goes up the center," the man said. "Straight for the jugular!"

McCall pretended to consider the offer for a moment. "Weel, lad, if you're that anxious t' part wi' your money, done! My hundred says he goes for the flank an' forces Wolf to come t' him! Alex? What would you do in the Colonel's place?"

"I, I'm not sure ... Davis." By previous agreement, the two were calling one another by their first names only, if for no other reason than they didn't want to be treated like celebrities by the other passengers. It was hard for Alex to get used to, though, calling McCall "Davis."

The fact that Davis Clay had been named for the Scotsman didn't help one bit. It made Alex uncomfortable, while resurrecting memories he really didn't want to deal with.

"Weel, noo," McCall said. "If you were in command there—"

"I wouldn't pull a flank march," Alex said abruptly. "If the enemy saw what I was doing, he could hit me with a concentrated formation while my 'Mechs were strung out across three or four kilometers. He could break my line in two, maybe even three pieces or more, and dispose of them one by one."

"That's right!" the man with the loud shirt said, grinning. "The kid's got a good head for tactics, Scotty, eh? Pow! Right down the middle!"

"So, Alex," McCall said, ignoring the man, "you've said what y' would nae do. What would y' do instead?"

"Take a strong defensive position," Alex said. "Make him come to me."

"Nope," the loud man said. "Not ol' Death's Head Carlyle! Pow! Right up the middle!"

"Tell me, sir," McCall said gently. "Seein' as how you're

such a student o' military tactics. Have you ever studied the real Battle of Gettysburg?"

"The *real* Gettysburg?" The man blinked. "Well, say, Scotty, I can't say I knew there was another one! Where was that? A world in the Draco Combine?"

"Och, aye. Weel, let's just see wha' develops then."

"It looks as though Colonel Carlyle is up to his old tricks, Linda," the smooth-voiced announcer was saying. "He's pulling off a flank march right under Jaime Wolf's nose."

"That's right, Rob. Of course, Jamie Wolf is—"

And then the sound went dead as the computer cut out some part of the commentary containing tactical information about Wolf's movements.

No matter. For good or for bad, Grayson was committed now to one of the most dangerous of all tactical maneuvers—splitting his force in the face of a numerically superior opponent.

The real General Lee had done just that at the Battle of Chancellorsville, and with considerable success. Longstreet, his most able lieutenant after the death of the immortal Stonewall Jackson, had strongly urged the same sort of maneuver two months later at Gettysburg for various reasons now lost in the mists of history, and Lee had chosen instead to launch a series of direct attacks, gambling that the enthusiasm of his veteran soldiers would be enough to overcome their Union enemies, dug in on high and well-sheltered ground.

But that was a tactic Grayson Carlyle rarely favored. He only used head-on attacks against a strong enemy when he was sure of having the advantage of surprise and morale, or when the assault was a part of some larger strategic deception. Guessing that Jaime Wolf would probe with his scouts across the open valley between the parallel Cemetery and Seminary Ridges, Grayson had advanced one entire company—twelve 'Mechs—out from the tree cover of Seminary Ridge and into the valley, supported by a full battalion of foot soldiers and light hovercraft. Almost immediately, his recon-in-force flushed Wolf's cavalry, a strong force of hover armor already moving across the Emmitsburg Pike toward the seminary, taking advantage of folds in the ground and scattered buildings to conceal their advance from Grayson's scouts.

A sharp and highly mobile battle developed in the fields between the two ridges, as hovercraft howled and snapped at one another in tight, spinning turns, and Grayson's 'Mechs laid down salvo after devastating salvo, covering their own foot infantry's advance. Grayson was risking a lot here; most of his cavalry—representing the forces of the historical General Stuart—had not yet arrived on the field, and those hovercraft comprised almost his entire available reconnaissance force. It was a calculated maneuver, however, one designed to pin Wolf's attention on *this* side of Seminary Ridge, while the bulk of Grayson's army moved elsewhere.

He'd left only about thirty of his 'Mechs in position, strung out from the foot of Culp's Hill in the northeast to the northern half of Seminary Ridge in the west. The vast majority of his force, comprising his entire I and III Divisions, most of the II, and as many reserve units as he could scrape together, were on the move, a long, sinuous column of BattleMechs marching south, sheltered by the trees lining Seminary Ridge. The hardest part was to stay out of the line of sight of any enemy observers—and there were certain to be such—hidden in the woods at the top of Big Round Top, a cone-shaped eminence that dominated the entire southern portion of the battleground.

This was an enormous gamble. Wolf was certain to be expecting something of the sort, if for no other reason than that Grayson Carlyle had the reputation for daring and unexpected maneuvers.

Know the enemy, know yourself; your victory will never be endangered. Grayson long ago had committed Sun Tsu's immortal *Art of War* to memory, for the basic precepts of strategy and tactics changed little with the ages, whether the weapons employed were crossbows or *Archers*. The two men, Wolf and Carlyle, alike in so many ways, had markedly different tactical styles in the field. Jaime Wolf tended to unfold complex plans, with strategies that employed multiple wheels within wheels, misdirection, and surprise. Grayson, on the other hand, tended to be more spontaneous, concentrating on maneuver, strike, and maneuver again, with a fluid and opportunistic fighting style that probed relentlessly for openings, then exploiting them with lightning speed and power when they were revealed.

Knowing what he did of Wolf's character and reputation, he suspected that his opponent would anchor himself to the fishhook's hills and ridges, as Meade had done historically, while preparing some sort of multilayered surprise in the sheltered vale beyond, out of Grayson's line of sight. A mirror-image flanking maneuver to Grayson's end run was a possibility, but not, he felt sure, a probable one. More likely, Wolf would stick to the high ground, forcing Grayson to come to him, conservative tactics for the flamboyant Jaime Wolf, to be sure, but the best use of his forces in a situation like this.

But if Grayson knew anything at all about his opponent, it was that the man was unpredictable . . . and that he would not long be fooled by Grayson's diversion in front of Cemetery Ridge. Grayson keyed in the command to increase the moving column's speed.

"I don't think we can wait anymore," Pardo said. The rifle, a deadly, smoothbore flechette launcher, was assembled, the electronic imaging sight snapped home and switched on. In the darkened press booth, the light from the targeting display cast a pale, yellow-green light across his eyes and the bridge of his nose. "I say pop the primary target. The secondary'll show up quick enough when he goes down, right?"

"Ice it, Pardo," the other man said. "Ice it down!" He checked the action of his needler with a quick nervous gesture. "We wait until I give the word, you got me?"

"Got you." Pardo returned his full attention to the display on his sight. At this range, with the magnification set to ten power, Carlyle's head nearly filled the screen, neatly quartered by glowing white cross hairs.

His finger tightened on the trigger ever so slightly. *Damn,* but he hated waiting!

The single most commanding feature on the battlefield was not a natural object like a ridge or a hill at all. Located a kilometer or two to the east of Cemetery Ridge, close by the Taneytown Road, was an imposing steel structure rising a hundred meters or more above the battlefield. Identified simply as the "National Tower," it was an ugly gray monstrosity of primitive engineering which Grayson doubted very much had existed during the original battle here. One of the problems with historical recreations, however, was the uncertainty of some of the research into older conflicts—in this case, a battle fought more than a thousand years ago. Many of the buildings present in and around the simulated town of Gettysburg were the product of guesswork and computer extrapolations, in particular the restaurants, motels, and souvenir shops.

And the National Tower.

That tower, however, whether it had been present in the original battle or not, was definitely a factor in this one. Wolf would have lookouts up there, and from that vantage point they could see most of the battlefield in all directions.

The tower had to go.

So far, Grayson had managed to keep his moving column out of the tower's line of sight by sticking to the woods and the hollow in the land behind Seminary Ridge. Soon, though, he would have to cross in the open; if Wolf had observers up there, they would see Grayson's 'Mechs for sure.

He checked the time. It should be any moment now. . . .

A roar sounded across the battlefield, echoed by the excited crowd watching. At the center of the field, the National Tower gave a shiver, then slowly, slowly, its saucer-shaped top swayed toward the east, falling, falling, then smashing into twisted steel wreckage across the Taneytown Road.

Now! Move! Grayson's fingers clattered furiously across his keyboard. This had been yet another gamble, but a vital one. As he'd begun his movement, he'd ordered a team of four soldiers clad in individual combat armor to penetrate Wolf's lines and set charges at the base of the National Tower. It wouldn't be long before Wolf had other eyes aloft—in the trees on the crest of Big Round Top if he didn't have them there already—but the tower's unexpected demolition might buy Grayson a few precious moments of relative security.

Racing now, risking overheating with an extended run, Grayson's "Confederate" BattleMechs broke into the open almost two kilometers south of the Round Tops, moving east at full speed. Even without the tower, the enemy's scouts would almost certainly spot them in the open, but it shouldn't matter now. In a classic shift to the right, Grayson had swung around Wolf's left flank and was sweeping around toward his rear. He would be encountering Wolf's outlying pickets any moment now. . . .

Contact! A scattering of light BattleMechs—*Jenner*s and *Locust*s, mostly—blocked the way. Grayson keyed in a command and his lead 'Mechs rushed the enemy line in a blaze of rocketfire and lasers. Hits were scored and 'Mechs disabled, but Grayson ordered his line to ignore the cripples and keep moving. Damaged or routed twenty-tonners would pose little threat in his rear, and now more than ever, speed was of the essence.

When the line of nearly two hundred BattleMechs was stretched from just south of Big Round Top clear to Rock Creek, Grayson gave another order, and each 'Mech simultaneously wheeled in formation to the left.

Moving in line abreast now, each 'Mech separated from its neighbors by sixty meters, the Confederate line swept toward the north, squarely into the Union rear and astride the enemy's supply lines to the south. They'd begun taking fire, too, mostly scattered shots from isolated units of foot infantry and light armored vehicles. Grayson was feeling a growing apprehension. Where were Jaime Wolf's heavy 'Mechs? He'd expected to encounter most of Wolf's simulated army here, in the valley east of Cemetery Ridge and the Round Tops, but so far ...

An alert sounded, followed by scrolling lines of text on his primary display. Enemy 'Mechs had entered the line of sight of some of his units, moving into the open.

There! Grayson choked down a sudden burst of laughter. Jaime Wolf's army had indeed moved into the open. As though attracted by the cavalry fight between the north-south ridges, his heavy and assault 'Mechs were spilling down off of Cemetery Ridge to the west, striking hard at the 'Mechs Grayson had left in position south of the seminary. The camera view Grayson was seeing now was coming from one of those few defending 'Mechs he'd left behind, as a savage firefight snarled and swirled across the open fields and among the restaurants and motels along the Emmitsburg Road at the edge of the town.

So ... Wolf had elected to take the more dangerous option, moving over to the offensive, risking everything by leaving prepared positions, but with far more to win if he guessed right. If he'd caught Grayson's force while it was still in the process of moving, that might have ended the battle right then.

But now the advantage was with Grayson. Already blocking Wolf's supply lines to the south, he could hunker down and force Wolf to turn and attack him, knowing that the advantage generally went to the defender; that, in fact, had been a large part of Grayson's plan all along. But there was a splendid opportunity here.

Typing furiously, Grayson urged his 'Mechs forward at full speed, racing up the Taneytown Road from the south, pivoting like a gate behind the Round Tops to begin closing on Cemetery Ridge from the southeast. As the line extended itself, fresh volleys of fire seared in from the northeast, striking 'Mech after 'Mech. Grayson, his viewpoint now planted in a Confederate *Marauder,* paused and surveyed the field to the north. Rockets were rising in tightly packed, fire-tipped clusters from a wooded hill on the northeast horizon. A quick check of a topo relief map on one of his displays made him smile. By ironic coincidence, that elevation from which the LRM fire was coming was historically known as Wolf's Hill, a low and thickly wooded rise positioned in the Union rear. More missile fire was probing down from the Round Tops as well; there must be several *Archer*s or *Apollo*s up there, lobbing LRMs in indirect fire up through the tree cover.

Stop and deal with them? Or press ahead? He made his decision almost before he could mentally voice the question. If he paused to engage each of the hardpoints Jaime had left scattered about the Union rear, he would become so bogged down in small, separate actions that his main force would never win free in time; Wolf would turn his main body about and return to Cemetery Ridge, guns, lasers, and missiles blazing. He would keep moving, accepting the casualties as enemy fire raked his flanks.

His goal now was Cemetery Ridge, less than two kilometers ahead. Simulated explosions flashed and thundered to left and right, and Grayson physically ducked his head to the side. Even in simulation, it was possible to get so caught up in the excitement, in the fluid movements of the scenes on screen, that the players flinched and ducked as rounds came too near. Another round exploded close by, and this time red warning lights winked on his primary display; his *Marauder* had just taken some heavy damage and was limping now, its right leg actuator nearly crippled.

Press on! Press on! Past the wreckage of the National Tower now and up the gentle slope beyond. According to the computer-simulated views relayed from his hold-out forces south of Gettysburg, Wolf's force had swarmed across the valley and was now rampaging in among the trees on Seminary Ridge. Most of Grayson's 'Mechs on that front had broken and fled or been reduced to smoldering pieces of simulated wreckage, but a few continued to snipe at the enemy as he advanced. Was Wolf completely unaware of the threat in his rear? The Confederates had been under fire for several minutes already; Wolf *must* know....

Ah! Some of the Union 'Mechs were turning now, taking up position in a battle line facing *east* now, instead of west. The movement was ponderously slow, however, and markedly disjointed. It took time, precious time, to reverse an army's course and attack towards its rear, especially when it was already engaged along its front.

On the third day of the real battle, Lee—unable to turn either enemy flank by his attacks of the day before—had made a suicidal gamble, sending some twelve thousand of his remaining fresh troops in a massed direct assault across that open valley, an attack that would forever afterward be immortalized as Pickett's Charge. Doomed from the beginning, the advancing Confederates had been cut down in row upon bloody row by concentrated fire from the crest of the ridge. Only a few hundred Confederates actually made it as far as the stone wall running north and south along the ridge, a place called The Angle—and of those who actually managed to scramble across the wall, not one made it back again. Perhaps sixty percent of the men who'd made that heroic charge were killed, wounded, or captured, with fewer than five thousand Confederates returning to their lines unhurt at the end.

Grayson had been determined to avoid the mistake Lee had made on the third day at Gettysburg. To his way of thinking, you *never* charge an entrenched enemy unless you outnumber him by at least four to one, and even then you'd better have a damned good reason. Now, however, chance and maneuver had played a fascinating trick on the two simulation combatants; Wolf, playing Meade, was charging Cemetery Ridge from the west, just as Lee had done in the real battle.

And at the same time, Grayson, playing Lee, was charging the same ridge from the east. It was a race, and whichever one reached the crest first would be in a position to loose a savage and devastating fire on his opponent below and on the other side....

* * *

Lori Kalmar Carlyle didn't like crowds, and, besides, the throng in the arena would have made it impossible to concentrate on the game. She'd decided instead to watch the battle not from one of the spectator seats, but in an office elsewhere in the building. While the room's wall-sized vidscreen gave her a good overall view of the terrain map, scattered now with hundreds of tiny, moving BattleMech images and computer graphics that showed movement and objectives, she actually had a much better view on a small hand computer screen resting on the desk. Tuning in a close-up angle of Grayson, she studied his face and smiled. The look of sheer, intense concentration was one that, after thirty-some years of marriage, she knew very well. She could see his head bob and weave from side to side as he fought his 'Mech, maneuvering it up the reverse slope of the ridge at the van of a long, strung-out line of BattleMechs wreathed in flame and flashing explosions.

He also looked tired, drained dry by the sheer power and focus of his concentration.

"This is certainly one for the strategy books, Linda," an announcer was saying in a voice-over. "The two armies have maneuvered around each other's flanks, completely reversing their initial positions. The Confederate forces under Colonel Carlyle are now advancing toward Cemetery Ridge from the *east*, while Wolf's Union force is advancing toward the same position from the west. I've never seen anything quite like this."

"That's right, Rob. It looks to me like the main bodies of both armies are going to collide right at the top of the ridge. . . ."

Other displays were showing the audience, which was in a manic frenzy as the action on the simulated battlefield heated up. Some people were standing now on their seats, jumping up and down and screaming at the tops of their lungs. Lori could see fistfuls of C-bills exchanging hands as wagers grew larger and larger. The people who ran Glengarry's organized gambling, she thought, must really be cleaning up with this event.

The contest was obviously coming to its climax, with the battle to be settled one way or another in a epic BattleMech clash within the next few moments. Lori decided she wanted to see the finish in person, even if it meant going down and mingling with the crowd.

Switching off the screens, she walked out of the room and down the hall. Her ID would be her pass for a seat, even if she had to fight someone for it.

She wanted to be there in person, though, when Grayson won.

"There!" the leader of the two assassins said, grabbing his partner's shoulder and pointing. "That's her!"

"Where? I don't see—"

"In that aisle, on the left, coming down to the front." The assassin had been using a small set of electronic binoculars to scan the crowd. "See her? Use your scope, for God's sake!"

Pardo swung his rifle to the left, scanning across the massed faces of the crowd. A memorized face flashed briefly across his imaging screen, vanished, then popped back into view as he reacquired the target.

"Well, well, well," Pardo said with a grin. "Our secondary target! She's making it easy for us!"

"Bitch must've been hiding out someplace."

"Typical politician, huh? She just shows up for the applause and the speeches at the end. Can I take her down?"

"Primary target first. We gotta be sure of Carlyle, or hitting the bitch doesn't do us a damned bit of good."

"You're the boss." Pardo swung the deadly rifle around again, until the back of Grayson Carlyle's head once more filled the targeting screen.

"Right, Pardo! Put him down! Now!"

Pardo's finger closed on the trigger. . . .

= 8 =

The Residence
Castle Hill, Dunkeld
Glengarry, Skye March
1342 Hours, 18 March 3057

His *Marauder* took another hit, a dazzling blue bolt from an enemy PPC, and Grayson instinctively flinched and ducked slightly to the right—

—and in that instant, his main computer screen flashed white as the glass surface disintegrated in a fine spray of shards, the monitor's plastic frame shredding and the electronics inside the case exploding in hissing sparks and hurtling fragments of circuit board. Something slammed into the smooth shiny surface of the console enclosure at Grayson's back, and he felt the hot wind as dozens of projectiles whizzed past his head with the high-pitched buzz of a swarm of insects.

Operating on combat-honed instinct, Grayson followed through with his initial flinch, diving forward and to the right just as a second swarm of deadly projectiles blasted his keyboard into hurtling plastic shrapnel and wildly scattering keys. He hit the floor hands first, dropped into a shoulder roll, and somersaulted beneath the overhanging edge of the terrain projection table as repeated blasts slammed through the noncorporeal holographic imagery and into the tough plastic surface of the tabletop itself.

He collided with the table's base, housing the projection electronics, and scrambled back another meter as fire continued to strike the table top centimeters above his head. His hand dropped to his sidearm, a KK98 laser pistol in the synthleather holster strapped to his leg. Drawing the weapon, he snicked on the power switch, but he couldn't shoot back, couldn't even find the target without exposing himself to that deadly hail of fire.

A burst missed the table and struck nearby, sending tiny, spent gray projectiles skittering across the floor. Flechettes—three centimeters long, probably fired from an autoshotgun of some kind. Each was a tiny arrow made of lead, with fins at the end to stabilize their flight. Fired in clusters of twenty or more at a time from each shotgun shell, they were deadly at ranges of a hundred meters or less.

Gunshots thundered, the steady, slow *thud-thud-thud* of an autoshotgun, and this time the fire was being directed at the audience.

The *audience*! People in the stands were screaming, shrieking, the crowd dissolving into raw panic. Grayson steeled himself. He couldn't cower here beneath the table and do *nothing*.

He felt a warm wetness on his left hand and looked down. Blood covered his left arm, soaking through the sleeve of his tunic. He'd been hit but hadn't even felt it. . . .

Pardo swept the aim of his weapon across the crowd, seeking the secondary target. Damn . . . where was she? He was pretty sure the primary had taken the hit, even though he'd rolled out of reach beneath the table. He'd seen blood fly as Carlyle jerked and went down. Now he had to kill the woman. *But where was she?*

Lori Carlyle had dropped and rolled with the first shot, a combat instinct impossible to overcome. By the time she'd risen to her knees, her Imperator 9mm autopistol drawn and with a round chambered, the gunfire was scything into the crowd all around her. She stayed where she was, safe behind the shelter of the crowd barrier that separated the main arena from the seats.

But the rest of the crowd was directly in the sniper's line of fire. People jammed into the seating area against Lori were dying horribly . . . in bloody clumps. An overweight woman in a fashionably ornate tan and orange jumpsuit threw up her hands and sagged backward against the people behind her, her clothing and her chest shredded in a bloody spray; an older man gaped at the scarlet fountain where his arm had been; a teenage boy dropped at Lori's side, his face ripped up and back from his skull. . . .

"Down!" she yelled at the people around her, trying to lift her voice above the thunder of the mob. "Get down behind your seats!"

She might as well have been shouting at a storm. The people who moments ago had been seated behind and to either side of her were screaming wildly, mindlessly pushing and shoving in a desperate attempt to escape. Lori was in terrible danger at that moment, not of being shot but of being trampled to death as the panicked crowd stampeded in every direction. The man who'd lost an arm vanished, knocked down by the surging crowd. Several bodies slammed Lori back against the unyielding plastic of the barrier and she gasped, unable to move, unable to breathe. She considered firing her pistol above their heads, but that would only have increased the panic. And in any case, the people squeezing against her had no place to go.

More gunfire thudded across the mob, and the screams increased in pitch and intensity as a weapon intended for use on the open stretches of a battlefield was unleashed against the packed crowd in the arena. Lori tried to push herself up above the sheltering barrier, both to breathe and because she wanted to see. She was pretty sure the shots must be coming from one of the media balconies suspended above the stadium seats, but she had to see to be sure.

A man pressing against her side shuddered, his blood splattering across Lori's head and shoulders. The pressure of the crowd increased, and she felt a sharp, biting pain in her side. . . .

Jaime Wolf, seated at his gaming station just thirty meters across the table from Grayson Carlyle, had also ducked with the first shot, but trained ears and instincts told him none of the gunfire was coming his way . . . at least, not yet. Drawing his sidearm, an old but serviceable Mark XXI Nova laser pistol, he switched it on and waited for the cycling chamber to power up. When he heard the high-pitched tone of a ready charge, he eased his eyes up above the level of the table, taking advantage of the illusory miniature hills and forests still projected upon it.

He sought the origin of the autoshotgun fire. It was coming from high up . . . yes! There! The media balcony, almost directly across the stadium from where he was seated. At this distance—well over one hundred meters—he couldn't make out details, but he could see the telltale shadow of a man's silhouette, crouched above the stock of a weapon as he fired it into the crowd to Jaime's right.

Carefully, moving slowly so as not to attract attention, he raised the Nova, gripping it solidly in both hands as he braced his forearms against the edge of the table. He took a breath . . . held it . . . and *squeezed.*

Pardo yelped as his leather jacket flared in a burst of incandescence, flame bursting from his right shoulder and smoke curling from his long, smoldering hair. "*Ayiee!* Boss! I'm on fire!"

"It's Wolf!" The other man leaned past him, aiming his needler. The handgun gave a ragged, fluttering sound as it spat a burst of high-speed slivers toward Wolf's side of the table, but the mercenary had already dropped from view when the packet scoured the edge of the table where he'd been hiding an instant before.

The man looked to the left, where a bloody gash had been carved through the struggling throng of civilians. Raising his electronic binoculars in one leather-gloved hand, he scanned the sprawled bodies and the writhing wounded but couldn't see Carlyle's woman. He couldn't see Carlyle either, though Pardo had been certain of a hit. *Damn!* He had to be sure. . . .

Grayson had decided that his wounds weren't serious, though loss of blood was certain to slow him down in another few moments. He had to act *now.* From the shape and timbre of the sounds around him, the unseen gunman had been firing into the crowd and abruptly stopped.

Judging by the angle of the incoming projectiles, the gunman was up high, probably in that media balcony suspended above the arena seats directly behind Grayson's

gaming station. Quickly, he checked the settings on his
KK98, making certain that the selector was switched to the
standard setting. He would have preferred using more power
to ensure a kill, but in this situation he couldn't depend on
accuracy so he would have to settle for as high a *volume* of
fire as possible.

Kicking off hard from the base of the table, Grayson slid
several meters across the slick floor, his laser pistol clutched
in both hands and already seeking a target. As soon as he
cleared the edge of the scenery table, he drew down on the
large window of the media balcony and triggered his first
shot, an intense flash so brief it was more felt than seen. A
rising hum told him the weapon was recycling; one and a
half seconds later a green light winked on and he fired
again. And again. . . .

The dead weight of a man's body rolled off of her as the
tide of panicked civilians ebbed up the steps and bleachers.
Gasping, clutching her side in pain, Lori finally pulled herself upright just in time to see both Wolf and Grayson firing
their lasers at the media balcony. Leaning against the crowd
barrier, she raised her Imperator, aimed at the balcony, and
opened fire.

A palm-sized portion of the balcony window two meters
away turned frosty white, then shattered from the diffused
heat of a laser pulse. Another laser pulse scored a black
streak across the ceiling. A bullet smashed glass; a second
punched through the structure's thin metal side and blew out
a lighting fixture. The balcony sharpshooter's box had
turned into a target—and a deathtrap.

"C'mon, let's get the hell outta here!" Pardo shouted. The
side of his face was cruelly blistered where that first laser
bolt had seared past just centimeters from his skin; his jacket
was still smoking where he'd been grazed. As he rose from
his hiding place behind the opened portion of the window,
another laser pulse flashed, and Pardo clutched at his face.
"My eyes! My eyes!"

There was no time to waste. Coolly, the other man tossed
his needler to the floor at Pardo's feet, peeled off his gloves,
then drew his other weapon, a heavy, military-model TK70
laser pistol. "Goodbye, Pardo."

He fired, sending a bolt squarely into the gunman's chest; one-tenth of a megajoule in a tenth-second pulse dumped energy equivalent to twenty grams of exploding TNT into the target. A fist-sized crater opened Pardo's chest in a burst of vaporizing blood and tissue.

Laser bursts and bullets from the arena continued to smash glass and pock random holes in the balcony wall. Ducking low, the laser still in hand, the man palmed open the door and backed out.

A railed walkway provided access to the enclosed balcony from a lounge area beyond the arena's curving, inner wall. Four Gray Death Legion troopers were just emerging from the lounge, laser rifles at the ready.

"Don't shoot!" the man shouted, still crouching, his TK70 held with the muzzle aimed at the ceiling. His voice cracked. This had been too close! "Don't shoot!"

"Drop the weapon!" an angry-looking soldier with sergeant's chevrons barked, and the man could *feel* the aim of the military laser rifles as he let his weapon fall to the walkway with a metallic clatter. "Hands up! Up! Up!"

The man complied. "I got him!" he said, breathing hard as he slowly straightened upright. "I got him, Sarge!"

The sergeant advanced, keeping the muzzle of his rifle centered on the man's head. "Got who, you son of a bitch?"

"The gunman, Sarge! I got him! He's inside!"

Doubt crossed the soldier's face behind the transparent visor of his helmet. "Who are you?"

"May I?"

"Careful! No sudden moves!"

Very, very slowly, the man reached into a pocket in his jacket. Then, holding it daintily between thumb and forefinger, he even more slowly withdrew his ID card, which he handed to the sergeant.

The other two soldiers pushed past and vanished into the balcony. One emerged a moment later, his face ash white. "Jesus, Sarge!" he said. "It's a mess in there!"

The sergeant handed the ID to the fourth soldier, standing at his back. "Blaine! Check this!"

Blaine dragged the card through a small magreader and studied the screen. "Says he's one of ours, Sarge! Lieutenant Walter Dupré, Second Company, Third Batt!"

"Lieutenant Dupré, huh?" the sergeant growled. "I don't know you."

"I'm new, Sarge," Dupré said. "Signed on two weeks ago."

"MechWarrior?"

"That's right. Used to be with the Lyran Guards, but I got smart and went merc. The Legion's more my style."

The sergeant relaxed just the slightest fraction, but the muzzle of his rifle stayed centered on Dupré's head. He shot a glance at Dupré's civilian clothing, then back to his face. "You're off duty?"

"That's right. Came down to watch the simgame."

"What happened here?"

Still moving slowly, Dupré pointed. "I was sitting down there, up high in the bleachers near that door."

The sergeant did not follow Dupré's gesture. "Go on."

"When the shooting started, I could tell it was coming from this box. I was wearing my sidearm, so I ducked quick through the door and came up here to see if I could help. Went through this door—lucky the guy hadn't locked it. Caught him just as he was turning away from the window in there. It . . . it looked like he already had taken out some people who were in there first."

"Turn around."

"Huh?"

"Turn around!"

Dupré did as he was told. Rough hands frisked him with thorough professionalism. Then his captor grabbed his raised right arm and pulled it down. Dupré felt the cold bite of a wrist shackle and heard the snick of the locking mechanism snapping home.

"Sorry to have to do this to you, buddy," the sergeant said, taking Dupré's left arm and cuffing it to the right behind his back. "Gotta make sure, though, you know?"

"Of course, Sarge. SOP. You have to check me out."

"That's right. You just hang easy, though. If your story checks out, guy, you're gonna be a hero!"

"I just did what I thought I had to do," Dupré said with a smile. He let the smile vanish. "Say! It looked like that guy was shooting at the Colonel! Did—"

"I saw the Colonel shootin' back," The sergeant said with a grin. "He can't be too badly dinged up, eh?"

"Oh! Good. That's . . . good!"

"It'll take more'n one lone crackpot with an autoshotgun

to lay the Colonel out," Blaine added. "That's for damned sure!"

"Shame you fried the bastard," one of the other troopers said. "Son of a bitch cut loose on a packed crowd with fletch-loads." He grimaced. "Bastard got off too easy, if y'ask me!"

"No one asked you, Cellini," the sergeant said. "Let's go, uh, Lieutenant. Security'll check you out . . . and if you're clean, the drinks're on me!"

"That, Sarge," Dupré said with a heartfelt sigh of relief, "would suit me just fine!"

"Dad!" Alex leaped up from his seat, eyes wide as the scene displayed on the lounge bulkhead dissolved in a chaos of screaming, surging, terrified people and thumping gunfire. The camera continued recording the scene with impassive and impartial clarity. Horrified, Alex watched rapid-fire shotgun blasts sweep across Grayson Carlyle's game station and—apparently—knock him from his seat and under the table. He saw the gunfire turned on the crowd, saw civilians die in bloody tangles, and wondered if his mother was there, somewhere in that panicking mob.

"Easy, son," McCall said, a gentle but firm hand on his shoulder. "There's not aye y' can do for them noo. . . ."

Alex almost choked with frustration, rage, and fear. "We've got to—"

"Lad, lad . . . what we're seein' here happened close on t' half an hour ago! Light lag, remember?"

The camera view zoomed back for a longer panoramic shot, and Alex continued watching, his breaths coming in short, hard pants. The image was so clear and clean, it was impossible to think that it wasn't happening now. But the signals carrying that scene had been crawling out from Glengarry for twenty-seven minutes before they'd reached the *Skye Song*.

The events he was seeing must be resolved by now. *Must* be, one way or the other. . . .

The gunman was in that media box above the crowd; Jaime Wolf made his appearance, firing his laser at an impossibly difficult range for a hand weapon. And there was Dad! Sliding out from beneath the table and snapping off several shots at the balcony. And Mom . . . she was there too, leaning over the crowd barrier, blazing away with her 9mm slug thrower. Several troopers around the perimeter of the arena were firing as well, all concentrating their return fire on the balcony, which jumped and shivered and erupted in clouds of sparkling shards of glass. Armed and armored foot soldiers could just be glimpsed storming onto the walkway that led to the back of the box. The camera angle was such that he couldn't see what was happening back there.

"Ladies and gentlemen!" the male announcer's voice said, rising above the roar of background crowd noises. "This is terrible . . . simply terrible! One minute we were watching a war game . . . and the next, oh God! God!"

The man's voice cracked and broke. The female announcer took over. "Rob, from here it looks like soldiers have broken into the balcony where the gunfire was coming from. It looks . . . yes! It looks like they may have captured the man who did it. I see them leading someone away with his hands tied. Ladies and gentlemen, we're trying to get some word on casualties. It looks—I repeat, it *looks* as though someone tried to assassinate Colonel Carlyle, opening fire on him from a balcony here at the Civic Arena. I can see MedTechs running out onto the arena floor. I see Colonel Carlyle. He's, yes! He's on his feet! It looks like he's been wounded, but he's on his feet, he's walking toward the crowd barrier now."

"Linda," Rob's voice interrupted, still sounding shaky and weak. "I've just had word from the floor. Dozens of civilians were killed or wounded in that vicious, unprovoked attack. Both Grayson Carlyle and Jaime Wolf are unhurt . . ."

"The Colonel *has* been wounded, Rob. I can see blood on his arm and face, but he's on his feet and making his way to the edge of the crowd. He's . . . I think . . . yes! I see his wife, Lieutenant Colonel Kalmar-Carlyle. She was in the bleachers just where the assassin fired into the crowd, and it looks like . . . God, it looks like she's covered with blood too and she's moving like she's hurt. . . ."

"I've got to get back," Alex said. He barely spoke the words aloud, but McCall heard.

"Alex, Alex, use what's inside your thick skull for once! We cannae turn about in mid-trajectory, am I right? An' there's nae a bit we can do aboot what's happening back there! What you're seeing there on tha' screen, what you're hearing . . . *it's already over!*"

Alex swallowed hard, his fists clenched at his side, his eyes burning, but he managed to nod. "Sorry, D-Davis."

"It's all right, lad. I feel th' same way. It's aye frustratin', havin' t' watch, bein' unable t' help."

"We can still radio a message," Alex said. "Can't we? Make sure . . . make sure they're both all right."

"Of course we can, lad."

"Say," the man with the loud shirt said, coming up behind McCall. "Did I hear that kid shout 'Dad' when the shooting started?"

"Eh? Oh, aye, aye. His father was in the audience. He's a mite worried aboot him, as y'can weel imagine."

"Oh yeah. That's real tough. Gosh, and it's too bad our little wager's off too, eh, Scotty? I mean, they never finished the game."

McCall reached out with one powerful arm and clamped down on the man's shoulder, his thumb grinding against his collarbone. "If I remember th' terms of our agreement," he said reasonably, "the wager was on whether or not the Colonel would charge straight on or go around the flank. I think we were able to settle that question before the excitement began, weren't we noo?"

"I . . . ow!" The man grimaced with pain. "Yah! Yeah, I guess so. Here!"

"Thank you, sir. It's aye a pleasure doin' business wi' th' likes of you!" McCall accepted the C-bills and riffled the edge of the stack with an expert thumb, counting. "One hundred, right. And, just by the by, sir, the name's *nae* 'Scotty'!"

"Colonel?" Gunnarson said. "He's here, sir."

"Send him in."

"You're lucky to have such men, Colonel," Jaime Wolf said from the other side of the room. "There's no telling how many would have died if it hadn't been for that man's quick thinking."

"Thank you, Commander. I'm just glad it wasn't worse."

Grayson Carlyle stood up behind his desk, glancing briefly at Lori who was sitting across from him. Both sported multiple bandages. Grayson's head was circled by a band of white gauze, and his left arm was in a sling to take pressure off his wounded shoulder. According to Ellen Jamison, who'd patched him up afterward, he'd caught just the fringe of a cloud of high-speed flechettes.

Strange. He'd never even felt the wounds until after the shooting and shouting had stopped. One had furrowed his left temple, another had snicked off part of his ear lobe, and three had punched clean through his left shoulder. Had he caught the full load square-on, his head and upper torso would have been shredded into bloody hamburger.

He'd gotten off remarkably lightly, actually. Lori had suffered the more serious injury, with two ribs cracked by the press of the crowd during the panic. Ellen had ordered her to stay in bed, but, typically of her, she'd insisted on coming here, taped up beneath her tunic like a mummy. She also wore bandages on her forehead and right hand, where she'd suffered some nasty abrasions in her close encounter with the crowd and the crowd barrier.

A man in a Legion lieutenant's uniform strode into the office, stopped, and rendered a crisp salute. "Lieutenant Dupré reporting as ordered, sir."

"At ease, Lieutenant," Grayson said. "At ease. May I present Supreme Commander Jaime Wolf?"

"Honored, sir."

"And you know our executive officer."

"Good evening, Colonel. I heard you were hurt as well."

"Nothing serious, Lieutenant," Lori replied. "Thank you."

"I'm told," Grayson continued, "that you're the one who nailed the gunman today. That was good work."

"Thank you, sir."

"Wasn't that a bit hair-brained, though, charging through a door armed with a laser pistol? What if there'd been more than one in there?"

"I only heard the one weapon, Colonel. I thought if there was more than one up there, they'd have a couple of heavy weapons."

"The gunman also had a needler," Jaime put in. "A nasty weapon. He killed three media correspondents with it, then broke out the shotgun. He also—" Wolf stopped, looking puzzled.

"Problem, Commander?" Grayson asked.

"Not really. I was curious, though, as to why the gunman

would stop shooting with the autoshotgun at one point and take a crack at me with the needler. Funny. I didn't think about it at the time."

"Perhaps his weapon jammed?" Lieutenant Dupré suggested. "Or he was out of ammo?"

"That could well explain it," Wolf said, nodding.

"In any case, we're grateful to you, Lieutenant," Grayson said.

"I'm only glad I could help, sir."

"Your security check showed you were an officer with the Fifteenth Lyran Guards," Lori said. "Eight years?"

"Almost nine, Colonel."

"They're stationed where? Hesperus II?"

"That's right."

"What made you leave?"

"Oh, the bureaucracy, I guess. The inflexibility. I needed an outfit where I could stretch out and swing a bit, y'know? So I went merc."

"I see. An ambitious man."

"Yes, ma'am. I aim to boss my own company, some day."

"I'm sure you will, *Captain*," Grayson said.

The man blinked, then broke into a broad smile. "Why, thank you, sir!"

"I'm sorry I can't give you a company to go with a company commander's rank, Captain Dupré," Grayson continued. "But Captain Rivera doesn't have time-in-grade for his next promotion yet, and I don't have any other vacant slots. Besides, I don't like advancing my officers to field command slots until I've seen them in action. In battlefield action, that is. However, consider yourself on the list for a company slot, as soon as I've seen you work and we have one open. I've also moved the refit on your *Zeus* up to top priority."

"Thank you very much, sir! I'll do my very best!"

"I know you will, son," Grayson said. "Dismissed."

Dupré saluted, whirled about, and strode out the door.

"Pleasant fellow," Wolf said. "Would he consider a transfer to the Dragoons, perhaps?"

"He might, Jaime," Grayson replied with a grin. "But I wouldn't. He's mine!"

They laughed.

* * *

In the outer office suite, Captain Walter Dupré checked out at the security point, then rode the lift down to the officers' quarters, exultant.

Yes! Yes! *Yes!*

9

"**S**o everything here is just fine," Lori said, smiling with warmth and affection. "Your father and I are both safe and well. Just a little wrinkled around the edges."

A burst of static passed through the translucent, three-D image standing on the holoprojector in the DropShip cabin Alex and McCall shared with four other male passengers. Alex was alone at the room's single, tiny desk and communications console, however, for McCall had gently but firmly ushered the other passengers into the passageway outside to give him some privacy.

A careless motion set him drifting, and he reached out with one hand to snag the edge of the desk, stopping his slight rotation. The *Skye Song* had been in zero-G now for nearly eight hours, ever since she'd docked with the Jump-Ship *Altair* early that morning, standard.

Microgravity was the proper word, of course, Alex absently corrected himself. He could have measured the local gravity—or the ship's thrust, which amounted to the same thing—had he possessed the proper instruments. JumpShips did not orbit the local star between jumps but hung suspended at zenith or nadir jump points, collecting the flood of radiation necessary to charge their Kearny-Fuchida drives in great, dead-black solar sails a kilometer or more across. For eight days now, the *Altair* had hung suspended at this point, her sail unfurled between herself and the sun, maintaining position with a gentle, almost unfelt thrust of charged particles streaming aft through the circle piercing the sail's center.

So slight was that thrust, however, that the passengers aboard the *Skye Song,* which now clung to one of the *Altair*'s docking collars like a tick on a much larger dog, were for all intents and purposes in zero-G. Hours ago, even the fractional acceleration of the station-keeping thrusters had ended as the ship began preparing for its jump to the Gladius system. Servomotors had carefully furled, folded, and stowed the sail. Glengarry's orange sun shone with a pale, wan ghost of its usual warmth, almost half a billion kilometers "below" the ship's stern, no longer blocked from view by the solar sail.

Through an image that had traveled twenty-eight minutes to reach him, Alex's mother kept speaking.

"Security thinks the attack was arranged by members of The Hand. The assassin was identified as a small-time hitman who'd worked for them in the past. We think The Hand must have had a lot of money riding on Commander Wolf in the sim tournament, and they had this man positioned so that if your father was about to win, he could shoot him and stop the game."

Alex raised his eyebrows at that. He wished he could reply to his mother directly, wished he could question her in detail about the attack, but the unbending laws of physics restricted even the most intimate conversations across such distances as these to one-way visual letters. Lori Carlyle had transmitted this message half an hour ago—more, actually, since what Alex was watching now was a recording downloaded to his console from the *Skye Song*'s comm center; it would be another half hour before his questions could reach her, and still another before he could hear her response.

And by that time, of course, he would no longer be here.

The Hand was the informal name given to the loose alliance of criminal gangs that ran Glengarry's underworld. Every inhabited planet in the Inner Sphere had some element of organized crime, often descended from similar groups that had followed the tide of man's outleap to the stars from Terra centuries ago. Like most such, The Hand was vicious, cutthroat, unprincipled, close-knit, secretive, vindictive, and quite dangerous. It was also *not* stupid, but what Alex had just heard sounded pretty damned stupid to him.

Would Glengarry's organized crime family risk something as dangerous to their continued existence as the attempted murder of the Baron of Glengarry—simply to avoid losing a paltry few million C-bills? That didn't make any sense at all!

"Security is checking into it, of course," Lori continued, unperturbed by Alex's frown of concentration since she couldn't see it. "They're rounding up some of the known leaders of The Hand for questioning, but we don't really expect any concrete results. The important thing is that your father and I are both safe.

"All together, twenty-six people were killed in the attack, and another hundred eighty-one were wounded. Vernon Artman thinks the guy who did it was 'just plain disconnected from his primary logic circuits,' to use his words. He doesn't think The Hand would risk killing so many people for no good reason. He's been wondering if there was some sort of deep, dark plot here."

Alex nodded. At least *somebody* back there was thinking! Good old Sarge!

"We're looking into that angle too, of course," she continued. "Both your father and I are being kept under close watch since the attack. You don't have to worry about us. They're taking good care of us.

"That's about all for right now, Alex. Thanks so much for your call. I'm sorry you were worried, and I wish we could've had at least a little time together. You can well imagine that your father is going to pay dearly for sending you off to Caledonia just two days before I got back! But we'll make it up when you return.

"Goodbye, Alex. Good luck on your mission, and give my best to Major McCall. We'll be looking forward to when you get back!"

The image remained there a moment, seeming to defy the directionless drift of free fall by remaining solidly anchored to the projection plate before dissolving in a burst of static.

Pushing off from the desk, Alex floated to the door and palmed it open. "Okay, Davis. I'm done."

McCall re-entered the cabin, followed by the four rather grumpy-looking men who were their roommates aboard the *Song*. "Well, lad?" He looked worried. "What's the word from home?"

"They're both fine," Alex said, and he smiled as McCall pursed his lips and gave a soundless whistle of relief. "They were both hurt, but it doesn't sound too bad." Alex cast a glance at the other men, then looked back to McCall, lowering his voice. "Mac? They think it was The Hand, trying to stop Dad from winning that game. Does that sound right to you?"

"Hmm. Perhaps, lad, if your maithair passed that bit a' news on, it was because she could tell you nae else over a transmission tha' could be intercepted. Do y' ken m' meaning?"

"Yeah. I think I do."

"Your parents are nae stupid, lad. They would nae ha' lived so long, the pair a' them, were it otherwise."

A buzzer sounded from a bulkhead speaker, a blast repeated three times, followed by a woman's voice. "Attention, attention, all passengers and crew. The *Altair* will be making its jump in twenty minutes. To avoid the disorientation of jump syndrome, all passengers are directed to remain strapped in your bunks until the all-clear has sounded. All ship's personnel, please man your jump stations."

"I know," Alex said. "I wish I could call again, though, and ask—"

"It's too late for that noo, Alex. You and me are on our own now . . . and so are they! Dinnae fash y'sel' aboot it. They'll work things out just fine!"

Twenty minutes later, solar sail furled and stowed, the energies stored in the *Altair*'s power cells unfolded across the reach of the ship's Kearny-Fuchida drive, crumpling the fabric of space within which she drifted. To an outside observer, the half-kilometer-long vessel would seem to shimmer, her form twisting and wavering in surreal optical distortions as the space around her warped. Abruptly, then, she vanished in a silent flare of light.

Her translation through hyperspace to the Gladius system, nearly twenty light years away, was, for all intents and purposes, instantaneous.

10

HQ, Third Davion Guards
Hesperus II, Tamarind March
Federated Commonwealth
2230 hours, 19 March 3057

Marshal Felix Zellner leaned back in his finely crafted automatic chair, his polished boots propped on the corner of his expensive hardwood desk. He enjoyed the comforts of his office here on Hesperus II almost as much as he was enjoying the discomfiture of his subordinate.

"But M-Marshal Zellner," the holographic image on the other side of the desk stammered. "This means the ruin of the Field Marshal's plan!"

"Gently, Thurman, gently," Zellner said with an easy smile. "Nothing has been ruined. In fact, in my opinion things will be better this way in the long run."

"And if the Gray Death's intel apparatus tracks the attempted assassination back to Field Marshal Gareth? Grayson Carlyle is popular, Marshal. Perhaps too popular, especially on Glengarry just now. That was why the assassination was ordered in the first place."

Zellner swung his boots off the desk and sat up, giving the communications console a quick glance. "This is a secure line," he reminded his subordinate. "Even so, General, I suggest you . . . be circumspect. Even internal transmissions can be tapped . . . or offices."

General Thurman Vaughn swallowed visibly, then mopped

his brow with a handkerchief. Even through the holographic transmission Zellner could see the sweat gleaming on his nearly bald head. Vaughn, Zellner thought with amusement, really wasn't cut out for this sort of thing.

But then, is any of us? For so long, military service, first under House Steiner, and for the past thirty years within the combined Federated Commonwealth, had been a predictable routine of career paths, fitness reports, and—with luck and skill—promotion, sometimes dangerous, usually boring or at least ordinary ... and rarely, if ever, colored by the melodrama of secret lives or covert operations. Once someone achieved senior rank—for Davion officers, that was generally colonel or above—promotion was always largely a matter of politics, of who you knew and what you could do for someone else's career. Zellner had certainly encountered his share of plotting along the way merely in managing his own promotions and those of certain officers in his clique, but intrigue on a scale as large as this, involving several worlds and hundreds of AFFC officers, was as new to him as it was to General Vaughn.

Or even, presumably, to Field Marshal Gareth.

Still, Zellner found himself reveling in the sense of power that came with knowing secrets that could destroy the careers of powerful fellow officers, or even more powerful politicians. For many years, he'd been chief aide to Marshal Caesar Steiner, a position that required complete devotion and loyalty, outwardly, at least. When he'd won his own coveted promotion from general to marshal, however, he'd found himself at last in a position to effectively use information garnered by people personally loyal to him throughout his career.

"I feel reasonably certain of the security of my office," Zellner continued. In fact, he had his office swept by sensitive devices that could ferret out even passively activated listening devices. "However, I cannot be sure about yours."

"I have complete confidence in my people," Vaughn said stiffly. But his eyes shifted back and forth uncertainly in his fleshy face as he spoke.

In fact, Zellner was as sure of Vaughn and Vaughn's office as he was of his own. Vaughn had *not* found Zellner's planted electronic ears, but since Zellner also had taps on the Security Office and in several other key offices within the Third Guard Headquarters facility, if anyone were about to launch an investigation of either Zellner or Vaughn, Zellner would hear about it.

"I have complete confidence in you, General," Zellner said with an easy smile. "And in your people. Please. Continue with your report."

"There is little else to say about it, Marshal. Field Marshal Gareth's plan appears to have failed completely. The mercenary, Grayson Carlyle, is alive, and one of the assassins is dead."

"And the other assassin?"

"I have no information on him, sir. Initial word was that he'd been captured, but I haven't been able to confirm that."

"If so, he doesn't know enough to harm us."

Zellner had no intention of letting Vaughn know that Captain Dupré had returned to duty . . . and with a promotion, no less. Some pieces of information, such as the fact that Zellner had been able to suborn one of Gareth's assassins, were best kept in reserve. Having an agent alive and in place within the Gray Death could be most useful to Zellner's future plans. . . .

Vaughn's holograph image shook its head unhappily. "Marshal . . . I'm afraid I'm just not cut out for this, this covert work. I have to tell you, I'm afraid of what the Field Marshal is trying to do. It's . . . it's too big. Too grand! And this attempt against Grayson Carlyle was dangerous. It could have brought us all down!"

"In what way, Thurman?"

"Carlyle is popular. Especially on Glengarry. The people love the guy, and his troops love him even more. If the assassins had carried it off, they would never have stopped until they found out who was behind it. I'm not so sure they won't try anyway, just knowing the attempt has been made! Marshal, do you know anything at all about this Gray Death?"

"What is there to know? They are mercenaries. . . ."

"Mercenaries, yes, though they've been constantly on retainer to the Commonwealth, well, since before the alliance. Thirty years, at least. They are widely admired throughout Steiner space, especially by military personnel. Heroes on some worlds, like Glengarry. Possibly on Caledonia as well, simply because those two worlds share a common ethnic heritage. The story of what the Legion did on Glengarry during the Second Skye Rebellion has already become a minor epic."

"General, General, I fear you're blowing this out of proportion."

"Marshal, with all due respect, I don't believe I've stated it strongly enough."

"Um. You are familiar with *The Prince*?"

Vaughn looked puzzled. "Prince Victor Davion?"

Zellner concealed a grimace. *What* were they teaching officers these days in staff college? "No, General. *The Prince* was a book written fifteen hundred years ago, by a man, a Renaissance Italian, named Niccolò Machiavelli." Idly, he keyed out a command on a small reader on the desk in front of him, entered a search command, then pressed another key. The wall screen on one side of the office lit up with the magnified view of a printed page, positioned where Vaughn could read it.

"If any one supports his state by the arms of mercenaries," the excerpt, which Zellner long ago had memorized, read, "he will never stand firm or sure, as they are disunited, ambitious, without discipline, faithless, bold amongst friends, cowardly amongst enemies, they have no fear of God, and keep no faith with men. Ruin is only deferred as long as the assault is postponed; in peace you are despoiled by them, and in war by the enemy. The cause of this is that they have no love or other motive to keep them in the field beyond a trifling wage, which is not enough to make them ready to die for you. They are quite willing to be your soldiers so long as you do not make war. . . ."

"That," Zellner said, snapping off the viewer, "is as true today as it was in the sixteenth century. Give me a strong, well-trained and well-disciplined regular army every time. One that owes its allegiance to *me,* and to the state I represent. Mercenaries owe allegiance to nothing but the almighty C-bill."

"With respect once more, sir," Vaughn said, "that's not entirely true in the Legion's case. The rank and file are utterly devoted to Carlyle. And as for Carlyle . . . he seems to be devoted to civilization."

"What . . . opera? Culture? The arts? Literature? What do you mean by 'civilization'?"

"I mean he fears that civilization is falling apart, that continued warfare will destroy all that the human race has built.

He's afraid that we'll lose even our ability to travel through space, that humanity will end up as bands of savages isolated on hundreds of separate planets scattered across the light years."

"Very poetic. Also, not very likely. How did you learn all of this?"

"I have my . . . sources."

Which means he has his own spies in Carlyle's camp, Zellner thought. *I'll have to look into that.*

"Grayson Carlyle," Zellner said slowly, "is good. Very good. But he is just a mercenary. When he dies, the people will forget him. His troops will forget him."

"But it's dangerous. I don't understand the Field Marshal's thinking here, and I'm worried about the Gray Death's intelligence wing. They're very good too!"

Zellner wondered how much to tell Vaughn. The man was, after all, only involved in Operation Excalibur in the most minor and peripheral of ways. And now that he was showing signs of wanting out . . .

Felix Zellner owed no particular loyalty to Field Marshal Brandal Gareth. True, he owed much of his recent success to the man. But that would not keep him from doing whatever was necessary to survive—better, to prosper—in the coming crisis.

Everybody, all of the senior officers of the Armed Forces of the Federated Commonwealth, knew that the Davion-Steiner alliance was facing serious internal strains. They said nothing about it publicly, of course, but privately they talked among themselves of little else but the possibility of civil war. Most dreaded the prospect, whether they were pro-Steiner, pro-Davion, or straddling the fence as pro-FedComs.

Dreaded or not, the possibility of outright civil war was all too real.

The Federated Commonwealth was not a natural entity; the old Lyran Commonwealth under the stewardship of House Steiner had itself been a union of three states, the Tamar Pact, the Protectorate of Donegal, and the Federation of Skye, coming together under a single government in 2341. That union, at least, had the legitimacy born of over seven centuries of success in trade, in productivity, in diplomacy, and in war, but even it had felt the restless urgings toward independence within its member states more than once.

The alliance of the Federated Suns and the Lyran Commonwealth had been far more sudden and unexpected, one sprung upon its populations virtually overnight, an alliance that had, in the course of a few short years, overturned many of the customs and accepted manners of doing things, especially within government and the military. The appointment of local planetary rulers by fiat, often as a reward for some service or outright bribe, as opposed to accepting candidates advanced by the local populations was one case in point.

The Skye Rebellion of the previous year, most senior AFFC officers were convinced, was nothing more than prelude to something bigger and far more serious.

A prelude, perhaps, to a civil war that would destroy the Federated Commonwealth.

If the alliance was again torn into two states, Davion and Steiner, then every advantage that had been won in the past thirty years could be lost . . . and more, since the dissolving union would spend incalculable precious resources and assets, military and civilian, fighting the war that brought it down.

Some few officers within the AFFC were already making detailed plans against the possibility that the worst was about to happen. In Gareth's case, the plan involved carving out a small empire in the heart of the restless worlds of the Skye March. The planets scattered across that reach were rich, many almost untouched by the last few centuries of war. And then there was Hesperus II, this world where he'd arranged to have himself stationed. With its complex of BattleMech factories in the formidable Myoo Mountains, Hesperus was *the* most important planet in the Steiner sector. Without BattleMechs nobody could remain in power for long.

"The Field Marshal felt that Carlyle's popularity on Glengarry and in the surrounding area could make him a rallying point for the opposition when Excalibur is launched. Getting him out of the way seemed to be the most expedient way of eliminating the Gray Death as a possible obstacle to our plans."

"Fine. Why the woman, then?"

"She is Carlyle's executive officer and would presumably take command if he died. The idea behind the assassination was to ensure that both were killed so that the Legion's number-three officer would take command."

"Who is that?"

"A Caledonian. One Major McCall."

"I don't know him. Why do you want him in command?"

"Tell me, General. Are you aware at all of the situation on Caledonia?"

"It's a relatively low-resource world a few parsecs from Hesperus II. That's its only strategic importance, so far as I know."

"Exactly so. And its governor is Field Marshal Gareth's man. He used to be Gareth's secretary and was given the governorship of Caledonia by Prince Victor at the Field Marshal's specific request."

"What does that have to do . . . Ah! You said this McCall was a Caledonian."

"And he is on his way back to his native world at this moment. The Field Marshal was convinced that should McCall receive command of the Gray Death, we would be in an excellent position to control him and through him the Legion."

"But how?" Vaughn shook his head. "I still don't understand this. As I said . . . I don't think I'm cut out for this sort of thing. I'm a simple man, and these rings within rings are too complex for me to be of much use to—"

"Nonsense, General! We need you, and we have every confidence in your ability to carry off your part in Excalibur!"

"I appreciate that, sir. Still, what will happen now that the Field Marshal's plan has failed?"

"Ah, but it hasn't failed. Not really. I admit that things would have been simpler had we been able to put the Carlyles out of the way. But as it is, we still have an excellent opportunity here to control the Gray Death . . . or to destroy it."

"Destroy it?"

"Either way, General Vaughn," Zellner said with a smile, "*our* needs will be served."

11

At the nadir jump point of the Gladius star system Alex and McCall had made their connection with the *Neptune*, an AFFC transport en route to neighboring Laiaka with space available for two hand-off passengers from the *Altair*. Three days later they made the jump to Laiaka, where, after several days of negotiations with the rather seedy-looking owner/captain of the independent freighter *Shoshone*, they were accepted as passengers and taken aboard for the hyperspace passage to Caledon.

The *Shoshone*'s DropShip *Tagalong* took Alex and McCall on the final leg of their voyage, touching down at the New Edinburgh spaceport on a fiery shaft of white-hot plasma as she settled into the port's Number Five grounding pit. It took less than an hour for Alex and McCall to pass through the obligatory customs check, to pick up their baggage, and to make arrangements for McCall's special freight consignment to be stored in a local warehouse after being offloaded from the *Tagalong*'s cargo hold.

It was just past local noon when they were ready to find transport to the home of McCall's family in Dundee. Caledonia's day was similar enough to Terra's in length that it used the same twenty-four-hour clock, with an extra fifty-three minutes added after local midnight. New Edinburgh, as the planet's capital, designated the Terra Mean Time Zone, just as on Glengarry.

The riot, they learned later, had already been going on for most of the day.

"I'm sorry, gentlemen," the heavily armed and armored trooper told them just inside the exit from the spaceport terminal. "It's not safe to go out on the streets today. You should try getting a room at the spaceport's hotel until things quiet down."

Alex looked back at the crowd already thronging the terminal lounge, hundreds of people occupying every available chair or bench, and many sitting in disconsolate clusters in out-of-the-way corners of the carpeted floors. It seemed unlikely that there would be hotel rooms vacant.

Not that McCall was in any mood to be delayed.

"Laddy," he said cheerfully, drawing a .50 caliber Starfire, the handgun he favored as a sidearm. "After comin' all this way, I'll nae be turned away from m' ain home by rabble! Step aside, noo!"

It might have been the small hand cannon McCall was holding, or it could have been something in the heavily accented voice. The young trooper started to speak, then shrugged and waved them through. "If that's the way you want it, fella. It's your funeral!"

The soldier, Alex noted, was wearing the black and yellow livery of Caledonia's Home Guard, a militia regiment under the direct command of the planet's governor. As the two of them stepped through sliding doors and into the cool afternoon air outside, Alex commented about it to McCall. "That soldier back there."

"Aye. They call them 'Blackjackets' here. Officious little so-and-so . . ."

"He didn't sound like you. No Scots burr."

"Aye, y' noticed that, did ye? Not all Caledonians have the same rich command of th' language as th' auld families. Still, true enough, he sounded like an ootlander t' me. Imported, most likely."

"Imported? By who?"

"His majesty the governor, of course. The poor wee man has trouble findin' support among th' natives, noo, so he has t' send oot for hired help. Ah. Watch y'self noo, Alex. This could get interestin'."

The spaceport rose from a flat plain on the outskirts of New Edinburgh, in a depressed-looking district of run-down housing, ramshackle warehouses and bulk storage centers, and manufactory facilities. Alex could see the silver-white ribbons of elevated highways rising above the slums and cheap, fabriplas constructs in the distance, but there were few groundcars in evidence. A subway station faced the entrance to the spaceport across a rubbish-littered park; a mob was issuing from the station doors and into the park's central plaza, some armed with clubs or improvised weapons, most unarmed. Numerous signs were visible above the angry, shouting heads. Alex saw several with the word MURDER-ERS! scrawled in red paint to mimic blood.

"This way, lad," McCall said, nudging him with an elbow. His hands were full, one holding the pistol, the other his shipcase, but he managed to steer Alex nonetheless, leading him away from the street fronting the park and down a side alley running along the spaceport's perimeter fence. The crowd, growing second by second, continued to spill into the park, overflowing the plaza and occupying most of the bare ground that had once been grass beyond.

One of the mob's leaders had sprung onto an improvised podium—the pedestal of a bronze statue rising from the plaza center. She was a young woman, Alex noted, with long brown hair held back from her face by a red headband. She wore plaid trews and a T-shirt with the clenched-fist emblem of the Steiners.

"Citizens!" she called out, her voice amplified by some unseen sound system. "Caledonians! Our rights and our liberties hae been first trampled an' then taken away, until we are little better than slaves to Wilmarth an' his cronies!"

Alex would have liked to hear more, but their path suddenly jinked left behind a warehouse, muffling the woman's voice to unintelligible booms and thumps from the amplifier bass circuits. The thunderous roar of approval as the crowd cheered something she'd said, however, still followed them clearly.

"I would like t' hear wha' the lass has to say m'self," McCall told Alex as they hurried along the alley, "but I think it might be best if we not associate wi' the likes a' them the moment we set foot on th' planet."

"I'm sure you're right." They took several more turns in rapid succession, weaving a confusing trail through a labyrinth of storage buildings. "Uh, you do know where we're going, Major, don't you?"

"Lad, this place has seen no growth or new construction in years. I played in these alleyways as a bairn full fifty years ago, noo."

"Really? My father said you were from a rich family here. And you were playing in alleys?"

"Aye, that I was. I was a bit of a rebel, even then. Came doon here every chance I could t' watch th' DropShips come an' go. There was somethin' romantic aboot those great, round ships climbin' to th' stars on their pillars of white flame, back then. Here we are. Watch your head." He dragged back a loose section of chain-link fence, opening a narrow way through. Alex squeezed through into yet another alley, whose far end opened onto a dirty, trash-littered street.

He could hear the troops coming long before he saw them.

McCall had holstered the pistol and set down his bag. "Let's wait a bit, Alex," he said. "Look friendly and peaceful. A harmless tourist."

They stood at the mouth of the alley as the armored column swept past, twelve open-topped hovercraft racing one after the other down the street on shrill, shrieking ducted fans. The wind howling from beneath their skirts set litter and trash in the street whirling, and pelted both men with showers of fine, air-blasted grit and cinders. The soldiers riding those troop carriers were black-armored, their faces invisible behind polarized helmet blast shields, but Alex could sense their incurious glances as they passed. Beside him, McCall grinned foolishly and waved.

As the last troop carrier in line howled past, Alex was about to move into the street, but McCall touched his shoulder. "Wait, lad." Then Alex, too, heard what McCall had heard, a familiar and unmistakable *hiss-wheeze-thump* of machinery in motion.

BattleMechs.

The lead 'Mech was a *Wasp,* painted head to foot in the Home Guard's black and yellow colors. Despite the paint, the machine, Alex could plainly see, was not in particularly good shape. Large streaks of rust or corrosion had been merely painted over, and they showed through the paint now like patches of decay. Missing access panels revealed clusters of brightly colored wire or bundles of myomer, weak chinks in the 'Mech's armor.

Still, even as a MechWarrior—*especially* as a Mech-Warrior—Alex had rarely been in a position to confront a potentially hostile 'Mech from this vantage point, unarmed and in the open as the machine towered above him. The *Wasp* was a twenty-tonner, standing eight meters tall—just over four times Alex's height. Though the machine was basically humanoid in design, the legs were longer than the rather squat torso; Alex would have had to stretch to reach up and touch its knee. The head, ridiculously tiny, haloed by its array of four Duotech comm antennas, mimicked human expression as it swung to scan the two humans standing at the side of the road. As the slit of its viewpoint swung to face them, Alex could see the neurohelmeted head of the pilot squeezed into the 'Mech's tiny cockpit. So cramped was the pilot's space in a *Wasp* that only his head and shoulders extended up out of the 'Mech's torso; the impression was more that of a man wearing a very large suit of armor than piloting a combat machine.

With a ponderous clanking and the *squeak-chirp* of metal chafing metal, the *Wasp* strode past, following the hovercraft troop carriers. During the trip from Glengarry, McCall had used the DropShip's comm equipment to play a recording of the news broadcast he'd downloaded from the net. Alex wondered if this was the same *Wasp* that had stomped on that lone protester in Malcom Plaza.

"Looks like they're headed for that park," Alex said.

"Aye, lad. Y' dinnae often see BattleMechs used for crowd control."

"Looked like a whole infantry battalion as well. Things must be pretty bad."

"Aye, lad. An' gettin' worse. We go *this* way."

Once they were clear of the area near the spaceport, New Edinburgh became less threatening, and less claustrophobic. The citizens in the streets seemed much the same as those of any other world Alex had visited. Perhaps a quarter of the men wore kilts displaying a variety of colorful tartans, while many of the women wore trews, loose-fitting slacks in patterns of plaid. There were no soldiers in evidence.

Malcom Plaza was a much larger and better-kept park than the one near the spaceport, and it seemed peaceful enough at the moment. Nevertheless, Alex noticed several telltale signs of battle, the pockmark craters of bullet holes on a ferrocrete wall, and a thin brownish stain on the street not yet entirely washed or worn away. Beyond the plaza was the terminal for a monorail system, part of the same network as the subway near the spaceport. Still lugging their baggage, Alex and McCall paid their fares, climbed aboard a waiting maglev transport, and within minutes were silently streaking through the heart of the city, past the encircling belts of manufactories and light industrial plants, and into the rolling green countryside beyond.

"Pretty country," Alex said, leaning back in the maglev car's seat and staring at the scenery drifting past.

"Aye, tha' it is."

"Are you happy to be back?"

"I might be," McCall admitted. "I would be in different circumstances, certainly. If we dinnae ha' *that* t' contend wi'." He pointed out the window. Turning, Alex saw the Citadel for the first time.

It was a structure much like the Castle back on Glengarry, with architecture fairly typical of the early centuries of the Star League. It was hard to see details at this distance, but it hugged the top of a cliff overlooking the chrome and glass towers of New Edinburgh like some immense, carnivorous black cat crouching above its prey. Most of it looked like it had been carved and polished from a titanic block of obsidian, for it drank the light of Caledonia's yellow-orange sun without giving up a single reflection. Towers stretched skyward from the perimeter wall; once they had housed powerful sensor suites, planetary-defense beam projectors, and anti-DropShip weapons. Now, they most likely housed human sentries and observers, for on Caledonia, as on so many other worlds throughout the Inner Sphere, the relentless loss of all technologies over the past centuries of unrelenting warfare had inevitably forced a greater and greater reliance on *human* sensors rather than on electronics.

"Quite a fortress," Alex said. "How do you get up there, anyway?"

"Oh, there's a road, of sorts. Winds up through those hills below the main cliff."

"Looks like it would be hard to attack."

"Aye. Its designers had tha' in mind, no doubt. There's only one way in on the ground, and tha' across a stone bridge over a sheer drop of thirty meters or so. The outer walls are ferrocrete and twenty meters tall. Not tall enough, perhaps, to stop a 'Mech wi' jump jets, but there's aye precious few places ootside to boost from that are close enough for a 'Mech to make a controlled jump. The foundation of the thing is native bedrock, melted out a' the heart of that mountain. Mount Alba, we call it."

"Alba. White?" The mountain was a dusky purple-gray even in full sunlight, and seemed darker beneath the black embrace of the Star League fortress.

"Eh? Och, aye, you're thinkin' of th' Latin word *albus*. Nae, 'Alba' is an auld Gaelic word for 'Scotland.' Could hae' been from th' Latin originally, I suppose, but that was a long, long time ago."

The maglev monorail swept through a shadow-dark patch of forest that blotted out the view of the Citadel. When it emerged into full light once more, they were already slowing for the town of Dundee.

A rural town of low, crystal domes and organic buildings that looked more like they'd been grown than built, Dundee lay nestled along a bay on the Firth of Lorn, sheltered from Caledon's occasional coriolis storms by the gray-brown loom of the rugged Isle of Mull. The hills encircling the city to the north and west rose swiftly to saw-toothed peaks that were snowcapped throughout the world's entire year, and sunlight off the Nevian Glacier struck white fire from those slopes on any clear and sunny day.

The McCall estates were in the hills to the northeast, overlooking both the town and the bay. A twenty-minute ride in a rented groundcar brought them to the ornate front gates.

"Good lord, Major," Alex said as they pulled up, seeing nothing visible beyond the gate except woods and steeply sloping hills. "You gave up living *here* to become a mercenary?"

"There were extenuatin' circumstances, Alex." McCall flashed a wry grin. "Besides, I always was a rebel."

The elderly gatekeeper who came out to meet them wore civilian clothing, but the sash running from left shoulder to right hip gave him a distinctly military air despite his obvious years; the sash was woven in the rather severe red and black tartan of Clan McCall. Seeing the face of the man at the groundcar's control stick, his eyes widened and his jaw dropped. "Young Davis!" he exclaimed. "You're back!"

"Aye, Myles, I am. Are they expectin' me on th' hill, d'ye think? I dinnae call ahead when we grounded."

"Not for a couple of weeks, a' least, sair. Ah know they got your transmission before y' left Glengarry, though. They was talkit aboot it an' little else for a week."

"What do you think? A friendly reception? Or like last time?"

"Friendly enough, I imagine, sair, though you're no doubt aware tha' there was some wee disagreement about your maither's calling you a' first."

"I can imagine. Any word about Angus?"

"Nothin', sair, except tha' a trial's yet t' be held. There's aye new trouble i' the city, though, an' Wilmarth's dungeons must be fair t' overflowin' by noo."

"I can imagine. We came through a wee bit a' disturbance on th' way here."

The gatekeeper looked from McCall's face to Alex, then back again. "An' this is your aide, you said? Young Alex Carlyle?"

"That he is, Myles."

"Weel, you two can go on through, then. I'll call ahead an' let them ken you're comin' up."

"A servant?" Alex asked as the gates swung open and McCall guided the groundcar through.

"A retainer, an' aye more than that. Myles has been wi' the family for as long as I can remember. He's always been a good friend t' me." He grinned. "He helped me get oot on m'own when I needed some fresh air, back when I was a bairn."

"Just how many retainers does your family have?"

"And how should I know that, lad? It's been a few years since I last was here."

The house lay deep in the woods, a series of beams and saucer shapes thrusting from the sheer-sided cliff and extending out into the air above a step-like cascade of small waterfalls in the rocky stream below.

"Alex!" A tall, attractive woman in her mid-forties was descending a curved sweep of steps as the car pulled to a stop beneath an overhanging awning. "They said you were on your way. It's good to see you again!"

"Hello, Marta."

"Come on in! The others are waiting for you inside."

"Well, might as weel go an' face th' music, then. Ah,

Marta? This is Alex Carlyle, my aide an' protégé. Alex? Allow me to present the loveliest a' th' McCall lovelies, Marta. She was daft enough t' marry m' brother Robert some years back, but tha' was aye after I was long gone, so she bears me no ill will. At least . . . as far as I ken?"

"Idiot," she said, smiling. "And the daftest of the lot of us besides. Come on. There's no ill will here *now*. Not with what's happened to Angus."

"The others" were two men, younger than Davis but displaying a distinct similarity in the angles of jaw and brow, in the sharp thrust of nose, in the cold blue-gray of eyes. Davis introduced them as his younger brothers, Robert and Ben. Besides Marta, three other women were there, Julia and Kristal—the wives of Ben and Angus—and an elderly woman whom Davis introduced as "Maither."

"An' your regiment, Davis," the old woman said as McCall completed the introduction. "Will it be a' comin' soon, then?"

"No, Maither," Davis said. "It's me an' the lad here."

Her face hardened. "Is tha' a', then? An' how is it you propose t' take on Wilmarth an' his whole army of off-world foreigners, eh? Wi' your ain two hands?"

"We know our message to you was cut off," Ben McCall said, with only a trace of the lilting Scots burr. "But we thought you'd have sense enough to bring your unit, Davis. Those people up in the Citadel are playing for keeps!"

"Aye, Ben," McCall said reasonably. "An' so am I. We dinnae need the Gray Death t' roust such a beggar as Nelson Wilmarth, even if bringin' them here were possible."

"Yes," Robert said with just a trace of smugness. "Your people are mercenaries, aren't they? We'd need to come up with quite a bit of money to hire them, I suppose. We *do* have some resources, you may remember. How much would you ask, Davis? How much to help your own family?"

Davis scowled. "Robert, the Gray Death is nae mine to give. But do ye truly believe y' need to purchase my services?"

"Please, boys," Marta said, pleading in her voice. "Let's not fight, not now! Robert, Davis came here to help. It's not like he has a BattleMech regiment of his own to order around like his own personal army!"

"Aye," Ben said. "It's Wilmarth who has that, and we have precious little of our own to face him with." He shook his head hopelessly. He looked at McCall and at Alex, a rueful expression on his face. "I don't imagine either of you two was even able to bring a BattleMech wi' you?"

"We need an army, Ben," Robert said. "And I don't know where we're supposed to find one!"

"Weel," McCall said slowly, "it seems t' me you hae the beginnin's of one, right here in New Edinburgh. We saw a group as we came in—"

"What?" Robert said. "That rabble? Hardly an army. Street demonstrators an' gutter sweepings, th' lot of 'em."

"You'd be surprised just what you can do with 'gutter sweepings,' " McCall said. "But our first job will be easier than tha'."

"What?" Kristal asked. She was a severe-looking woman with a hard set to her jaw. "What is it you plan to do, Davis?"

"Why, lass," McCall said cheerfully. "I think that first thing tomorrow, Alex here and I are going to pay a courtesy call on our friend Wilmarth!"

"What? We're going to the Citadel?" Alex asked.

"Aye, unless you think we'd be better off inviting him here. Somehow, though, I don't think he'd come."

"Are you as daft as that, then?" Robert asked. "Folks around here don't go to that place, not voluntarily. And those that do go, well, they don't usually come back again."

Kristal gave a stifled sob, then rose and rushed out of the room. "Damn you, Robert," Julia said as she hurried after the other woman.

"I heard you and Ben went there, after Angus was taken," McCall said in the awkward silence that followed.

"Aye," Ben said. "We did, but they wouldn't let us through the front gate. Told us that Angus would be held for trial, that he would be an example for all of Caledonia, and that there was nothing we could do about it."

"Who'd you talk to. A guard?"

"Actually, it was Wilmarth's chief liaison with the FedCom military," Robert said. "A poisonous toad of a man called Folker."

"Folker?" McCall said, eyes narrowing. "Tha' would nae be a particular toad named Kellen Folker, would it?"

"Major Kellen Folker," Ben said, nodding. "That was him. What, you know the man?"

"He was nae a major when I knew him last," McCall said.

"But then, neither was I. Yes, I know 'Killer Kellen' vurra weel indeed."

"Is that good?" Alex asked. "I mean, can you talk to him, get him to let us in to see the governor?"

"I'll see what I can do," McCall said slowly, thoughtfully. "It may be tha' our acquaintanceship will do just that little thing. . . ."

"Yes?"

"Unless, of course, one of us kills the other one first."

The Citadel
Caledonia, Skye March
Federated Commonwealth
0920 hours, 1 April 3057

They drove the groundcar up the winding road toward the crest of Mount Alba. Alex sat in the front passenger seat, checking their hand weapons, while McCall sat at the stick. Though not deliberately looking for trouble, both men were wearing combat fatigues and load vests instead of the civilian garb they'd worn the day before. As McCall had pointed out to his brothers that morning, civilians had already tried approaching Wilmarth with no appreciable success. Now they would try a more military approach.

They'd already passed several no-trespassing signs and a concrete pylon that almost certainly housed remote sensors. As the mountain's crown of black walls and turrets rose before them, Alex had the distinct impression that they were being closely watched.

"So where did you meet this Killer Kellen guy?" Alex asked, probing.

"Furillo."

"That was back, when? Before you joined the Legion."

"Aye. Tha' would hae been aboot '17, maybe '18. Tell me, lad. Hae' y' never heard of th' Guardians a' Cameron?"

Alex considered the name. "I don't— Wait. Merc unit? Had a cutesy rep?"

"Tha' they did. A strange bunch, tha' lot."

Hundreds, perhaps thousands of mercenary units were scattered across the Inner Sphere, augmenting the military forces of the various Great Houses and of individual worlds, and dozens more appeared every year. Some few—the Gray Death and Jaime Wolf's Dragoons were two—had survived and even prospered during the past few bloody decades. Many had vanished utterly, disbanded when they couldn't meet their contracts or pay their bills, or else been so badly crushed in combat that they simply never recovered.

The rest struggled on, desperate for munitions, for new equipment, for new men. A handful, in an attempt to provide some unifying motif for their units, adopted unusual dress, recruiting standards, philosophies, or even hobbies intended to distinguish them from the rest. Most combat vets cast a baleful eye on such gimmicks. Alex had heard of one unit that collected archaeological artifacts. Another supposedly recruited only beautiful women, though that story was almost certainly apocryphal, one of the stranger popular myths that floated through the MechWarrior community.

"So what was their gimmick?"

"Their CO had this strange notion a' warfare," McCall replied. "Chivalry. Honor. Fighting for lost causes, even when th' employer could not pay."

Alex nodded. *Chivalry will get you dead* was a favorite expression of Sarge's, back on Glengarry, though there were those even in this day and age who still thought that war was a kind of glamorous contact sport, synonymous with terms like "honor" and "glory." Most of those people, Alex reflected, had never faced a real 'Mech on the field . . . or else they were politicians or wore a general's rank insignia. In the popular mind, BattleMechs were frequently linked with such concepts, at least on worlds that hadn't suffered repeated invasions by 'Mech armies that reduced their cities, factories, and farms to smoking ruin. Among the uninitiated, and for a few veterans who gloried in the image of single combat, MechWarriors remained modern knights of the battlefield, jousting with one another in one-on-one tests of bravery and skill.

"As a result," McCall continued, "th' Guardians dinnae do so weel, a' least in a financial way."

What was left unspoken, though, was the obvious fact that McCall had joined the unit in the first place, years before.

Alex remembered the story he'd told on himself of sneaking off to New Edinburgh Spaceport to watch the DropShips lift. Gimmick or not, the Guardians of Cameron must have appealed somehow to an impressionable young Caledonian.

It was a side of Davis McCall's nature that Alex had never seen revealed before.

"And this Kellen Folker guy?"

"Aye. He was one a' th' auld hands, when I was just fresh oot a' trainin'. There was a wee bit of a dust-up between him an' me on Furillo. We were fightin' Marik tech raiders, a drop-an'-snatch aimed at a power plant factory ootside the capital. Killer took some rounds from a wee village an' went berserk. Burned down half th' town, killed God knows how many civilians. The Guardians' CO would nae have him in th' unit after that."

"You said there was a dust-up between the two of you. That sounds personal."

"Oh, aye, it was. I was in his lance, a raw newbie in my first real fight. I was th' one tha' testified against him at his court-martial."

"Ah."

"I've heard of him from time t' time since, even run into him once or twice, on Gladius an' elsewhere. He had the rep a' bein' a hard-cast freelancer, a merc who'll do *anything* for C-bills enoo'."

Alex thought about the charge he'd heard leveled at McCall by his brother the afternoon before, about being unwilling to help his family without being paid for it. The accusation seemed even more unfair and uncalled-for now than it had then.

"Tell me, Major. Uh . . ." He stopped. How could he ask the man such a question?

"Oot wi' it, lad. I think I know wha' you have on your mind."

"I'm not sure how to say it in a diplomatic way."

"You dinnae need t' play th' diplomat wi' me. I've known you an' your father both for too long."

"Mmm. I was just wondering how . . . how completely you can trust them? Your family, I mean."

"A fair question. There's been aye some bad blood there, over th' years."

"We're using them for our home base . . . the radio." They'd set up their transmitter equipment that morning in the loft of a McCall barn. If and when the Gray Death arrived, they should be able to make contact—or pick up an automated transmission with a recorded log of everything that had happened up until that point.

But the possibility of betrayal to the government forces was very real.

"I don't believe they'll try to exchange me for Angus, if tha' is what you mean," McCall said. "They hate Wilmarth, as I'm sure you heard. Perhaps they hate him enough t' even trust th' likes a' us."

"I hope so."

"It's a fact, lad. The Scots like t' fight among themselves. When there's no other clan to trounce a' th' time, they'll tear a' one another within the family like nestling cragclaws. But threaten them wi' an ootsider, an' look out!"

The groundcar rounded a final bend in the road, slowed, then stopped. The Citadel rose directly before them now, on the far side of a bridge spanning a rock-bound gulf some fifty meters wide and thirty deep. A trooper in black and yellow armor stopped them with an upraised hand; others advanced with weapons at port arms. Alex reached unobtrusively for the laser pistol holstered to his thigh, but McCall caught the motion. "Easy, lad. Keep your hands where they can see 'em."

One soldier, with the sleeve chevrons of a sergeant painted on his old-fashioned kevlar armor, walked up to the driver's side of the car. "Okay, you two," he growled. "Where do you think you're going?"

"Why, t' pay a wee social call on th' governor," McCall said in a cheerful voice. "An' t' say hello to an auld comrade-at-arms, if he's still here."

"And who might that be, Scotty?"

"Major Kellen Folker," McCall replied. "Though we used t' call him 'Killer.' "

The sergeant's swagger dwindled a bit at that name. "And your name, sir?"

"Major McCall. Of the Gray Death Legion."

The sergeant looked at Alex, who met the visored gaze evenly. "Captain Alex Carlyle," Alex said without being asked. "Also of the Gray Death."

"A moment, please, sirs," the sergeant said, and he took a step back as he used his armor's comm unit to talk to someone in the Citadel. After several tense moments, during which the guards surrounding the car fidgeted with their weapons, the sergeant stepped forward again. "You can go on through," he told McCall. "Someone will meet you in the gatehouse."

"Aye, thank you, lad."

The car moved slowly across the bridge, as double gates slid aside for them directly ahead. The gate tower was the tallest and most imposing of the wall defenses, rising fifty meters above the foundations and flanked by evil-looking turrets boasting quad-mounted high-speed autocannons that tracked the two men as they approached.

Up close, though, the crumbling facade of the outer walls suggested that the owners of this place had stopped trying to provide proper upkeep a long time ago, and that almost certainly meant that the technology, too, had been allowed to decay. As they passed through the gate and into the shadowy interior of the barbican, Alex saw numerous open recesses in the stone walls to either side that once must have held sensor arrays or cameras, but which now were vacant. In some cases, it looked as though wires had been stripped out of conduits, probably for the resale price of the metal or fiber optic cables.

Most of the soldiers waiting for them in the gatehouse were like those outside, wearing mismatched and ill-fitting pieces of black and yellow kevlar. One, though, was a tall, imposing figure in the full dress finery of a Federated Commonwealth major.

"Weel, noo, Killer," McCall said as he and Alex climbed out of the car. "It's been a year or two, hasn't it?"

"Well, if it isn't the Boy Scout," the other said with a gravel-rough voice. Though clearly older than McCall by at least ten years, his hair and neatly trimmed beard were glossy black. "What the hell brings you to this jerkwater dirt ball?"

"It's my home, for one. Your new boss in there for another."

"The Governor?" Folker snorted. "*He's* not my boss."

"Aye, you're wearin' a new uniform, I see. FedCom?"

"And senior military advisor to the Governor of Caledonia." Folker brushed lightly at the staff command insignia on his breast, above the rows of campaign and service medals. "As you can see, Davis, I've improved my station in life considerably. Your weapons, please."

"Eh?"

"Your weapons. Leave them here. No one goes into the Governor's presence armed."

McCall reached for his belt buckle. "Nervous type, eh?"

"These are dangerous times, Scout. Fanatics have tried to assassinate the man three times already. There's a revolution brewing on this world, or hadn't you heard?"

"Oh, I'd heard all right." McCall handed his gun belt to a guard.

Alex removed his gun belt as well. "What's that, kid?" Folker demanded, pointing at a sheathed combat knife clipped hilt-down to Alex's combat vest.

"Vibroblade," Alex replied. He patted his right breast pocket. "And in here I have a monothread. You want those too?"

"Nah, keep your toys," the man said, grinning. "Lasers and slug-throwers make the old man jumpy, but, believe me, you'll never get close enough to use a blade on *him*! This way, gentlemen, if you please."

"Wha' aboot you?"

"Eh? What about me?"

"Don't you leave your sidearm here too?"

"That rule is for natives, and for strangers. I happen to be one of the Governor's most trusted aides."

"Oh, aye? An' just what is it you aid him with?"

Folker drew himself up a bit straighter. "I am here, gentlemen, as special military liaison to the Governor of Caledonia. Basically, that means I am his military advisor. I've been helping him train his militia, repair his 'Mechs ..."

"An' wi' you bein' a fine an' experienced MechWarrior as weel ..."

"Yes, I've piloted his 'Mechs. Usually I take his *Wasp* out."

"Aye, I thought I recognized your style when I saw a vid of a *Wasp* in New Edinburgh a few weeks back."

"What, the riot in Malcom Square?" Folker chuckled. "Yeah, that was me. The rabble really ran, didn't they?"

"Aye, tha' they did. Most of 'em."

"Were you in the *Wasp* we saw in the city yesterday, Major?" Alex asked.

"I usually have more important things to do than arresting malcontents, boy. I was guiding the operation from the Citadel, here."

Accompanied by Folker and an escort of four armored troopers, they passed through the gate tower and entered the courtyard beyond. "God in heaven!" Alex murmured, stunned. McCall said nothing, but Alex could see his fists clench, the tendons standing out stark white and taut on the backs of McCall's hands.

The bodies of half a dozen men hung in the courtyard, impaled through the back or beneath the jaw on upright, three-meter-tall iron stakes. Some of the bodies had been exposed that way longer than others; the stink in the air was suffocatingly heavy and sweet. One stake held nothing but human heads, threaded on rusty iron one atop another like beads on a needle. The ones at the bottom were nothing but shiny white bone; the ones at the top were fresh, still possessing hair and skin and staring eyes.

Compounding horror with horror, numerous people—soldiers, technicians, even a few civilian laborers, giving lie to what Robert had said about "folks around here"—were going about their business in the shadow of those grisly trophies as though nothing whatsoever was wrong. Two soldiers were leaning on a wall within three meters of one bloody stake, swapping stories punctuated by bursts of raw laughter.

Standing over the scene of horror was a single BattleMech, the black and yellow *Wasp* they'd seen the day before.

The old Star League fortress's inner keep was the governor's residence proper, a thick-walled bastion topped by weapons turrets and commo antennas. Inside, past an antechamber and several layers of office suites and administrative personnel, sliding doors opened on a long, gloom-shadowed audience chamber with two lines of stone pillars and a vaulted ceiling that reminded Alex forcibly of the interior of some ancient stone cathedral. Perhaps this place had once been a chapel for the Star League troopers stationed here; pews and altar had long ago been removed, however, and the Governor used it now for meeting supplicants and for entertaining guests.

Especially, Alex thought with a hard-edged black humor, the entertaining. The place was a horror-house, with skeletons and mummified corpses shackled to the pillars like macabre sentries standing at their posts to either side of the worn red carpet running down the center aisle. Another, fresher corpse hung from a strand of piano-wire, slowly turning, as naked and bloody as freshly butchered meat. Alex had heard that people hung that way died from slow strangulation, rather than a quick, clean snap of the neck. What kind of sick monster was this Wilmarth, anyway?

At the far end of the room, the governor's seat was raised like a throne on a pedestal set on a low stage. Towering overhead and behind the throne, a close fit even in this high-ceilinged room and dominating the entire chamber, stood a black and yellow *Locust*, its unexpected presence indoors giving it a shadowy, demonic look.

As they approached the throne, several paces behind Folker, Alex saw a new horror that nearly made him miss a step. With a hiss of indrawn breath, he touched McCall's elbow.

"I see them, lad," McCall said in a low murmur, walking smoothly down the red carpet. "Take it in stride. Don't show it botherin' ye."

Take it in stride? How? Two prisoners, a man and a woman, had been brought to the chamber for execution where, just a few meters away, Nelson Wilmarth sat enjoying his midday meal. Stripped, bound, gagged, they stood barefooted on half-meter-thick blocks of ice, with piano-wire nooses cinched around their throats and the free ends drawn taut and secured to a wooden beam high overhead. Neither dared move, though Alex saw their eyes shifting toward him, desperate, pleading. The woman, already straining high on the balls of her feet to keep the deadly, slicing pressure off her throat, was trembling with cold, exhaustion, or fear—most likely all three. Alex doubted she would be able to keep her precarious footing on the fast-melting ice block much longer. The man beside her stood rock-steady, though his bare legs had a ghost-blue pallor to them.

"Well, Major," Nelson Wilmarth said from behind the table. "Is this the man you told me of? Your old comrade?"

"He is indeed, sir. Governor, may I present Major McCall and his aide, Captain Carlyle. Gentlemen, this is Nelson Wilmarth, Federated Commonwealth Governor of the Caledonian system."

Nelson Wilmarth was a ponderously fat, sallow-skinned man with dark eyes, unkempt hair, and dough-soft features almost lost in layers of sweat-sheened fat. The table before him was piled high with food, and he seemed to be enjoying his meal with rather carelessly messy gusto.

"Charmed, gentlemen, I'm sure," Wilmarth said, wiping his mouth with the back of one fat hand. "Carlyle. That would be the son of the leader of the notorious Gray Death Legion?"

"That's right," Alex said. He jerked a thumb at the two prisoners. "You sadistic bastard! What the hell is the meaning of this?"

"Easy, lad," McCall said. "Gently, noo—"

"Rebel scum," Wilmarth said, shrugging. "Taken just yesterday, as a matter of fact. They were instigators of a demonstration near the spaceport, and I decided to make an example of them."

Alex looked at them again. He didn't recognize the man, but he was suddenly aware that he'd seen the dark-haired woman before—wearing a red headband, a T-shirt, and Caledonian trews as she addressed the crowd near the spaceport.

"Damn it, you can't do things like *this*!"

"Really?" Wilmarth seemed unconcerned by Alex's outburst. "As Governor of this world, boy, I have both responsibilities and a certain measure of power. It is my responsibility to keep the peace here for the Federated Commonwealth by any means I deem necessary. And that includes, Major McCall, putting your older brother on trial for inciting a riot, endangerment of public morals, and treason. I assume that he is the *real* reason that you are here, of course, and not the likes of *these* two."

"About my brother," McCall said easily. "I assume there's somethin' you want, since y' would nae ha' waited so long otherwise. Did y' give *these* two a trial before trussing them up like tha'?"

Wilmarth looked at Folker and smiled. "You said he was smart, Major."

Folker grinned back. "In most ways, Governor. If we could just break him of that nasty idealistic streak ..."

The Governor looked back to McCall, still smiling. "There is indeed something you could do for us, Major. We've, ah, heard that your regiment will be ordered here soon."

"Aye, y' did, did ye?" McCall said, and his smile was as cold and tight as death itself. "An' you think th' Gray Death may be able to help you wi' the locals if the Federated Commonwealth picks up our contract an' sends us here."

"They *will* order you here, Major," Folker said. "We've

had definite word on that, shortly after we put in a call to Tharkad for help in the face of this revolt."

"Then, Governor, I can't see where you need *my* help, noo. I'm nothin' but one of Grayson Carlyle's officers, after a' . . ."

"Oh, don't be so modest, Major," Folker said. "You're number three in the line of command. And you're one of Colonel Carlyle's oldest friends. Not to mention that your family is quite important on this world. We expect you have a certain amount of influence with them. And they have a certain influence over Caledonia's population."

"Aye, so that's the way of it, eh?"

Alex heard the deadliness in McCall's voice and took his cue from the glance, so quick it almost wasn't there at all, that the Caledonian flashed his way from the corner of his eye. He knew that look. *Get ready! Watch me!*

"I want to see m' brother," McCall declared, his voice hard and low. He took a step forward . . . and Alex heard the sharp *snick-snack* of a heavy weapon being readied, followed by a high-pitched whine of machinery. Above and behind the governor, the two weapons pods raised to either side of the *Locust*'s torso had shifted position, bringing the muzzles of their heavy machine guns to bear on McCall.

Alex stiffened. The two of them stood directly beneath the looming gaze of the eight-meter-tall combat machine. On one side of the room, a panel slid open in the wall, and three men with assault rifles appeared.

Alex wasn't sure what was next, but it suddenly looked like there would soon be some additional entertainment in this room, with him and McCall as the featured players.

13

The Citadel
Caledonia, Skye March
Federated Commonwealth
1035 hours, 1 April 3057

The *Locust* shifted position again, its sharply back-angled knees flexing to bring its body a bit lower. The machine-gun pods to either side of the cockpit remained fixed on Alex and McCall.

"Don't move!" Folker ordered.

"I would come no closer, if I were you," the Governor added. "Lieutenant Dahlgren, here, tends to react badly to anything he perceives as a threat to my person. Isn't that right, Lieutenant?"

"Right, Governor," a voice boomed from the *Locust*'s external speaker overhead. "I got the bastard covered."

"Aye, an' now I'll do the talkin' an' you'll listen to me, y' fat, slicket weasel." McCall seemed totally oblivious to the BattleMech standing a few meters in front of him. "You will release my brother, an' you'll release these two people here, an' you'll release all th' other folk y' been keepin' inside your foul house. I'll do wha' I can t' quiet things down, aye, but I'll nae be able t' stop this revolt until y' stop washin' your hands in the people's blood! Alex! Cut those two down."

"Stop!" Wilmarth demanded, rising in his chair. "I'll have you—"

"You'll have me wha', y' puir sick bastard? Shoot me, worse, shoot this lad here, an' when the Gray Death *does* ground here, no power on Caledon would stop 'em from renderin' your fat carcass down to aye a kilogram or three a' lard! You'll want to pull this mountain down a' top of ye to hid from th' likes a' Colonel Carlyle, and I'll tell you somethin'. He'd *still* find you, lad, an' make you curse th' day you were born! Alex! Do it noo!"

With a clean, swift movement, Alex freed his vibroblade from its vest sheath and keyed the power switch. A low hum sounded in the room, and the slender blade, its atomic structure set to vibrating by powerful oscillating mag fields, began glowing, leaping up the spectrum until it was white-hot. Spinning, he slashed the blade just above the bound woman's head, parting the wire with a loud ping. He took a step as she sagged, catching her on his left arm and lowering her gently down from the ice. Reaching up again, he snicked the wire looped around the man's neck. Both prisoners were trembling now as they slumped on the carpet, and he didn't want to risk burning them with the hot blade. Sheathing it once more, he pulled out the monowire, two button-sized reels of heavy metal that, when drawn a few centimeters apart, exposed the dangerously fine, almost invisible monofilament thread. With quick, deliberate movements, he used it to slice neatly through the metal shackles binding their wrists behind their backs. The fragments clinked cheerfully as they hit the floor.

"Y-y-y-you can't do this!" Wilmarth screamed, pointing, his pudgy hand shaking up and down. "Folker! Dahlgren! *Do something!*"

Kellen Folker was drawing his sidearm, a heavy laser pistol. Alex saw McCall move . . . a lightning snap of body and hands almost too fast to follow. Before either Folker or the *Locust* pilot could react, McCall was standing behind Folker, his arms thrust across the man's shoulders, his clenched fists held rigidly just in front of the man's face.

Nobody moved.

"G-God, Davis," Folker said, breaking the silence. He still held the laser pistol, its muzzle aimed now at the room's ceiling. "Don't—"

"Why don't y' lay your wee toy there on th' table, noo?"

Moving very slowly, Folker did as he was told, clearly terrified of what McCall held in his hands. Alex recognized the stance. McCall had pulled out a monowire of his own and was holding it taut between his fists. One misstep on Folker's part, and that invisible thread would snick back through his neck and send his head bouncing across the floor.

"Alex?" McCall said. "Do me a favor an' retrieve the Major's gun."

When Alex had the pistol, McCall stepped back, the monofilament reels vanished somewhere into his vest. "Keep th' gun on our friend, here. You! You! Ay, an' you too!" He pointed at the trio of Blackjacket guards who'd appeared out of the side doorway. "Let's have your weapons, as weel."

"Lieutenant Dahlgren!" Wilmarth screamed. "Step on that little bastard!"

Alex snapped the muzzle of the laser pistol from Folker's head to the Governor's. "I'd countermand that, were I you, Governor!"

Wilmarth squeaked. The *Locust* shifted back slightly but did not otherwise move. With the gun no longer pointed at his head, Folker stiffened and started to turn, but Alex brought the pistol back and tapped him behind the ear. "Don't. Sir. I'd hate to stain the Governor's nice carpet."

McCall, by this time, had snatched an assault rifle from one guard's hands and brought the weapon up to his shoulder. "I wouldn't worry m'sel' too much about that, Alex," he said. "Th' carpet's red, after a'. You two," he called to the two former prisoners. "Can ye handle a rifle?"

"Try us!" the woman cried, pulling an assault rifle from the hands of another of the guards.

"We'll take this bluidy damned place apart," the man said in a heavy burr, picking up the third weapon where the trooper had dropped it and snapping back the bolt, chambering a round. Both of the ex-prisoners were still trembling, but now Alex sensed that the trembling was a barely suppressed rage. The woman, especially, bore a flame in her eyes and a hunger in the expression behind her bared teeth that must have been terrifying to her former captors. Whirling suddenly, she dropped one of the soldiers to his knees with a sharp rifle-butt thrust to his kidney.

"Easy there, lass," McCall told her. "Why don't you both find y'sel's somethin' to wear. It's a bit nippy ootside. Boots, too. We hae a bit of a walk ahead of us, an' a drive after that."

As the prisoners relieved two of the guards of various articles of clothing, McCall turned back to face Wilmarth, who was seated on his throne, fists clenched as he glowered at the scene being played out before his unbelieving eyes. "Lad, we're goin' to walk oot a' here, an' we'll be takin' your wee F-C friend here wi' us for a bit a' the way, as insurance, y' ken. I suggest you sit vurra still where you are for as long as you can see us. I assure you tha' I could pop off the top of your head wi' this rifle all the way from the front door a' this place.

"An' while you're watchin' us go, I suggest you think aboot jus' wha' might happen to you if the lad here or I ended up bein' killed or wounded because you were foolish enough to try to stop us ootside. Colonel Carlyle is nae so forgivin' an' gentle a man as I am."

"I want that son of a bitch," the woman said. Dressed now in black boots, trousers, and a combat jacket, she took a step forward, raising her rifle to aim at the governor.

"No, lass," McCall warned. "There'd be no stoppin' the hornet's nest if y' did that."

"You don't know what these bastards *did*!"

"Aye, I have a pretty fair idea, lass, an' I'm sorry. But this is nae th' time t' settle auld scores. Or the place."

"What about your brother?" Alex asked him.

Alex could see McCall assessing options, weighing the chances. The Caledonian shook his head slightly. "No, lad. We'll hae t' come back for him. D' ye hear that, Governor? I'll be back for Angus McCall, an' when I come, ye'd best hae him safe an' sound an' ready t' come wi' me!"

They backed out of the room together, Alex, McCall, and the two ex-captives, with Folker still in tow, the muzzle of Alex's laser pistol prodding him along. The governor, the *Locust,* and the three disarmed guards watched them go, unmoving.

No one tried to stop them as they hurried through the outer offices or when they emerged into blinding sunlight in the courtyard outside.

"I don't understand, Major," Alex said as they hurried across the courtyard. "Wasn't that our best chance to get your brother out? Wilmarth's going to be waiting for you now. Worse, what if he decides to just kill Angus?"

"I don't think he'll do anything as foolish as tha',"

McCall said. "What' d' ye say, Major? Is the governor tha' stupid?"

"You've made a bitter enemy there, McCall," Folker said. "You made him lose face in front of his own people, and he's not going to forget that. God, I'd hate to be in your boots when Wilmarth gets hold of you."

"I don't intend to let him get hold of me. But tha' was nae th' question, lad."

Alex prodded Folker harder with the laser. "Answer the question, Major."

"Your brother is safe," Folker admitted. "For now, anyway. You were smart not to press your luck back there, though. He's well guarded. You'd never have made it to him."

"Aye, tha' was my thought a' th' time. But, y' ken, I cannae let tha' wee bastard keep Angus as a gun against my head."

"I don't see what you can do about it."

"Weel, noo. I could bring the Gray Death in, a company or so a' heavy 'Mechs. Wha' would he say t' tha'?"

"That when your mercenaries are brought in to Caledonia, they'll be under contract to the Armed Forces of the Federated Commonwealth. To *me*, in other words, Major, and subject to my orders. Break your contract, and you and your mercenaries are finished!"

"Still, it might be fun to see how far we could press your boss, wi' a BattleMech or four a' our backs. Here we are. You won't mind seein' us t' the bottom of the hill noo, will ye?"

Together, they entered the gatehouse where the groundcar was still parked. Under the impassive gaze of a dozen armed soldiers, the five of them squeezed into the vehicle, with Folker pinned uncomfortably between the two freed Caledonians in the back seat. No one tried to stop them as they drove out of the barbican, across the bridge, and down the mountain road. Alex was turned in his seat, watching the quad-mount autocannons tracking them, but there was no last-second burst of flame, no sudden ripple of explosions to hurry them on their way.

Ten minutes later, they reached the outskirts of New Edinburgh, and McCall pulled off the road to release Folker.

"No!" the man in the back seat said. "We should take him back to—"

"James!" the woman snapped. "Shut up!"

"We can question him! He could tell us how many 'Mechs and soldiers—"

"I dinnae think tha' is such a good idea, lad," McCall said. "Major, you're free t' go."

"That's decent of you, McCall," Folker said. " 'Mercenary's honor,' eh?"

"If y' like t' think so, aye. Get oot! An' Major!" McCall added as Folker clambered out of the back seat. "One more thing. You remind tha' governor a' yours tha' he's just liable t' find he's ridin' a tiger, here."

"What's a tiger?"

"Like an Arcturan razorcat," Alex told him, drawing on a bit of lore picked up from an education vid about extinct Terran animals some years before. "Only bigger."

"Aye, an' faster an' meaner," McCall said. "Wilmarth's goin' t' hae a wee bit a trouble haulin' his fat carcass doon off th' beast again wi'oot turnin' into dinner."

He touched the accelerator, and with a rising hum the groundcar swung back onto the road and off into the city, leaving Kellen Folker standing there at the side of the road.

"Well done, Major!" Alex exclaimed, leaning back in the seat. "I thought they had us boxed there for a while!"

"Aye, lad. It was a bit tight there for a second or two." Half turning in the seat, McCall grinned back at the two passengers. "I'm afraid we nae hae had th' time for proper introductions. I'm Major McCall, an' this good-lookin' lad here is Captain Carlyle."

"Delighted to meet you both," the man said. "I mean, *really* delighted! I'm James Graham."

"Allyn McIntyre," the woman said. "You two came along just in time, Major. My feet were so frozen on that ice, I couldn't feel a thing from my knees down."

"Glad to be of service," McCall said. "I take it you two were in tha' gatherin' by the spaceport yesterday."

"She was the woman standing on that statue," Alex pointed out.

"Aye, we were there," the woman said. "An' the bluidy Sasunnach bastards came at us wi' their hovercraft infantry an' a thunderin' great BattleMech. James an' me were caught by the soldiers before we could get clear."

"How many more prisoners in the Citadel now?" Alex asked.

"I dinnae ken for sure, Captain," Graham replied. "But a goodly many. Perhaps as many as a hundred. If . . . if your brother's there, Major, I'm afraid I don't know who he was."

"We weren't kept wi' the others long," Allyn explained. "Wilmarth dragged us oot early this morning t' hae his fun wi' us. Told us our bodies would be dumped in Malcom Square when he was done wi' us as a warnin' t' others."

"The Governor appears to be playin' for keeps," McCall said. "I take it you've got an organization behind you, lass?"

"What makes y' think tha,' Major?" James said.

"The way y' both handled th' weapons back there," McCall said easily. "You've both had some experience, I could see. You've got some vets wi' you, I would guess, t' show you how to handle assault rifles at least. An' you, James, vurra nearly let the cat oot a' the bag when you told our friend back there tha' you wanted to take him somewhere for questionin'. Tha' tells me you hae an intelligence apparatus of some sort."

"Not a very good one," Allyn admitted. "Not yet, anyway. But you're right. We hae a group. We call ourselves the Reivers."

"How many are you?" Alex asked.

"Enough t' make a start," James said. "Jacobites, most of us."

"Aye," Allyn added. "An' Jihaders."

"The Word of Jihad?" Alex asked.

James nodded. "They hae a personal reason for takin' on Fat Willie's BattleMechs, y' ken. See themselves doin' God's work by takin' the machines down."

"I cannae say I agree wi' the Jihaders' ideas," McCall said. "But I'd like t' meet them an' your people just the same. I'm a Jacobite m'sel'. Or *was*. It's been a few years since I was home."

"You're a McCall a' *the* McCalls," Allyn said. Her eyes widened. "Oh. *Tha'* Major McCall! I dinnae connect you wi' what I'd heard, at first."

"We heard you walked oot on your family an' clan," James said slowly. "Tha' you'd been disowned."

"Perhaps. But I'm back noo."

"We'll certainly want to take him to the General," Allyn told James. "He could help th' Reivers a lot."

"Unless . . ." James stopped, thought a moment, then shook his head. "Major, don't get me wrong, but I heard the talk between you an tha' bastard Folker. If your unit comes here, will it be t' fight against us? T' put down the rebellion? Because if they do, it will be you against us, an' we're not goin' to simply lay down our arms t' be butchered by tha' bluidy monster in the Citadel!"

"Lad, d' you think I'd fight for a madman like tha' Wilmarth?" He shook his head. "I hae to live wi' m'sel', y' ken."

"I think my father would shoot the Major if he even suggested such a thing," Alex added. "That's one reason we're here, anyway. To find out whose side we *should* be on!"

"Mercenaries who care which side they're on?" Allyn asked, her eyebrows raising. "That's a new one!"

"Not so new," Alex told her. "We pick our fights when we can. We wouldn't last long, as a unit or as a business, if it were otherwise."

"Aye, but this contract Folker mentioned. Between your unit an' the FedCom. How do you expect to get around tha'?"

"There are ways, lad," McCall said. "But we're not in th' habit a' discussin' trade secrets wi' folks we've just rescued from the enemy."

"Y' know," James said, relaxing slightly with a grin. "I *like* these men, Allyn." He laughed. "Major, that was a slick piece of work you pulled with that monowire on Folker."

"Never saw you move so fast, Major!" Alex said, laughing. He patted the combat vest pocket that held his own paired reels of monothread. "I didn't know you had one of these with you."

McCall gave him a wry grin. "Aye. An' who said I did?"

Alex's jaw dropped. "That was a *bluff?*"

"Weel, noo. Monothread's aye a wee bit hard t' see, unless it catches the light just so." Holding the car's stick for a moment between his knees, McCall held up his fists a few centimeters apart. "An' if y' think I might be holdin' the reels in each hand, just in front of your throat, weel, it's possible y' could see things that weren't really there."

"Steer the car," Alex said, shaking his head. "Good God, you talked a merc into giving up his laser with a bluff!"

"It's good t' have you on our side, Major," Allyn said. Her eyes were bright. "James, I think we should take them to see the General tonight."

"Ah, but lassie," McCall said. "I'm afraid we might hae a bit of a scheduling problem. We cannae go wi' you tonight."

"Why?" Alex asked. "What are we doing instead?"

"Why, we're payin' a wee visit on our friends oop there in the Citadel tonight."

James looked confused. "But, you said you'd be coming back with the Gray Death and with BattleMechs. Are you saying your people are already here?"

"We heard nothin' about it," Allyn said. "Are they very far?"

"Is sixty light years very far?" Alex asked.

"But—"

"Weel, noo, lass, I didn't exactly say the Legion was *here* then, did I?"

"Another bluff!" Allyn said, laughing.

"Just a bit of a wee diversion," McCall replied. "A word or two a' misdirection can aye work wonders sometimes."

"That's why he insisted on letting Folker go," Alex said. "Back at the Citadel, they'll be thinking in terms of incoming DropShips and BattleMech deployments. Major Folker may put an HPG call in to Tharkad, asking for instructions. They'll be checking on whether the Legion has left Glengarry yet and on when it might be arriving."

"Aye. All of which means they won't be expectin' the likes of us t' be puttin' in another appearance tonight. We'll go just as soon as it's full dark."

"But . . . do you have BattleMechs?" James asked. "Here?"

"You'll need 'Mechs to take on that army up there," Allyn said. "I can't tell you exactly how many troops he has, but we've seen at least four kinds of 'Mechs."

"Aye," McCall said. "We've seen the *Wasp* and the *Locust.*"

"*Locust?* Which one is that?"

"Tha' wee 'Mech keepin' watch over you in that room back there, while you were gettin' cold feet," McCall told her. "What else does he have?"

"I don't really know the different types, just by the look of them," James said. "I've heard of something called an *UrbanMech,* however."

"And a *Commando,*" Allyn added. "I've heard the General talking about a 'Mech called a *Commando.*"

"Are there more than one of any of these?"

"I think so," Allyn told him. "But we really don't know much in the way of numbers."

"Aye," McCall said. "We should be able t' get a better idea tonight, lad."

"But how?" James asked. "They've got at least four BattleMechs up there and plenty of other defenses besides. How can the two of you fight all of that?"

"Alex an' I will get along just fine," McCall told him. "All we need is t' swing by the cargo storage vault at the spaceport."

"What have you got there?" Allyn asked. "BattleMechs?"

"Not 'Mechs," Alex told her. "But something almost as good."

"Aye," McCall added. "We'll need t' pick up our wee bairns. . . ."

14

Slopes of Mount Alba
Caledonia, Skye March
Federated Commonwealth
2145 hours, 1 April 3057

"You'd better not come any closer," Alex said. "They'll have sensors up there that can pick you out of the night if you do."

"I wish we could come with you!" Allyn said, her voice low and fierce.

Alex turned to face her, aware of the hiss and whine of servomotors as his combat armor shifted position. With the visual sensors set to project IR imagery, Allyn appeared through his visor as a woman-shaped smear of color, all warm oranges and yellows in her face and torso and upper thighs, shading to cooler greens and blues at her extremities. Projecting alphanumerics on the right side of his visor, a HUD data feed told him she was .42 meter away at a bearing of 142 absolute, massing 58 kilos and carrying a fully charged laser rifle. The scanners were sensitive enough at this range to pick up the steady throb of her heart in her chest, echoed by the warm flutter of her pulse at her throat.

"I know, Allyn," Alex said. His voice, picked up by the suit's electronics and relayed to an external speaker, had an odd, metallic quality to it. He used his tongue to shift the HUD imaging to normal lighting; the colored smear gave way to Allyn's face, streaked with camouflage paint, her eyes showing her worry. "But the Major and I will stand a better chance if we go in alone." He rapped carballoy-clad knuckles against the side of his suit, eliciting a metallic clank. "In these."

Powered combat armor. The thought didn't much appeal to Alex, but he knew that the power suit might be the technological innovation that would one day end the reign of the BattleMech in ground combat. The old Star League had used various types of PCA, particularly for scouting and as mobile infantry support for the ponderous 'Mech units. The Clans, when they'd first struck the Inner Sphere with unexpected ferocity and dazzling technological superiority, had introduced to warfare something called Elemental armor—man-sized, jump-capable powered suits nearly as tough and as deadly as a 'Mech. There were cases on record of whole swarms of Elementals leaping onto a 'Mech in battle and beginning literally to tear it apart.

During the past few years, though, combat armor had been making an appearance with Inner Sphere forces as well, either manufactured locally with newly rediscovered techniques, or discovered in forgotten Star League arms caches. Few mercenary units could afford the things, but the Gray Death had been lucky enough to acquire a number of Inner Sphere units almost as soon as they'd become available. More recently, the Legion had struck it rich when Major Frye's Third Battalion had uncovered a number of crated, mint-condition Mark XXI Nighthawk suits in an underground Star League cache on Karbala, during a mission across the old Lyran Commonwealth border into the Rasalhague Free Republic. Legion techs had been modifying the technology and had come up with two versions of their own, a combat suit and a lighter, more maneuverable one for scouting. The scout suits were the ones Alex and McCall wore now.

"We'll be waiting, Alex," Allyn told him. "You can count on us!"

"We are."

The Reivers turned out to number at least four or five hundred men and women, though General Ambrose McBee and his officers were reluctant to discuss exact numbers. Alex didn't blame them; they'd already suffered heavy casualties in militia raids and dragnets. Switching his infrared scanners back on, he turned again, searching for McCall's

Nighthawk suit. Compared to the dancing flames of infrared radiated by the rebel troops around him, McCall's suit was very nearly invisible. Like Alex's, it emitted almost no heat at low-activity levels, and its armor employed electronic stealth technology similar to that of chameleon suits, constantly monitoring ambient patterns of color, light, and shadow, and adjusting the surface color and apparent texture to match. That didn't make the suits invisible by any means, but it made them very, very hard to spot at a distance or in poor light.

Especially if you weren't expecting them.

"Well, Major," Alex said, walking up to the other suited figure. He used his helmet's sonic transmitter rather than radio; there was too great a chance that radio communications were being monitored from the Citadel. "Do you have the information you need?"

"Enough, I think," McCall replied. "Tha' Citadel's a damn big labyrinth, but a few of the Reivers hae been inside an' oot again. As prisoners, or on one errand or another. Robert was wrong about tha', at least."

"There were those civilians we saw inside this morning."

"Aye. Folks will be folks, nae matter wha'. Turn around. Let's check our power systems again."

"Yes, sir."

Alex and McCall had retrieved the two suits, carefully foam-packed inside two-meter crates labeled "machine parts" and stored in a starport warehouse in New Edinburgh. They'd spent most of the afternoon back at the McCall estate, tuning the units and installing their power cores, checking weapons and program loads, and readying them for combat. Donned like unusually heavy and bulky space suits, the Nighthawks were surprisingly light to wear. Sensors embedded inside the suit's legs and arms felt the wearer's movements and responded with a myomer-assisted movement of the same degree. A man in a Nighthawk was not only nearly invisible, he was immensely strong. Both men carried laser rifles and microgrenade launchers, as well as an assortment of munitions. McCall also carried several satchel charges packed with polydetaline and equipped with pullring detonators, as what he referred to jocularly as "lockpicks."

They'd spent long hours going over all their gear before the mission, with the suits' backpack power cells receiving special attention. After McCall had run a final diagnostic check on Alex's unit and declared him fully operational, he turned around and let Alex perform the same service on him.

"You're set," Alex said. "I think it's time we moved out."

"Aye. Tha' it is."

The Reivers had escorted the two men this far, to a patch of woods on the lower slopes of Mount Alba, about five kilometers from the road that wound up to the bridge across the canyon. They left the Caledonian rebels there, strung out in a rough skirmish line in the woods, and began making their way through the heavy underbrush, climbing steadily toward the unseen Citadel.

They didn't speak; more than likely, there were channel scanners and RF detectors in the area that would pick up even tightly beamed radio signals, and sensitive sound-activated mikes that would pick up human speech. Conversation was not necessary, though. They'd gone over this plan numerous times that afternoon while working on the suits.

The Reivers seemed an unlikely group of rebels—farmers and merchants, most of them, with only a handful who'd ever seen military action. Allyn, for instance, the daughter of a New Edinburgh vintner, worked in a New Edinburgh factory that manufactured AgroMechs—civilian machines that worked Caledonia's farms. James Graham, a bootmaker from a village not far from Dundee, was himself the son of a family that bred fertile neomules. Even the General, who Alex and McCall had met late that afternoon after all, was a pharmacist in what he jokingly called his real life. A big, jolly man almost as given to excess mass as was Wilmarth, Ambrose McBee had admitted to them both over dinner that he'd served only briefly in the military. Years and years before, he'd been a captain with the First Crucis Lancers before returning to Caledonia to serve with the planetary militia, which in those days bore the proud name Caledonian Reivers. Like many other locals, though, he'd resigned his commission not long after Wilmarth was appointed governor some five years ago. There'd been too many changes being made in the old Reivers . . . and too many outsiders being brought in to suit Ambrose McBee.

Most worlds maintained their own planetary defense militias, regimental-sized groups of locals who trained and drilled together in addition to any regular or mercenary units that might be stationed on the world with them. Militias tended to be indifferently trained and poorly equipped; inevitably, the best equipment always went to active line units, and there was never enough money to purchase BattleMechs or top-of-the-line weaponry. Even so, more than one raid, even outright planetary invasions, had been repulsed by determined men and women serving in their local militias. The key was that they were locals, fighting on their own soil and for their own homes and families.

During the past five years, however, sweeping changes had been wrought in the Caledonian Reivers. More and more of its members, it seemed, were being imported from off-world, mercenaries . . . or had simply been recruited from the sweepings of various spaceports, promised pay and loot in exchange for easy duty. They'd abandoned their traditional colors—the ancient Black Watch tartan—for black and yellow, and eventually had changed even their name. They called themselves the Bloodspillers now and acted more like some vicious urban gang than a military unit. Increasingly arrogant, increasingly violent, they roamed the streets of Caledon's larger cities, extorting, assaulting, raping almost at will. Their excesses had led to the resurrection of the Reivers, but as a kind of secret society that met in a different home each week and kept its weapons buried in hidden caches around the countryside.

Many of the changes in the old Reivers had been introduced by Wilmarth personally. It was said that he'd come from Robinson originally, an oft-fought-over world on the Davion side of the Federated Commonwealth, and it was thought that many of the Bloodspiller officers came from there as well, old friends and cronies of "Wee Willie," as he was derisively called.

There was more to Wilmarth's psychotic behavior than was immediately apparent, Alex thought. The man wielded too much control for someone as obviously mentally unbalanced as he was. Who was the real power behind Caledonia's government now . . . Folker? That hardly seemed likely, though it was clear that the man was controlling—or at least guiding—Caledonia's putative governor. There had to be someone higher on this particular government totem pole, someone who was really calling the shots.

I wonder what Dad would do if he was here? That question had been bothering Alex a lot for the past hours. What he and McCall were about to do was illegal—outrageously, flagrantly so. Yet McCall had summed up Alex's own feel-

ings with a shrug. "Tha' wee struttin' bastard hae put himself above th' law, Alex," he'd said. "We'll be giving him
naught but wha' he deserves."

Strangely, the thought of soon going into combat again
wasn't bothering Alex at all. He'd thought the very prospect
of battle would have him trembling, but the truth was he'd
simply been too busy ever since he and McCall had
grounded on Caledon to give the matter much thought.

And *now* was certainly no time to start thinking about it.

The underbrush ahead thinned out. Moments later, Alex
emerged from the woods a few meters from the edge of the
canyon. Directly ahead and fifty meters away, the walls of
the Citadel rose like shiny black cliffs from the far edge of
the chasm. The bridge and the road from the city were to the
right; McCall's scout suit stood motionless to Alex's left, almost impossible to pick out from the foliage and weather-
worn rock around it. Scanning the upper reaches of the
Citadel walls, Alex could see the heat glow of several sentries moving along the ramparts.

McCall raised one armored hand, giving a cumbersome
thumbs-up. Alex returned the gesture, then crouched, tensing
his upper leg muscles and keying a release inside his left
gauntlet to initiate his jump sequence.

Then he jumped, the movement translated by the suit's
electronics into a soaring leap that carried him out over the
edge of the cliff. An instant later, his jump jets kicked in,
sending blasts of superheated air shrieking from ducted
vents on either side of his backpack. Seconds later, he
grounded on the top of the rampart, dropping into a crouch
with his laser ready. McCall alighted on top of the wall
twenty meters away, then lightly jumped down to the parapet
walkway beneath. The shriek of his jets had almost certainly
alerted the sentries, but unless the Citadel's defenses were a
lot better than Alex and McCall gave them credit for,
chances were good that they'd made it unobserved.

Yellow patches of color shifted across Alex's HUD; soldiers were hurrying along the rampart, coming toward them.
Swiftly, he leaped off the top of the rampart, then again onto
a lower parapet overlooking the inner courtyard. Lights inside the compound cast pools of white radiance across the
wide, ferrocrete pavement, but the shadows on the parapets
above were night black and impenetrable, save by IR electronics.

"What was that?" someone said nearby, the words picked up by Alex's external mikes. "Hey! What's goin' on out there?"

"Ah, probably the wind," another voice replied.

Seconds later, the two speakers walked past within two meters of the spot where Alex was standing, pressed back against a black ferrocrete wall, neither of the men so much as glancing in his direction. Even if he'd not been wearing the scout suit, Alex thought, they probably wouldn't have seen him. The bright lights of the inner courtyard would have ruined their night vision.

"All right, Alex," McCall said softly, using his suit's external sound speaker rather than radio. "I'd best be makin' my move."

"Roger that," Alex replied. "Good luck!"

He never saw or heard McCall's departure.

Alex found a spot on the inner rampart walkway where he had a good view of the inner courtyard, and settled down to wait.

McCall had switched his visor HUD from IR to normal, with enhanced low-light imaging to allow him to see better in the night and had quickly found what he was looking for. A young Reiver who'd worked in the Citadel for several months had told him about the door, which bypassed the main entrance to the Citadel's inner keep. Tucked away in a corner of the keep wall just below the second tallest of the building's multiple towers, it led to the kitchen area; the Residence staff used it to bring in supplies to the food-storage lockers. The door was kept locked, and McCall was tempted to use one of his high-explosive lockpicks, but there was a quieter way. With his enhanced musculature, he easily yanked the cover off an electronic access panel nearby, jacked in several wires from a power-feed controller on his suit's belt, and cycled through several tens of thousands of binary bit combinations in mere seconds, until the proper code was transmitted and the door quietly slid open.

A guard stood inside, his assault rifle slung over his shoulder. McCall's armored fist slashed forward faster than a striking snake, splintering the man's jaw and crushing his windpipe in a single, near-silent blow. Lowering the corpse to the floor, McCall then palmed the control that slid the door shut behind him. So far, so good.

The trick was to see how far he could penetrate the facility before the alarm was sounded. Perhaps as many as a thousand people lived in the Citadel or in the barracks that ringed the courtyard surrounding the keep—including the several hundred soldiers who comprised the Bloodspiller Militia. Sooner or later he would be spotted, but until then he had the descriptions of the Citadel's inner twistings provided to him by people who'd worked there. This passageway sloped down beneath the center of the keep and emerged in the kitchen; a side passage, however, would take him through a supply room, bypassing areas where civilians were likely to be working.

There! Another pass with his electronic skeleton key, and McCall had access to the storeroom.

The back stairs leading down to the cellars where the prisoners were kept should be just ahead. . . .

"What's that? Up there!"

Alex froze in place, but it was too late. A group of militia troopers had emerged from a doorway on the parapet walkway thirty meters away, and one, at least, was wearing a helmet with IR scanners and a HUD visor as efficient as Alex's own. Though the Nighthawk suit cut down significantly on IR emissions, he'd been wearing the thing for hours now, had engaged in a tough, uphill climb over broken terrain, and capped the approach off with a burst from his jump jets. He was definitely no longer invisible to IR sensors.

"Halt!" a voice cried out. "You! Stop where you are!"

Alex vaulted from the parapet. It was a ten-meter drop to the ferrocrete pavement below, and he triggered his jump jets at the last instant, cushioning his landing. A burst of autofire crackled from the ramparts; bullets snapped past his head and one struck his chest, singing off his armor in a shrill ricochet.

Swinging about, Alex scanned the rampart above, his visor HUD picking out swiftly moving heat sources and bracketing them in flashing cursors. As he raised his laser rifle and aimed at the nearest of the IR targets, his suit electronics relayed targeting information to his HUD. Crosshairs intersected the cursor and flashed green.

He squeezed the trigger. There was a flash, and his external pickups caught the man's shriek as his clothing and kevlar armor caught fire. Alex shifted targets as the man tumbled backward off the wall; a second trooper running along the walkway took a pulse of coherent light squarely in the chest, and the explosion of vaporizing body fluids and tissue also pitched him backward and off the rampart.

Alex triggered another burst from his jets, vaulting to the cover of a line of parked vehicles and coming to ground again in a hissing shriek and a swirling cloud of dust. Just ahead, a pair of soldiers emerged from the doorway of a barracks, armed but carrying their weapons in relaxed, no-hurry poses. Alex chopped down the one on the right, but the other yelped and backpedaled into the open barracks door, screaming an alarm.

So much for maintaining a covert presence.

Well, it had been too much to hope that the two of them could actually penetrate the Citadel's defenses and remain undiscovered for long, not with so many soldiers and base personnel wandering around. An alarm was sounding somewhere in the depths of the Citadel's central keep, a rasping buzz that set the teeth on edge. Atop the gate tower, off to Alex's right, a quad-mount gun turret pivoted about with a mechanical whine, its twin pairs of autocannons dipping to bear on the invader. Alex triggered a shot from his laser, sending a blue-green pulse of light slashing through the night, searing off one of the gun barrels and boiling away a fist-sized crater in a burst of hot vapor.

Gunfire answered from the remaining weapons; explosions ripped across the pavement where Alex had been standing an instant before—but he'd already flexed his legs and taken flight once more, rocketing into the night as he sent a fresh salvo of laser bursts into the turret's target acquisition and tracking antenna array. Landing again, he ducked for cover, unclipping the Imperator-Delta autogrenade launcher strapped to his equipment harness. He chambered the first round, a high-explosive microgrenade, selected an aim point across the courtyard, and let fly. Explosions ripped through parked vehicles and stacks of equipment crates.

Suddenly, the courtyard had become a war zone wreathed in drifting smoke and torn by explosions. Armored soldiers appeared from every direction as the alarm continued to sound. In the keep itself, beneath the tallest of its spires, the main doors to the building's 'Mech bay, fifteen meters tall and cast in solid diacarb-tempered steel, were grinding slowly open on greased rails, revealing the pulse of a red warning light flashing on and off in the depths of the access tunnel beyond. Men in light combat armor or fatigues raced up the sloping ferrocrete ramp from inside the keep and into the open, only to crumble and die in the flash of multiple grenade explosions.

Alex tongued the control that gave him an active radio channel. "Gray Skull One, this is Gray Skull Two," he called. "It's starting to get hot out here. Do you copy? Over."

There was no answer, save for a burst of automatic rifle fire from the shadows on the far side of the courtyard. Alex tracked the heat signature of the gunman and returned fire, a burst of laser light that cut the running figure down.

"Gray Skull One! Gray Skull One! Do you copy?"

The night was filled with flame and noise, but no response from Davis McCall.

=== 15 ===

Citadel Keep
Caledonia, Skye March
Federated Commonwealth
2308 hours, 1 April 3057

Davis McCall had heard nothing over his radio communications channel, but he was deep enough underground now that the powerful little transceivers built into his headgear wouldn't be able to penetrate. He hadn't heard any gunfire, either, but he had heard the alarm when it went off, the raucous buzz grating through every level of the Citadel.

He dodged one group of soldiers when he heard them at a door in the passageway just ahead. Springing straight up, he grabbed hold of some bundled power cables and conduits attached to the stone ceiling four meters above the floor, hooked his legs above a cluster of water pipes, and hung on motionless as the door slid open and soldiers came charging through, their helmeted heads just a man's height beneath McCall's shoulders.

In that position he couldn't see them, of course, but he could track each trooper by the noises he was making—pounding boots and clanking gear, nervous chatter between mates, and labored breathing. When the last sound had died away, McCall released his grip and dropped lightly back to the floor, his power suit camouflage already losing the surreal pattern of wires and pipes and shadows that it had shown a moment before. Congratulating himself on avoiding a nasty encounter, he unslung his laser rifle, palmed open the door and nearly collided with a pair of surprised-looking soldiers who were coming through after the rest of their comrades.

Instinctively, McCall raised his rifle one-handed, triggering a dazzling flash of blue-green light that exploded the head of the first soldier in a messy splatter of blood, bone, and gray matter.

The second man snatched his weapon—a viciously snub-nosed submachine gun—to the ready, clamping down hard on the trigger and sending a long burst rattling into McCall's chest at point-blank range. The impact staggered McCall, punching him back a step as bullets shrieked and whined off his breastplate. He shifted his aim but didn't fire, for the subgunner was twisting and jumping like a puppet on a madly jerking string, riddled by a dozen or so of his own bullets as they ricocheted back off McCall's armor. Finger still holding down the trigger, the gunman toppled over, his last few rounds chewing their way across the ceiling before the magazine ran dry.

McCall stepped across the two bloody bodies and into a large, round, low-ceilinged room with many doors. In the center of the room was a doughnut-shaped control console occupied by yet another soldier, a Bloodspiller officer, who was rising to his feet and groping for his sidearm.

"Don't!" McCall ordered, bringing his laser to bear squarely on the officer's chest. A slight pressure from his finger triggered the laser at a very low wattage, painting a bright blue-green dot on the man's sternum. "All I have to do is close my fist, lad, an' you're dead!"

The officer gaped down at his chest, eyes goggling, then slowly raised his hands above his head. "Don't shoot!" he cried. "Please!"

Keeping the targeting laser on the man, McCall moved closer, glancing at the console. Dozens of small monitors were there, each showing scenes of men and women sitting in stone-'walled cells, alone or in small, disheveled groups. "Open 'em up," McCall ordered. "Let 'em go!"

The man complied, touching a master release. With a hiss, the doors around the room's perimeter slid open as one. With a sudden movement, the officer dropped his hand to the laser pistol holstered on his hip, but McCall fired first.

The man screamed once, a sharp, short yelp, and his body fell, smoking, to the floor.

"Come on oot!" McCall boomed over his external speaker when no one immediately ventured out. "You're all free!"

One woman poked her head out the door of her cell. A moment later, a couple of men stepped uncertainly through the door of theirs, followed closely by three more.

"Who are you?" one of the men demanded.

"Never mind tha'," McCall said. "Listen to me vurra closely, people. I'm here for Angus McCall! Is he here?"

"I'm here," came a voice, and McCall turned, tracking the sound. His brother was scarcely recognizable, a dirty scarecrow of a man in tattered white rags and an unkempt beard. "D-Davis? Is tha' *you* in that thing?"

"Aye, Angus. An' what hae y' done t' get y'sel' in trouble noo?"

"I don't . . . I don't believe it!"

"Maither sent me t' get ye, Angus," McCall said with a tight grin. "She says it's aye time t' be gettin' home!"

"I'll agree wi' y' there, Davis."

Somewhere far overhead, thunder rolled.

Alex needed to find a way to buy himself and McCall a few precious moments of complete confusion among the Citadel's defenders, and he was pretty sure he'd found just that. A number of vehicles—groundcars and lightly armored hovercraft—were parked in ranks just behind the vertical thrust of the gate tower. Among them was the silvery form of a small tanker truck. Alex couldn't tell what the vehicle was carrying, or even whether or not it was full, but there was plenty of water on Caledon, so whatever the tank's contents were, they were likely to be nasty. Even if the tank was empty, trapped fumes from jet fuel or volatile petroleum products could turn it into a very large bomb under the right conditions.

He decided to create the right conditions. Reaching down with his left hand, Alex plucked a timed scatter toss from his suit's carry harness. A twist set the timer, one minute. His throw, amplified by the suit's electronic musculature, sent the silver-gray cylinder flying eighty meters before striking a back wall and clattering off the cab roof of a hover transport and onto the pavement, ten meters away from the tanker.

Before the tosser stopped rolling, Alex had stepped backward into the pitch-black shadow of the Citadel's walls, crouched slightly to take advantage of the cover afforded by a rusty, paint-chipped Pegasus hover tank and a stack of plastic supply crates. As he froze motionless in place, his suit's chameleon circuitry shifted his armor's color into patterns of black and dark gray.

Seconds later, a team of laser-armed soldiers raced past, pounding across the compound in search of the reported intruders. The immediate noise of battle had died away for the moment, but the night was a confusion of shouting men and of boots scuffing and thudding across the pavement. The alarm buzzer continued to sound, and the throbbing warning light from the open doorway to the keep cast a surreally shifting alternation of red and black across the Citadel's walled enclosure.

"Where are they?" one voice yelled from the vicinity of a fuel truck parked near a shed. "Which way did they go?"

"I don't think they're inside, Rodriguez," another voice answered. "Th' Cap'n said they was just lobbin' missiles into the compound."

"Who was?"

"The rebel bastards, of course! Who else? Tryin' t' get even with us for yesterday."

A soldier in combat fatigues and lugging a heavy assault rifle stepped into the space between the Pegasus and the supply crates, peering carefully into the darkness. Alex found himself staring straight into the man's fear-widened eyes, close enough to see the beads of sweat trickling down his face. The temptation to move, to defend himself, to *shoot* was almost overpowering, but Alex forced himself to remain absolutely motionless ... and the soldier's eyes slid past him, up the stack of crates to the left, and then the man had turned away and gone.

"Johnny said he saw one over this way," a voice called from nearby.

"Aw, Johnny couldn't see a BattleMech if it stepped on his—"

Across the courtyard, the tosser went off, a rippling chatter of detonating submunitions hurling tiny bomblets across that half of the compound. Explosions banged and thuttered like crackling fireworks or shrieked through the air on fiery streaks; a sheet of flame went up among the parked vehicles, and, an instant later, the tanker exploded in a blinding, deafening blast.

Orange flame mushroomed into the night, its glare obliterating the illumination from spotlights and lamps, its roar as loud as bellowing thunder. Pieces of parked vehicle rained across the compound, trailing smoke; a screaming soldier ran wildly into the open, his jacket furiously burning. Another vehicle exploded . . . and then another, a chain reaction that jolted Alex's feet through the pavement each time a blast went off. Several of the high-intensity lamps ringing the enclosure went out as blast effects shattered their lenses. The compound was in utter, flaming confusion now as explosions continued to detonate in every direction.

Alex crouched lower as the night in the courtyard turned to searing day.

"The rest of you, noo," McCall said, addressing the others who were moving into the room in increasing numbers. There must have been eighty or ninety men and women there, all together. "You're all aye free, but I cannae promise you a safe trip oot a' the Citadel! It sounds like there's gunplay ootside, an' it's likely t' be dangerous."

"No more dangerous than staying in here!" one dirty-faced, raggedly dressed woman shouted back. "Tha' bastard Wilmarth's promised t' kill most of us here!"

"Aye," another woman said, "An' the blessed hope a' tha' was all tha' was keepin' some of us goin'!"

Some of the others laughed, and McCall grinned to himself. Wilmarth and Bloodspillers and dungeons hadn't broken the spirit of this lot, not by ten light years! "Any of you who want t' stay an' take your chances wi' Wilmarth, you can do so," he said. "If you're not missin' from your cells, he cannae accuse you of takin' part in a jailbreak.

"If you want to go, though, you'll hae t' take your chances wi' Wilmarth's troops ootside. If you can get past the walls and th' front gate, there are Reivers in the woods, ready to take care of you. But gettin' to them is liable t' be a wee bit tricky. . . ."

"Better tha' than Wilmarth's damned interrogators!" a man snapped. He took a step forward and spat on the officer's body. "I say, let's tell Wilmarth wha' we think of his filthy hospitality!"

A resounding cheer answered . . . punctuated by a deep,

rumbling boom from somewhere overhead. The light in the room dimmed ominously, and a fine mist of dust drifted down from the ceiling.

"Who kens how t' use this?" McCall asked, holding up the officer's laser pistol. Dozens of hands, men's and women's, thrust up or reached out. "Aye," McCall said, handing the weapon butt-first to a bearded man with a vividly fluorescent tattoo on his right deltoid—a BattleMech holding a giant hammer aloft. Recognizing the insignia as one popular with some enlisted MechWarriors, McCall guessed that the man had seen military service. "You a vet?"

"Twelve years pilotin' steel with the Fifth Crucis Lancers," the man growled. "That vet enough for you?"

The Fifth Crucis was one of the best. "Good enough. Name?"

"Ross."

"Okay, Ross. You bring up the rear an' make sure everyone who wants t' get out does. Don't stop to play. Anyone who stops gets left behind! I'll lead from the front."

"Right." Ross took the laser and stripped back the charge lever, checking the power coil with an obviously experienced eye.

"Angus! Where are you?"

"Here, Davis." His brother still looked dazed, as though unable to fully comprehend what was happening. "Is . . . is it really you?"

"Aye, lad. It really is."

"You *came* for me. . . ."

"I've done a lot of aye stupid things in m' time. Stay close to me noo. I would nae want t' lose ye after all this trouble!"

Thunder barked again overhead, louder and more insistent this time, and the lights dimmed again. "Wha' is it? Did y' bring your mercenary BattleMech friends wi' ye, then?"

"Just the one," McCall replied. "But he's more than a match for what Wee Willie can throw at him. Come on, people! Line up! We're movin' oot!"

The crowd surged toward the doorway leading out.

Alex crouched in the cover provided by the Pegasus hover tank and a portion of the keep's outer wall as explosions continued to boom and rumble across the compound. Most of the parked vehicles on the far side of the compound were flaming piles of wreckage now. There were perhaps a half dozen vehicles on the near side, though, including the old Pegasus. It would be nice to take them out too before the raiders left. Wilmarth would be a long time rebuilding his military infrastructure after tonight!

Next on his scheduled list was the barbican and the gate leading out of the Citadel's walls. He could see the entrance from here ... standing open on the courtyard side, though the outer gate was closed. Snapping a fresh clip of ten microgrenades into the receiver of his autolauncher, he chambered the first round, raised the weapon to his shoulder, and squeezed off a long, chattering burst directly at the open inner gate.

The inside of the barbican lit up brighter than day with a popping, rippling chain of flashes. Windows blew out, and a larger, more massive secondary explosion blasted out a portion of the gate tower wall as some vehicle or ammo store inside detonated. Dust and smoke boiled from the gaping scar in the tower's face, but no return fire came from the walls or the upper windows. Just to be certain, Alex reloaded again, then fired carefully aimed, deliberately placed microgrenades through individual windows and firing ports. Flames were licking from one open window at the parapet level, but still there was no sign of life from the barbican defenses.

Raising up higher behind his patch of shelter, Alex surveyed the rampart walls to either side of the gate tower. Both autocannon turrets appeared to be out of action, their fire control circuits fried or damaged, their gun barrels cocked at odd and useless angles. In the courtyard itself, bodies lay everywhere, mingled with wrecked equipment and scattered rubble. A few of the bodies were those of Wilmarth's victims, his courtyard trophies, but those few were far outnumbered by the carnage Alex had wrought in just the past few minutes.

Some of those sprawled human forms were still alive, too, and the sounds of their screams added a chilling and surreal background to the scene. Alex raised his right arm and lasered one man who might have been wounded, but who'd been cradling a laser rifle in his arms. There was no room here for gallantry, not when the margin between success and death was so narrow.

With the barbican and gate towers apparently secure, his

major concern now was the open, fifteen-meter doorway
leading into the Citadel's heart. Wilmarth possessed at least
four 'Mechs for sure. Chances were, they were stored in a
'Mech bay somewhere behind those carballoy steel doors
and would be emerging from them any moment now. It had
been several moments since Alex had detected any movement in that direction. Several bodies in the opening marked
the last attempt by Wilmarth's troopers to rush through the
door into the open.

It would take time to ready a 'Mech to deal with the intruders. Only about ten minutes had passed since the first
shot had been fired—an eternity in combat, but too short a
time to saddle up a 'Mech and get it rolling if it was down
and cold. Unless Wilmarth had one waiting on ready-ten—
rather unlikely given the level of professionalism of most of
his troops, but Alex and McCall had been forced to consider
the possibility—the two raiders would be long gone by the
time the Governor's warriors could climb into their machines, power them up, and get it moving. Still, each
passing moment made it more likely that one or more of the
Bloodspiller 'Mechs would be putting in an appearance
soon. Alex consulted the time readout displayed on his visor
HUD: 2316 . . . no, 2317 now. *Come on, McCall! Where the
hell are—*

"Gray Skull Two! Gray Skull Two!" McCall's voice said
suddenly over Alex's headset. "We're comin' up. What's it
look like oot there?"

"Major!" he cried. "Thank God! It's been pretty hot up
here, but there's not much going on right now. Barbican and
gate tower are neutralized, along with the gun turrets."

"Good job! I've got something like eighty people here,"
McCall said. "Can we make it to the front gate, do you
think?"

"It's clear at the moment," Alex replied, taking one last
look around. "But the Citadel's main door is open, and I
imagine they'll be sending some scary stuff through pretty
soon now."

"Roger that. Get ready, laddie. We're coming out! Now!"

Alex raised the grenade launcher, aiming it squarely at the
open Citadel door. "Got you covered, Major. Go! Go!"

McCall palmed open the kitchen access door and stepped
across the body of the soldier still lying there on the floor,

his arm up and shifting quickly left and right as he checked each corner, each shadow beyond for ambush or the unexpected. The courtyard beyond was blanketed by smoke, a battle fog so thick that the Citadel's gate tower and ramparts were visible only as vague black shadows behind the glare of a few remaining spotlights and some burning vehicles. The scene was completely transformed from what it had been like when McCall had ventured through this door minutes earlier. Alex Carlyle had been busy....

There was no movement, no sign of any life at all. "The man says go," McCall told the crowd of people filling the passageway at his back. "You!" He pointed to Angus. "See the gate tower, right through there?"

"Yes, Davis. I see it."

"Head for it, and don't stop for anything. You!" He pointed to the woman next in line. "Follow him. The rest of you, follow the one in front, one at a time. Fast as you can, now. Go! Go! *Go!*"

Alex saw the first of the released prisoners emerge from the shadows at the base of the Citadel keep, followed closely by another, and another ... a long chain of ragged, staggering humanity striking out across the smoke-wreathed plain of the ferrocrete-paved courtyard. They were crossing from his left to his right, passing between his station next to the Pegasus and the Citadel's open main doors.

That was a mistake. If Wilmarth's troopers emerged from the Citadel now, the freed prisoners would be squarely in the crossfire. Too late to correct for that now, though. Lightly, Alex vaulted up onto the rear deck of the Pegasus to get a better view.

It was almost impossible to see anything. Alex shifted his helmet electronics from IR to light amplification to straight optics but could make out little beyond the line of running people and the pulsing red glow of the red-alert lights still strobing inside the entrance to the keep. From his new observation post, Alex had a good, clear line of sight to the keep's gates, but the smoke from burning vehicles was so thick he could see almost nothing.

Movement ...

He shifted back to IR, grimaced, and shifted once more, trying to get a computer enhancement of what he'd thought he'd seen. Was it ... yes! A shadow. A towering, impossible shadow moving across the throb of the red light inside the keep's entranceway tunnel.

Gunfire flashed in the opening; several of the running civilians in the courtyard screamed and dropped to the pavement. Beyond them, in the main doors, something very large was moving, with a familiar *hiss-chirp* of grating ferrofibrous armor.

Then the BattleMech lumbered into view, neatly framed by the open keep doors.

And the fleeing civilians began to panic.

16

It was an *UrbanMech,* squat and ugly, looking more like some monstrous, round-topped kitchen appliance on legs than a BattleMech. Instead of arms and hands it had weapons, an Imperator-B autocannon on the right, a Harmon small laser on the left. It was closely trailed by a dozen armored troopers as it lurched into the open.

*UrbanMech*s massed only thirty tons, but they were slow for their size and difficult to maneuver. Created for combat in close, built-up areas and narrow streets hemmed in by tall buildings, their design concentrated on armor rather than speed, on firepower rather than maneuverability. In 'Mech-to-'Mech combat, most MechWarriors thought of them as dead meat—easy kills. Against ground troops, however—or against a scattering mob of former prisoners fleeing for their lives—they were deadly.

Alex let fly with a long, full-auto burst from his grenade launcher, firing above the heads of the civilians, but the volley was to knock down the troops following the *UrbanMech* into the courtyard, not to damage the 'Mech itself. Even an *UrbanMech* had armor enough to harmlessly deflect the blasts of microgrenades—or the baby laser Alex had strapped to his arm.

A line of explosions uprooted chunks of pavement in the *UrbanMech*'s wake and sent Wilmarth's troops tumbling left and right. The 'Mech stopped, its upper torso pivoting with a grating whine of machinery, the big autocannon swinging into line with Alex's position. Its pilot probably couldn't see Alex's Nighthawk suit, but the 'Mech's Dalban tracking and targeting computer would have picked up his muzzle flash and painted it on the MechWarrior's HUD inside a flashing red cursor.

Time to leave.

Triggering his jump jets, Alex rose from the deck of the Pegasus, sailing low across several other parked vehicles as the *UrbanMech*'s autocannon opened fire with a rolling, crackling burst of fire.

Pieces of vehicle sprayed through the air; a light truck exploded in flames, and eye-dazzling blasts gouged craters in the ferrocrete wall beyond. Alex was already clear, however, lightly touching down close by the inner door of the barbican. McCall was there already, braced against the inner door, waving civilians through with an urgent, up-and-down pumping of his arm.

"You get him?" Alex called.

"Aye," McCall said, and Alex saw him grin behind his narrow helmet visor. "Aye, though we dinnae hae time for a reunion. He's already ootside."

Alex looked into the gate tower. The outer door was already open, he saw, its security control panel inside the barbican ripped open and hot-wired to bypass the locking codes. Civilians were racing past the two Legion officers and into the night outside the Citadel, but a good many others had scattered to hiding places inside the courtyard, their retreat cut off by the thirty-ton 'Mech. Standing in the smoke-wreathed courtyard, twisting its torso back and forth as it scanned for its vanished target, the 'Mech almost gave the impression of being confused. Still, unarmored humans would stand no chance if they tried to run through that monster's field of fire.

"How many more civilians are there?" Alex asked McCall.

"I dinnae ken, lad," McCall replied. "I dinnae hae time for an exact count. But there's thirty or forty at least who didn't make it past tha' hulkin' brute."

"We can't just leave them." He gestured toward one of the

stakes in the courtyard with a human body impaled on it like a side of meat hanging from a hook. "If Wilmarth gets his bloody hooks into them again . . ."

"Aye. But can th' two of us take on a 'Mech?" McCall gestured at the *UrbanMech,* still standing like a somewhat befuddled giant in front of the keep's main doors. "Even the likes a' *tha'* silly thing?"

Their operational plan had depended on getting in and out of the Citadel before Wilmarth could get his 'Mechs up and running. According to what they'd worked out that afternoon, it was time now to slip out the front gate and vanish into the night. Any moment now, more 'Mechs would arrive from the depths of Wilmarth's fortress, and then the courtyard would become a killing ground.

But all those people . . .

"There's one way," Alex said, gripping the elbow of McCall's power suit. "Stay here to guide the rest of them out. I'll take care of the 'Mech."

"Alex! What d' ye think you're doin'?"

"Trust me, Major! I'll be right back!" Alex pulled away before McCall could try to stop him, triggering his jump jets and sailing back across the courtyard. The *UrbanMech* sensed the movement and pivoted sharply, laser and autocannon firing in rapid, alternating bursts. Touching down behind the overturned hull of a wrecked armored car, Alex pulled out a scatter toss, set the timer for fifteen seconds, and hurled it as hard as he could past the looming shadow of the *UrbanMech.* The thirty-ton monster was advancing on him now, step upon ponderous step, its upper torso swiveling back and forth with a power-tool whine. The seconds ticked away . . . and then the scatter toss erupted in a clattering chain of explosions among the wreckage and debris behind the slow-moving 'Mech. Shrapnel pinged off its rear hull armor; a burned-out groundcar chassis toppled over with a crash.

The *UrbanMech* paused, almost as if it was considering this new piece of input, then slowly swung about to face the chattering pops and blasts of the submunitions grenade. Alex was up and running once more, zigzagging through the wreckage back to the Pegasus scout tank even before the machine had completely turned away. There it was! Autocannon rounds had slammed into its port-side armor, piercing its skirts and opening several ugly craters in the polished upper hull, but the vehicle's paired dorsal missile turrets were still intact, the blunt tips of the Starstreak heavy SRMs visible in the launch tubes.

Alex vaulted onto the upper deck, looking for the hatch. There ... just forward of the launchers! It was locked, of course, requiring a keycard or a coded radio signal to open it up. Bending over, Alex grasped the hatch handhold and began pulling with a heavy, steady pressure.

The actuators of his power suit whined protest as he threw his back into the effort, harder ... harder ... and still *harder*. He'd just begun wondering if he'd misjudged the strength of the hatch-locking mechanism when there was a sharp *ping*, and then a ratcheting crash as a locking bar tore free and the hatch swung up and open.

Dropping inside, he palmed a pressure plate to switch on the cockpit lights, then took a quick look around.

The Pegasus was still one of the most popular and common of all reconnaissance vehicles throughout the Inner Sphere, though, like this one, it was increasingly found in service with backwater militias. Normally, it carried a crew of four—driver, gunner, radioman/scanner tech, and commander, but it could be handled easily enough by one man. The cockpit area was surprisingly roomy, though Alex had to stoop low as he made his way forward to the main control console. Squeezing into the driver's seat, he ran his gauntleted fingers across the touch-sensitive input boards and was rewarded by a galaxy of red and amber lights and a rising power hum as the machine went into its automated start-up cycle. Monitors switched on one after the other, each displaying a different view of the flame-seared night outside, some in visual optic ranges, others in IR or starlight.

Weapons might well be a problem, since he didn't have the proper authorization and release codes, but there might be another way. As the Pegasus continued powering up, the red and amber lights shifting block by block to green, Alex leaned over to the gunner's station, reached beneath the console, and pulled off an access panel.

A spaghetti tangle of wires and circuit boards spilled onto the deck. Alex fished among the power feeds and cables for a moment, before finding a test jack-pad wired to the main bus feed.

Three power feed cables that unreeled from a panel on Alex's backpack clicked smoothly into external jackports.

Flipping open a protective cover on a ten-key numeric pad mounted on his left arm, Alex entered a series of digits. His suit's computer took over from there, sending a series of test codes through the Pegasus's fire-control system at lightning speed.

It was more than possible this wouldn't work. If it didn't, Alex would be reduced to using the tank itself as a giant, low-flying missile. That might be necessary in any case, but things would be a lot easier if he could tap into the hover vehicle's considerable on-board firepower.

A roar thundered through the hover tank's hull, and the vehicle rocked violently, slamming Alex from one side of the console station to the other and back. He glanced up at one of the monitors, and saw the *UrbanMech* standing less than fifty meters away, its autocannon bearing straight at the parked tank as it blazed away, hurling round after round. Explosions detonated on the Pegasus's hull. The *UrbanMech*'s sensors must have picked up the power surge from the hover tank's systems, and its pilot was trying to destroy the vehicle before Alex could bring all of its drive and weapons systems on-line.

A trio of savage explosions bucked the Pegasus hard to the right, rocking the vehicle from side to side. With a rising whine of turbine fans, the tank's skirts began to fill as the plenum chamber pressurized. Another explosion struck the hull, and this time the vehicle skittered to the right, floating on air rather than scraping across the pavement. Quickly, Alex grabbed the steering tiller and corrected for the drift. The Pegasus was listing at a ten-degree angle to the left and slightly bow down ... the result, he realized, of air spilling out of the plenum chamber through a skirt that had been holed on that side like swiss cheese. On the monitor, he could see the 'Mech striding forward, autocannon blazing. A dozen lights on Alex's consoles were flashing red, indicating damage to hull armor, to commo antennas, to scanners and headlights ...

Then a new pattern of winking lights flashed green, these projected across the left-hand side of his helmet's visor HUD, reporting that his code feed had been received by the Pegasus's weapons computer, that the tank's SRMs were safety-off and ready for launch.

With one hand, he steadied the hovercraft's tiller; with the other, he keyed in a firing code. Alone, without a gunner, he had to aim the tank's twin turrets by a rough-and-ready point-and-shoot guestimate, pointing the entire tank rather than each turret independently, but at this range, precision of aim wasn't all that necessary for accuracy.

Alex punched in the final release, sending a coded signal through the feedjacks. The hover tank shuddered as its portside missile launcher lit up his surroundings in a day-bright glare, and the first short-range missile slid off its launch rail and streaked across the compound.

He waited, marking the flight of the first round, watching, then exulting as it slammed squarely into the *UrbanMech*'s right side, just below the Imperator cannon's armored mount. In rapid-fire succession, he triggered five more shots. The second warhead missed, streaking on a trail of fire past the *UrbanMech*'s right leg and exploding inside the tunnel entrance, where it scattered the infantrymen who were still cowering there. The next four hammered into the 'Mech's side and torso one after the other, the strobe of detonating warheads popping in the half-darkness like flashbulbs. Armor plate tore and spun away. The *UrbanMech* returned fire with a steady *thud-thud-thud* from its autocannon, sending high-explosive shells crashing indiscriminately into parked vehicles and the rampart walls and the Pegasus's armored hull. Alex engaged the tank's main thruster fans, angling the craft forward, out from under the scything blast of the 'Mech's autocannon fire.

The hover tank's bow scraped the pavement with a grating screech and flashing sparks, but Alex got the vehicle moving, steering it around a parked cargo carrier and into the open. The *UrbanMech* followed, clumsily. It triggered its laser, and a beam flared across the hover tank's starboard side, scouring armor.

Alex dragged the tiller hard to the right, and the Pegasus rotated in place, bringing its second loaded SRM turret to bear. The *UrbanMech* lurched forward just as he triggered a second volley of SRMs at nearly point-blank range. The blasts were so close that the Pegasus was buffeted by the shock waves, which sent the machine drifting backward on its hissing cushion of air. Alex pulled the tiller back, bringing the unexpected motion under control, then using it, putting even more distance between himself and his clumsy pursuer.

The *UrbanMech* followed, and Alex grinned. His maneuvering had drawn the enemy 'Mech away from the center of the courtyard, and he could see the remaining civilians, the men and women who'd been trapped inside the Citadel courtyard by the *UrbanMech*'s arrival, making their way in small groups toward the gate tower and freedom.

He kept backing away, luring the *UrbanMech* farther and farther from the Citadel's front gate. The key to taking on any BattleMech one-on-one was maneuverability; if the 'Mech could pin its tormentor long enough to deliver a hammering volley of high explosives, enough to peel open the tank's deck armor and get at the delicate internal systems, the match would be over. Alex simply had to keep one step ahead of the ponderous, thirty-ton machine.

Alex was surprised, however, and pleased, to note that his combat instincts appeared to be back. There was no hesitation, no confusion or second thoughts as he made each combat decision with a cold, sure edge, unflustered by the heat of battle ... or by memory. He scanned his readouts, then squinted up at the image of the 'Mech filling his forward viewscreen. It looked like the *UrbanMech* had been hurt by that second volley of SRMs. Blue sparks danced in a gaping crater just beneath the right-arm autocannon. As the heavy weapon continued firing, spraying explosive rounds indiscriminately across the compound, Alex realized that its electronic triggering mechanism had fused shut, that it was continuing to pump out shell after shell in an uncontrollable fusillade. Several explosions banged off the Pegasus's hull, but most ripped into the wall of the keep towering to the vehicle's left and rear.

Alex skittered back to the right as gravel and spent shrapnel clattered off the deck of his tank. Abruptly, the *UrbanMech*'s autocannon fell silent, either jammed or out of ammo, but the 'Mech's light laser was still operational, slashing across the Pegasus's bow armor in dazzling flashes of light. Alex's monitors flared and went black as some part of the scanner system overloaded and went down.

With a curse Alex reached up and forward, palming the driver's hatch release. The hatch slid open and Alex levered himself up, poking his head part way out of the tank's hull so that he could see.

Viewed directly instead of on the console monitors, the *UrbanMech* seemed far bigger and more menacing ... as well as closer. A laser beam danced across the Pegasus's starboard turret, and Alex winced and ducked.

Another missile volley might settle the issue, but Alex—or rather his scout suit's computer—was having trouble finding the electronic code that would tell the Pegasus to reload its empty SRM tubes. The Pegasus also possessed a bow laser as powerful as the 'Mech's right-arm weapon, but he couldn't access that fire-control system either, not while he was trying to pilot the tank at the same time.

That left Alex only one weapon in his rather limited arsenal, and he decided to use it.

Still steering by poking his head up through the driver's hatch, he rammed the tiller full forward. The Pegasus accelerated, blasting dirt and dust and small bits of debris as its driver fans howled, hurtling across the vanishing space between the two antagonists at high speed. At the last instant, Alex ducked back inside the Pegasus; a second later, the hover tank slammed into the *UrbanMech*'s legs with a grinding, splintering clash of steel on steel. The jolt slammed Alex into the driver's station console; if he'd not been wearing the Nighthawk suit, he almost certainly would have been killed.

As it was, however, the impact slammed him forward, then bounced him off the ceiling as the Pegasus canted wildly to starboard. The cabin lights went out, plunging Alex into total darkness. After a stunned moment, he switched on his suit's light, painting a bright white circle of radiance on the cabin's floor overhead.

The Pegasus had come to rest upside down. Painfully—his ribs were bruised and sore where he'd slammed into that console despite the suit's protective swaddling—Alex crawled along the ceiling in the direction of the driver's hatch. It was partly blocked by the driver's seat, which had been uprooted by the crash, but he managed to wiggle through, using his enhanced strength to lever the seat aside and pry the warped door back and out of the way. Dropping headfirst onto the ground, he rolled out from beneath the wrecked Pegasus and looked around.

The *UrbanMech* lay on its back, nine meters of ferrofibrous steel and carballoy sprawled across a mound of rubble and twisted I-beams. The Pegasus lay halfway across its legs, which had been twisted far out of alignment by the collision. Readying his suit's laser, he staggered toward the

'Mech's cockpit. If the pilot was still alive, he would either be trying to get out and thus a threat, or he would be trying to get his 'Mech's systems back on-line, which would be an even greater threat.

When Alex reached the 'Mech's cockpit, however, he saw that there would be no threat from this machine, or its pilot, now. It was hard to see past the film of blood inside the armored cockpit windscreen, but it looked as though the instrument console had broken free when the 'Mech fell on its back, landing squarely on the MechWarrior's chest.

"You okay, buddy?"

Alex turned at the words, his laser raised. The man, a bald, tough-looking sort with a fluorescent tattoo of a 'Mech on his bare shoulder, wore no armor or uniform, but he was holding a laser pistol, muzzle pointed at the sky. It took a moment for Alex to connect with the realization that this was one of the prisoners McCall had freed, that he'd come back to search the wreckage for survivors.

"Yeah," Alex said, a little surprised at the sound of his own voice. "Yeah, I'm fine!"

"Then let's get the hell outta here," the man said, glancing back over his shoulder. "There's more bad guys comin' through, an' your buddy ain't gonna be able to keep 'em pinned for long."

"More troops?"

"Yeah, and worse. More BattleMechs."

The man gave Alex a hand as he clambered down off the wrecked *UrbanMech*. Together, through thick swirling smoke, they hurried across the courtyard toward the Citadel's front gate. "Did all the prisoners get away?" Alex asked.

"Yeah, thanks t' you. A few got killed goin' out, and there's maybe eighteen, twenty wounded. But *none* of 'em would've got clear if you hadn't tangled with that *Urbie*."

As they reached the barbican's courtyard entrance, Alex stopped and turned. The court was still empty of Wilmarth's troops—of living ones, anyway—but there were fresh signs of life from the Citadel's keep, new shadows moving against the smoke and flashing alert lights.

McCall joined them. "You all right, Alex?"

"I'm fine. Just a bit dinged up, is all."

"When y' slammed into tha' *UrbanMech*, lad, I thought we'd seen th' last of you!"

Alex was still staring back at the keep's open fifteen-meter doors. "My God," he said. "Wilmarth's sending out his reserves!"

With the steady *clank-clank* of shifting actuators, a towering shadow emerged from the open door, a ten-meter shape more humanlike, and more menacing, than the ugly little *UrbanMech*. Alex recognized that heavy-shouldered, round-headed silhouette immediately and wondered where in all possible hells Wilmarth could have found hardware like that.

The *Victor*, eighty tons of armor and death, creaked and whined clear of the open 'Mech bay doors. Close behind the first came a second *Victor*, its head turning as it surveyed the battle wreckage of the courtyard.

Victors! It had been all Alex could do to take down that single, lightweight *UrbanMech*. Two *Victors* ... stopping them was not something a pair of lightly armed humans could even attempt.

"I think, lad, we'd best get the hell oot a' here," McCall said.

"Couldn't have put it better myself, Major. Let's move!"

But the *Victors* were crashing toward the barbican as fast as their massive legs could carry them.

Escape was impossible.

Citadel Front Gate
Caledonia, Skye March
Federated Commonwealth
2327 hours, 1 April 3057

Victors massed eighty tons, placing them squarely in the heavyweight category for BattleMechs, but they were not as heavily armed as other 'Mechs of their size. Weaponry had been sacrificed to give them jump jet capability; each of the monsters mounted paired medium lasers in its left arm, a Gauss rifle in its right, and four SRM tubes set high in the left side of its chest, like a row of military medals.

Alex, McCall, and the veteran with the laser pistol ducked back from the barbican's courtyard gate just as a pair of SRMs slammed into the gate tower wall. The blast slammed at Alex and nearly knocked him down. It did send the laser-toting ex-prisoner tumbling. Alex reached down and helped him up. "You all right?"

"Fine! Fine! Let's get the hell outta here!"

Together, they ducked through the open outer gate, following the last of the escaping prisoners out and onto the bridge across the canyon beyond.

Alex was not quite halfway across the bridge when he heard a shrill hiss and the roar of air superheated to white-hot plasma. Turning, he was just in time to see one of the Victors descending outside the Citadel wall on flaring jump jets, landing squarely in the center of the bridge just in front of the main gates. Its left arm came up, and the twin lasers set into the forearm flared. Trees across the canyon burst into flame, and a heavy branch burned through and fell into the gulf with a splintering crack of shattered wood. The second *Victor* appeared inside the open gate, following the first more cautiously, ducking slightly to slip beneath the open gate's portcullis.

These were no militia 'Mechs, Alex thought as he watched the first advance across the bridge with ground-devouring steps; they lacked the black and yellow paint schemes borne by Wilmarth's combat machines as well as their marks of wear, tear, and age. There were unit numbers and insignia, but Alex didn't recognize them—hardly surprising given the enormous number of active 'Mech units, regular and mercenary, operating in the Inner Sphere.

But this was no time to worry about who the *Victor*s belonged to. Clearly, they were both in the service of Wilmarth and the Bloodspillers, and they were moving now to punish the invasion of Wilmarth's domain.

"Get to the forest, lad!" McCall snapped, facing the advancing giant.

"Eh? But—"

"Dinnae argue! Move your ass, damn it!"

Alex tore himself free of the almost hypnotic view of the advancing *Victor*s, turned, and fired his jump jets, soaring down the length of the bridge and grounding on the road at the edge of the forest. The vet was already there, crouched behind a fallen log, his laser pistol raised and braced against the rough bark of the trunk. "My God," the man said as Alex reached him. "The man's lost his freaking mind!"

Turning once more, Alex saw Davis McCall lying flat on his belly next to the bridge abutment. He'd thought McCall was right behind him, but the Caledonian was facing down the advancing 'Mechs, his autogrenade launcher pressed to his shoulder as he fired a stream of microgrenades. Explosions crashed and popped and banged around the *Victor*'s lower legs. No grenade—not even a macro—could more than scratch a BattleMech's armor, but it was obvious that McCall had something else in mind than bagging an eighty-ton Mech with a lightweight grenade launcher.

With a chain of loud, flat bangs, rectangular antipersonnel charges strapped to the *Victor*'s feet and lower legs went off in sympathetic detonation, spraying clouds of steel bearings

in broad swaths a meter off the bridge pavement. Smoke
boiled around the *Victor*'s feet, partly obscuring the monster.

Suddenly, McCall was on his feet and running.

But he was running *toward* the lead *Victor* . . . not
away. . . .

Davis McCall knew he couldn't stop both *Victors*, but he
had at least an outside chance of stopping one. If he could
manage that, the second 'Mech might withdraw . . . or at
least pull back to await the arrival of supporting 'Mechs or
infantry. BattleMechs, as Grayson Carlyle had proved decades ago, could be vulnerable to infantry attacks.

"Major!" Alex's voice called in his headset. "Major, what
are you doing?"

"We'll hae no peace an' quiet a' all wi' these bastards
clumpin' around," McCall replied. "Keep me covered!"

The stunt he was trying was deadly, especially without
heavy support back-up of his own. Ever since 'Mechs had
first begun falling victim to massed infantry attacks, most
had begun mounting external explosive packs loaded with
steel shot on their lower legs specifically to foil close-assault
tactics. Infantry, even infantrymen wearing combat suits,
could be torn to bits by the savage, shotgun-blast deadliness
of an antipersonnel claymore triggered either on command
from the 'Mech's cockpit, or by heat, mass, or radar proximity.

Davis McCall was an expert at anti-'Mech tactics, however,
and had been ready with the counter. The burst of microgrenades from his launcher hosing across the nearest *Victor*'s
lower works had wrecked proximity triggers and power feeds,
not to mention setting off most of the charges prematurely
through sympathetic detonation. Once the charges had been
fired, the 'Mech was vulnerable to the Carlyle close-assault
tactic known as "kneecapping."

Leaping to his feet, bending nearly double as he ran,
McCall made use of the swirling smoke as cover as he ran
toward the 'Mech, reaching up with his left hand to grab
hold of the poleyn—the squared-off armor plate protecting
the 'Mech's knee—and then vaulting onto its left foot. Timing was critical, for the foot and leg were in motion as he
grabbed hold and, in the same motion, unslung his satchel of
polydetaline. As the 'Mech brought its leg forward and

down, a space opened up behind the poleyn. Davis crammed the satchel home, snatched one of the pull-ring detonators protruding from beneath its flap, and yanked it.

The entire maneuver, from the time he'd leaped up and charged to the instant he fired the fuse, had taken perhaps three seconds. The *Victor*'s pilot was just becoming aware of his presence, possibly as his companion radioed urgent warnings over their tactical link. The 'Mech's torso whined as it rotated some four meters above McCall's head. The *Victor* stooped forward, its gigantic, steel-alloy left hand reaching down out of the fog of smoke and darkness, fingers extending to grab McCall and pluck him from its leg.

Davis triggered his jump jets as he let go of the 'Mech's massive knee and let himself fall backward. The thrust kicked him clear, sending him sailing out over the canyon.

A laser beam seared past his head—not from one of the 'Mechs, but from a turret high up in one of the spires rising over the Citadel keep. Twisting over in midair, he fired his suit's jets again, angling now toward the woods beyond the rim of the canyon.

More laser fire snapped and hissed past him, some of it striking the woods ahead with flares of yellow flame. Unlike the confines of the courtyard, here in the open beyond the fortress walls the invaders were in precisely surveyed fire zones swept by the Citadel's main defensive weapons. Turrets atop the keep itself sent slashing beams of laser light spearing through the darkness and exploding among the trees of the forest beyond. One beam reached out of the night, touched Davis's backpack with a flash, and speared through the armor over his left shoulder. Flinching, he felt something like a white-hot wire dragged across his skin, and the movement sent him tumbling out of control.

In the same instant, the four-second fuse on the pull-ring detonator burned out, and the explosives stuffed up against the *Victor*'s knee went off. The night around the bridge was briefly illuminated by the blast, which was compressed and focused back into the vulnerable knee joint by the armor poleyn like a tamped charge. Shards of metal tore free, whistling through the air. The *Victor* took one more step, bringing its full mass down on its left foot, and the left knee buckled as drivers, frame, actuator leads, and myomer bundles shredded.

McCall hit the ground clumsily, on his back at the very edge of the cliff. Loose rocks at the rim gave way with the impact and he started to fall, snagging a trailing length of vine and twisted branches as he slid over the edge. He triggered his jump jets again, but this time there was no response. Either the laser hit or his collision with the cliff had damaged the control mechanism.

"Major!" Alex's voice yelled over the tactical link. "Major, are you all right?"

"Aye, lad. I'm fine! Stay put!" Legs flailing over emptiness, McCall clung to his precarious handhold as rocks the size of his head bounced and clattered past his armor. He was a perfect target for the 'Mechs and expected one of them to pick him off at any moment. Twisting about, he could see the *Victor* just twenty-five meters away, wobbling uncertainly on its damaged leg. With a groan of yielding metal, the 'Mech twisted to its left, gave an unpleasant shudder, then pitched forward as its leg support gave way completely. Its pilot tried to stop the fall, reaching out with both arms, but the 'Mech struck the bridge pavement face down and, unable to control its sideways momentum, smashed through the bridge railing in a noisy spray of ferrocrete and scrap iron and rolled off the edge.

With an avalanche of raw noise, the *Victor* plummeted into the moat-like valley in front of the Citadel, scraping and banging down the rocks and bridge pilings all the way to the bottom. Hanging above that gulf, McCall looked down, watching as its pilot tried to right the falling machine so he could use its jump jets, failed, and struck the rocks on the canyon floor, the 'Mech giving a final rag-doll bounce as it hit.

Laser fire stuttered across the moat, striking rocks and vegetation at the top of the cliff. Reaching up as high as he could, McCall tried to pull himself further up on his precarious perch, only to lurch downward almost a meter as the matted tangle of branches, limbs, and vines he was clinging to partly gave way. Black-and-yellow-armored troops were spilling out of the Citadel's gate tower now, rushing past the stationary form of the remaining *Victor,* blazing away wildly with lasers and submachine-gun fire.

Bullets slapped into the back of his armor, screaming as they ricocheted clear. Others struck the tangle of brush and vines he was clinging to, and he felt something over his head give way. With a lurch, he dropped another half meter, his feet twisting helplessly over the gulf.

Without jump jets, he would be killed by that fall, Nighthawk or no Nighthawk. He felt the vines starting to give way . . .

Alex had watched McCall's lone assault against the *Victor,* had seen him fire his jump jets and arrow back toward the near side of the canyon, only to be caressed by one of the laser beams, tumble over in midair, and strike the edge of the crater. McCall's order to stay put had kept Alex in place for a few seconds, but then the Major hadn't reappeared on hissing jump jets, and militia soldiers had started pouring through the Citadel's gate behind the remaining Battle-Mech.

Breaking from cover, Alex ran to the edge of the cliff, ignoring the bullets that sang off his armor or cracked and whistled from the rocks around him. Looking over the canyon rim, he could see McCall's arms and the top of his helmet three meters below, as the man clung to a shredding mat of partly uprooted vegetation.

"Hang on, Major!" Alex stepped off the edge of the cliff, firing his jump jets as he dropped.

"Alex! Wha' the blazes are y' doin' oot here? I told you t' stay put!"

"Saving your life, Major." Reaching out, Alex slipped one hand beneath each of McCall's arms and clamped down hard. "Don't wiggle, now. I wouldn't want to drop you!"

He used his tongue controls to increase thrust. His jump jets were already straining to support the mass of two sets of armor, and now he was trying to find the power to lift the two of them together up the crumbling face of the cliff. For a moment, Alex wondered if they were going to make it. Still supporting McCall, he managed to squirm out of the sling to his grenade launcher and to unsnap the harness pouch containing the rest of the microgrenade ammunition. When he dropped his laser as well, he and McCall began slowly moving upward.

As they rose out of the canyon, Alex could see the entire face of the forest ahead lit by flickering muzzle flashes. He and McCall were squarely between two large bodies of infantry engaged in an all-out gun battle, the Bloodspiller militiamen rushing onto the bridge and Reivers hidden in the woods.

Bullets screamed off Alex's armor. His jump jets shrieked as he struggled to keep the two of them aloft. Fortunately, they didn't have far to go. The ungainly duo cleared the top of the cliff with a meter to spare and crashed forward into the underbrush. Gunfire barked and crackled around them as Alex untangled himself from McCall and stood up. A moment later, troops were all around them, extending helping hands, pulling them along to cover. The vet soldier freed in the Citadel was there, and so was Allyn McIntyre.

"Thought I told you folks t' stay back where we left you," McCall said. Over the tactical channel, his voice sounded tight with pain.

"Well, excuse me," Allyn said, grinning at him. "I didn't realize you were our commanding officer!"

"He gets a bit touchy when people don't do what he tells them," Alex explained. Missiles were arcing toward them from the Citadel. "Damn! Let's get out of range!"

"I'll go along with that," the vet growled as they started to drag McCall toward the shelter of the trees. "We're kinda exposed out here on this cliff!"

In fact, though, the battle was already over; half a dozen of Wilmarth's troops had been cut down on the bridge by the gunfire from the forest, and the rest were fleeing back to the safety of the Citadel's walls. The remaining *Victor*, after peering over the side of the bridge in an almost laughably human manner to check on its fallen companion, had withdrawn as well, pausing only to hose the woods one last time with laser and autocannon fire.

They carried McCall further back into the woods, coming at last to a clearing well out of the range of the laser turrets atop the Citadel towers.

"You destroyed that giant Mech!" Allyn said, her face flushed with excitement. "I've never seen anything like that! I never knew it could even be done!"

"Probably can't, lass," McCall replied as they lowered him gently to the ground. "It'd take more than a wee fall like tha' to ruin a *Victor*. Mind, the MechWarrior pilotin' the thing's probably smeared all over the inside of the cockpit like strawberry jam, but they'll hae a recovery team down there by mornin' to drag the thing free."

" 'Mechs are too valuable to just leave lying around," Alex added, checking McCall's shoulder. It didn't look like the laser had penetrated, but the ferrofibrous armor shell protecting the shoulder had been partly melted by the beam and was twisted like soft putty.

He needed a delicate touch for this, more delicate than was possible for the Nighthawk suit. He hit his helmet release and cracked it open, tasting the cool night air for the first time in hours. Then he unlocked his gauntlets and discarded them, before he started opening up McCall's Nighthawk suit.

"But he wrecked its leg!" Allyn protested.

"Not likely!" McCall said through tightly clenched teeth, sounding like he was talking now to keep his mind off the pain. *God* but that shoulder must hurt! "If they hae a spare knee actuator an' a myomer bundle patch kit, they'll hae tha' little nick mended in no time. If we were aye lucky, th' Gauss rifle an' lasers were smashed up enough not to work anymore, an' they dinnae hae the spares. But I'm thinking tha' those two *Victor*s were well cared for, better than anything I saw in Wilmarth's stable. They'll probably hae all the parts they need."

"Then, that was for nothing?" Allyn asked, something close to despair on her face.

"Oh, I had a reason, all right."

"If he hadn't knocked out one *Victor* and discouraged the other," Alex explained, breaking open the armor's chestplate and exposing McCall's upper torso, "those two 'Mechs would be scouring these woods right now, looking for us. As it is, I guess the Major here convinced them that discretion is the better part of valor after all."

"Aye," McCall said. "I've been thinking. It would be nice, though, if we could get some idea a' who those bluidy *Victor*s belong to!"

"I was wondering about that," a new voice said.

"General McBee!" Alex said.

"You didn't expect me to stay back at the farm and miss all the excitement, did you? How is he?"

"I've been burned worse," McCall said.

"The beam melted part of his armor," Alex told him, studying the wound. The skin was blistered over most of McCall's shoulder, with one area badly charred. The stink of burnt meat made him gag. For just a moment, Alex remembered another Davis, charred to death in his burning 'Mech . . .

Then the memory was pushed aside by more urgent needs. A first aid medipatch slapped onto the base of McCall's neck between the burn and his head gave a low hum as it began interrupting the pain messages flowing to McCall's brain. The Caledonian relaxed almost immediately, his eyes glazing slightly.

"What hit him was a jet of molten metal, not the beam itself," he told the others, pulling a tube of burn cream from his suit's first aid kit and squeezing the contents into the charred area. "Second and third degree burns, but nothing so serious a medkit won't fix him up."

"I'll see what we have in supply," McBee said. "I'll also send a team down to check out that 'Mech you damaged. We don't have much in the way of explosives, so we probably can't smash it bad enough to finish it off, but we might find out something useful, like where the damned things came from!"

"That . . . would help . . . a lot, General," McCall said, the words slurred by the anesthetic effect of the medipatch. "Thanks. . . ."

A dull pop sounded in the distance, and the area was raggedly illuminated by a drifting star shell high above the fortress.

"We'd better find out just exactly who our enemies are back there," Alex said thoughtfully, "or we're going to be fighting them totally in the dark."

"Alex?"

"I'm right here, Major."

"Jus' thought . . . somethin'. Important."

"What's that?"

"The . . . date, lad."

"What about it?"

"It's the Day . . . of Heroes. . . ."

Alex's eyes widened as McCall slipped away into anesthesia. He'd not thought about the date at all, but McCall was right. This was the Day of Heroes, the day the Gray Death Legion set aside every year to honor the memory of those Legionnaires who'd given their lives, their friends and comrades fallen in combat.

18

Third Davion Guard Headquarters
Maria's Elegy, Hesperus II
Tamarind March
Federated Commonwealth
1045 hours, 2 April 3057

"**W**e lost two Mechs," the holographic image of Kellen Folker said, a flicker of scanning static running down its length. "One of Wilmarth's *UrbanMech*s and one of our *Victor*s."

"One of the *Victor*s!" General Karst exploded. "How could they—"

Marshal Felix Zellner impatiently waved the man to silence. The HPG transmission was one-way and could not be interrupted.

"The *UrbanMech*'s probably headed for scrap recycling," Folker continued. "Wilmarth doesn't have much in the way of spares, though the *Urbie* wouldn't be hard to get running again if he had the right parts and a halfway decent technical crew. I think we can get the *Victor* operational again, but Charley tells me it'll need two new legs, a new Gauss rifle, and a replacement articulating mainbrace for the torso endoskeletal supports." Folker cocked a wry grin at the camera. "You can put all of that on your list of stuff to bring with you.

"The attack was carried out by at least fifteen commandos, heavily armed and wearing advanced combat armor, and operating in close conjunction with the local rebels. We don't yet have a confirmed ID on them. Apparently, they carried off all their dead and wounded after the fight, and Wilmarth hasn't been able to recover any bodies. But I'm as certain as I can be without formal confirmation that they belonged to the Gray Death Legion. As I told you in my last report, Carlyle's third-in-command is here, as well as his son. I've seen them both, talked to them, even. And McCall, especially, has a rep for this kind of action. I hate to admit it, but he's good.

"The situation here, in my opinion, is becoming serious. They succeeded in releasing over eighty of Wilmarth's prisoners—a few tax evaders, and the rest agitators and troublemakers scooped up at various antigovernment demonstrations. Rebel morale will have been boosted considerably by this raid on Wilmarth's headquarters. And if you were hoping to involve the Gray Death against the local rebels, I'd say you're too late. They've already entered the fight but against us. They're going to be a serious obstacle to Field Marshal Gareth's plans.

"Marshal, I urgently request full military assistance to break the back of this rebellion once and for all. Wilmarth can't do it, and the 'Mechs in my command aren't going to be enough to deal with this situation, especially since one of my *Victor*s is going to be out of operation until you get here anyway.

"This is Folker, signing off."

With a final flicker of static, the holographic projection wavered, then winked out. Zellner remained in his chair, contemplating the empty projection plate for a moment. On the other side of the desk, General Vinton Karst stirred uncomfortably in his chair, as though unwilling to be the one to break the momentary silence.

"We will leave for Caledonia at once, General," Zellner said at last. "Have your unit ready to board the DropShips within forty-eight hours."

"We can be ready in twenty-four, Marshal," Karst said. "My people have been on full alert since last week. But, with respect, sir, I still wonder if you know what you're doing."

Zellner considered Karst narrowly for a moment, wondering if he'd made a mistake in promoting this particular man. He was far more able than his predecessor, more intelligent, more the career soldier than the politician, and less self-centered and self-serving than Thurman Vaughn had been. In short, he was an excellent officer, but the qualities that made him excellent also made him difficult to control. The man had a brain, and that made him potentially dangerous.

His predecessor, the late, lamented General Vaughn, had died a few weeks before. Few knew that Vaughn's death had not been an accident . . . that his private aircraft had crashed and exploded during takeoff from the capital's airport because he'd become undependable at a time when Gareth and Zellner and the other conspirators of Operation Excalibur needed dependable men.

"The Jacobite rebellion on Caledon," Zellner said quietly, "offers the Federated Commonwealth, offers *us,* a unique opportunity."

"So I've heard you say, sir. But I fail to see how engaging my unit on a jerkwater world like Caledonia is going to help Excalibur. In any case, the rebellion there offers no direct threat to us. They have no 'Mechs of their own, no equipment, no DropShips."

"The rebels themselves offer no serious military threat, but there are other rebels in the district that do."

"The Skye separatists."

"And others. But the separatists are the most serious danger, not only to the Federated Commonwealth but to what we're trying to do here."

"You know, Marshal, it strikes me that in some ways the separatists are on our side. Don't misunderstand me on this, but they seek autonomy for the Skye March, as we do. They're seeking a secure niche for themselves as the Federated Commonwealth's authority crumbles, as we do. And they seek order and safety for this part of the Inner Sphere. I wonder if we shouldn't consider working with them, instead of against them."

"We have no 'side,' General, save our own. The problem with the separatists is that their activities undercut ours and focus the government's attention on this district when it would be better for us if they were occupied elsewhere." He folded his arms, leaning back in his chair. Webs within webs; wheels within wheels within yet more wheels.

As a supposedly loyal officer of the Armed Forces of the Federated Commonwealth, it was Zellner's responsibility to ruthlessly suppress independence-minded agitations by Skye separatists or anyone else who challenged the Federated Commonwealth's authority. Fulfilling that responsibility was the best way he knew to convince his superiors back on Tharkad that he *was* a loyal AFFC officer.

But as one of the highest-ranking of the conspirators within Operation Excalibur, he had the double-edged responsibility of convincing Tharkad that he was still loyal to the Federated Commonwealth and of not alienating the population he hoped to govern soon. Many Skye separatists were members of the military, of course, but they came from worlds in the Skye March, worlds like Caledonia and Glengarry, like New Earth and Arcadia and Skye. Feeling was running high against the Federated Commonwealth on those worlds and dozens of others. If Zellner moved to crush the separatists in either his official role as a Marshal of the AFFC, or as a leader of Excalibur, he would be alienating the very people he would later need for support in the long, dark days to come. It looked to him and the other members of Excalibur that the days of the famous alliance between Steiner and Davion were numbered. Who knew what the future might bring? Civil war, death, destruction . . . If he was to save anything, anything at all of these worlds, he would have to ally himself with the separatists.

But gently . . . gently. He could not reveal his true loyalties to Tharkad too soon, or everything so painstakingly built up thus far would be lost. He studied Karst carefully. He was more than half certain that General Karst was himself a secret Skye separatist, an officer who'd either not declared himself during last year's rebellion, or whose political convictions had changed as a result of what had happened. The purges within every level of the AFFC had shaken many good men, Zellner reflected. That made them vulnerable, both to political disaffection and to recruitment by cabals like Excalibur.

He suspected that Karst hoped to recruit him for another officers' separatist coup attempt. Well, that wasn't a bad thing at all. Excalibur would need good, solid lines of communication to the separatist camp, whether they ultimately ended up joining them . . . or exterminating them.

"In fact, General," he told Karst, "it is my hope to work with the separatists when the time is right. We do share many of the same goals. My only real argument with them is in their sense of timing. They launched their rebellion last

year far too soon . . . and they seriously miscalculated in trying to take on the Gray Death Legion with an insufficient
appreciation of that regiment's abilities."

Karst looked surprised. "I thought you didn't care for
mercenaries."

"I don't. Most of them are rabble, ill-trained, ill-
disciplined, greedy, and loyal only to their own leaders, and
to C-bills. Some few are well-trained and highly motivated,
however, and that makes them dangerous. Still, once you understand how the mercenary mind works, you can use them
. . . let them do your dirty work for you so that you can
emerge playing the part of the hero."

"And this is what you mean when you talk about using the
Gray Death on Caledonia?"

"Exactly. Field Marshal Gareth hoped to cripple the Legion by removing its senior officers. While that option might
still prove to be necessary, I think we can use the Gray
Death to put down this populist uprising on Caledonia. A
show of force, a *powerful* show of force on Caledonia, will
convince the Skye separatists of the Federated Commonwealth's will to hold onto the region by any means necessary. But suppressing the Jacobites will not harm us with the
separatists. The Jacobites are, after all, a fanatic and ill-
disciplined mob." Zellner chuckled. "Even the most ardent
of the separatists would have to admit that the Jacobites
must be suppressed for the common good. You know, this
may be a way of inducing the separatists to join us when the
time comes!"

Karst—if he was a separatist sympathizer—refused to rise
to the bait. "And the Jihadists?" he asked. "Destroying them
could work against us, make us seem intolerant, even tyran-
nical. The Federated Commonwealth has the reputation for
allowing religious diversity, you know."

"True . . . when that diversity does not threaten the rights
of other citizens." Zellner shrugged, a careless gesture. "The
Jihadists are heretics. No one will care what we do to them."

Karst's eyebrows went up. "Heretics? That's a strange
word to hear in this day and age!"

"They are heretics by the standards of the Unfinished
Book that they claim as their origin."

The Unfinished Book Movement was the attempt by Father Jasper Ovidon to create a genuine, pan-human faith that
would unite the splintered religions that divided a star-

scattered humanity. The "unfinished" aspect referred to their creed that revelation was a continuing and ongoing process, that no one faith could have the last and complete word, for there was always more to learn.

"The Jihadists claim," Zellner continued, "that all spiritual revelation is complete and that the end of civilization is at hand, which is completely counter to the Unfinished Book. The most extremist among them call for a complete end to all reliance on any machinery more complicated than a plow, an end to war machines and armaments, an end to space travel ... and you can imagine how well *that* would go over with the big corporations! They even argue among themselves over the proper interpretation of their own prophecies and writings. They're reviled by civilized and technic cultures everywhere in the Inner Sphere. Their destruction will be applauded by all supporters of law and order, as well as help to convince the separatists of the AFFC's resolve."

"And destroying a bunch of Jacobites and religious fanatics is going to help us with Excalibur?"

"That's right. And the key to our success will be the Gray Death Legion."

"Which is what I still don't understand. The original plan, as I understood it, called for Tharkad to order the Legion to Caledonia to put down the revolt there. From what we're hearing from Folker, that is no longer an option. If anything, this new situation just complicates things for us. We're going to have to fight, not only the Caledonian rebels, but a mutinous mercenary regiment as well!"

"Possibly. It all hinges on what the Baron of Glengarry will do."

"Carlyle?"

"The same." Zellner grinned. "Delicious, isn't it? Carlyle has a reputation for siding with the common man, the little people, the popular causes. He would detest working for a small-minded monster like Wilmarth. And yet, if he wants to maintain his position as Baron of Glengarry, he'll have to follow the letter of his contract, which requires him to obey the legal orders put to him by State Command on Tharkad."

Karst gestured at the empty holographic projection plate. "Folker seemed to think Carlyle's already thrown in with the rebels."

"His third-in-command probably has. McCall is a Caledonian, after all, and would have no love for the likes of Wilmarth. He may recommend that Carlyle side with the rebels, no matter what that means to his title."

"Do you imagine that Carlyle would fight against his own son and one of his most senior officers?"

"The tactics of duty, General, can be harsh and uncompromising. I have no idea what orders these Gray Death commandos on Caledonia are under, but likely they're there simply to scout out the situation, find out who is fighting for what, that sort of thing. Any arrangement McCall or the younger Carlyle entered into would not be binding, not if it was in contradiction to the elder Carlyle's responsibilities as Baron of Glengarry or as the holder of a long-term contract to House Steiner. If Carlyle does his duty, he will arrive on Caledonia, ignore any agreement with the local rabble, and carry out the orders given him by the government's duly authorized representative on the planet."

"Wilmarth."

"Officially, yes. The real voice for Tharkad, though, is our friend Folker. But since Major Folker has been pulling Wilmarth's strings for some time now, it all amounts to the same thing.

"In any case," Zellner continued, "he will have his orders . . . to put down the rebellion of Jacobite extremists and religious zealots on Caledonia. If Carlyle and the Gray Death carry out their orders, well, we will have demonstrated our resolve to maintain peace and order throughout the Skye March. Furthermore, any wrath the Caledonian population might feel after this popular insurrection is put down will be turned against a *mercenary* unit, a unit that we can distance ourselves from politically. They will be seen as tools of that idiot Wilmarth, and any burned cities or roasted babies they may complain about will be the Gray Death's fault.

"When *we* arrive, we will declare Wilmarth to be a traitor, you will take charge of the Caledonian government as we've already discussed, and the people will hail you, hail *us* as liberators."

"Granted. But if Carlyle does join the rebels, against Wilmarth? Against us? It could happen. This man has a reputation for doing . . . the unexpected. We would find ourselves forced to destroy the Gray Death, rather than using it as originally planned."

"Then we will kill Carlyle and destroy the Gray Death Legion *and* the rebellion. And, once again, we will be the heroes. Not on Caledonia, perhaps. But this will look good, very good, on Tharkad. Consider the report! A rebel uprising . . . and a mercenary unit supposedly loyal to House Steiner joins the revolt! Then you and I and the Third Davion Guards go in, crush the mutiny, and bring order. Tharkad is happy with us, while the Skye separatists—who will be watching this action closely, you may depend on that—will see that we will tolerate no challenge to our will to maintain order. You will be military governor of Caledonia, which will prove to be an important staging area for Excalibur's next planned move."

"Hesperus II."

"Exactly. When we control Hesperus, we will control the military muscle and sinew of all of House Steiner space. The two systems are adjacent, a single jump, only a few light years apart. We can arrange for units of uncertain loyalty to be dispatched to Caledonia to keep the peace, while our loyal forces are redeployed here. By the beginning of next year, I suspect, no later, we will be in a position to seize Hesperus II for Excalibur and carve out our own little domain among the worlds of the Skye March."

Rising from his chair, Zellner walked around the desk to the room's wallscreen, which was set now to show an external view. The city of Maria's Elegy, capital of Hesperus II, was surprisingly small, and for all of the technology associated with the 'Mech plants and factories located on this world, surprisingly primitive-looking. A huddled collection of geodesic domes and tiered, multilevel enclosures of glass and aluminum, it looked small and vulnerable set against the overwhelming spectacle of the mountains. The world's F-class sun, shrunken and chill at this distance, set blue-white highlights sparkling in the glaciers at the higher elevations and gave the sky a deep blue-violet cast.

Hesperus II was known for two things, its mountains, which rose rugged and forbidding in labyrinthine folds across all four of the world's continents, and its factories, which were nothing less than the military-industrial heart of the entire Lyran Commonwealth. In its history, Hesperus II had endured no fewer than fourteen separate military invasions and unnumbered raids; there were never less than two full battalions of top-line 'Mechs guarding its principal cities, spaceports, and manufactory centers.

Zellner did not command all of those forces. Not yet. But very soon he would. For a long moment, he stood before the viewscreen, hands clasped behind his back, looking up at the mountains that encircled the tiny human landhold known as Maria's Elegy.

"Which do you think it will be, sir?"

"Eh?"

"What do you think Carlyle will do? Fight for Wilmarth? Or join the rebels?"

"It actually hardly matters, one way or the other," Zellner said with a shrug. "I confess, I'm curious. The man was created Baron of Glengarry by Prince Victor Davion himself. Davion rules the Federated Commonwealth, and so Carlyle is bound to the man—even if following orders means doing the bidding of a fat, bloody-minded toad like Wilmarth. But, as I said, he has the reputation for following populist causes. The man really is an incurable romantic. He should have been born a thousand years ago, back in the romantic age of flights to Terra's moon and covered wagons and chivalrous knights." Turning suddenly from the wallscreen, he faced Karst. "The Gray Death should be en route to Caledonia by now."

"Folker seemed to think they were already there, sir."

"An advance scouting party," Zellner said, dismissing Folker's report. "Nothing more than that. They cannot have moved much in the way of heavy equipment to Caledonia, or my agent with the Legion would have noticed. According to his last report, which was over a week ago, the Legion's DropShips were being loaded on Glengarry."

Dupré had been sending back a steady stream of coded HPG reports on the readiness and disposition of the Legion. Zellner congratulated himself again on his own foresight in securing the man as a private source.

"Your agent, yes," Karst said. "And he is your ace in the hole, I imagine, if it turns out we do have to take Carlyle out of the way."

"Just so. I doubt we'll need to exercise that particular option, however, even if Carlyle decides to take sides against us."

"Really? Why, sir?"

"Because his landhold on Glengarry is hostage to his unit's good behavior. If the Baron of Glengarry should revolt, his unit mutiny, well, Victor Davion will have no choice at all save to turn Glengarry over to another party."

"You, Marshal?"

"Field Marshal Gareth, actually, though we have discussed the possibility of my assuming the title of Baron of Glengarry, should Carlyle betray his contract. The point is, Carlyle won't be able to carry his mutiny very far, not if we control the families his men have left behind. Do you follow me?"

"I believe I do. Sir." Karst smiled. "Carlyle and his Gray Death will be yours no matter what he chooses to do!"

"That, my dear General Karst, is the essence of successful politics. It is always best to leave *nothing* to chance!"

19

JumpShip Rubicon
Zenith Jump Point
Caledonia System, Skye March
Federated Commonwealth
1347 hours, 7 April 3057

Space rippled, and the background of stars seemed to crawl and twist as the gravitational fabric of one small area of the cosmos folded back upon itself. Light flared out of nothingness, a torrent of free photons loosed as titanic energies relaxed their grip on one part of the cosmos and touched another. The shape that materialized, a shadow against the fading glare, was titanic, three quarters of a kilometer in length and massing some 380,000 tons. With flaring thrusters, it aligned its tail toward the Caledonian sun; over the course of the next several minutes, the ship's sail ring, rotating to keep the deployment rigging taut, began sliding off its mount encircling the JumpShip's primary station-keeping drive.

Despite the merging of Federated Suns and Lyran Commonwealth, the *Monolith* Class JumpShip *Rubicon* was still of Lyran registry, and the insignia displayed on the inner face of the unfolding energy-collection sail was the clenched fist of the old Lyran Commonwealth and House Steiner. For fairly obvious reasons, the Great Houses of the Inner Sphere retained individual control of what were euphemistically referred to as House assets. Alliance, clearly, had not brought total trust and cooperation, even—or especially—when the Federated Suns was increasingly perceived as the senior partner of the two states, and with greater control of the joint AFFC military.

The huge *Rubicon* was capable of carrying nine Drop-Ships attached to the docking collars arrayed along its long, central shaft. On this passage, however, jump had been completed with only five riders—a pair of merchant DropShips and three military vessels, *Union* Class DropShips bearing the gray-and-black skull logo of the Gray Death Legion.

Aboard the DropShip *Endeavor,* Colonel Grayson Carlyle unstrapped himself from his couch on the bridge deck and, with a shove, drifted across to the complex of display screens and consoles that comprised the Battalion Operations Center a few meters away. Catching himself on a bundle of wiring threaded across the deck overhead, he braced himself alongside the couch occupied by Major Jonathan Frye. "Well, Jon," he said. "We made it this far, at least."

Frye, a craggy-faced man with a thin mustache, grimaced as he uncinched his couch harness. "If you mean, Colonel, that we made it this far without getting caught in the crossfire of a civil war, I agree. But the news we picked up at Gladius didn't sound any too good. We may not have much longer."

"Affirmative. I want to get this one cleaned up as fast as possible," Grayson said. "I don't like having the regiment scattered across sixty-five light years."

"Do you think Glengarry is vulnerable?"

"Lori can handle whatever happens there," Grayson replied, despite the small stab of worry the question raised. "It's the old tactical dilemma of splitting your forces in the face of the enemy."

Frye grinned. "Like you did at Gettysburg?"

"Um. Trouble there is that a simulation, no matter how complex, can't be totally accurate. I split my forces at Gettysburg, sure, but I was also running both halves of my forces, and I always knew what both were doing. In a real fight, I'd have to send ... well, you, for instance, on a wide flank march. After you'd vanished over the horizon with half of my BattleMechs, all I could do would be to hope to hell you knew what you were doing!"

Frye chuckled. "Well, Colonel, me and Third Batt did pretty well by ourselves on Ueda and Karbala."

"That you did, Major. I never intended to suggest that I couldn't trust you out of my sight! I *am* worried about the people we left back on Glengarry, though. The political situation right now is . . . pretty strange. Anything could happen."

"I'm sure it wasn't easy trying to decide whether to stay with the landhold on Glengarry or take off for Caledonia to check up on Alex and Davis."

Grayson shrugged slightly as though to say it hadn't really been a choice. He jerked a thumb over his shoulder. "Let's get up to Ship Ops."

The *Endeavor*'s bridge was designed in two levels, with Ship Operations run from a circular deck with an open center set just above the larger area reserved for Battalion Operations. When the ship was grounded on a planet, the bridge was reached by ladder or elevator running up to Ship Ops's central opening; in zero-G, however, moving from one level to the next was a matter of giving a practiced kick and gliding through empty space to the next handhold.

Catching himself on a bulkhead wiring conduit, Carlyle bobbed in midair alongside the control console occupied by Captain Jennifer Walters, the *Endeavor*'s commander. "Hello, Jennie," he said. "What's the feed?"

"Well, Colonel, it looks like the *Rubicon* came through in one piece," she replied. Her blond hair, worn a bit longer than shipboard regulations generally permitted, swirled in a fine, golden haze about her head and shoulders as she turned. "They're deploying the sail now, and we have priority clearance for release and drop as soon as sail evolution is complete."

A bank of broad, thick windows ringed the bridge at this level, giving a three-sixty view around the DropShip. The window set above Captain Walters's station was looking aft down the length of the *Rubicon*'s central spine. The Legion DropShip *Defiant* was next in line, and a half a kilometer farther off, the sail was slowly opening beyond the splayed reach of the *Rubicon*'s towering deployment masts. Half a dozen monitors at Walters's station repeated the scene from various alternate angles, relayed to the *Endeavor* from cameras mounted elsewhere along the *Rubicon*'s enormous length. Caledonia's yellow-orange sun gleamed in a burst of dazzling luminosity through the circular opening at the sail's center.

Caledonia itself was invisible, though a representation of the world appeared on one of Walters's screens. It would be five days more before the Gray Death's Third Battalion would touch down on the world.

Five days until Grayson saw his son again.

The communications officer's station was located next to the DropShip captain's. Lieutenant Xavier Mendez was pressing the earphone of his headset tightly against his ear, a look of intense concentration on his face. "Colonel?"

"Yes, Lieutenant."

"We don't seem to be getting anything from Caledonia. No news, no vid carriers, nothing but a computer voice message that says all communications have been temporarily interrupted."

"Anything on the Legion's tac frequencies?"

"Just static, sir. I think the whole spectrum is being jammed."

"*That* doesn't sound promising," Frye said, floating alongside with one hand on a console support.

"Agreed." Some thirty light minutes from Caledonia, of course, two-way communications were impossible, but if Alex or Davis had some vital information to communicate to the Legion when the unit arrived in-system, they might have set their transmitter to broadcasting the same coded burst over and over.

But someone was blanketing all of the standard military frequencies—the civilian frequencies, too—making reception of even one-way recorded messages impossible.

"Anything in the message about why service has been cut off?" Frye asked Mendez.

"No, sir. Just the temporarily interrupted bit. And the other freaks are definitely being jammed. We won't be able to transmit through them, either."

"Then we'll be going in blind," Grayson said. This didn't sound good.

"Colonel?" Frye said. "When we get to Caledonia, what then? Are we really going to be fighting the Jacobites?"

Carlyle sighed. That question had been looming larger and larger in his mind for some time, and the jamming of Caledonia's comm frequencies didn't reassure him. "Our orders are to restore order," he said. "Let's wait until we can establish contact with Alex and Davis, and see what they have to say, first."

But he was already sure enough of what the situation would be, based on the last HPG report from McCall. The Caledonian's worst fears, it seemed, had materialized, and it was entirely possible that the Legion would soon find itself fighting McCall's friends and family.

Carlyle's grip on the wiring conduit tightened until his knuckles showed white. The Baron of Glengarry was already questioning his basic loyalty to the state that had hired him.

Would this, he wondered, be the first battle of the long-threatened civil war?

He didn't like that thought at all.

Lieutenant Mendez turned in his seat. "Colonel?"

"Yes, Lieutenant?"

"Sir, the planet's being blanketed, but regular ship-to-ship communications are still open. A call just got relayed to us from the *Rubicon*'s skipper. There's a small shuttle waiting at the jump point. Apparently they're waiting for us."

"That's interesting." Could it be Alex? Or McCall? Where would they get a shuttle? Did this have anything to do with the jamming at Caledon? "Any word on who's aboard or what they want?"

"Let me check, sir."

Mendez began speaking quietly over his headset as Grayson digested this bit of news. Whoever it was waiting for them had taken a bit of a risk. Every star system had two standard jump points, one at the system's zenith, one at the nadir. However, any starship with adequate navigation charts and system ephemerides could also make use of non-standard points, the so-called "pirate points." True, Jump-Ships, especially the big ones like the *Rubicon,* tended to stick with established and published schedules. It did, after all, save both time and money if DropShips planning to join a JumpShip at a given system were waiting at the right spot when the starship arrived, and not sitting hundreds of millions of kilometers away on the other side of the local star.

But schedules did change, and military vessels in particular often made a practice of being as unpredictable as possible.

It was safer that way.

"The vessel is an ST-46-class shuttle," Mendez said. "Federated Commonwealth military registry. One hundred tons. It's carrying three passengers besides the pilot. Fed-

Com clearance, code green three. They only say that they have urgent business with you."

"Me?"

"They asked for you by rank and name, sir."

Grayson frowned. Code green three meant a liaison officer or medium-ranking attaché. If Alex or Davis had been aboard, they would have said so. But the only other people who would know that he was here would be the people who'd sent him here.

Field Marshal Gareth, of the Lyran State Command in Tharkad.

"Well, I don't mind seeing them if the *Rubicon*'s skipper doesn't. Coordinate the docking with him, will you?"

"Of course, Colonel."

JumpShip skippers had to be careful about the approach of strange vessels at jump points. Attacking any JumpShip was a direct violation of the Ares Conventions, but that particular measure aimed at slowing the relentless slide into atechnic barbarism had been ignored more and more frequently in the past few years. Some DropShips could carry hundreds of troops, and something as big and as valuable as a JumpShip always made a tempting target—especially when it was stuck helplessly at a jump point, its Kearny-Fuchida capacitors drained and not yet recharged.

An ST-46 ought to be safe enough, however. Captain Walters already had a warbook display on the shuttle, which showed a rotating, full-color computer graphic of a flat, delta flyer that was almost all wing, with a one-man crew, the pilot, and room for up to nine passengers. There could be a bomb aboard the thing, of course, but there was no way that four people were going to take out a JumpShip the size of the *Rubicon*.

"The *Rubicon*'s skipper has agreed, Colonel," Mendez said. "The shuttle will be docking at three-forward, as soon as sail deployment is complete."

"Very well."

"The skipper says we can use the conference room on the number-two carousel deck to conduct your business."

"My compliments to the *Rubicon*'s skipper," Grayson said. "And my thanks. Tell him I'll be up as soon as the sail's unfurled."

"Aye, sir."

"Uh, Colonel?"

Grayson turned. Caitlin DeVries was standing a few meters behind him, looking small and trim and very appealing in her dark gray, form-hugging jumpsuit. "Hello, Sergeant," he said. "What can I do for you?"

"I was just . . . wondering, sir, if there was any word about our people on Caledonia."

Grayson sighed. He was well aware of the feeling Alex and Caitlin had for one another. He was also well aware that the two of them had quarreled, and bitterly, just before Alex had left Glengarry on his mission to McCall's homeworld. He suspected, in fact, that the fight was part of the reason Alex had agreed to go.

Still, when Grayson had been putting together the Third Battalion's deployment orders in preparation for this mission, it was Caitlin who'd come to him with the suggestion that they include First Battalion's First Company 'Mechs and equipment on the roster as well. The First of the First's Command Lance currently consisted of Grayson's *Victor*, Alex's *Archer*, Davis McCall's *Highlander* . . .

. . . and Caitlin DeVries's *Griffin*.

Grayson had already been planning on coming along, and both Alex's and Davis's 'Mechs were stored in the *Endeavor*'s cargo hold. Caitlin had simply wanted to make sure that she was included as well.

Grayson had mixed feelings about the relationship between Caitlin and Alex. He liked the girl, liked her a lot, in fact. She was smart, she knew what she was doing, and she hadn't let the fact that she was the daughter of the former governor of Glengarry spoil her. She also knew how to go after what she wanted; she'd joined the Legion despite her father's rather vehement protests.

But Grayson was Alex's father, and he knew what the death of young Davis Clay had done to his son at the Battle of Ryco Pass. It was never a good idea, he thought, to have two people who were especially close assigned to the same outfit. Too often, they paired off and began looking out for one another—and worrying about one another—to the exclusion of the others in their unit.

It also made it a hell of a lot tougher when one of them was killed or seriously hurt. Still, Lori had started out in Grayson's unit, back when he'd just been getting the Legion started, and every man and woman in the modern Legion knew that story well. It didn't make sense for him to try to enforce rules that he'd not followed himself.

"I'm sorry, Caitlin," he told her. "There hasn't been a word. All of the regular communications frequencies with Caledonia are being jammed, and we still don't know why."

"The last we heard, sir," she said, "Alex and Major McCall were consulting with the locals. But we don't really know what's going on down there, do we?"

"Not really. But I'm willing to trust those two to do the right thing. We wouldn't have been able to get much data from them anyway, even without the jamming. You never know who's listening in. But Alex knows we're coming—we told him that much in our last HPG transmission—and I'm sure they'll have the situation pretty well sorted out for us."

"Yes, sir. Thank you."

"I'm counting on them to brief us on the real situation on Caledon."

Though their mysterious visitors in the shuttle might have some useful information as well.

Grayson sincerely hoped so.

Several hours later, Grayson was waiting in the *Rubicon*'s conference room, *standing* on the deck for a change, instead of floating free. The carousel deck was one of two circular structures mounted on the *Monolith*'s forward hab module, angled in such a way that the out-is-down spin gravity generated by the carousel's rotation canceled the almost insignificant acceleration gravity induced by the ship's station-keeping thruster. Though the coriolis effect could produce some queasy effects in the stomach if you stood up or moved too quickly, the carousel deck afforded a chance for the Jump-Ship's crew to exercise and stretch their legs in a full gravity—vital if they were to be able to walk again once they returned to the surface of a planet after a long series of jumps.

The conference room was small—space aboard even the largest JumpShip was always at a premium—and nearly filled by the table mounted on the slightly curving deck. One bulkhead was taken up by a deck-to-overhead wallscreen that could be used to display computer data or a vidcom image, but which at the moment displayed a view of the now fully deployed jump sail astern of the *Rubicon*. He was staring at the stars beyond the black eclipse of the sail when the room's door hissed open.

"Colonel Carlyle?"

"I'm Carlyle. And you are . . . ?"

The first man into the room was tall, with a closely trimmed beard and glossy jet-black hair, and wearing an ornate, full-dress F-C staff officer's uniform. Close on his heels were another, younger man, and an attractive woman, both wearing combat fatigues instead of full dress. "I'm Major Kellen Folker, sir," the man in the dress uniform said. "Have, er, have you heard of me?"

"Can't say that I have, Major." Carlyle looked the officer up and down, noting the details of his uniform. It was heavy with braid and multiple loops of gold aiguillettes across his shoulder. A device worn above the rows of campaign ribbons on his left breast identified him as staff liaison to a planetary government. "I take it you're Governor Wilmarth's liaison with the AFFC."

"Exactly right, Colonel. And may I present my staff assistants, Lieutenant Churnowski and Lieutenant Dahlgren."

"A pleasure. I understand you wanted to meet with me. I didn't expect to talk with anyone official until after we'd touched down."

"It was, ah, necessary, Colonel, to see you at once and apprise you of the deteriorating situation on Caledonia."

"Indeed? Does this have anything to do with the communications blackout that appears to be in force?"

"Yes, sir. We regret that. I, ah, realize that you have people already on Caledonia. I'm sure you must wish to get into immediate communication with them."

"That would be appreciated."

"I'm very much afraid, however, that it will not be possible. You see, we have reason to believe that the unit you've already deployed here has been operating against the Governor's militia. Two of his BattleMechs were damaged in a skirmish in front of the official residence. The purpose of my meeting with you here, now, is to ascertain from you directly just what your intentions are. It is possible that the Gray Death Legion is already in violation of its mercenary contract with the Federated Commonwealth. Needless to say, the Governor would like to straighten out any potential, ah, misunderstandings now, before there are further incidents."

"Whoa! Hold on a second. What do you mean, 'the unit' I've deployed? I have two men on Caledonia, one of them a native of the planet who was here on what amounted to compassionate leave. I admit that I asked them to look around and prepare reports on the political situation on Caledonia. At the time, there was a good chance that the Gray Death was going to be deployed here, and it always helps to have an idea of the political situation before blundering in with a battalion of 'Mechs."

"I see." Folker reached into a pocket and extracted a computer memory clip. "May I?"

"Of course."

The liaison officer placed the clip in the reader slot on the table. The wallscreen at Grayson's back flickered, then dissolved from the view of the *Rubicon*'s energy sail to another scene, equally dark. Apparently shot from a camera positioned high up in a tower of an old Star League fortress, the view angled down across a cluster of towers in a high wall and was focused on the activity on a stone bridge across a canyon beyond. It was night, though the image had been enhanced through a nightscope. Gunfire flashed and snapped from a black line of trees beyond the canyon as a pair of *Victor*s moved slowly across the bridge, leaving the castle's front gate. There was no sound, and the silence lent a surreal and dreamlike quality to the unfolding drama.

Clearly, a pitched battle was underway. Equally clearly, the battle had been going on for some time. Smoke boiled up from the courtyard inside the walls, where numerous fires and hot metal left blurred, dazzling white after images in the nightscope's electronics. It looked as though the interior of the castle had been under heavy bombardment, though the smoke was so thick that Grayson could get only intermediate glimpses, never a good enough look to tell exactly what might have happened.

Folker sprawled into one of the chairs at the conference table. "This was taken late on the evening of April first, Colonel. A large number of raiders in advanced combat armor attacked the Citadel without provocation. At this point, they have already knocked out one of the Governor's *Urban-Mech*s. Watch the lead *Victor* on the bridge, there."

Despite the enhancement and light amplification, it was almost impossible to see what was happening. The *Victor*'s legs and lower torso were engulfed in the unheard *pop-pop-pop* of microgrenades mingled with the larger blasts of defensive antipersonnel charges. An instant later, something landed on the *Victor*'s left foot.

"Freeze," Folker said. "Enhance image."

The conference room computer obeyed, zeroing in on the shadowy something clinging to the *Victor*'s leg. Even though Grayson knew exactly what he was looking at, it was impossible to make out much at all save a dark shadow; the chameleon circuitry of Nighthawk armor was damned effective, especially at night.

Who was he seeing there, Alex or McCall? Almost certainly that blurred shadow was Major McCall; this sort of close assault was virtually a trademark of his, a technique he had helped to perfect many years and many campaigns ago.

"As you can see, Colonel," Folker continued, "troops in highly sophisticated combat armor are using close-assault infantry tactics on the Governor's 'Mechs. Slow motion, one to five, continue."

The shadow sprang back from the *Victor*'s foot, the flare from the Nighthawk suit's thrusters briefly reflected by dark metal. Laser fire from the Citadel towers drew interlacing patterns of blue-green and white light across the screen, one of which briefly caressed the shadow and sent it into a tumble. The figure struck the far side of the canyon, then slid back over the steeply sloping rim, vanishing from sight.

"As you can see, we did get some of the attackers, Colonel," Folker said. He was staring hard at Grayson, apparently trying to read the emotion on his face. "We were unable to recover any of the bodies, however. The locals appear to have dragged them all off."

"I . . . see. How many did you hit?"

"We're unsure of the exact number. According to the after-action reports I've seen, we had five confirmed kills."

"Good for you. How many casualties did you have?"

"Eight dead, fifteen wounded. Of course, the Governor's people weren't wearing armor. The attack came as a complete surprise, without provocation."

"Yes. So you said."

Grayson searched the scene, now moving in a dragged-out slow motion, wondering if the figure who'd fallen into the canyon had survived. Had he just witnessed Davis McCall's death?

Then an explosion suddenly lit up the panorama, a brilliant white flash squarely behind the protective armor plate over the *Victor*'s left knee. The 'Mech wobbled and gave a half turn, then collapsed face down onto the bridge. Abruptly, the scene cut off.

"Colonel, I don't want to put too fine a point on this, but Governor Wilmarth is furious. Your people came to our world, which was already in a state of unrest—virtually open rebellion—and appear to have helped the locals mount a major attack against the Governor's residence. For that reason, we've imposed a total news and communications blackout on Caledonia. I needn't add that Tharkad and New Avalon both are concerned about what is happening here, *quite* concerned. We were ... we still are counting on you and your men to restore order, *Baron*."

Grayson turned on the man, angry. "Don't give me that Baron bunk! Major, I assure you that I had no more than two men on your planet. What you have just shown me was the death of either a very good friend ... or of my son. I don't know who else attacked the residence, and I don't know why. But Field Marshal Gareth directed me to come to Caledonia to help restore order, and that is precisely what I intend to do."

"Fair enough. In light of what has happened, however, I'm sure you will not be surprised to hear that the Governor has requested additional forces as well. A battalion of the Third Davion Guards will be arriving here from Hesperus II within the next few days...."

But Grayson didn't hear the man.

He was wondering if McCall was really dead, and if Alex was all right....

$=$ 20 $=$

Riever Headquarters
Morayport
Caledonia, Skye March
Federated Commonwealth
2115 hours, 8 April 3057

Alex was excited. Even now, a full week after the penetration of the Citadel, he was still flushed with victory, alert, and filled with an almost irrational joy of simply being alive. It was more, he was sure, than simply relief at having survived the firefight at the Citadel. That emotion would have evaporated with his initial surge of adrenaline, scant hours after the battle's conclusion.

No, this was a different kind of a joy, one born of the sure and certain knowledge that it had all come back—his combat instincts, the keen edge of his training, everything he'd lost, everything he'd missed since the disastrous hours at Ryco Pass, had been there when he needed it.

Alex and McCall had been meeting with the local rebel forces during the past week, each gathering larger than the last as rebel cells from farther and farther afield were contacted and brought into the growing network. The Reivers, of necessity, had to keep their meeting places on the move, which was the reason for tonight's being held in the supply shed of a Morayport fisherman. The room was long and high-ceilinged, cluttered with engine parts and tools, the walls draped with nets hung for repairs, the far end of the building taken up by the rusty, torpedo-shaped bulk of a third-hand family submarine. Perhaps fifty men and women were in attendance this night—a larger number than either Alex or Davis felt comfortable with.

The more people in the group, the more likely that some would be spies or traitors. That, of course, was the most ancient and basic problem of all popular rebellions. Even a patently psychotic monster like Wilmarth had a few local people willing to sell out friends and neighbors for C-bills.

Despite the danger, however, the two Legionnaires had agreed to meet with this larger group tonight. The Gray Death Legion would be in-system soon; indeed the Legion force ought to have arrived yesterday and be en route to Caledonia now. The incessant jamming that had been blocking all radio communications channels for the past week prevented all but laser messages from passing between the jump points and the planet, and Alex and McCall had not brought any laser comm gear with them. Still, if things were going according to plan, at least one battalion of the Gray Death ought to make planetfall within another few days.

And this time, his father's arrival would be less a rescue than a reunion, a difference greatly contributing to Alex's buoyant spirits. In the meantime, he and Davis had only a few days to pull things together with the locals.

Perhaps as few as four days, in fact, to mend a serious breach that by itself threatened to undo everything the Caledonian rebels had been fighting for.

"They should be on their way noo," McCall was telling the group from an improvised stage atop the forward deck of the small family sub. "We last talked t' th' Carlyle by HPG shortly after we arrived. The Gray Death Legion, or a part a' it, is being deployed here by State Command in Tharkad."

McCall still had his left arm in a sling to keep his burned shoulder immobilized. A couple of days in a medsleeve had regenerated much of the skin and muscle tissue burned by the molten armor, but it would be several weeks before he'd recovered full function and mobility. His face looked worn, however. The strain both of the wound and of what amounted to an intensive political campaign during the past week was taking its toll.

"Aye, an' then what, Major?" General McBee said from the front row of the audience. "Prince Victor intends for the Legion to put *us* down, not the legal Governor. We're the rebels here, an' the troublemakers. Or had y' forgotten that?"

"I'd nae forgotten, General," McCall said with an easy grin. "Let's just say I have a wee bit a' influence wi' th' Carlyle. Noo tha' Alex an' I hae seen the real cause a' th' trouble here, I think I can promise that the Legion will nae be used against you. Alex an' I will be talkin' to th' Carlyle about wha' we can do about Wilmarth."

"What if the Governor, or the Governor's people, get to him first?" Sergeant Ross—the big, tattooed soldier they'd rescued in the Citadel—crossed muscular arms and did not look convinced.

"I don't see how that would be possible," Alex said. "They'd have to send someone out with a ship, and our people have been watching the spaceport."

"There's more than one spaceport on Caledon," Allyn said. "They could send someone out to rendezvous with the Legion's JumpShip."

"Sure, but what would be the point?" Alex asked. "The Legion will be coming under orders from Tharkad. What's Wilmarth going to do, tell them to go back where they came from?"

"And what's this Colonel of yours going to do when he gets here?" Angus McCall wanted to know. "Sure, he'll listen to what you say, Davis, but he's a mercenary. We don't have the money to pay for a full, front-line merc regiment like the Gray Death!"

"Weel, lad, I'll tell you," Davis replied. "Th' Carlyle would noo' stand for this wee, tin-plated dictator Wilmarth an' his army a' thugs. He jus' might be persuaded t' settle for a contingency contract."

"Contingency contract," Allyn said. "What's that?"

She was sitting beside Alex in the front row of chairs that had been grouped in concentric semicircles about the make-shift stage.

"Loot," Alex told her. He shrugged when she looked at him in surprise. "Wilmarth has stuff in that castle of his that we could use. His 'Mechs aren't in very good shape, so I doubt he has much in the way of spare parts, but he does have some. And tools. And expendables like short-range missiles and power packs and the like."

"Aye, laddie," McCall said from the stage with a grin. "It's too bad you took out most a' Wilmarth's motor pool last week! I imagine Cindy would hae liked t' get her hands on some a' those hovercraft y' scrapped!" Cindy was Lieutenant Cindy Sashimoto, CO of the Legion's motor and service company.

His statement was answered by scattered laughter from the audience. "So your people would be satisfied with whatever booty you could take from the Citadel, as payment for helping us?" someone asked as the laughter died away.

"Why?" The speaker was a man in a dark, high-collared jacket and maroon traveling cloak standing at the back of the room. He'd been introduced to Alex and McCall earlier that evening simply as Bryson Caruthers, but they already knew he was the focal point of the dissent growing within the rebellion. He'd been listening to the proceedings so far with a distinct air of disapproval, his features set in an unpleasant frown, as though he were smelling a whiff of something foul.

"Wha' do y' mean, sir?" McCall replied. "Why *what*?"

"Why would these mercenaries of yours be willing to help us?" Caruthers shook his head, the frown deepening. "Brothers," he said, now addressing the Caledonians sitting around and in front of him, "it seems to me tha' one band a' invaders is just as bad as another. One *army* of BattleMechs is as bad as another, trampling our fields, burning our crops, smashing our buildings."

"And how do you propose we make them all stay away, Bry?" McBee said. "Your Jihaders haven't come up with a plan for kicking Wilmarth and his men off Caledonia that doesn't require at least a company of 'Mechs."

" 'Rely not upon the machine,' " Caruthers intoned, apparently quoting some text Alex didn't recognize, " 'for the way of the machine is death. Walk instead the way of life, which dwells within us all.' "

"Thus says the Word," another voice chimed in from the other side of the room, and Alex heard several low-voiced murmurs that could have been assent.

"Major . . . Captain," McBee said, "Bryson here is a Jihad proclaimer. Not all of us see quite eye to eye wi' him an' his ideas about machines, but they're good people and good neighbors."

"So I take it," Alex said, turning in his seat to face Caruthers across several rows of listeners, "that you don't care for machines."

"I am a proclaimer of the Word of Jihad," Caruthers said, in the tones of a teacher correcting a student. "Nothing more. It is not my intent to tell you all how to run your revolution. But it ... distresses me to see so much reliance on demon technos. In the short run, the death machines might help our cause. In the long run, however, they will steal our very souls."

"Aye, lad," McCall said softly from the stage. "That vurra weel might be. But y' hae t' survive the short run t' worry about the long. An' without BattleMechs, I promise you, you'll nae last long agin' Wilmarth an' his people."

" 'The righteous need not the stink and clank of machines,' " another man in the audience quoted. " 'Trust ye in heart and soul and the precious gift of life, for it is written that in the end, the green shall always overcome the gray.' "

"Thus says the Word!" several other voices echoed.

"Major, not all of us feel the way the damned proclaimers do," Allyn said. She snapped an angry glance back over her shoulder at Caruthers. "Their so-called Word hasn't done a thing to lift Wilmarth's oppression, and that little bastard's been ruling Caledon from his black tower for five years now! Platitudes and high-sounding proclamations about green overcoming gray are all fine, but we don't stand a chance in hell of beating Wilmarth's 'Mechs."

"Especially when he seems to have gotten reinforcements lately," Ross added, rubbing his jaw. "Those *Victor*s ..."

"Third Davion Guard," Alex added, shaking his head. "Not good at all."

"Are those 'Mechs really from Hesperus II, Captain?" someone wanted to know. "Could your Gray Death stop them?"

"Depends on how many there are ... and how many 'Mechs the Gray Death sends, of course. The Third Guards is a good unit, with a fair amount of combat experience." Alex grinned. "Of course, they're not as good as the Gray Death."

"People, people," Caruthers said, standing now and pleading with the assembly, his arms spread wide. "Don't you see? Violence breeds violence, machines breed machines! If we don't stop this insane dependence on the clanking monstrosities, we will never be rid of them, never! Humans will be slaves to the monsters for all eternity!"

McCall was shaking his head. "I suppose, then, tha' you'll nae be wantin' the help of the Gray Death's wee 'Mechs."

"You fought Wilmarth's 'Mechs without one of your own!" one young woman sitting next to Caruthers argued. "We saw it! You could teach us how to do the same thing!"

A pained expression passed over McCall's face. "Lass, y' dinnae ken what you're sayin'."

"Unarmored, with nothing but a satchel charge," Alex said. "You'd be dead before you got within fifty meters of a BattleMech."

"The point is," the woman shot back, "that you two did what you did without relying on a ten-meter monster of steel and electricity! You weren't depending on machines to fight your battle!"

"I don't mean t' stand here an' refute you point blank, lass, but aye, I was depending on machines," McCall reminded her. "If I'd nae had tha' Nighthawk power suit, I would hae been chewed to bloody mash oot there before two minutes were past."

"Besides, Janet," one of the rebels added, laughing, "a satchel charge is a kind of machine too. Isn't that right, Proclaimer? Or does the Word have an answer for that?"

The words were spoken lightly, but Alex heard the undercurrent of tension. The alliance between Caledonia's Jacobites and the Word of Jihad was a fragile one, and the friction between the two had been growing during the past few days. The Jacobites were willing to go to any lengths to free their world from Wilmarth and his thugs; the Jihadists were unwilling to help if it meant forming an alliance with machines—specifically with BattleMechs. The problem was, if this revolution was to succeed, it required the broad support and cooperation of as many of Caledonia's people as could be recruited—and that included the Jihadists. The once obscure anti-technic sect had been growing in power and in influence all across Caledonia during the past five years, especially in rural areas away from the larger cities.

"Y' ken, I've been aye wondering about tha', sir," McCall told the proclaimer. "Just where do you folks draw the line between what's machine an' what is not? Or would y' hae us all shed our clothes an' frolic naked in the forest?"

"Certainly not!" the man said, looking shocked.

"Ah, weel, I'm relieved t' hear tha'. Caledonian winters can be aye a mite cold, an' nuts an' berries are hard t' come by when the snow's up to your chin. But, d' y' nae see? The clothing you wear an' the processed food y' eat are both products of our demonic technological culture, would y' nae agree, lad?"

"The Word proclaims that there is a difference between tools that serve the maker, and machines that rule him." He plucked at the hem of the cloak he wore. "Even a piece of clothing can become a master, though, if it so rules our thoughts and our souls that we become slaves to it. To fashion. To rich garments or clothing that proves we're better than our neighbor. Better to live naked, then, or clad in tree bark, than to be slaves to a *thing*!"

"Aye, aye," McCall said. "An' I must admit I hae nothin' against idealism, or against idealistic stands. I've made one or two in my own life. But I tell y' noo tha' there's a time for faith in your Word, an' a time t' get off your ass an' get things done."

"*All* good works proceed from faith," Caruthers said. "You can't separate the one from the other."

"Do you really believe you can attack BattleMechs wi' your bare hands?"

Caruthers glanced down at the woman who'd talked about McCall not needing a BattleMech and gave her a condescending smile. "Janet here spoke emotionally, Major. The way to final triumph and salvation is essentially a passive one. We will resist peacefully. We will answer hatred with love. And love will triumph in the end."

"I see," McCall said thoughtfully. "Aye. Let me ask you all somethin', then. How many here believe that machines are evil?"

Fully twenty hands went up around the shed, from nearly half of the gathered rebels.

"That you'd be better off fighting Wilmarth wi' your faith? Fighting BattleMechs wi' love?"

A number of the raised hands wavered at that, and several dropped.

One of the men who'd kept his hand up rose to his feet, hand still firmly in the air. "There's aye plenty a' Jihadists joinin' the Jacobites, Major," he said, "an' plenty more every day. The Word prophesies three centuries when ordinary people will be ground down under th' heel of the machine in blood and war, followed by a time of tribulation, when the faithful will be tested. An' after that comes th' time of cleansing, when ordinary people who have the faith will rise up and destroy the machines forever!" He paused, looking around the room, defiant. "Well, it appears t' me that we've had our three centuries, more or less. An' Wee Willie has certainly provided the tribulation!" Low-voiced murmurs of approval sounded around the room, intermingled with scattered applause.

"I'll tell y' all th' truth then, people," McCall said. "I hae never had much tolerance for the idea that technology is evil. Oh, aye, it's fashionable from time t' time to up an' say that science makes more problems than it solves, tha' technology is evil, tha' machines are dehumanizing. We humans hae been flirting wi' tha' nonsense since the steam engine . . . no, since we first learned how t' make fire. But it's nae the machines tha' define our humanity. We're slaves to machines only when we oursel's *want* to be. When we *let* them rule our lives. There's nae shame or loss of faith in using tools when you need them, whether it's a textile manufactory t' make the clothes t' keep you warm or a BattleMech t' defend your homes an' your bairns. Proclaimer Caruthers is right aboot one thing. War an' hatred are aye parts of a deadly circle, an if there's a way to get off the damned thing, I have nae heard it yet.

"But I'll tell y' this, an' this from bluidy experience because I've seen it wi' these eyes on worlds tha' hae lost the ability t' make things, t' build an' grow an' *dream*. Take away th' technology, an' it will nae be the bucolic agroparadise th' Jihadie prophets claim it'll be. You'll hae disease an' famine an' war an' death, aye, the Four Horsemen themselves, an' you'll never be rid of them till you an' all your bairns an' their bairns after them lie dead together in th' rubble!"

There was no applause when McCall stopped speaking, only a deep and full silence that in its own way was louder than applause would have been. Alex listened to that silence, and he felt the mood of the audience shifting. A majority, he was pretty sure, agreed with what McCall had just said . . . a majority even of the Jihadists.

Alex marveled. Davis McCall knew how to *lead*!

"I suggest," General McBee said after a long silence, "tha' we vote on the matter. 'Aye,' if we're t' accept the help of th' Gray Death Legion, even if it means BattleMechs. 'Nay' if y' choose to find another way."

"Thou shalt make no covenant with evil!" Caruthers cried from the back of the room. "Surely there is room here for negotiation, for compromise!"

"With the likes of Wilmarth?" Allyn called out, her voice bitter in the silence that followed the proclaimer's plea. She stood up, then turned to face the audience, and there was fire in her eyes. "I was *there,* Proclaimer, in his dungeons, for no greater crime than voicing my protest of his high-handed and bloody rule! I was arrested, beaten, stripped naked, abused, humiliated, tied and gagged, raped, and then strung up in a wire noose and left to die on a melting block of ice! Look me in the face and tell me that compromise with Wilmarth is less of an evil than accepting the Gray Death's help!"

The vote was forty-one ayes, with only a handful abstaining or voting nay.

"Aye," McCall said softly to Alex, after the votes had been counted. "We hae ourselves a wee army now. I jus' hope t' God we can convince the Colonel t' side wi' us when he gets here."

"I'm not too worried about that," Alex said. "He'll do what's right." He looked around the room at the people gathered there, talking now in small, urgent groups of two and three. "But what's going to happen to these people? No weapons to speak of, no armor."

"Aye," McCall said. "But a vurra great deal of *heart.*"

21

DropShip
Approaches to New Edinburgh Spaceport
Caledonia, Skye March
Federated Commonwealth
1412 hours, 13 April 3057

Balanced on shrieking, thrusting spears of white-hot plasma, the *Union* Class DropShips *Endeavor, Valiant,* and *Defiant* drifted down out of a cloudless sky. Spherical, painted black and gray, each massed 3,500 tons and was being gentled toward Caledonia's surface on thundering Star League V250 plasma thrusters, which gulped down tons of atmosphere, superheated it in parallel-linked fusion plants, and spewed it out astern at temperatures approaching those of the core of a star. Four nacelles evenly spaced about their thrusters split open, disgorging the heavy, cylindrical feet of their landing legs.

Closer and closer they came toward the starport, dropping past five kilometers now. Four of the Legion's aerospace fighters, released while the flight of DropShips was still in space, circled at a distance, protecting their larger, clumsier charges from air attack, scanning the area for any military threat from air or ground.

Aboard the DropShip *Endeavor,* Grayson Carlyle stood in Ship Operations, ignoring the thrumming vibration of the drive rattling against the soles of his feet through the steel deck, studying the screen of a large monitor set to display the view from one of the ship's external cameras. Regulations directed all personnel to remain in their acceleration couches during atmospheric maneuvers and until the pilot sounded the all-clear, but the *Endeavor* had already completed its necessary heavy-duty maneuvers and was descending at only a few meters per second. No sudden maneuvers were expected or necessary, and Grayson wanted to take advantage of the ship's dwindling altitude to get a good look at the city of New Edinburgh.

"Left five," he said, speaking for the benefit of the console's voice-command circuits. "And enhance."

The picture from an altitude of twenty kilometers was remarkably clear and steady; the camera was computer-controlled to maintain the image despite the DropShip's movements or the buffeting of the wind. At Grayson's spoken command, a square appeared in the center of the screen, shifted left, then expanded swiftly to zoom in on the selected region. The view showed a portion of the spaceport spread out beneath the slowly descending DropShip as well as a nearby park or public square surrounded by buildings. The square was filled to overflowing with a great, black mass that seemed to quiver and seethe as Grayson watched it.

"Magnify," he said. "Times five."

Again a graphic square appeared on screen, then expanded, magnifying the view. Now the black mass was revealed as individual people, standing shoulder to shoulder in a great, seething mob.

A riot . . . or a massive demonstration. He widened the angle of his scan and ran a search for large heat sources . . . there! Three of them, BattleMechs, moving toward the town plaza. Make that four. A fourth heat source appeared to be lurking among the warehouses on the northeast side of the spaceport, some distance away from the main demonstration. Why was it all the way over there? A backup for the others in case the crowd broke that way? An ambush?

Major Frye came up behind him, looking over his shoulder at the screen. "Trouble, Colonel?"

"Looks like. Better pass the word for the ground troops to go out armed and in armor. They are not, repeat, *not* to engage, however, unless and until they're fired upon."

We still don't know for sure who the enemy is here. . . .

Grayson thought again about Alex and McCall. There was still no word from either one, still no break in the government's jamming of all radio frequencies. He'd been almost frantic for the several hours after he'd seen Folker's film of the battle at the Citadel. Somehow, somehow, he'd remained *almost* impassive, though it had been all he could do not to deck Kellen Folker then and there. In the hours that followed, however, Grayson had arrived at several conclusions.

One, the fact that he'd seen a man in what looked like Nighthawk armor get shot and fall into a canyon did not necessarily mean that the man was either Davis McCall or his son. It could have been someone else.

Two, the fact that the person had fallen into a canyon after being shot didn't necessarily mean that he was dead. There was no way to tell from that brief glimpse on video how deep that canyon was, and Nighthawk suits were astonishingly tough.

Three, Grayson had decided that he didn't trust Folker—not when the man was the representative of a government that clearly preferred to control all information about itself in order to control its own people. Folker had a sliminess about him, about his manner that set Grayson's teeth on edge, and Grayson could easily believe that the man might have staged or forged that entire video sequence.

Why? Grayson still wasn't sure, but he had the distinct impression that Folker was trying to tie Grayson and the Gray Death more closely to Wilmarth and the governor's stewardship of Caledonia. Rather than returning to Caledon in the shuttle, Folker had remained aboard the *Endeavor*, where he'd spent much of the past five days in attempts to convince Grayson that the Jacobite/Jihadist rebellion was the work of anarchists, of enemies of the Governor, and of enemies of the Federated Commonwealth.

The Legion, Folker had insisted, was one of two Battle-Mech units being deployed to Caledonia—an indication, he claimed, of just how important this world was to the Federated Commonwealth—in order to keep the peace. He'd brought with him several memory clips filled with hundreds of gigabytes of data, with detailed operational orders for the Legion to deploy from New Edinburgh spaceport, secure New Edinburgh, and then initiate martial law. The second unit, Folker said, would be a battalion of the Third Davion Guards, formerly stationed on neighboring Hesperus II but soon to arrive in-system for deployment either at New Edinburgh or at the city of Stirling, to the north.

Grayson had done a lot of thinking about the situation during the final leg of the passage to Caledonia. He was in a damned tight position, both politically and ethically. As the Baron of Glengarry, he owed his primary allegiance to Victor Davion, Prince and ruler of the Federated Commonwealth. That title of nobility, however, meant little to him personally. The Legion was his life, and his life's work.

So far as his allegiance as a mercenary was concerned, that had been purchased decades ago by House Steiner. Though mercenary units didn't necessarily stay loyal to one employer—those that did were, in fact, rarities—Grayson Carlyle's political sympathies lay more with the Steiners than with any of the other Great Houses of the Inner Sphere. The Steiner world of Verthandi had given the Gray Death its first contract those many years ago when Grayson had first formed the unit. And in their current stint, he had actually signed on with Katrina Steiner before she'd abdicated in favor of her daughter Melissa. His contract had never officially been with House Davion or the Federated Commonwealth. He sympathized with the disaffection many Lyrans felt for the Davion emphasis being given to the alliance of their two great realms. Prince Victor was currently ruling from New Avalon and seemed to be more concerned with maintaining his power than being fair to all his subjects.

Quite apart from the politics of the matter, though, Grayson disliked it when people in power—those accustomed to having their own way—attempted to use the Gray Death Legion for their own political ends. That had happened more than once in the past, and Grayson was certain that someone was trying to do it again. Who? And for what purpose? Not Folker, certainly. The man was a go-between, not a mover. Wilmarth? Possible, but from what he'd heard so far, unlikely. Field Marshal Gareth? A distinct possibility. That one certainly had ambitions . . . and sympathy for the Skye separatists as well.

But there was no way to sort out his conflicting emotions, or loyalties, before he reached Caledonia and found out for himself what the situation there was.

One thing was certain. Major Kellen Folker was not making it easier to feel sympathy for the legitimate government of Caledonia. The man was there at Grayson's side at every opportunity, attempting to sway him, reminding him that the

Jacobites and Jihadists were in rebellion against their legally appointed Governor and against the rightful authority of the Federated Commonwealth. He continually harped on the same theme: *"You are the Baron of Glengarry, Colonel. You owe your oath of fealty to Prince Victor. We are facing the Prince's enemies here, and it is your sworn duty to destroy them!"*

By the time they'd completed their final deorbit burn and entered Caledon's atmosphere, Grayson had no idea who was right and who was wrong on that world. All he knew was that the first thing he must do was find Davis and Alex. And if they were alive, he would learn from them the true situation on Caledonia.

If they were not, then someone was going to pay for their deaths, and pay very dearly indeed.

"There they are!" Alex said, pointing excitedly into the sky.

McCall, one-handed, held a set of electronic binoculars to his eyes and peered up toward the zenith. Three brilliant white stars set against the blue of the afternoon sky were drifting swiftly down. Through the binoculars he could make out details of hull and laser turret, and the stylized skull of the Gray Death.

"Aye, lad, tha's them. Looks like the *Endeavor,* the *Defiant,* and the *Valiant,* all three of Third Batt's DropShips, though I would nae be surprised t' see your father wi' 'em."

"Now all we have to do is figure out how to contact them."

Wearing their Nighthawk armor but with the helmets removed, the two men were seated together in the high, open cockpit of a spider-legged AgroMech, a relic of a CK-3 *CherryPicker* at least two centuries old that had been volunteered to the cause by a Dundee farmer. The man was a Jihadist and a pacifist, but, as he'd put it when he'd showed up at the Reiver camp the morning after that meeting in Morayport, "I'm aye a peaceable man, but enough is enough! These bastards can takit their damned tribulation a' the righteous elsewhere!"

The *CherryPicker* had been equipped with machine guns and a jury-rigged laser—the igniter from a small, household fusion plant with the safeties stripped off and the output boosted by removing the governor. The device was now the equivalent of a small laser, and though no one could promise that it would fire more than once or twice before burning out, it gave the CK-3 at least that many shots before the AgroMech was smashed to pieces.

McCall hoped the thing wouldn't have to see combat this afternoon, but he knew better than to take *that* as a given. He'd been certain that the Legion DropShips were arriving when Reiver lookouts had reported that Bloodspiller troops had begun getting into position around the spaceport several hours ago. Wilmarth obviously wanted to keep the rebels away from the Gray Death forces, at least until he was sure that the Legion was on his side.

The rebels' response had been suggested by the two Legionnaires with them—another huge demonstration to be held in the plaza outside the New Edinburgh spaceport terminal. Nearly twenty thousand people were expected, a crowd that would test Wilmarth's crowd-control capabilities to their limits and distract them long enough for McCall and Alex to make the sprint to the DropShips.

The AgroMech had been partly disassembled three days ago and moved by truck and cargo hovercraft to the spaceport's warehouse district. There, inside a warehouse donated by another secret member of the Reivers, the CK-3 had been reassembled and its makeshift weaponry mounted. That jury-rigged firepower would be useless in a tangle with a real BattleMech, but if Wilmarth's troops tried pursuing them out onto the landing field, a burst of machine-gun or laser fire might discourage them.

Now, McCall and Alex were sitting inside the 'Mech, waiting for their chance. The roof and south wall of the warehouse had been rolled open by the half dozen armed Reivers waiting there with them, and, once the building's interior was open to the sky, the two Legionnaires could watch the DropShips' final approach.

The squat, spheroidal shapes were close enough now that McCall could see details of their hulls and markings even without the binoculars. If he and Alex only had some laser comm gear, they could've flashed a message to the *Endeavor* right now. . . .

The distant rumble of the demonstration off to the west was swiftly drowned out by the piercing, shrieking thunder of the descending trio of DropShips. Once again, he wished they could use their radios to contact the Colonel directly, but the planet was still blanketed with heavy jamming. Narrow windows had been reserved for government communications, but without the necessary codes and frequency sets, there was no way for the Reivers to take advantage of them. Laser communications would have been better yet. Even though limited to line-of-sight ranges, there was no way you could jam a lasercom. That equipment, however, rare and valuable, was simply not available.

Actually, McCall thought with a wry grin to himself, there was another way they could have used laser communications, though it was too late to do it. Hand lasers took too long to recycle after each shot to be useful in transmitting a code, but there were targeting lasers and ranging devices that could have been adapted. Aimed at the *Endeavor* and switched rapidly on and off, they would have attracted immediate attention from the DropShip's defense computers, which registered any laser energy striking the ship's hull. If the ship's weapons officer had noted the irregular pattern of dots and dashes ...

Unfortunately, McCall hadn't thought of that in time to set something up. No matter. The mere sight of a spindly-legged AgroMech striding across the tarmac would alert the Colonel. After all, it was Grayson Carlyle himself who'd pioneered the use of jury-rigged Agros on Verthandi, over three decades ago, and he'd know what was up.

Just so long as some trigger-happy newbie in the Legion didn't get the wrong idea and shoot first, before the Colonel had a chance to tell him not to. . . .

In swirling clouds of superheated steam, the three DropShips gentled one after the other into yawning starport receiving bays, refractory, ferrocrete-rimmed craters half filled with water to cool the walls after they were licked by the flaming, starcore fury of the ships' main thrusters. Settling deeply into the yield of the shock-absorbing legs, the hulls shuddered for a moment as the thrusters powered down.

Then they were still. Enclosed boarding ramps slid out from the receiving bay walls, magnetically locking to each ship's primary entry port. This was luxury; on most combat drops, DropShips landed in open fields and didn't have the luxury of air-conditioned ways leading to underground slidewalks, maglev transports, and the cool, brightly lit interior of the starport terminal.

Now the 'Mech loading bays on the sides of the Drop-

Ships slid slowly open, and the debarkation elevators began trundling the first of the battalion's massive battle machines to the ground. Ramps descending into each landing pit gave the 'Mechs easy access to the open tarmac of the port field.

It never failed to amaze McCall, even after all his years of experience, just how *huge* a DropShip actually was. Their interiors were so cramped that a single company of Mech-Warriors, techs, and auxiliary personnel were crowded into a stinking, claustrophobic, elbow-in-my-eye intimacy that swiftly became intolerable after just a few days of inter-system boost. Aboard ship, there were never enough lavatories, fewer showers, and men and women were crowded together in the troop bays without even the memory of what privacy was like. Civilian transports were somewhat better, but military jobs couldn't afford to cater to humans when every single kilo saved on measures for comfort or privacy could be applied to another kilo of expendables, of 'Mech parts, of military equipment.

Seen from outside, however, even from well over a kilometer away and with the lower halves of each ship hidden in its landing cradle, DropShips were enormous, especially when their BattleMechs began moving about outside to give them a sense of scale. McCall knew 'Mechs better than he did DropShips, knew their sheer mass and bulk and complexity, but a *Union* Class DropShip, measuring seventy-eight meters from stern thrusters to bridge dome, towered almost eight times taller than a 'Mech and dwarfed the largest *Atlas* by its sheer bulk. Even nestled in their landing craters, the upper halves of the DropShips towered above the deploying BattleMechs.

McCall studied the deployment through his binoculars. There was a *Vindicator,* a *Catapult,* and a *Hunchback,* obviously working together as part of a lance. That would be Lieutenant Anders's Combat Lance, in First Company of the Third Batt.

He saw no sign of Grayson Carlyle's *Victor.*

"Weel, lad, there's no sense in waitin' longer. I was hopin' to spot your father first, but tha's Larry Anders's *Catapult* over there. I think he can be trusted not t' shoot first an' ask questions later. Still, I wish I could spot the Colonel's *Victor.* It would be nice to walk up t' him, 'Mech to 'Mech."

"We can wait a bit longer," Alex said. "In fact, we probably should. There's no sign yet that the Bloodspiller

'Mechs have started moving against the demonstrators." The signal, arranged early that morning, was to be a green flare fired over the plaza. Once Wilmarth's 'Mechs were moving toward the plaza, the AgroMech could scamper across the tarmac in relative safety. If McCall and Alex broke from cover too soon, it was possible that the government 'Mechs, which had been positioned about the spaceport in order to guard the approaches to the landing area itself, would see the little AgroMech and move to block it. The thing was un-armored. A single solid hit would probably take it down.

"All right, lad," McCall said, deciding. "We can wait an-other ten minutes. Then we'll go, whether your father is paradin' aboot in his *Victor* or no."

Grayson was not in his 'Mech. Instead, he, Major Frye, and a half dozen Legion staff officers had accompanied Ma-jor Folker and his two lieutenants through the boarding tube, then gone by underground maglev to the starport terminal a kilometer to the north. There were militia guards in black and yellow armor everywhere throughout the terminal, and Grayson had the impression they'd been there for some time.

"Just what is it you want us to see, Major?" Grayson asked as they stepped into a circular, glass-enclosed lounge. A brief elevator ride had taken them up a slender tower to the saucer-shaped observation area, which gave a splendid three-sixty-degree view of the entire port, as well as the city of New Edinburgh sprawling across gently rolling ground to the north and east. Grayson took one brief glance toward the south, verifying that the Third Batt's 'Mechs were indeed deploying as he'd ordered, then followed Folker and the oth-ers toward the north side of the lounge.

"This, Colonel," Folker said. "I got word by radio as we were landing."

"You've been in radio communication with your superi-ors?" Grayson was angry. "Damn it, man, I've been asking for access to your people for five days!"

"I told you, Colonel. *I* am to be your liaison with the Gov-ernor. I was informed this morning that a demonstration had begun outside of the spaceport terminal. Now, though, it ap-pears to be getting out of hand. I thought this would give you the best view...."

Folker was right. From almost one hundred meters up,

Grayson and the others could look down onto the plaza in front of the starport terminal almost directly below, getting an aerial view even more close and detailed than that afforded by the *Endeavor*'s scanners during the descent. The crowds had filled the plaza with a black sea of people pocked everywhere by the colorful, dancing points of waving flags and hand-carried signs. Grayson couldn't read the signs at this distance but could imagine what many of them said: DOWN WITH WILMARTH, perhaps, and MACHINES = DEATH.

There was no sign of the four BattleMechs he'd spotted from the DropShip. Perhaps Wilmarth's troops were holding off until things really got out of hand.

"As you can see, Colonel," Folker said gesturing out the window, "things have become impossible here. The Governor only has a few 'Mechs and a few armored vehicles available . . . and two of the 'Mechs and a number of transports were knocked out last week by your people. I remind you, sir, that you were brought here to restore order."

"What is it you want of me, Major Folker?"

The Major waved at the window. "You have 'Mechs. Your orders are to deploy your battalion into the city, seize it, and disperse the rioters."

Grayson's eyes widened. "Major Folker, are you suggesting that I turn *BattleMechs* against those people down there?"

"Those people, Colonel, are in rebellion against the duly constituted government of this world." Folker drew himself up straighter, his mouth a hard line, his eyes dark. "Colonel Carlyle, as the personal representative both of Governor Wilmarth and of Field Marshal Gareth, I *order* you to deploy your full force against this rebellion, even if it means total destruction of this city!"

"Good God, man, do you hear yourself? Do you have any idea what you're saying?"

"I'm ordering you to destroy the city and crush the Jacobite rebellion!"

Grayson took a deep breath. There were some orders that must be obeyed, even though obeying them meant death. There were others, though, that meant the death of a man's spirit, of his soul.

"No."

"What did you say?"

"I said, 'no.' I refuse that order."

"*Damn* you, Carlyle! This is an emergency! The Governor has already declared martial law. You can't refuse a direct order made on the Governor's authority!"

"I just did. I will *not* see my Legion used to incinerate civilians. What you're asking isn't war. It's a civilian massacre."

"I can have you and your whole damned Legion listed as outlaws!" Folker shouted. "As contract breakers! I'll see you broken for this! You'll never get another mercenary assignment, never! No one in the Inner Sphere would hire a man, would *trust* a man, who'd refused a legal order from his employer!"

Grayson crossed his arms. "I can't accept the order, Major, and you know it. I couldn't accept it if your Governor Wilmarth were here to deliver it himself."

Folker exchanged a hard glance with his two lieutenants, then gave a nod. His hand dropped to his holstered sidearm, dragging the weapon free with an ugly rasp of steel on leather.

"In that case, Colonel, I'm going to have to place you under arrest. Your weapons please, all of you!"

Grayson's hand had moved automatically to the butt of his own laser, but at the same instant, he heard the snick of drawn bolts all around the public lounge. The small group of Gray Death officers was surrounded by black and yellow armored militiamen, who had them covered from every side.

"The Gray Death Legion," Folker said with a dark grin, "is now under *my* command and you will do *exactly* as I say . . ."

22

New Edinburgh Spaceport
Caledonia, Skye March
Federated Commonwealth
1436 hours, 13 April 3057

They rode the elevator back down to the main terminal level. There'd only been room for Grayson and Major Frye, Major Folker, and two armored militia troopers as guards. The rest were still in the observation lounge, waiting for another car.

"Tell me something, Major," Grayson said as they dropped to the main level. "Would *you* issue an order like that if you were Governor? Fire on women and children, just because they're protesting what they see as murder?"

"Of course I would. If they're interfering with the proper functions of the state? If they're threatening the smooth functioning of government? Damn right I would. The people have no business telling the ruling class how to rule!"

"Funny," Frye said. "I always thought that was what democracy was all about."

"Democracy, my dear Major Frye, is a much overrated sham to placate the masses. Too much democracy is nothing more than mob rule, and dangerous. . . ."

Grayson glanced at Frye as the elevator slowed to a halt. "Major Frye?"

"Yes, sir."

"I've heard enough of this, haven't you?"

"Damned straight. Sir."

The door hissed open. Grayson stepped out, followed closely by Frye. "Security," Grayson said, his voice scarcely rising above a murmur. "Carlyle. Take them. Now."

A half dozen men in dark gray armor stepped up close, ringing the party in with the ugly, heat-pitted muzzles of laser rifles and pistols. The two militia guards gaped their astonishment and meekly gave up their weapons, raising their hands. Frye pulled the laser pistol out of Folker's hand and checked him for other weapons. "He's clean."

"No," Grayson said, taking back his sidearm from one of the guards. "He's filthy. But we'll discuss his personal habits later."

"Orders, Colonel?" one of the Legion security men said.

Grayson glanced around the terminal. It was crowded with both civilians and Legion personnel, but there were none of the militia troops in black-and-yellow that had been so evident earlier. "You get this level cleaned out?"

"Yes, sir. Some of them, uh, resisted. We weren't too gentle with 'em, I'm afraid."

"Radio communications?"

"Okay for short range line-of-sight stuff, sir. We're still looking for the source of the jamming."

"What the hell is the meaning of this, Carlyle!" Folker demanded.

"Command Sergeant Lafferty here is my chief of security, Major. He tends to get concerned when I'm out of his sight for too long." Grayson turned to face the security chief. "Lafferty, there are eight more of these militia troopers upstairs in the lounge, holding six of my officers. Some may be coming down already in another elevator. Send a team up to secure things."

"Already done, sir. O'Grady took a team up by the maintenance stairs a few moments ago when I decided you'd been out of sight for too long."

"Well done!"

Folker was looking around the terminal with an expression of complete bewilderment.

"But . . . my men . . ."

"I gave orders to my people to secure this terminal building before you took me on that little sightseeing tour, Major. I dislike having two different armed units controlling the same area. Makes me nervous. There's too much chance for misunderstanding."

"What! You have no right—"

"I am following my orders, Major, and to the letter. My orders are to restore order in the New Edinburgh area, and I have decided to begin with this spaceport. We have dealt with that threat and now control the installation. You can assist us by giving orders to switch off the jamming, which is hindering my forces far more than it could possibly be hindering the rebels."

"Your orders, Colonel, were to place yourself under the direct command of Governor Wilmarth. . . ."

"Whom we still haven't seen. And who, I think, we'd better pay a visit to, right away."

"*I* am the governor's representative, with full—"

"Sergeant Lafferty, be good enough to place the Governor's representative under arrest. Lock him up aboard the *Defiant,* and keep him under guard."

"Yes, sir. A pleasure!"

The explosion shook the entire building, sending a fine spray of glass hurtling across the terminal lounge. Grayson tumbled to the floor, knocked down by the concussion and momentarily stunned. A woman screamed, and men were shouting as white dust boiled through the air. Most of the Legion security men were down as well. Major Frye staggered to his feet, then turned to help Grayson.

"Folker!" Grayson snapped. "He's getting away!"

Folker was running, knocking two women aside as he bolted for a side door. Lafferty drew his laser and took careful aim, but Grayson reached out and lifted the muzzle.

"Too many civilians about," Grayson told him. "Someone might get hurt. Let the son of a bitch go."

Folker plowed through several more civilians in the confusion created by the explosion and vanished through the door. "I hate to see that bastard walk," Frye said, holstering his weapon.

"Looked more like a flat-out run to me, Major. Don't worry about it. We have other things to worry about right now. Sounds like we have 'Mechs out there."

Shouts and warnings echoed through the terminal, punctuated by sharp gunfire. Behind the noise and confusion, the creak and clank of heavy machinery could be heard . . . coming closer.

"Major!" Carlyle ordered. "This building isn't hardened. Get our people back into the lower levels."

"Yes, sir."

"And see if you can clear the civilians out too."

"They'll be in our way. . . ."

"I know. But we can't leave them to be buried or burned up here."

"I wasn't protesting the order, Colonel. Just pointing out a fact. Benford! Imura! Round up those people on that side! Start falling back to the underground levels!"

Through the hole now gaping in the north wall of the terminal, beyond the piles of rubble and broken glass, a black and yellow *Wasp* could be seen moving slowly across the center of the plaza toward the terminal. Its right arm, with the menacing bulk of a laser, was raised. Beyond it, a second 'Mech, a *Locust,* was walking with delicate and mincing steps across the plaza.

Grayson trotted across the terminal floor to a position sheltered by a massive stone pillar, from which he could look out through the gaping hole and into the plaza beyond. Moments ago, that plaza had been packed with people, with demonstrators and agitators protesting Wilmarth's rule. Now, there were still people everywhere, but the mob had broken and scattered. There were people running, people screaming, injured or dead or unconscious lying sprawled on the pavement, a handful of people facing the oncoming *Wasp* with handguns and rocks. . . .

High above the plaza, a green flare streaked into the sky.

What the hell was that all about?

"Colonel!" Frye said behind him. "Our people are falling back to the lower levels. You should get out of here!"

"I'll be along in a minute."

"But sir—"

"Major, what is the status on our 'Mechs?"

"About half are deployed, Colonel. The rest should be out and clear within ten or fifteen minutes." He looked puzzled. "Uh, but . . ."

"But what?"

"Sir, you're *not* going to attack the city, are you?"

"Hell no! But I'm sure as hell going to restore order!"

* * *

"There's the signal!" Alex cried, pointing. Overhead, a brilliant green star fell across the sky, trailing white smoke from the general direction of the spaceport terminal.

" 'Mechs on the move!" McCall said.

"Ready when you are, Major," Alex said, reaching down to key in a line of power plant switches. The AgroMech, already powered up, began to hum and vibrate as the actuators switched on. Alex picked up his Nighthawk helmet and snapped it in place on his suit's shoulder girdle with a sharp half-twist, then gripped the handholds of the jury-rigged laser and thumbed the power feed on. "Ready, Major!"

"Let's move out then," McCall said. He was having some trouble with his own helmet, which was almost impossible to don one-handed.

"Let me help with that," Alex said. "Damn, this was a screwball idea. You shouldn't be trying to work in armor with that shoulder."

"Nonsense, lad." McCall winced as Alex twisted the helmet home in the locking collar. "This shell'll keep me from bangin' the thing worse."

Helmet in place and visor locked down, McCall gave a thumbs-up to the Reiver troops around the AgroMech's feet, then engaged its walker drive. There was a loud popping sound, followed by the clatter of ancient valves. Though power was provided by a fairly modern bank of fuel cells, the main drive was a relic, a smoky, wheezing internal combustion engine.

The machine was clumsy, and moved with an annoying, lurching awkwardness. Unlike a military 'Mech the *Cherry-Picker* didn't have a neurohelmet link to provide balance and orientation feedback directly to the pilot's brain, so operating the thing was more like driving a truck—a bulky, slow, and dull-witted truck—than piloting a BattleMech. A half dozen strides of its four spindly legs and it was out of the warehouse and stepping across the chainlink fence that marked the north edge of the spaceport field.

"Hang on, lad!" McCall cried, nudging the mechanical beast's throttle to full forward. "Let's see what she'll do on th' open road!"

"I think Wilmarth's 'Mechs must've moved faster than the Reivers expected," Alex said. "Look!"

A 'Mech was just visible beyond the bulk of the terminal

building, a black and yellow *Wasp* that appeared to have just opened fire on the crowd. People were fleeing in every direction in blind and terrified panic as the 'Mech began to advance upon the terminal.

Laser fire seared the air just above Alex's head. Spinning, he saw to his horror that the fire had come from the *Defiant*, now looming up above the rim of its grounding pit only a few hundred meters away.

"Watch it!" McCall yelled, and the AgroMech lurched heavily to the left. White contrails scrawled their way across the sky, arcing from the grounded DropShip. Explosions roared on the tarmac nearby.

Gravel clattered off the back of the *CherryPicker* and bounced off Alex's helmet. "Those idiots think we're attacking them!" Alex cried.

"Those *idiots* are doing exactly the right thing," McCall replied, struggling one-handed with the clumsy AgroMech's steering bar. "If there's a battle on and a contraption like this heads for one of *my* DropShips, they'd damn well better shoot."

The original idea had been for the AgroMech to strike out toward the DropShips before any actual shooting started. The 'Mechs guarding the DropShip perimeter should have stopped the intruder, at which point Alex and McCall could have identified themselves.

But in combat, things very rarely, if ever, go exactly as planned. The sudden and unexpected attack by the *Wasp* had pushed the DropShip's defenses to full red alert, and any unidentified piece of equipment coming too close would be subject to fire without warning.

As resources and as unit assets, DropShips were far too precious for it to be otherwise.

"We'd better pull back," Alex said. "We're gonna get flambéed if we keep heading for the DropShips!"

"Aye, lad. I agree." McCall pointed. "We'll make for those supply sheds over there, and see wha' else we can try."

Another explosion thundered close behind the AgroMech, which rode out the shock by dipping sharply to the right on telescoping, jointed legs. Something snapped inside one of the legs, and the 'Mech's number three driver made an ugly, grating noise. Red lights flared on the control panel and the AgroMech took a staggering, halting step before freezing in place. The engine coughed, rattled, and then died with a wheezing sigh. "What do we do now?" Alex asked.

"We surrender," Davis replied. "If they'll let us."

Caitlin DeVries leaned as far forward as she could within the close embrace of her *Griffin*'s command seat, hands on the 'Mech's controls, peering through her viewport. The attack didn't look like much. The *Griffin*'s warbook program couldn't identify the machine stalking across the ferrocrete pavement half a kilometer ahead, but from here it looked like some sort of civilian 'Mech, probably customized for low-intensity combat—a guerrilla special. The political situation on Caledonia was still so damned confused there was no certainty about who might be friendly and who was not. With a sharp, upward slap of her hand, she armed the *Griffin*'s battery of Doombud LRMs.

She swivelled her cockpit assembly left, turning the 'Mech's head as machinery whined around her. Lieutenant Anders's lance, the Combat Lance of First Company/Third Batt, was deployed in an uneven line of three to her left. Hers was the only One-one 'Mech off-loaded so far; the Colonel hadn't debarked yet, and of course Alex and Major McCall were still . . . out there, somewhere. No matter. She would stick tight to the One-three, until she could pick up a wingman. 'Mechs that operated alone in combat, even—or especially?—in guerrilla fights against infantry—tended to end up dead.

"Ah, Combat Three-one," she called over the tactical frequency. Jamming was still bad on all channels, but in line of sight and at close range, the transmissions could still be sorted from the background noise. "This is DeVries, from Command One-one. Mind if I tag along and make your lance an honest foursome?" Combat Lance Three-one had been short one 'Mech, since losing Albrecht Weiss's *Hunchback* on Ueda a few months back.

"Hello, Caitlin," Lawrence Anders's baritone came back, meshed with the static hiss of the jamming. His *Catapult*, a massive, sixty-five-tonner with a sleek fuselage atop splay-footed, back-angled, digitigrade legs, was taking the lead, with Tom Vandermier's *Hunchback* in support. "Welcome aboard. You stick with Sharon while she checks out that intruder."

Sharon was Sergeant Sharon Kilroy, in an old and battered-looking *Vindicator*.

"Hey, Lieutenant," Sharon Kilroy's voice called. "I'm getting hostile 'Mechs, north side of the terminal."

"They're not on my scope yet," Vandermier said.

"Don't worry about the militia 'Mechs," Anders said. "We're to block that intruder. Sharon? You guys have a better angle. How about the two of you move in close, see what we've got."

"Combat Three-one, this is *Endeavor* Combat Command. Watch yourselves. We're reading a laser in that jury-rigged job. It's probably a makeshift ranged weapon . . .

". . . but it could be a trigger for a bomb," Sharon said, completing the unpleasant thought. "Roger that. We'll be careful, mama. C'mon, DeVries. Let's check that buggy out."

"Roger." Caitlin put her *Griffin* into step with Sergeant Kilroy's slightly smaller *Vindicator,* and the two 'Mechs strode across the ferrocrete, bearing down on the distant AgroMech.

Grayson Carlyle reached the *Endeavor*'s 'Mech bay on the run, sliding down the railings of a shipboard ladder rather than taking a slower lift platform. The DropShip's cavernous 'Mech bay was a cluttered tangle of shadowy metal parts, the crisscrossing frameworks of multiple gantries and catwalks, and the great, hulking shapes of the 'Mechs themselves, half lost in the shadows, with highlights here and there picked out by spotlights set into bulkheads and on elevated access walkways. The bay deck was made hazardous by the speeding, weaving electric carts trundling out loads of rockets and cassettes of autocannon shells from munitions lockers to 'Mechs. Everywhere, techs and assistant techs were working with the frantic yet meticulously choreographed urgency of imminent combat. On the far side of the bay, daylight dazzled the eye as an external hatch slid open; a *Guillotine* was moving into the debarkation elevator, its movements cast as shifting black silhouettes against the glare from outside.

Grayson's VTR-9K *Victor* had already been broken out of its storage cocoon and rigged in its ready gantry. It stood there in the shadows lifeless, limp as a puppet strung from a rack, a slouch to its shoulders and torso and its arms dangling free at its sides. The Legion's current crew chief, Tech Sergeant Brunner tossed him a jaunty, two-fingered salute as Grayson trotted up to the boarding lift and hit the button on the frame.

"She's ready and charged, Colonel!" Brunner called up to Grayson as he rose. "Take it easy on the jumps, though. I'm still worried about the lower-leg shocks!"

Those leg shocks had been worrying Brunner for months. Eighty-ton BattleMechs weren't really meant for jump-jet flights, and a *Victor's* touchdown after flight could be hard on the hydraulics that cushioned the landings.

"Don't worry, Jim!" Grayson shouted down in reply. "I'll bring your baby back in one piece!"

The cockpit hatch was open, splitting the *Victor's* rounded helm to reveal the close-set complexity of consoles, screens, and instrumentation within. Grayson slid down into the control seat feet first, slapped the cockpit power, and hit the hatch close switch.

All around him, lights showed green or amber, and electronics gave off a faint and reassuring hum. Reaching up and back, he grasped the neurohelmet from its rack above and behind the seat and swung it down, positioning it over his shoulders and checking the connectors. He was still wearing his shipboard jumpsuit; there'd been no time to change to cooling vest or other MechWarrior paraphernalia, but this wasn't likely to be a long or grueling engagement, not against the 'Mechs Wilmarth would be likely to field.

The *Victor* had an unusually large cockpit display, with a tall, reinforced transparent fiber-plastic alloy windscreen forward, and large viewscreens mounted to left and right to give an almost seamless, unparalleled breadth of view. Though his primary control console blocked part of the forward window, he could look down between his knees and see through the 'Mech's chin port. Brunner waved up at him, gave him a thumbs-up, then hurried to the side, out of the way.

"This is Command One-one," Grayson said, speaking into the neurohelmet's mike. "Coming on line."

"Command One-one, this is *Endeavor* Tactical Command. We have you on-line, 'Mech Bay One, and ready to march."

"Request debarkation queue interrupt, command priority." Grayson continued to run through the checklist as he spoke, switching on systems, bringing the *Victor* from standby to full operational combat mode. Left arm twin lasers . . . powered up and check. SRM 4s, tubes loaded, safeties on. Check. Gauss rifle . . . power on, magnetics engaged, safeties on. Check. Matabushi Sentinel targeting/tracking system . . . operational, powered up, diagnostics clear, DropShip telecommunications relays engaged. Check. Communications, go . . . though the jamming would render his Siphur Security Plus unit useless more than a few kilometers out. Good enough for close work, though. Check.

"Command One-one, Tactical Command. You are clear for immediate debarkation. You may march when ready."

"Roger that. Command One-one, moving."

Gently, Grayson set the ponderous, eighty-ton 'Mech in forward motion, taking one step clear of the support gantry, then another. Spinning about in their hoods, warning beacons on the gantry walkways flashed and pulsed at the *Victor*'s knee level, sending crescent-shaped smears of bright yellow illumination chasing one another across the irregular surfaces of deck and gantry and other 'Mechs, clearing the bright yellow munitions trucks and fast-moving technicians and 'Mech crews from his path. A half-dozen steps took him across the open deck and up to the elevator, which was just rising into place to accept the *Victor*'s weight. Stepping aboard, Grayson used the 'Mech's left hand to steady himself on a support strut. With a high-pitched whine of machinery, the platform trundled down its framework, dropping Grayson into daylight. He emerged from beneath the vast and overhanging loom of the spherical DropShip on the floor of the landing pit. A ferrocrete ramp just ahead rose forty meters to the landing field outside the pit.

Data flickered across his monitors and down the right side of his HUD. Three hostile 'Mechs had been detected, two north of the terminal—but he knew about them already—and another that had broken onto the landing field and was approaching the DropShip *Defiant,* about three kilometers east from Grayson's position.

That 'Mech appeared to have been stopped, and the Legion's defensive perimeter had walled it off. Much closer to Grayson's current position were the *Wasp* and the *Locust,* both of which at last report were still attacking the panicked mob in front of the terminal.

He had to stop that slaughter.

He fired his jump jets, and the thunder echoed across the

spaceport, the air dancing and shimmering in the wash of heat from his venturis. Slowly, the huge 'Mech rose into the sky, drifting past the port's observation tower and just clearing the terminal roof. He came down, flexing the 'Mech's knees and increasing the thrust at the last moment, trying to keep the stress off the *Victor*'s bad hydraulics.

Ahead, eighty meters distant, the black and yellow *Wasp* loomed above the panicked crowd of civilians. Grayson moved forward, walking slowly but with meticulous deliberation, taking care not to step on anyone. The *Wasp* turned to face him, and Grayson could see something in its attitude that seemed to reflect the puzzlement its pilot must be feeling. Wilmarth's people had no doubt been told that the Legion would be fighting on their side, but the *Victor*'s menacing advance must have him wondering.

At the last moment, the Bloodspiller pilot panicked and began backpedaling his *Wasp*, its medium laser swinging up to fire. Grayson fired first. With a shrill, harsh chirp and then a thundercrack that shattered glass for hundreds of meters around, the Gauss rifle mounted on his right arm accelerated a massive nickle-iron slug with a core of depleted uranium to hypersonic velocities.

The round slammed into the *Wasp*'s upper right torso, opening a gash of a crater, ripping off the right arm entirely and sending it spinning end over end across the street. The shock staggered the little 'Mech and nearly knocked it down. Correcting his aim, Grayson sent a second hypersonic screamer squarely into the *Wasp*'s center of mass. The impact picked the twenty-ton machine up and dropped it on its back; it slid across black pavement, striking sparks for ten meters before it came to rest.

Grayson advanced closer, his Gauss rifle raised and ready for another shot, but the *Wasp* was already dead. Blue lightnings played in the two holes in its chest and danced from the severed power leads dangling from its shattered shoulder.

"Striker, Striker, this is Command One," Grayson called over the infantry channel. "Let's have this one open."

He should be close enough, still, for radio contact with Lafferty. . . .

"Command One, Striker," Lafferty's voice replied, barely audible through the squeal and hiss of static. "A team's on the way."

Grayson stood above the fallen body of the *Wasp*. The question was whether or not the pilot still lived. The *Wasp*'s pilot might know something about that Nighthawk-clad man who'd fallen into the canyon before the Citadel. . . .

Something made him stop. Thinking furiously, he called up a map on his tactical display. That intruder at the spaceport had come from a different direction than these other two. The *Wasp* and the *Locust* could have been a diversion, of course, and yet . . .

"Tactical Command, Command One-one," Grayson called. "What do you have on a hostile intruder moving onto the spaceport field, uh, that would be map coordinates three-five-one by one-one-two. Over?"

"Command, Tactical. Negative on hard data yet for the intruder. It appears to be a jury-rigged Agro. It was moving toward the *Defiant* when the shooting started. The *Defiant* returned fire, and it has moved back, possibly damaged, though we can't tell for sure. We have a lance out that way now, investigating."

"Tactical Command, this is Air Show One," another voice called. "We have the intru—"

The transmission was lost in a fresh burst of static.

Damn! What was going on out there? Grayson was filled with a sudden, deep forboding. A jury-rigged AgroMech?

Davis McCall . . . and Alex. If they needed to reach the DropShips fast, there weren't that many ways to pull it off . . .

. . . save, possibly, to rig up an old AgroMech to carry you across the open ferrocrete at a fast clip. Hell, the demonstration could have been the diversion, set to keep Wilmarth's people busy while they made their break.

"Air Show, Air Show," he called. "This is Command One-one. Do you copy?"

"Command, this is Air Show One." The voice was badly broken by static. They *had* to do something about this jamming! He lost several words in the surf-crash of white noise. ". . . attack run. I'm going in!"

"Negative, Air Show! Negative! Do not attack! Repeat, do not attack the AgroMech!"

The only reply from Carla Staedler in her *Corsair* was the hiss of static.

* * *

Lieutenant Carla Staedler pushed the stick of her CSR-V12 *Corsair* forward, watching the horizon swing up above the nose of her fighter as she plunged toward the spaceport field like a swooping bird of prey. The battlefield was spread out beneath her gaze like a gameboard, all small, neat pieces, not yet soiled and cluttered by the smoke, burning buildings, and scattered wreckage that marked a battle later in its evolution. The jamming had just cut her off from Legion Tactical Command, but that scarcely mattered now. She could see the Gray Death 'Mechs forming up to her left, throwing out a defensive line between the intruder and the grounded DropShips. Directly ahead, the spaceport terminal appeared to have taken several hits from the militia BattleMechs still moving through the plaza. The real threat, though, to her mind, was the lone, toylike AgroMech stilting its way across the spaceport landing field. Carla had been an aerospace pilot assigned to the Gray Death Legion DropShip *Endeavor* for only two years, now. She'd made her lieutenancy just six months ago, after the Glengarry campaign, but she'd been a DropShip aerospace jock long enough to pick up the cardinal rule of that breed: *always* protect your DropShip! Even an AgroMech could do serious damage to hatchways and seals and communications gear if it managed to get too close to a grounded Dropper.

Target acquisition . . . the HUD cross hairs dropping across the target, then flashing to signify a lock. She flipped the switch that engaged both medium and large lasers, bringing them on line. Target lock! *Fire!*

Her thumb came down on the firing switch, and the AgroMech, so toylike as the *Corsair* bore down on it in glorious, booming thunder, was engulfed in flame. . . .

23

New Edinburgh Spaceport
Caledonia, Skye March
Federated Commonwealth
1451 hours, 13 April 3057

The AgroMech had frozen in place, one leg raised clear of the ground, the other three locked and unmoving. Agricultural machinery had to be tough, but was rarely built strong enough to stand up to combat.

For several moments, McCall and Alex had stayed where they were, watching the relentless advance of two Legion 'Mechs across the spaceport—a *Vindicator* and a *Griffin*. Alex was pretty sure from the numbers and hull markings that the *Vindie* was Sergeant Kilroy's First Company Combat Lance machine, but who was the *Griffin*?

And just as he realized who that 'Mech's pilot must be, McCall grabbed his shoulder, pointing to the south. "Trouble, lad! Punch out! Now!"

Alex saw the oncoming aerofighter just as a stuttering barrage of laser bursts bracketed the AgroMech, shearing through one of the legs as cleanly as any vibroblade. The balky internal-combustion engine burst into flames and thick, oily smoke.

Flexing his knees, Alex fired his Nighthawk suit's jump jets. The cockpit filled with swirling smoke and superheated air, and then, jets howling, he was sailing across the tarmac just as a Gray Death Legion *Corsair*, its needle nose painted with a vivid shark's face, thundered low overhead, hurtling north.

Where were those BattleMechs? There! Shifting his weight to the right, he adjusted his course slightly, then increased his speed. . . .

"Launch! I've got a hostile launch!" Caitlin yelled over the intercom. She'd seen the AgroMech explode. Pieces of the thing were still raining down across the black ferrocrete pavement of the spaceport. At the last possible instant, though, something had streaked up out of the agricultural machine and veered straight toward her *Griffin*. It was moving too slowly to be a missile, though it could be some sort of remote control device. She pivoted her *Griffin*'s upper torso right, raising her right arm as she turned to acquire the target. The thing was coming too fast for her to dodge out of the way, but she might still knock it down with a burst of autocannon or laser fire.

Then she realized what she was seeing. "Negative! Negative on that launch! Don't fire!"

Even thirty meters away, the Nighthawk suit seemed to blur its own outline and was difficult to follow with the eye. It was moving much more slowly now, and Caitlin could make out the man's overall form and recognize the design of the suit.

"All units!" she announced. "I've got one of them! I've got one of them!" It wasn't exactly a concise or informative report, but everyone in the unit would know what she was talking about.

One of the men posted to Caledonia had just been spotted.

The man-shape slowed to a hover, the last bit of thrust from his jump very nearly exhausted. Nursing his dwindling thrust across those last few meters, he closed on Caitlin's *Griffin*, then collided with her upper torso with a metallic clang.

Caitlin found herself staring into her own face reflected in the shiny visor of the Nighthawk's helmet. Then the visor slid up, and she was looking into Alex's clear, blue eyes.

"Caitlin!" he yelled, his voice picked up on her external mikes. "Caitlin, I know you must still be mad, but please don't shoot me! I've changed! Really I have! . . ."

* * *

Grayson urged his *Victor* forward. He was too far away to pick out details, but he'd seen the low, strafing run by the *Corsair*, seen the explosion of the AgroMech that was now sending a greasy black pall into the blue afternoon sky over the starport.

"All units!" a voice said over his headset. "This is Caitlin DeVries! I've got Alex here! He's safe!"

Something sagged deep within Grayson, and the *Victor* very nearly faltered. Alex ... safe ...

Somehow, he kept his voice level and his response to business. "Caitlin! This is Colonel Carlyle. Any sign of Major McCall?"

"Negative, Colonel. Alex says they were together. He thinks the Major jumped the same time he did, but he didn't see for sure."

"Did you see anything?"

"No, Colonel. I just saw Alex jump clear an instant before that junker exploded."

Davis couldn't be dead. Not from friendly fire! No, it wasn't possible ...

"All Legion 'Mechs, keep an eye out for Major McCall! He may be out on the ground somewhere, and he may be hurt! Advance the perimeter line and try to find him!"

Grayson had brought his *Victor* around the terminal, passing through the spaceport perimeter fence, shredding steel mesh like so many threads. Now, he urged the big 'Mech ahead, angling toward the smoking ruin of the AgroMech. Overhead, two *Corsairs* circled.

"God, Colonel," a woman's voice said, blasted by static. "I'm sorry! I thought I had a fire order!"

"Don't worry about it, Air Show. Just keep the real hostiles off our backs while we complete our search!"

"Roger that! The enemy *Locust* appears to be withdrawing. He may have been frightened off by your 'Mech deployment."

"Frighten him some more, if you can do it without hitting any civilians in the street."

"Roger, Command One-one."

And then Grayson saw him, a lone figure made fuzzy by the chameleon armor he wore. The figure was moving across the endless black flatness of the spaceport field, walking away from the smoking pyre of the AgroMech.

Grayson edged his *Victor* closer, until he towered two meters above the Nighthawk-suited man. "That had better be you inside that suit, McCall," he said, using his eternal voice circuits rather than the radio. They should have agreed on tactical frequencies before the mission, Grayson thought with some small disgust. Neither McCall nor Alex would have been able to radio the 'Mechs directly, and with the jamming, they'd been too far to get a clear signal through to the DropShips.

"Aye, sir," the figure said, and he raised his visor. "It's me. But I'm afraid m' wee bairn here is a bit th' worse for wear!"

He turned around, and Grayson saw that the entire back-pack unit, housing power supply and jump jets, had been mangled by the *Corsair*'s laser beam.

"I got aboot three meters clear a' the AgroMech," McCall continued, "an' suddenly, this bluidy thing was nae workin' a' all! I ended up heels over head, wi' the 'Mech goin' up in flames aboot me!"

"Just so *you're* working, Davis. I don't think I could manage without you. Welcome back to the Gray Death!"

Four hours later, the Gray Death was in complete control of New Edinburgh, the spaceport, and the approaches to Mount Alba and the Citadel. Grayson returned to the *Endeavor* and there, in the DropShip's small conference room, he at last clasped the arm of Davis McCall and fiercely embraced his son.

"To say I'm glad to see you two would be pushing the art of understatement a bit far," he told them. Both men looked drawn and haggard, and McCall's arm was immobilized in a sling. "What the hell happened to you, Davis?"

"Th' wee bastards winged m' arm, sair," McCall said, letting his burr drip the broad Highland vowels and rolled Rs. "But it takes more than tha' t' downcheck th' likes a' me."

"Five days ago, I was ... shown a vid of someone in a Nighthawk suit kneecapping a *Victor*, then getting hit by laser fire while he was evading. Was that you?"

"Aye, sir, it was, I'm ashamed to admit. I must be losin' m' touch, for the Sasunnach to hae their way wi' me like tha'."

Grayson smiled. "I thought I recognized your combat style there, Major. Well, I'm glad you made it, glad both of you made it. Davis ... I owe you an apology. I shouldn't have sent you here in the first place. Not the way things have worked out."

"Actually, they've worked out vurra well, Colonel. We got my brother out a' th' governor's vacation home, Alex an' me. Thanks t' tha', I may be on speakin' terms wi' a' least some of my family noo."

"Some of them, eh? Well, that's good news." Grayson turned to his son. "Alex? You're looking ... well." He couldn't quite put his finger on the difference, but there was one. His son seemed more confident, more self-assured than he had in many months.

Alex grinned at him. "Maybe I just got some priorities straight." The grin faded and he shook his head. "There's some bad business going down around here, Dad. They *wanted* the Gray Death to come here, and I think they meant to use us against the local population, to keep them quiet and in line."

"More than that," Grayson said, noting his son's use of the word *us*. "I received direct orders this afternoon to raze the city and turn our weapons against the people. I don't know what's going on here, but it looks to me like someone—Folker or the Governor—wanted the Legion implicated in a massacre."

"Like Sirius V all over again," McCall said, rubbing his bearded chin with his good hand.

Grayson nodded. Decades ago, a faction within House Marik had caused the Legion to be blacklisted and disgraced by cracking the dome of Tiantan on Sirius V, a poisonous hellhole of a world, in a plot to seize the Legion's landhold on Helm. Success all too often bred enemies, and when those enemies were both powerful and greedy they would go to any lengths to secure what they wanted.

"Y' know, sir," McCall added, "I believe it goes a wee bit higher than Wee Willie. Folker is a cheap thug who struck it big time, God knows why. And Wilmarth is insane."

"Is that a clinical diagnosis, Major?"

"Near enough. The man kills for th' fun of it an' enjoys power for its own sake."

"You could say that about a lot of MechWarriors."

"The Major's right, Dad." Briefly, and with an obvious effort, Alex began describing what he and McCall had seen during their visit to the Citadel two weeks ago.

"He rules by sheer terror and arbitrary bloody-mindedness," Alex concluded. "My impression was that

Folker was providing any efficiency this government might have and that he was acting on orders from someone else."

"Can you substantiate any of that? That he's acting on orders?"

Alex shook his head. "No, sir. I can't. But I can give you ten thousand more eye-witness accounts of what Wilmarth's rule has been like for the past few years. Dad, we've got to help these people!"

Grayson sighed, folding his arms across his chest. "I don't deny that. I do find myself, find the Legion, in a hellishly difficult spot, though." He cocked an eye at McCall. "Major, I dislike being manipulated. I dislike seeing the Legion manipulated. That, more than anything else, is what turned me against Folker in the first place. It was clear to me he wanted to use us for his own power politics, or those of his superior. But you were worse than he was."

"Sir!"

"Dad!"

"The two of you made promises to these people that were in direct opposition to the orders I received from Tharkad. I find myself forced to choose between breaking those promises, and ordering this unit to go rogue and attack our employer's forces."

"Dad, we never meant—"

"I know, I know." Grayson was suddenly very tired. He brought both hands to his face, rubbing his eyes. "I would very much like to know what we're supposed to do now."

McCall scowled. "Sir, it seems t' me tha' there is no argument here. *I* made the promises to the rebels. You can disavow my actions an' court-martial me for exceedin' my authority. Perhaps you'd aye best do just tha' when this is over, no matter what else happens. But you can nae attack these people. They are fightin' for their own, for their homes, their families, their security, an' their freedom. T' back the likes a' Folker an' Wilmarth against them, well, sir, as much as it pains me t' say it, you'd have to fight me as well, because I would be oot there wi' 'em."

"That goes for me too, Dad," Alex said. His face was hard, and worried. "Throwing in with Wilmarth is just plain *wrong*."

"Alex, Davis, both of you know that it's impossible to run a mercenary regiment on good feelings, pretty words, or chivalric sentiment. This is a *business*, and not a crusade."

Grayson paused a moment, watching the dismay on their faces. "But ..." He stopped again, then shrugged. "There are also some things that have to be done, because not doing them would be to deny yourself and who you are. There will be no court-martial, Major. From what you've described, I would have made the same decision if it had been me here and not you. I would have made the same decision if Folker had ordered me to fire even if I hadn't suspected that you two were still out there, somewhere, working with the resistance. But—just for the future, mind you—you will both remember that intelligence operations are not conducted for the purpose of choosing sides or for volunteering our time and resources!"

"Aye, sir."

"Yes, sir."

"In particular, I dislike contingency contracts. I doubt that we're going to recover a tenth of what we expend on this op ... and by the time we're done, no one in the Federated Commonwealth will ever hire us again." He thought for a moment of Francis Collins, the Gray Death's Disbursing Officer, and Dobbs, the Supply Officer. "Collins and Dobbs are going to have my hide on this one!"

A chime sounded. "Come," Grayson called.

Captain Allison Lang entered the conference room. Major Frye's executive officer and number two in his Command Lance, she was a trim, attractive, and highly competent woman who also served as Third Battalion's intelligence officer.

"Yes, Captain?"

"Sorry for the interruption, Colonel," she said. "But radar has just picked up high-altitude ionization trails in the stratosphere, coming down beyond the curve of the planet to the northwest."

"Descending?"

"Yes, sir. Ops thinks they're DropShips, inbound."

"You have a hard trajectory on them yet?"

"They went down well beyond the horizon, Colonel, so we couldn't get a precise fix. Best guess, though, is the Stirling area."

"Just about one thousand kilometers to the northwest, Colonel, gi' or take a few," McCall said. "An' there's a spaceport there almost as big as New Edinburgh's."

"Folker told me Wilmarth was bringing in another unit," Grayson said. "The Third Davion Guards."

"Aye, an' they've already got 'Mechs deployed here. Those two *Victor*s y' saw in tha' video segment were Third Guard. Some of th' locals went down and got tha' information for us."

"Damn!"

"How'd they get all the way to Caledonia without our seeing them?" Alex wanted to know.

"Tha' would nae be a problem, lad," McCall said. "They could hae come through a' the nadir jump point. We would nae hae seen 'em a' all."

"More likely they used a pirate point," Grayson said. "The impression I had from Wilmarth was that they wouldn't be here for several days yet. But if they were loaded and ready to go at Hesperus, and if their navigational data were sharp enough to let them arrive at a pirate point within a day's flight or so of Caledon ..."

"Those ion trails," Lang said, "are consistent with a pirate-point approach. They re-entered over Caledonia's night side and closer to the equatorial plane than a flight coming down the hypotenuse from the zenith or nadir system points."

"Any chance we can get these people on our side?" Alex asked.

"We'll give it a try," Grayson said. "But don't hold your breath. If Third Guard 'Mechs are already here and working for the government, it's because some sort of deal has already been struck." He cracked a wry smile. "Just because we're willing to go chasing off on some damn fool crusade for justice, it doesn't mean everybody else on the planet is going to do the same!"

"Well, it looks like the vacation is over, Colonel," Allison Lang said. "The local militia isn't good for much more than target practice, but the Third Davion is a top-notch outfit."

"Yes, it is. Captain, I want a complete report on the Third Guard. Command staff. Assessments. Whatever you can find in Third Batt's data base."

"Yes, sir."

"Immediately."

"Ten minutes, sir."

"Good enough." As Lang left the conference room, Grayson reached over to the table-top console and keyed in a request. The wall screen switched on, showing a computer-enhanced view of the Citadel seen from the air.

"Well, gentlemen," he said. "We will assume that the Third Guard is landing at Stirling and that we're going to be its target. First things first, however. This position has to be neutralized. Our communications people have confirmed that it's the source of the jamming we've been struggling with, and it's the key to controlling everything between the Alba Mountains and the Firth of Moray. Furthermore, I will not move north against the Third Guard with a strongpoint like this in my rear. Gentlemen? Do either of you have any idea as to how we can take this place down, with minimum losses to ourselves?"

They began discussing the tactical possibilities.

24

The Citadel
Caledonia, Skye March
Federated Commonwealth
0200 hours, 14 April 3057

The capture of the Citadel in the dark hours of the following morning was almost anticlimactic. Grayson led one company, twelve 'Mechs, up the mountain road, dispersing them through the woods before they reached the canyon. Jamming was still heavy—and getting stronger as they neared its source—but the MechWarriors had rehearsed their moves many times already, using holographic simulations aboard the *Endeavor*.

The Citadel was laid out in such a way that 'Mechs trying to use jump jets to clear the walls would be excellent targets for the batteries of turret-mounted lasers in the towers above wall and barbican and keep. Grayson had elected to use a different strategy, however. From the cover of the woods, the Fire Lance of Third Batt's Second Company—an *Apollo* and two *Catapults*, with a *JagerMech* providing support—opened up with everything they had, sending a cloud of missiles streaking through the night sky of Caledonia. From inside the black walls of the Citadel, explosions flashed and thundered. One tower took a direct hit that detonated ammo stores, the pyrotechnics lighting the face of the mountain and leaving the tower a jaggedly truncated stump.

And as the bombardment continued, Grayson marched his

Victor to the near side of the bridge, raised his Gauss rifle, and sent round after hypersonic round slamming through the massive gate. The rounds possessed no explosive, no warheads, but kinetic energy alone battered the massive gates back on warped tracks, set solid duralloy steel to glowing white hot, and brought down an avalanche of crumbling stone from the surrounding walls. The laser batteries atop the barbican had been knocked out by Alex and Davis during their raid two weeks before and had not been repaired. The closer Grayson's *Victor* came to the gate, still hammering away at it with round after round, the less the defensive batteries atop the keep could bear. As the *Victor* smashed aside the remnant of those gates, Second Company's Medium Lance charged, rushing the bridge, crowding past Grayson's 'Mech and through the open barbican, and bursting into the courtyard beyond.

A signal flare burned through the night. With a roar, the two *Catapults* of the Fire Lance soared up out of the woods on white-hot thrusters, crossing the canyon and coming to roost like enormous and highly improbable birds atop the Citadel walls. Laser fire lanced down from the keep, but the rain of missiles and the fire from the courtyard had knocked that line of Wilmarth's defenses down to almost nothing. Now, with a direct line of sight on the surviving batteries, round after round, salvo after salvo, streaked through the air and slammed home in savage, blinding detonations that hurled thunder echoing down off the mountainside.

The final assault, however, came from twenty Nighthawk-armored commandos who earlier in the night had positioned themselves among the rocks and cliffs behind and above the keep. With the Citadel's defenses focused entirely on the frontal attack by the Legion's 'Mechs, the commandos used their jump jets to descend out of the night, land atop the keep's roof, and blast their way through locked and guarded doorways. With McCall's arm keeping him out of the action, Alex headed up the commandos. Using his knowledge of the stronghold—both what he had gathered on his own and what had been passed on by Reivers rebels—he lead his team down through the heart of the keep and seized the main command center.

After that, the battle became an interlocking series of minor skirmishes, as hold-outs were discovered and snipers flushed. Another thirty prisoners were released from

Wilmarth's dungeon—several who'd stayed behind during the prison break engineered by Alex and McCall, and the men and women scooped up by the Bloodspillers during the riot the previous day, before the Gray Death 'Mechs had deployed and spoiled their fun.

There was no sign of Wilmarth, of Folker, or of their staffs. The Citadel's defense had been entrusted to some two hundred Bloodspiller infantrymen, under the command of a captain, now dead. Those who surrendered knew nothing about the Governor's future plans, nor had they been told anything about the DropShip landings at Stirling. Their leaders had fled hours before the Gray Death's assault, leaving the troops to defend the fortress on their own without even a single BattleMech to back them up.

Lieutenant Rodney Leitner, however, proved to be a platinum mine of information.

Leitner was the pilot of the *Wasp* Grayson had taken out in front of the spaceport terminal. Pulled unconscious from the close confines of his cockpit, he'd been taken first to the *Endeavor*'s sickbay for treatment, and then, once the Citadel was taken, to the far better medical facilities there. He was not badly injured, it turned out, and though at first he had refused to talk, Captain Lang's quiet promise to have him turned over to the people of Caledonia for trial as a war criminal broke the last of his resistance. Lang further ensured Leitner's cooperation by showing his prisoner three-D vids of some of the horrors discovered inside the Citadel, suggesting that these might be used as evidence at his trial.

A citizen of Gladius originally, the lieutenant had served with the Third Davion Guards for five years, having spent most of that time on Hesperus II. He'd been one of twenty-five Guardsmen who'd volunteered for special duty—and the extra pay that had come with the assignment.

That posting, he'd told Gray's intelligence staff, had been viewed as easy duty, with the Guardsmen and the pilots and techs for two *Victor*s serving as advisors to the scumbag troops of a backwater militia. While on Caledonia, he said, they'd taken their orders from Major Folker. But on Hesperus, their commanding officer, the man who'd given them their assignment and their briefings, was Marshal Felix Zellner. Normally, Leitner explained, he piloted a *Jager-Mech*, but his 'Mech hadn't been brought along on this operation, and for the most part he'd served as an advisor to

Wilmarth's 'Mech techs. Usually, either the regular militia pilot or Folker himself operated Wilmarth's *Wasp*, but the Bloodspiller had been killed in the courtyard the night of the raid, and Folker had been otherwise employed during the fight at the spaceport, so he'd filled in. He hadn't *liked* the orders to fire on an unarmed crowd, Leitner said, but disobeying orders would have meant death . . . or worse. Wilmarth had personally and slowly executed two of the volunteers the previous week for what he'd perceived as their inadequacies in the defense of the Citadel against Caledonian rebels.

The chilling part of the story, at least from Grayson's perspective, was the fact that there was really nothing special about Leitner. The man seemed perfectly commonplace; he had a wife and two children back on Hesperus II, a good combat record, and marks on his proficiency reports ranging from fair to good, with one gig for having gone AWOL two years before. That someone so *ordinary* should be able to close his eyes to the extraordinary horrors perpetrated in the Citadel by Wilmarth and his torturers . . .

In any case, Leitner had provided the Gray Death's intelligence staff with an invaluable and up-to-date picture of the Third Davion Guards. They were described as veteran troops in most force listings, but after hearing Captain Lang's report, Grayson thought it likely that they'd lost some of their edge after several years of garrison duty on Hesperus II. Their commanding officer was Marshal James Seymour, a political appointee, but by all accounts a talented if somewhat predictable officer capable of inspiring near-fanatical devotion in his people. The Guards would be tough opponents, garrison duty or not.

By the time the sun was rising on the morning of the fourteenth, Grayson was inside the still smoke-stinking cavern of the Citadel's Command Center with his battle staff, going over every detail of local planetography to which they had access.

There would be a battle with the Third Guards, he was certain of that. Though no hard data were in yet, the number of ion trails sent to the northwest suggested well over a battalion of 'Mechs inbound—possibly even the entire regiment—and it would not be long before they linked up with whatever was left of the Bloodspiller militia. As usual, the Legion would be badly outnumbered.

The only way they could win was if Grayson could choose carefully the ground of the battle.

Alex led Caitlin by the hand up a narrow, rocky path through thickly wooded slopes on the south face of Mount Alba, just above the Citadel. There was almost no hope whatsoever of finding a quiet, private place for an intimate hour or two aboard a DropShip, and Alex had long since given up trying to find one. Nor did he care for the Citadel as a rendezvous for the two of them; the bodies hanging in the courtyard and strung from the rafters of Wilmarth's throne room had been taken down and buried early that morning by a delegation from New Edinburgh, but the stink of the place lingered still, and the blood-awful memory of what he'd seen there would remain long after the smell was gone.

He'd found this place last night, when he'd led his team of commandos up through the woods and around behind the Citadel, to a point where they could fly down out of the trees, across the fortress's north wall, and onto the roof of the keep.

The path opened onto a rocky ledge, its top sheared off by some ancient landslide, an eyrie providing a spectacular view to the south. Almost below their feet was the Citadel, still black and imposing, but bustling now with both Gray Death troops and with a working party of civilians sent up from the town to inspect the place, record Wilmarth's crimes, and clean it out. Beyond, the canyon that served as moat for the Citadel opened up into a broad and wooded valley, while New Edinburgh and its suburbs lay in a majestic sprawl on the shores of the Firth of Moray. The spaceport was a vast, dark smudge on the horizon, with the three DropShips just barely visible in their grounding pits.

They sat on a boulder back a little ways from the edge, admiring the view.

"You *have* changed, Alex," Caitlin said, taking his hand. "What happened to you?"

Alex tried to smile, but the effects of nearly thirty hours without sleep were beginning to catch up with him. It reminded him that his father *had* ordered him to get some sleep; technically, he was violating orders ... again.

"I'm still not entirely sure, Cait," he said, stifling a yawn with the back of his fist. "I think, though, it has to do with commitment."

"How?"

"I guess I've always wondered if Davis Clay died for nothing, died because he was trying to help me, and only succeeded in getting himself killed. I've been, well, hypersensitive since then about how my orders, my decisions, the things I do or don't do, might lead to getting people I care about killed or hurt."

"I think it's called accepting responsibility, Alex."

"Yeah, well, I never really had a choice about whether I wanted to be saddled with that responsibility. I was always, you know, Grayson Carlyle's son, the next great Gray Death Mechwarrior."

"You've told me. What's different now?"

Reaching down, Alex picked up a rock on the ground next to the boulder they were sitting on. It was part crystal, the natural facets catching the orange sunlight and striking fire against his hand. "I think, Cait, what I needed to know was that what I did, me, Alex Carlyle, really could count for something, apart from what my title or rank or who my father was. I needed to know I wasn't just going through the motions, a robot following orders like that Leitner creep. I needed to know I was, well, this sounds corny, but I needed to know that I was on the *side* of good. Making a difference." He chucked the rock over the ledge, watching it sparkle as it plunged into emptiness. "Otherwise, everything I did . . . everything people like Davis Clay died for, it was for nothing, see?"

Caitlin reached out, put her arms around Alex, and kissed him deeply. He relaxed in her warm and fragrant embrace, savoring her softness.

"You know," he said, after a long while. "We really shouldn't, um, get involved out here. I'm so tired, I can hardly stand up. . . ."

"Then you should take a nap," she whispered in his ear. "Right here."

He could feel her fingers unsnapping the catches in his clothing.

"But—"

"Lie down. I'll help you. . . ."

They had no blanket, but their clothing would pad the rough spots on the ground. Soon they were totally absorbed in one another, and even Alex's tiredness could not block his enjoyment of this loving woman.

Neither of them saw the RX-30 SpyEye perched among the branches of a tree ten meters away.

"Baby, baby, *baby*! . . ."

The words were low and murmured, barely audible, a softly chanted litany of lust.

George Sidney Groton was a 'Mech tech, a native of Glengarry who'd joined the Legion less than a year ago. Though his duties normally kept him occupied in a Legion 'Mech Bay, his technical expertise with electronics occasionally got him out of the 'Mech drek and behind a sensor or electronics suite. That was how he happened to be in the Citadel command center today, operating an RX-30.

SpyEyes, as they were popularly known, were small gadgets used by governments and militaries throughout the Inner Sphere, especially by the various security agencies. They were little more than a camera and a transmitter mounted on six walking legs, a primitive, battery-powered robot small enough to hold in the palm of your hand. Too slow and too fragile to be efficient as scouts in battle, they were invaluable as silent, near-invisible sentries around a military base—especially out in the wilderness where they could scuttle behind rocks or vegetation or, with the aid of small, sharp hooks on their feet, even climb trees.

And right now, Groton had SpyEye Seven in a tree about three meters off the ground, and he was focusing in on Caitlin—a gorgeous girl, daughter of the Governor of Glengarry, no less, that he'd drooled over in his fantasies even before either of them had joined the Legion—while she did a number on the Colonel's kid.

"Oh baby, baby, ba—"

A hand and arm dropped across his field of vision, blocking the view of a great deal of lovely, pale skin and snicking off the camera feed with an angry stab of one finger.

"Give me one good reason, Mister, why I shouldn't arrest you on the spot."

"C-Colonel! I'm, I mean, I, I, I didn't see you—"

"Obviously." Carlyle snicked off an entire line of switches on the console, killing the power in the distant remote. "Voyeurism isn't a crime in the Legion," Carlyle said darkly. "With no privacy to begin with, rules to make slimes like you keep their eyes to themselves are a bit silly. However, when individuals go out of their way to spy on brother and sister Legionnaires, I'm damned tempted to add it to the sixteen farms."

Groton swallowed hard and had to work to keep from falling out of his chair. To most techs, Grayson Carlyle was a bigger-than-life figure, heroic, remote, talked about but rarely seen. To have the man descend on you like this was worse than facing a BattleMech unarmed and unarmored. The "sixteen farms" Carlyle had mentioned were the sixteen paragraphs in the Gray Death's *Regimental General Orders* that ended with the ominous phrase, "shall be punishable by death, or by such other punishment as a court-martial may direct."

The sixteen ways a man could "buy the farm" in the Legion, short of actually getting killed in combat, things like murder, rape, betrayal of unit secrets to the enemy, or refusing a direct order in combat.

"What's your name, Mister?"

"G-Gordon. Sir. 'Mech tech, Third Battalion."

Carlyle made an entry in his hand computer. "Groton, you are on report. Dereliction of duty. Inattentiveness on watch. Conduct prejudicial to good order and discipline."

"Sir, I can explain! I just—"

"Explain it at mast. You're relieved of duty. Now. Get out of my sight!"

Grayson watched the technician hurry off, his face burning a bright red. He looked back at the RX-30 station's blank monitor screens and shook his head. Leaving this one station dead would not seriously jeopardize the Legion's perimeter. Damn it, though, those two should be more careful! Half the Command Center crew might have been looking over Groton's shoulder and cheering the pair of them on if he hadn't happened by. If Alex and Caitlin wanted to provide a free show to the more libidinous members of the command staff, fine ... but that kind of mass distraction could put a serious hole in their defenses, not to mention shooting unit morale to hell. There was a definite morale problem in the general knowledge of the CO's son being intimately involved with a woman under his command. If nothing else, people might think Caitlin's next promotion was due to some factor other than her efficiency and skill as a Mech-

Warrior. Grayson wondered how he could stop Groton from spreading juicy stories around the unit.

Impossible, probably, sort of shooting the man. *Damn* it all! Once upon a time, about a million years ago, he'd thought running his own merc unit might be fun. . . .

He still didn't think he approved of Alex's relationship with DeVries. If something happened to either of them, the other would be ruined as well.

And they would be in combat very soon. Perhaps as soon as two days from now.

But he also knew that they needed each other. "Enjoy yourselves, you two," Grayson said to the blank monitor, very, very quietly. "I'm afraid you won't have many more opportunities like this. . . ."

Two men talked together in the similitude of privacy offered by the vastness of the 'Mech bay of the Citadel. The huge chamber was filled with the bustle of men working on BattleMechs arrayed like so many suits of armor in their maintenance gantries. The flare and hiss of welding torches, the crash of armor on armor, the ratcheting clash of heavy cranes and travelers, all conspired to make conversation difficult and eavesdropping nearly impossible.

"So, Groton," the officer said with an easy smile. "I heard you got gigged the other day by the Old Man himself."

Groton looked up from the circuit test bed he was working on, then snorted. "Damned long-nosed son of a bitch. I wasn't doing anything wrong!"

"Hey, easy, pal. Easy. I know that. You think you're the first tech to get nailed by that SOB? Sometimes Grayson Carlyle thinks he's Almighty God or something. All this merc hero stuff over the years has gone to his head!"

"Yeah. It wasn't like I was asleep at my post or nothin! I was watching my display all the time!"

The other laughed. "Yeah. Selby up in Command Control said you got an eyeful of something good. What'd you see, anyway?"

"Ha!" Groton started to say, then stopped, suddenly uncertain. "Uh, look, sir. I'm probably in enough trouble already. . . ."

"Hey, tell me your troubles. Do I look like the kind of guy who'd rat on his buddies?" He snapped his fingers. "I don't give *that* for that officer-and-gentleman drek. I started off as an enlisted grunt."

"I didn't mean—"

"Look, I got some people in Admin who owe me some favors, right? I may be able to get things squared with you."

"No drek! Really?"

"Sure. I'd need a favor or two in return, of course."

"Hey, anything, sir! Anything! It wasn't like I was asleep or—"

"Well, tell me, for the love of Blake. What'd you see that ticked Carlyle off so bad?"

"Well . . . you know that looker in Command Lance One-one? The daughter of the Governor back on Glengarry?"

"Sure."

Grinning, Groton began describing what he'd seen on the monitor in loving, libidinous, and anatomically explicit detail.

"Man, that's juicy. With the CO's son, huh?"

"That's right, sir. They was really goin' at it!"

"Yeah, well. I guess rank hath its privileges, huh?"

"Sure as hell does. Uh, meanin' no disrespect, of course, Captain."

The officer laughed. "Drek, Groton. Do you think captains get any special privileges in this damned unit? Except for Captain Carlyle, of course! The rest of us? We're bottom of the ol' pyramid, just like you. Well, except for ensigns and lieutenants. But they don't count!"

"Never thought of it that way, sir. Least it's good to know some officers are *human*."

"Ha! Not like some we could name!"

"Damned straight!"

"Listen, Groton. You're a good man. And I do need a favor. Now, I don't want to make it like I wouldn't help you if you don't help me, but . . ."

"Hey, no problem, Captain. That's the way the military works. You scratch mine, I'll scratch yours, right?"

"Right." The officer glanced back and forth, as though checking for unseen listeners. "Okay, you've got access to a jack key, right?"

"Huh? Sure. But what would you want with one of those?"

"Well, it's like this. In a way, see, I've got the same problem with the Colonel that you do. The guy can kinda sneak up on you even when you're both inside BattleMechs!"

"I can believe that. He's got eyes in the back of his head!"

"There are times, when I'm out in my 'Mech, that I need a little extra room, know what I mean?"

"No, sir. I don't think I do."

"Contraband, son. Goodies from the locals. Things like candy and fresh fruit and dopesticks and stimmers that'll fetch a good price on the market . . . meaning, of course, the rest of the battalion."

"Smuggling, you mean."

"What's the matter, Groton? You have a problem with that?"

"Nah. I enjoy a stimmer hit once in a while, same as the next guy. I just don't like weaseling around the point, know what I mean?"

"I know exactly what you mean. Well, the point is, when we're out on patrol, or a march like this, I sometimes have the opportunity to pick up a little something on the side. Problem is, if Carlyle catches me, it's a court-martial, maybe even a bounce out of the Legion. I don't know why they're so damned tough on stimmers and such. I mean, everybody does it, right?"

"Just about. So anyway, how does a jack key help you?"

A jack key was a magnetic disk that, applied against a key spot on a 'Mech's armor, opened a small hatch to give techs access to wiring nodes or service tunnels.

"A jack key and a few minutes alone in the 'Mech bay where the Colonel's 'Mech is being stored lets me open up one of his access panels, say, in the leg. It lets me wire in a little device as big as my hand that acts like a radar transponder. Sends out a coded signal that only I can pick up, and lets me know when the Colonel's in the area."

"Slick!" Groton nodded, but he was still looking uncertain. "That's not somethin' an enemy 'Mech could use, is it? To home in on him, like?"

"Nah! Strictly short range, and the only way it shows up out of background emissions is when you have the descrambler, like I would in my 'Mech's tracking system."

"Those keys are restricted, you know. They're not supposed to leave the 'Mech bay, and we have to sign for them. Unauthorized people aren't supposed to even see 'em. Just the techs and the individual warriors."

"*I'm* a MechWarrior."

"Yeah, but you're not supposed to have access to anybody else's key."

"Why do you think I'm asking you? I figure a smart guy like you would let his crew chief know he was doing some late work, tonight, maybe? You could let me in, let me plant my package, and I'd be gone again in ten minutes. Maybe five. And ... you know, Groton, I could make it worth your while. Besides getting the charges against you quashed. I could cut you in for a piece of the action."

"Yeah? How much, you figure?"

"Hard to say. Couple thousand C-bills the first month, though, easy. That's your share. Say ... twenty percent of the net?"

"It would have to be late tonight. Oh-two-hundred, maybe, when the late shift changes. Not so many folks around to wonder what an officer is doing poking around the 'Mech gantries."

"Fine by me. I'll be up late tonight anyway."

"And ... you'll kill the mast on me?"

"Absolutely." The officer stuck out his hand. "My word on it!"

Groton grinned and accepted the hand. "Done, then! Uh ... sir."

"And done! I'll be over there ... that entrance, at oh-two hundred tonight. Don't fail me, Groton!"

"I won't, Captain Dupré! You can count on me!"

25

Advance Deployment Base Delta
Twenty kilometers south of Falkirk
Caledonia, Skye March
Federated Commonwealth
1305 hours, 16 April 3057

The bubble dome had been inflated earlier that afternoon, and the electronics jacked into the small, portable fusion plant outside. Armor plate had been added over the plastic framework, though it would provide protection against nothing heavier than small-arms fire or shrapnel. As a semi-mobile field headquarters, the dome was far more luxurious in terms of space than one of the big, twenty-five-ton, eighteen-wheeler HQ trucks sometimes used by larger BattleMech formations, but was decidedly less mobile and more vulnerable.

One major advantage of the dome over mobile HQ trucks was space . . . space enough, in this instance, to allow Grayson's regimental command staff to set up a large holographic projection map table in the center of the dome's main work area.

The table was nowhere near as large or as detailed as the map projection he'd used in his simulator match against Jaime Wolf. Measuring just two meters by three, it was large enough for the battalion's company commanders to gather around and study the projection at close quarters. Present were all of the unit's captains and majors, plus several lieutenants on the command staff. The imagery had been gathered from Caledonian data banks—the Legion had no reconnaissance satellites at the moment—and showed a rolling section of terrain as it might have appeared from a few thousand meters up, with roads, hills, forests, and a small town all portrayed in lovingly intricate, fractally generated detail. Rather than projecting BattleMechs as small, intricate models, however, military units were shown as traditional military symbols glowing with red or blue laser-painted illumination. Scale could be changed easily through a computer keyboard or voice circuit, and additional data about particular features was always available from the data base.

The biggest disadvantage of such systems, Grayson thought, was that the complexity of the presentation could actually mask deficiencies in intelligence. When you could actually look down into the village of Falkirk and see individual buildings—a church steeple, a shopping complex, a textile manufactory—it was easy to assume that you had the entire picture. In fact, that manufactory could have been torn down months before and replaced by a battery of ten-inch Gauss rifles, but if no one had fed the data to the computer, the information could not be displayed.

"They have to come this way," Grayson said, using a pen-sized laser pointer to indicate a pass through the Grampian Mountains just north of Falkirk. "The only other easy routes through these mountains are way off here to the east, and that would add two days marching time at least. Besides, they can't count on support from the population for food and other supplies. They'll need bases along the way, supply dumps. And Falkirk would offer them plenty of food, water, and POLs."

Even with portable fusion plants, POLs—petroleum, oil, and lubricants—were still vital for any mechanized army in the field. Some vehicles still ran on internal combustion engines, and all machines needed oil or polysilicarb lubricants.

"Aye," McCall said darkly. "Y' mean loot an' the spoils a' pillage."

"Could we block them at that pass?" Major Frye asked. "Maybe even come around through the mountains, here, and get behind them?"

"I was thinking about that, but that approach could pose some real problems. The pass itself is fairly broad, almost ten kilometers wide here at Falkirk, way too wide for us to simply cordon it off with the 'Mechs we have available. If we simply lined up to snipe at them along the sides of the valley farther north, where it's narrower, we'd knock out a few but the rest would breeze right past . . . and then we'd have *them* maneuvering in *our* rear.

"No, I think what we have to do is try to predict just what they'll do at Falkirk. They're headed in this direction, we know. Our scouts say they should be through the pass by late this afternoon. Gentlemen? What will they do next?"

"Encamp for the night," Frye said. "Definitely. The terrain gets rugged farther south, and they must know we're lurking down here somewhere. Only a maniac is going to push 'Mechs forward over unknown ground at night."

"And from what we've seen of their profiles," Captain Lang said, "neither Zellner nor Seymour is a maniac. Wilmarth might try it. . . ."

"They won't let Wilmarth gie th' orders," McCall said. "They probably put Wee Willie in th' rear someplace wi' a cold drink an' a monitor. Let him gie all the orders he wants, but keep him out a' the way."

"That's the way I read it," Grayson said, nodding. "They're going to want to push hard to get out of the mountains before night. If they don't, that would be an open invitation for us to bottle them up. Once they reach Falkirk, though, they're not going to be too eager to push ahead. It'll be getting dark soon, and there aren't too many good positions for quite a distance to the south. So. They encamp for the night here, at Falkirk."

Captain Ann Warfield, commander of the Third Batt's Second Company, used a laser pointer to trace a bright red line along some hills running east to west about two kilometers south of the town. "This is interesting terrain here," she said. "Provides high ground for anyone holding it and facing a possible advance from the south. If I were leading a 'Mech column south, I'd grab Falkirk and set up camp . . . here, maybe." She indicated a broad plain south of the town, perhaps a kilometer behind the line of hills. "Send my tax collectors out to raise the supplies I'd need. And dig in my 'Mechs along these hills."

Captain Duane Gallery, "Shooter" to his friends, and the CO of the battalion's Third Company, pointed out a low rise on the plain between town and hills, nestled in against some woods to the west. "Look," he said. "This would be a good place for a supply dump. Let's say I come through town, set up camp over here. I'd need a dump somewhere near Falkirk, because I know I'm going to run up against the dreaded Gray Death Legion in the next hundred kilometers or so. It's only two hundred klicks more to New Edinburgh, and I know the Gray Death is out there somewhere."

"Right," Frye said, nodding. He looked up at Grayson. "This whole area would be a great spot for an advance base, before launching the final strike toward the capital. It's a bit far, but the Third Davion has a reputation for moving fast. Whoever is in command could feed his front lines from a supply dump here easily enough, and it would provide a lot of flexibility if he was forced to fall back to the defense."

"I concur," Grayson said.

He'd arrived at much the same conclusion back at the Command Center, but he'd found that the planning went more smoothly when his subordinates came up with the answers for themselves. It wouldn't do to train them to simply wait for him to make his pronouncements. In fact, he'd first spotted that line of hills that Captain Warfield had noted the night before. Their arrangement, two groups of low, bare-topped hills anchoring a long ridge stretched between them, reminded him eerily of the terrain he'd fought over at Gettysburg, in his sim match with Jaime Wolf.

The terrain was different in detail, of course. The hills and ridgeline formed more of a round-ended crescent shape than a fishhook, and it ran east-west instead of north-south, but the topology was similar enough that he'd immediately considered it both as a potential defensive position and as a potential objective for an assault. The ridge lay across the road coming north from New Edinburgh, which passed over it through a saddle at its eastern end, in the shadow of two large hills.

"Just in case you need confirmation," Gray continued, "our recon forces have reported seeing Third Davion 'Mechs in the area. Light stuff, so far, *Locust*s and *Mercury*s. But they may be scouting the terrain. They spotted a *Mercury* up here on this hill early this morning, apparently taking laser survey sightings of the ground."

"You know," Alex said, "we should probably have names for some of these features to avoid confusion."

"Is there anything in the data base?" Shooter wanted to know.

"The forest to the west is called the Tanglewood," Lang said. She worked the table-top keyboard in front of her for a moment, and the name appeared above the holographic trees in glowing white letters. "This open area south of town is called Meadow Grove. We don't have anything for that ridgeline, though. There's probably a local name that never made it into the data base."

Grayson gave a wry smile and reached for his own keyboard. "I suggest this. . . ."

Typing quickly, he entered his own names for the features. Culp's Hill and Cemetery Hill to the west. Big and Little Round Top to the east. And stretched between the two, crossing through the saddle close to the Round Tops by the New Edinburgh Road, Cemetery Ridge.

"Looks familiar," McCall said with a grin, and the others laughed.

Grayson keyed in some more commands, and red lights appeared on the ridgeline, on the rise between the ridge and the town, and inside the town itself. "Here's our best guess so far," Grayson said. "Zellner—I'm assuming the force will be under Zellner's command until we know differently—will put his main force up here on the ridge and the hills. He'd be an idiot not to. Supply dump, back here, probably on this rise at the western end of Meadow Grove close to the . . . what's the road?"

"Tanglewood Road," Lang said.

"Right. We won't count on the dump being here, though. Could be anywhere in this general area. Observers and probably a command post up here in the town." More colored lights appeared on the map, this time in blue. "We will advance from the south, along this road. We will deploy for frontal assault when we meet them . . . as they would expect us too."

"Uh . . . Colonel?" Lieutenant Aleksanyen said, puzzled. "Did you say, 'as they *expect* us to'?"

"That's right, Grigor. We need to keep them busy. Keep them occupied." Grayson flicked his laser pointer across the map to the west, indicating the Tanglewood, which started two kilometers south of the ridgeline, ran parallel to it to the west, then took a sharp swing to the north, edging Meadow Grove and very nearly reaching the town itself.

"Our scouts report that in places these woods are damn near impenetrable," Grayson said. "Tanglewood describes it perfectly. Swamps. Trees so thick that BattleMechs wouldn't make it through in a year. But there are also thinner areas, as well as a number of roads, especially the Tanglewood Road, which crosses the forest from southwest to northeast on its way to Falkirk. The important thing is that a strong column of 'Mechs could move through here undetected from the air."

"If our people don't know the ground, though . . ." Captain Lang said, her forehead creasing.

Grayson gestured at McCall, who was standing at the other side of the table. "Major McCall over there has already volunteered to seek out some locals who'd be willing to serve as guides. Major?"

"Aye. We'll hae help from our Reiver contingent as well, sir. Some of them know this area, or have relatives nearby who do. We'll get through all right."

"So," Grayson continued, "we'll have civilian auxiliaries who can lead our flanking force through the woods . . . looping around the enemy's right flank, to here." His pointer touched the rise and its supply depot symbol with red fire. "They will emerge somewhere along this treeline. With luck, the enemy won't see them coming, won't have a clue they're even in the area."

"We'll have to allow for the possibility of pickets thrown out along the Tanglewood Road," Alex pointed out.

"If the unit moves fast, though, that shouldn't be a problem.

"Now, the flanking force will have two primary goals. First, and most important, when they come charging out of these woods they'll be squarely behind the enemy's right flank, or close to it. The attack will cause considerable confusion in the enemy's ranks, maybe enough to rout him if we can drive him forward into the main body's rear. It will certainly be enough to create openings along the front that the main force will be able to exploit, as Zellner turns to meet this new threat to his rear and flank.

"The second goal, of course, will be the disruption of the enemy's supply lines. If they do establish a supply dump in this area, our flanking force should be able to capture or destroy a large quantity of expendables . . . expendables the enemy will have to send clear back to Stirling and their DropShips to replace. Whatever we can destroy in the supply dump, he can't use against us on the field."

"How big a flanking force did you have in mind?" Alex asked.

"Captain Frank? What's our TO looking like?"

The Gray Death Legion's senior Tech officer consulted his ever-present hand computer. "We have thirty-seven 'Mechs up and on-line, Colonel," he said. "That includes the four Command One-one 'Mechs, with five Third Batt 'Mechs downgrudged. We might be able to get two of those running, if we work all night and cannibalize from the others."

"Get on it. For now, we'll assume thirty-six, a full battalion. The main thrust of our offensive will be this left hook, so that's where we have to concentrate our power. I'd say two companies, twenty-four 'Mechs."

"That's going to leave us damned thin on the line south of the ridge," Frye pointed out.

"I know. We'll have just twelve 'Mechs, plus whatever Captain Frank can scavenge for us, to make a noise like an army."

"General McBee's people can help there, Colonel," McCall said.

"I'm counting on it, but we'll be sending most of them with the flankers. Our armored infantry too, I think. I want this flanking force to materialize out of thin air, squarely behind the enemy's main body, across his supply lines, and between his front lines and his command staff. They're going to need enough muscle to make a quick kill, then hold on against all comers while the rest of our force moves up from the south."

"So who's going to lead the flanking force, sir?" Captain Warfield wanted to know.

Grayson had been weighing that very question for some time. "Normally, the choice would be obvious," he said. "Major McCall has the experience and the confidence of the entire battalion. That arm of his, though, is going to keep him out of—"

"Sir!" Davis said, shocked. "If I can wear a Nighthawk, then there's nae reason I can nae pilot m' *Highlander*!"

"Sorry, Major. You'll be in your 'Mech, but I want you with me. You won't be able to move or fight as freely with that arm immobilized as you would otherwise."

"But, sair—"

"No arguments, Major. I can't afford to lose you because you can't sidestep or pivot as fast as you need to. Major

Frye? I'll want you with the scouts. We're going to need to carefully coordinate our operations south of the ridgeline, and you know your people better than I do."

"Yes, sir." The major nodded understanding, but there was a twinge of bitterness in his voice. Frye's inner ear had been damaged in battle. As a result, he couldn't wear a neurohelmet—and could no longer pilot a 'Mech. In battle, Frye commanded his battalion either from a DropShip Ops console or from the deck of one of the legion's Pegasus scout tanks.

Grayson wondered how the man had held on. To tell a MechWarrior he couldn't strap into a BattleMech was telling a bird it could not fly.

"I want to leave each company commander where he or she is," Grayson continued. "I don't want to disrupt formations or unit integrity." He looked up, picking his son out from among the other faces watching him across the table. "Alex, I guess that leaves you. You want the job?"

Grayson watched various emotions chasing one another across Alex's face. None of those emotions, though, appeared to be doubt.

"Yes, *sir*!" Alex said. He grinned.

"I think the flanking force will consist of Third Battalion's Second and Third Companies. Warfield's Warriors and the Gray Raiders. Any questions? Problems? Speak now, or forever hold your peace."

There were some low-voiced murmurs among several of the assembled officers, but no one spoke up.

"Good. Provisionally, the First Company, Major Frye's Firestormers, will demonstrate along this front south of the ridge. If it seems advisable, Major, we may shift east and north to threaten the Round Tops. We might even be able to move with the Round Tops for cover if we can sweep hostile observers off their crests."

"Kind of like what you did at your Gettysburg sim on Glengarry, eh, Colonel?" Frye said. "A flank around the enemy's left, up and behind the Round Tops."

Grayson smiled. "Hell, who knows? Maybe Zellner saw the broadcast of that match. If so, he'll be thinking about that . . . and not about Captain Carlyle coming through the woods."

"What about timing?" Captain Lang wanted to know.

"It's almost thirteen-thirty hours now," Grayson said. "Sunset is . . . what?"

"Twenty-forty-five hours, this time of year," Lang replied.

"So, seven hours of daylight left. Alex? How long for you to get around that flank?"

"That depends a lot on what the terrain is *really* like out there," Alex replied. "I don't like trusting the projection data base. But I'd think four hours ought to be plenty. Four hours from when we move out."

"Let's plan on a departure by fourteen-thirty hours, then," Grayson said. "That puts you in the woods west of Meadow Grove at eighteen-thirty hours, with better than two hours of daylight left. That sounds good to you?"

"Perfect." Alex was studying the woods to the west and the faint network of roads and trails he would have to negotiate. "One thing, though, Colonel. Suppose we come charging out of the woods and no one's there? I mean, this whole plan is based on our assumptions about what Zellner might do."

"Aye," McCall added. "An' we all ken vurra weel tha' th' enemy never does just what y' expect him to!"

"In that case," Grayson said with a shrug, "we do what we do best. We improvise. The plan is subject to revision at any time, of course, should we learn the enemy is out of position . . . and of course field commanders have full freedom to make new operational decisions if they feel it necessary. But this"—he waved a hand across the holographic landscape— "this is good ground, the best in the whole area. If I was running the Third Guard south, I would certainly make use of that ridge. I'd be stupid not to."

"How would you deploy differently, Colonel?" Shooter wanted to know. "Or would you?"

"Good question. I probably wouldn't trust those woods on my right. To maintain operational flexibility, I might dig in on the hills with a minimum of 'Mechs, one company, say, and hold the main body in reserve closer to the town, ready to shift in any direction. Of course, I could be biased here, knowing what the Gray Death is planning ahead of time." The others chuckled. "Encamping my main body up here in Meadow Grove, though, would put me in position to defend against an attack either from the woods to the west, or from behind the Round Tops to the southeast." He studied the new dispositions for a moment. "Even if Zellner does it this way, though, he'll be in a tight position. When Alex hits him from the west, he'll have to shift that way to meet him with his full force . . ."

". . . and First Company comes charging over the ridge and onto his left flank," Frye completed. "Neat."

Grayson hesitated then, considering what to say next. "Now, people. Humor me for a short lecture, please. I don't usually go in for pre-battle pep talks. You know that. But this is a bad position we're in right now, fighting against a tough unit with decent leadership, and it's a unit that, until recently, anyway, was on our side.

"I know how some of you people here feel, and how many of the people under your command still feel, about House Davion. Hell, when I was growing up, the Federated Suns and the Lyran Commonwealth both were always, I don't know, a kind of icon for me. The good guys. The heroes who were holding the line against the Draconis Combine.

"But politics change, people. Alliances change, leaders change, whole nations and worlds and empires can change their very characters . . . especially if there's rot from within. I don't need to remind any of you of your duty. I will remind you, though, that some of our people may find themselves having second thoughts when they stop and think that these are *Davion* 'Mechs in their sights, instead of Dracs or Liaos or Clanners.

"I still hope we can stop this fight. Battalion Commo has been transmitting requests for a parlay for the past twelve hours, and it was my hope that we might convince Seymour and Zellner to talk, maybe stand down, instead of fight. But we haven't heard a peep in reply, so we've got to assume that Folker and Wilmarth have joined the Guards, that they're operating under what they believe to be legitimate orders, and that those orders are to bring the Gray Death to battle and destroy it.

"I want all of you to impress upon your people that it won't make any difference tomorrow that we're fighting FedCom troops. They'll be playing for keeps, and so will we."

"Hell, Colonel," Davis McCall said, rubbing his bad shoulder. "When has it been any different? Th' bluidy Sasunnach aye want our heads on sticks, but we're going t' gie 'em their own back, medium rare!"

The others cheered and applauded that, and Grayson knew his people were ready.

All that was needed, he thought wryly, was for Zellner to do what he was *supposed* to do. . . .

The hilltop, partly wooded, partly rocky and broken, rose to the west of Advance Deployment Base Delta, providing an excellent view of the terrain in all directions. South and east, in the direction of New Edinburgh, the land was rolling and heavily wooded, all the way back to the slopes of the Mount Alba. On the northern horizon, the Grampian Mountains rose purple against a clear blue sky. Falkirk, of course, was invisible at this distance, as was the collection of ridges and hills that was the Gray Death's objective.

Much closer by, almost in the shadow of the knobby hill, the Gray Death's advance camp, the dome of the headquarters building, and the mobile gantries for the 'Mech service array nearly filled the forest clearing. BattleMechs were already out and moving, slipping along a road toward the west in single file.

Captain Alexander Carlyle and his flanking force, heading into the depths of the Tanglewood.

Grayson Carlyle had been dead right about one thing in the briefing, the man standing on the hilltop thought. This terrain would make any major 'Mech fight a real bitch. Falkirk would be the battleground, without a doubt.

Swiftly, he knelt on a flat slab of a boulder and opened a small case. The antenna unfolded by itself, the dish unfurling and automatically swinging toward the southern sky, like a dayflower seeking the sun. In this case, though, the target was not the local sun, but a reconnaissance and communications satellite in synchronous orbit with the planet. He waited ten seconds for the unit to come to full power. When a green light winked on the small console, he pressed a button, and the coded message, already stored in the unit's memory, was fed through an intense burst of laser energy fired into the sky.

Undetectable, untraceable, lasting only a fraction of a second, the message would be relayed to Marshal Felix Zellner, revealing to him everything that had transpired in the briefing just a hour earlier.

Alex Carlyle would be in for a bit of a surprise when he

emerged from the woods some four hours from now. The ambusher was about to become the ambushed.

When the transmission was completed, Captain Walter Dupré, currently assigned to First Company of the Third Battalion, folded up the equipment, checked the area to make certain he'd not been observed, then started back down the hill.

═══ 26 ═══

Observation Post One
Falkirk, Caledonia
Federated Commonwealth
1940 hours, 16 April 3057

"**A**ll right, Marshal Zellner," Marshal James Seymour said, hands on hips and an I-told-you-so look in his eye. "Where the hell is it?"

"I don't know," Zellner admitted. "I just don't the hell know."

They were standing in the bell tower of the First Caledonian Church of the Cosmic All, the tallest structure in the town of Falkirk that afforded a decent view of the terrain to the south. Four broad, tall windows, one in each wall encircling the single, massive bronze bell, offered a good view of the surrounding terrain, one better than battlefield teleremotes in that it could not be jammed.

South, a battle was raging, *had* been raging, for the past two hours.

"We've planned our defenses around the information provided by your agent in the Gray Death's camp," Seymour said. "And this devastating flank attack he warned you about hasn't materialized. *As* I expected."

"It's only an hour late," Zellner pointed out. But he too, was beginning to have second thoughts.

"I think, Marshal," Seymour said, "that you should consider the following possibilities." He began ticking them off on his fingers. "One. Your man was mistaken. Two. The enemy knew your man was an agent and deliberately fed him misinformation. Three. Your man has been turned and is working for the Gray Death's intelligence. Four. Your man was discovered shortly after sending that message, Colonel Carlyle realized that his plan had been compromised, and he changed the plan to take into account that we know the original plan."

"Five," Zellner added. "*Captain* Carlyle got lost in the woods and could show up any moment now!"

"Maybe. But I must say, the Gray Death Legion doesn't exactly have a reputation for getting *lost,* Marshal. I strongly suggest a ruse of some kind here, and I don't want to risk more than half my command on the word of one hireling spy!"

"That 'hireling spy' is a good man."

"I don't doubt that. But he *is* only one man. We're up against a full battalion of one of the best mercenary units in the field." Seymour pointed to the south, where explosions were flashing and cracking along the length of the ridge straddled by the New Edinburgh Road. "We're obviously facing nothing more than a demonstration over there. The volume of fire from the woods beyond is far too light to be an entire battalion. My people tell me they're fighting a company there, maybe less. Now, if Captain Carlyle *isn't* sneaking up on us from the Tanglewood, he must be somewhere else." He gestured carelessly over his shoulder, toward the woods and marshes east of Meadow Grove. "Maybe over there. Hell, maybe circling up through the mountains and coming down on our rear!"

"I think you're giving the man too much credit." Zellner thought a moment, then picked up his mapboard, a computerized panel the size of a clipboard that showed the surrounding terrain on an electronic display. "Wait a minute," he said. "Carlyle—the old man, I mean, not the son—is known for pulling the unexpected. You have scouts out in the Tanglewood, I take it?"

"Of course. You don't think I'd overlook something that obvious, do you? I've got a full company out there, hunting for this mysterious flank march. So far, they haven't found a damned thing. Frankly, I think they'd serve us better if we pulled them back and put them into our reserve. If young

Carlyle is out there, I suspect he's given up on coming in by way of the Tanglewood Road. He's going to bypass our pickets and hit us from some other direction."

The sounds of battle to the south were redoubling. With a savage thunder and the searing hiss of outgoing missiles, the artillery and rocket launchers set up at Fire Base Alpha in Meadow Grove just south of town cut loose with a savage bombardment. Zellner leaned against the ledge of the opening in the belfry a moment, watching the volley clear the ridge and plunge toward the enemy lines somewhere beyond. So far, the battle was being prosecuted with an almost lackadaisical gentleness. Most of the Expeditionary Force had been drawn up in a temporary base alongside a supply dump that was still being assembled just south of the town, between Zellner's OP and Fire Base Alpha. An infantry encampment was in the process of being set up next to the forest to the southwest.

A communicator warbled, and Seymour picked up the headset resting on the ledge below the gallery of the bell chamber's east window. "Seymour." He listened for a moment, before adding, "Very well. Hold your positions, but keep an eye on them. Command out."

"What was that?"

"Malishnikov, on Hill Two-twelve. He's spotted what he thinks is a large body of 'Mechs moving through the woods to the southeast."

Zellner checked his mapboard again. Hill 212 was the taller of the two large, rounded hills lying east and northeast of the ridge that were the anchor for the Davion Guard's left flank. One company of light and medium 'Mechs had been posted there, with orders to hold the high ground at all costs. If Malishnikov had sighted enemy 'Mechs further to the east . . .

"Are you thinking what I'm thinking, Marshal?" Seymour was smiling.

"Carlyle almost suckered his opposition again." *Almost.*

"Five gets you twenty Captain Carlyle's flanking force is coming around from the east."

"What do you suggest?" Zellner was feeling a bit lost. He'd planned this part of the battle meticulously, relentlessly, hazarding all on what he'd been certain Carlyle was going to try. Now it was all coming unraveled.

"We pull Third Battalion out of camp and deploy them

behind Hill Two-twelve and Hill One-ninety. We leave Second Battalion in reserve and reinforce our line on the ridge. I suspect Carlyle might be about to hit us in the front, as a diversion. We should let him think his diversion is working."

Zellner shifted blocks of colored light about on his mapboard for a moment more. "Yeah. Yeah, looks good." He laughed, feeling relieved now that the suspense of not knowing was broken. "We're gonna *nail* this bastard, Jim!"

"Don't celebrate the victory just yet, Marshal," Seymour warned. "Carlyle is one opponent I wouldn't want to underestimate!"

"Of course, of course," Zellner said, but he couldn't be discouraged now. Up until this moment, the one factor that could have spoiled everything was not knowing for sure what the Gray Death was going to do . . . especially after he'd been so damned certain that he *had* known Carlyle's plan. Now that he knew, however, now that he could move with confidence, knowing where that old bastard Carlyle was going to be coming from, he could rely on simple numbers alone. According to Dupré—and his report had been verified by numerous sources—the Gray Death could muster no more than thirty-five to forty 'Mechs on Caledonia, essentially one battalion. Zellner's expeditionary force numbered sixty-eight 'Mechs, two full battalions minus a handful of downcheckers, plus a regimental headquarters company, an artillery company, and an infantry support regiment.

And there was also the possibility that Dupré had indeed been successful in planting his little surprise in Grayson Carlyle's 'Mech. His message had indicated that he'd managed to get access to Carlyle's *Victor* two nights ago. Now, if Dupré had been turned, of course, that piece of information was a lie, but if it *wasn't* . . .

The Gray Death's Third Battalion didn't stand a chance, outnumbered as it was.

And when Colonel Grayson Carlyle was killed in battle, that would seal the fate of the Gray Death Legion.

Secure in the cockpit of his *Victor* despite the ping and clatter of smoking shell fragments off his armor, Grayson Carlyle stood at the edge of the treeline, using his computer enhancement to study the enemy positions on the ridgeline two kilometers to the north. Alex should have been in position and launching his attack an hour ago, *over* an hour ago, and still there was no sign whatsoever that the pace of the enemy's battle management had been slowed or even disturbed. A signal had been arranged—two green flares for a successful attack, two red if the attack met determined and dug-in resistance. No flares simply meant that Alex hadn't reached his jump-off point yet.

What the hell had happened to Alex?

Grayson cursed the radio silence that prevented communication with the other half of the unit. He also cursed for not leaving Frye to handle the operation here while taking charge of the flanking march himself.

The volume of fire from beyond the enemy-held ridge was growing heavier, artillery rounds and long-range rockets, for the most part. Most of the rounds fell short, tearing the southern end of the field just in front of him into broken clods of shot-blasted earth. A few passed overhead, landing in the woods at his back, each thunderous detonation hurling trees, branches, and leaves into the sky like jackstraws. BattleMechs on both sides continued to take potshots at one another, though without any real hope of actually hitting anything, save by wildest chance. The air, the very sky overhead, was alive with whispering shards of metal. High up, far above the battlefield, Grayson's scanners could just pick up the twisting knots of white thread, contrails of an aerospace battle at high altitude.

He wished just one of his aerofighters would get freed up. He could use a detailed scan of the battlefield behind the ridge to the north.

Damn, *where* was Alex?

Another 'Mech moved up through the shadows of the trees to Grayson's left, a blocky-looking *Highlander* with scratched and battle-worn armor. "Hello, Davis," Grayson called over the secure tactical frequency. "How's the arm holding up inside that thing?"

"Well enough, Colonel. It's aye sore, bu' I can manage. I should hae gone on th' flank march."

"We're only an hour past his ETA. Maybe our data on the roads wasn't as up to date as we thought."

"Maybe." It sounded as though McCall wanted to say more but hesitated to utter the words.

Because it was Grayson's son out there.

"He'll make it all right, Major," Grayson said. "If there'd been real trouble, we'd have heard something by now. We still have forty-five minutes to sunset."

"Aye, sir. But it leaves us in a kind of tight spot. How long can we dither here, wi' out making a real attack?"

"As long as we have to. Any casualties yet?"

"No, sir. Infantry's all down an' weel under cover. Sergeant Gonzalez's *Guillotine* took a bit a' damage in th' arm an' side from a near miss, but he's still on his feet."

"Then we'll stick it out a bit longer. Anyway, Major Frye still has his two lances and the hoverscouts out east of the Round Tops."

"Aye. Makin' noises like a full battalion."

"Let's hope so. Let's hope the enemy thinks so." Grayson glanced wistfully at the monitor showing the sky overhead again. "The hardest part is going on with this, not knowing for sure how the enemy is deployed over there."

"Aye. We'll know more when young Alex comes out a' the woods."

When Alex comes out of the woods. How much longer would that be? 'Mech warfare was primarily maneuver, with the goal of getting as close as possible to the other guy and finishing him fast. Sooner or later, those people over there would guess that he didn't have more than a company or so hidden in the woods. When that happened, there wasn't much at all the Gray Death could do, save retreat to keep from being surrounded and destroyed.

Damn it all, where *was* he?

Damn it, when was something going to *happen*?

Walter Dupré stretched in the seat of his *Zeus,* trying to work out the kinks of muscles held too long in one position. He'd managed to stay with Carlyle and the command section; the fact that his eighty-ton *Zeus* was among the heaviest 'Mechs fielded by the Gray Death here on Caledonia had helped, since most of the machines sent off with Frye's diversionary force had been mediums and lights.

They'd spent the last several hours right here, however, moving in and out among the thickly scattered trees, firing at targets of opportunity when they showed themselves along the skyline above that distant ridge, but mostly just dodging the randomly falling fire that was slowly but relentlessly turning this patch of forest into a plowed field with wood-chip mulch.

Carlyle's *Victor* was currently some five hundred meters to the west, according to the tracking signal he was picking up on his map display. His last signal from Zellner, received hours ago, had been a single word: Completion.

He was to finish the job he'd almost accomplished that day on Glengarry. He wondered if he should just move in close and do it right now. . . .

No. Patience . . . patience. That alone would win the game and ensure that he lived to tell about it. The man who'd killed the great Grayson Carlyle! Now *that* was a story that could be told a few times over drinks in a spaceport bar! Of course, he would leave out the part about the device planted inside the right knee of Carlyle's *Victor*. That bit didn't seem quite so sporting—or it wouldn't when the story was retold.

But he couldn't do anything until Carlyle decided to move . . . specifically until he decided to use the *Victor*'s jump jets.

An artillery rocket howled overhead, smashing into a tree fifty meters behind the *Zeus*. The flash was bright enough to momentarily cast shadows among the other trees, the bang loud enough to set Dupré's ears ringing despite the cut-outs in his headset. Something heavy slammed into the side of his 'Mech, staggering him—a full three meters of tree trunk, the ends jagged and blackened by fire.

Don't keep us waiting out here all evening, Carlyle, or I'll come over and kill you now, escape or no escape!

Well, that was nothing more than bravado, and Dupré knew it. Still, he wished the waiting would end. . . .

Alex had gotten lost.

Well . . . not *lost*, exactly, but definitely mislaid. Less than two hours into their flank march that afternoon, Task Force Striker had encountered a flooded area in the woods that none of the data banks had described, nor had it been expected by any of the guides. The best guess was that rain during the past week had made a river overflow its banks, flooding this part of the Tanglewood and turning it into a treacherous swamp. Roads that showed up as passable on the electronic map could be seen descending into the black, oily

water; men who volunteered to wade out and test the depth
had returned with reports of a soft, mucky ooze without a
bottom—at least, none they could reach with four-meter
poles. It was *possible* a BattleMech wouldn't sink out of
sight if it waded into that muck. Equally possible it wouldn't
become so mired in four meters of mud that it would need
a recovery vehicle to haul it free again.

But those were possibilities that Alex didn't care to gamble on, not when the Gray Death had so few 'Mechs to begin
with. After consulting with his civilian guides, several of
whom had been born and raised not far from Falkirk, he decided it would be smarter, and safer, to try to find a detour
around the flooding.

They'd struck out toward the west, moving farther and yet
farther from the battlefield, until finally scouts reported a
track of dry ground through thinning trees leading north. By
1930 hours, they eventually reached a highway running
northeast. It *ought* to be the Tanglewood Road, but they'd
been forced to go so far off course that it could well have
been anything.

Taking a chance then, realizing that it was rapidly growing
dark in the woods even before the actual moment of sunset,
Alex led the twenty-four 'Mechs of Task Force Striker in
two long columns down the highway, trotting now to make
up for lost time.

By 2000 hours, the shadows were so deep even on the
road that several MechWarriors asked for permission to
switch on their machines' lights. Alex refused. The Davions
would almost certainly have sentries or pickets posted along
this highway, and he didn't intend to alert them to the flanking force's presence any sooner than necessary.

In swiftly gathering darkness, then, the two companies of
'Mechs crashed down the highway, flanged, carballoy feet
clashing with each step, striking sparks from the pavement.
A glow could be seen against the horizon and behind the
trees to the northeast, especially with light enhancement—
the glow of Falkirk, possibly, or of the Third Guard encampment.

"Okay, Strikers," Alex called over the tactical band,
breaking radio silence for the first time. "Arm! Safeties off!
Deploy!"

If there were hostiles listening on that frequency, or using broad band scanners, they would hear only scrambled code, but he still wanted to keep any transmissions to a tight, absolute minimum. He snapped off the safeties on his *Archer*'s control console, readying his medium pulse lasers for firing.

Gunshots cracked from the shadows to the right. "Striker One, Raider Five!" a voice called. "I'm taking small-arms fire from the woods."

"Take 'em down!" Alex growled, and the clatter of machine gun fire rattled among the deepening shadows. They were committed now, no matter what was waiting for them up there, no matter how late they were already.

Suddenly, a stilt-legged shape moved across Alex's forward view. A squat, rounded body with ungainly arms.

A *Mercury* . . . not one of his . . .

A PPC fired to Alex's right, and a blue-white bolt of charged plasma streaked into the unfortunate twenty-ton scout 'Mech, blowing a massive chunk out of its side. One arm spun away into the woods as lightning danced and sparked across its body and arced to the ground.

To his right, the Legion *Marauder* that had fired the first PPC shot loosed a second bolt, slamming the round into the *Mercury*'s leg. The clumsy-looking machine teetered for a moment, then plunged to the ground. Two more PPC bolts smashed into the wreckage, fusing it into a glowing, smoking mass.

That *Marauder* was one of Third Company's Combat Lance 'Mechs, piloted by MechWarrior Sergei Golovanov. "Nice shooting, Sergei," Alex called.

"*Spasebaw,*" the Skye-born Russian replied. "Like shooting ducks in a barrel, yes?"

"Something like that." Alex checked the time readout on his *Archer*'s HUD and grimaced. The battle had just begun at 2038 hours—only two hours late. The real problem was the fact that the sun would be setting in another few minutes, and it would be full dark within half an hour. BattleMechs did fight at night, but only rarely, and with good reason. In order to see a target, you generally had to go active with your sensors—even if those were nothing more than spotlights—and when you did that, you made yourself a target as well. Passive sensors, light amplifiers, and passive IR, could be used to some degree, but working and fighting a 'Mech over uneven ground in the dark was no joke. His unit was likely to take as many casualties from falls and stumbles as from enemy fire.

But Alex was discounting that. If 'Mechs didn't usually fight at night, well, that would be part of the surprise. Possibly they could arrange things so that it was the enemy doing all of the moving—and stumbling—in the dark.

"Strikers! Full frontal deployment!" he called. "Warriors on the left. Raiders on the right! Spread out!"

The names were those of his two companies, Warfield's Warriors and the Gray Raiders.

A missile shrieked out of the darkness to the south, trailing orange sparks. A shoulder-launched missile, it looked like ... and a miss. An explosion flashed among the trees, backlighting trunks and interlacing branches.

The edge of the forest *ought* to be up here somewhere, pretty close. . . .

Sunset. The western sky was a blazing glory of red and orange and green, and still there'd been no flares, green or red, and no indication at all that Alex had completed his circuit through the woods to attack the rear of Zellner's right flank.

Grayson considered his options. It would be dark within thirty minutes or so, and while the Gray Death had engaged in night battles, a large-scale engagement like this could easily become a confused free-for-all, with friends firing on friends as often as they fired at enemies. With no clear idea of the enemy's disposition, it would be suicide to risk an advance as far north as Cemetery Ridge.

"Command One-one," a voice said over his tactical net. "This is Firestorm. I'm coming in from your right."

Pivoting the torso of his *Victor* to the right, Grayson saw Major Frye's Pegasus approaching through the trees, the hurricane of its hoverjets whirling branches and saplings aside. Close behind came one of the *Marauder*s of Frye's battalion.

"Hello, Major," Grayson called. "I see you. Come ahead."

He felt a familiar pang at the sight of the hulking, fat-armed MAD-3R trailing the small scout hovercraft. Until the Battle of Sudeten in 3050, Grayson Carlyle's trademark BattleMech had been an old *Marauder* that had carried him through more battles than he really cared to think about. That machine had been savaged in the fighting against the Clans and been abandoned on Sudeten. He'd rebuilt the Legion after that, with extensive use of Star League memory core data and captured Clan technology; he'd acquired the VTR-9K *Victor* and used it ever since.

Perhaps it was simply the habit of thirty-plus years of combat, but after seven years he still preferred the *Marauder,* even when the old design was clearly outclassed by the new, uprated models.

As Frye's Pegasus came up alongside, artillery continued to crash and bang in the distance, further to the west. Zellner's people had lost contact with the Gray Death 'Mechs and were shelling an innocent stretch of forest.

"I'm glad you're back," Grayson told him, though Frye's return only reinforced his concern for Alex. "What do you see?"

"We've got a large concentration of 'Mechs moving around north of Big Round Top," Frye told him. "I'd estimate two to three companies, with pickets and patrols out in the woods to the east. Looks to me like Zellner's center of mass has been drawn pretty far out of line."

"You were seen?"

"Oh, yeah. There's no way they would have missed us. I'm pretty sure they have a fair-sized force on top of both Round Tops, and they have a clear line of sight for a good, oh, fifteen or twenty kilometers in all directions. We kept showing ourselves at various points east and even northeast of the hills. Zellner ought to be pretty well convinced we're coming from that direction."

Laser light flared, igniting tree limbs overhead. Grayson spun back to the left, scanning toward the north. There were Davion Guard 'Mechs there, coming down from the ridge. Strung out in a long line, they numbered twelve—a full company—and they were heading straight toward the Gray Death's line. They moved slowly, coming step by step, almost as though bracing themselves for an expected fusillade of fire from the treeline to their front.

For a moment, Grayson was vividly reminded of Jaime Wolf's charge from Cemetery Ridge, during their sim. Pickett's Charge, in reverse.

But this time, the flanking movement had failed to materialize, and that company-strength probe would quickly ascertain that only a company occupied the woods in front of them.

Options?

Grayson Carlyle was rapidly running out of those.

Meadow Grove
Caledonia, Skye March
Federated Commonwealth
2048 hours, 16 April 3057

Marshal Felix Zellner was climbing down out of his 'Mech, a recently refurbished *Atlas* that had been outfitted as his personal command 'Mech. After his survey of the battlefield from the church tower earlier, he'd come down to the base camp set up along the New Edinburgh road south of Falkirk. There, he'd climbed into the 'Mech, sitting there for the next hour while trying to monitor the evolving battle.

And with every passing minute he was growing less sure of himself. His Expeditionary Force was becoming increasingly strung out. Its right flank was anchored by the woods and the 'Mech reserve, but fully half of their 'Mechs were some three kilometers away, off on the left, and too far to immediately support the right if there was trouble. Seymour was gone, off in his *Stalker* to check on that battalion.

The battle along the ridgeline to the south, meanwhile, had been gradually dying away, as gunners reported fewer and fewer hostiles to fire at across the clearing beyond. Zellner had sent a company forward to probe the woods to the south, but so far there'd been no report back, and he expected none for some minutes yet. There was no sign of the expected attack around the left flank, either; the 'Mechs Malishnikov had reported an hour ago had failed to materialize. Were they still there, encamping for the night for an attack at dawn? Or had it been a feint?

And now . . . this. . . .

The soldier was muddy and dishevelled, his face filthy, his eyes wide and bright in the deepening twilight. He was also breathing hard, as though he'd been running hard and fast. One of Zellner's staff officers had brought him over just a moment before.

"Just how many enemy 'Mechs did you see, anyway?" Zellner demanded.

"I . . . I ain't sure, sir. Lots, though. More than a company. And they was heading this way at a full run!"

"Fool. If *they* were running, how did you get here ahead of them?"

The man turned and pointed west. The sunset sky was a brilliant red and orange beyond the blue-black shadows of the Tanglewood. "I came straight through there. They was coming up the road, to the north. I dunno. Maybe they stopped to form up. Maybe they're movin' through the woods now, slow like. But they're there, and they're comin', Marshal. Damn me if they ain't!"

A crackle of gunfire sounded to the west and the insistent yammer of a machine gun. Zellner kept staring into the forest, as though willing himself to see through the impenetrable wall of trees. *What* was going on out there? The man had seen something, that was certain. His was the fifth report in the last ten minutes, reports by infantry scouts and his communications staff and by one *Mercury* still on picket duty on the Tanglewood Road. The *Mercury*'s report had ended in midtransmission, with no clear warning of anything but something moving on the road, and Zellner had assumed a radio failure. Now, though, it was clear that enemy units were moving out there.

But a company or more? It didn't seem possible, not given what was known about the Gray Death's numbers on Caledonia. And at *night*?

Ridiculous!

The likeliest explanation, especially in light of the reports of large numbers of 'Mechs moving to the east, was that a few 'Mechs, possibly a recon lance of *Stingers* and *Locusts*, had been deployed through the Tanglewood either to act as fire observers for the main attack, or to serve as decoys, a diversion to pull Zellner's main strength back to Meadow Grove.

Something broke from cover, skittering across the open ground. Now what?

There was another. And another. In a moment, there were hundreds of the things, small, brown or black furred animals of some kind, leaping and bounding swiftly as they dashed out of the woods and across the open ground toward the east.

Zellner turned slowly, surveying the area. He was in the main encampment, where dozens of BattleMechs had been drawn together for servicing, arming, and preparation for the battle everyone expected in the morning. The infantry camp lay to the west, tucked in next to the woods, and he could see against the shadows of the trees dozens of campfires lit by men preparing evening meals. Further north was the supply dump, and row upon row of parked vehicles, supply trucks, ammo carriers . . . and suddenly it all seemed terribly, terribly vulnerable.

More of the furred animals crashed out of the underbrush, running frantically. *Something* sure had scared them, back in the woods. . . .

The first Gray Death BattleMech emerged from the forest less than a hundred meters from Zellner's position, striding out from among the trees and into the middle of the infantry encampment. Soldiers bolted and ran, a few in armor, some wearing fatigues or even underwear. The 'Mech, a *Locust*, strode through the camp with the look of some ugly, demonic insect eight meters tall, balanced on two slender legs that stilted across campfires and tents and scattering men. Zellner could see the black and gray skull emblem painted on its upper works. The 'Mech's twin laser mounts opened fire, and men began to fall.

To his own surprise, the appearance of the *Locust* steadied Zellner. A twenty-ton scout machine? Was *that* all? His *Atlas* could kick it to the next continent. Swiftly he climbed back up the access ladder, struggling to reach the safety of his cockpit before the *Locust* came closer.

Along the line of the woods, now, other 'Mechs were emerging. . . .

Alex saw the trees thinning ahead and urged his *Archer* along faster, crashing through the smaller trees and saplings, squeezing once between two larger trees, partly uprooting both as his seventy-ton machine forced them apart. An explosion erupted ahead and to the left; machine gun fire chattered. Shifting briefly to IR imagery, Alex saw dozens of small, bright blobs of life scurrying ahead of his footsteps—small Caledonian animals of some kind startled by the onslaught of 'Mechs, and sent fleeing ahead of the attack and out of the woods.

"I'd run too," Alex silently told the fugitives, "if I had this bunch on my tail!" His primary monitor showed two 'Mech formations to the north and south of the Tanglewood Road, arrayed six and six each. Alex was with Third Batt's Third Company, the Gray Raiders. The unit's CO, Captain Gallery, was maneuvering his *Shadow Hawk* through the woods to Alex's left; Sergei Golovanov in his *Marauder* was crashing ahead to his right. Alex shifted course slightly, moving a bit closer to Shooter Gallery, putting a bit more distance between himself and the *Marauder*'s PPCs, as well as providing additional fire support for the lighter *Shadow Hawk*.

Then he was through the final line of trees and bursting into the open.

It was twilight, with the sky still a pale and radiant green-blue and both of Caledonia's moons hanging in the southern sky. He'd emerged two hundred meters south of the road, and almost squarely in the center of a camp. Tents were strewn about everywhere, some still standing, many knocked down either by 'Mechs or by fleeing troops. Bruce Lazenby's *Locust* was moving ahead, dragging the white canvas of a tent that had snagged on his 'Mech's left foot. A few hundred meters ahead, the gantry rigging and portable cranes of a small 'Mech maintenance area showed where the Third Davion Guard had positioned its reserves. Several artillery field pieces were drawn up behind sandbag parapets, aimed at a point well above the ridge to the south.

Several nearby Third Guard 'Mechs turned to face the sudden strike from their right and rear. A *JagerMech* was caught in a crossfire by Sergeant Hank Corby's *Victor* and Golovanov's *Marauder,* twisting back and forth in a horrible parody of a dance as laser and particle beams stabbed and slashed through its armor. Then Corby cut loose with his Gauss rifle, and the crack of the ferrous-encased depleted uranium breaking the sound barrier echoed across the landscape. The round struck the *JagerMech* in the left side, peeling back a wad of armor as big as the 'Mech's arm, and exposing the sparking, flashing leads and circuitry of its internal wiring. As another fusillade of laser fire struck home, the domed top of the *JagerMech*'s squat torso popped open in a cloud of smoke, and an instant later the pilot rocketed clear, his ejection seat propelled skyward by a battery of powerful jets.

Alex noted the 'Mech's destruction but had no time for more than a glance as the *JagerMech* exploded into orange flame. He was already tagging targets for his LRMs. The artillery park first . . . followed by the field maintenance area. The more Third Guard 'Mechs he could put holes in while they were standing there helpless, without their MechWarriors, the better.

Pivoting right, the protective cowlings on both of the *Archer*'s LRM batteries folding back, Alex planted both of his 'Mech's feet solidly in the ground, then loosed a shrieking school of deadly Doombud LRMs. Their contrails arched away through the sky, descending on and around the long-range artillery pieces, which until that moment had been continuing to hurl high explosives over the ridge to the south.

Explosions blossomed among the artillery pieces; the tree trunk-sized barrel of a 155mm cannon spun end over end as it flew straight up in the air, hesitated a moment, then plunged earthward into the expanding smoke cloud of its carriage's destruction. The blasts continued after the last of Alex's rockets struck; secondary explosions were touched off among stored munitions behind the sandbag revetments. Abruptly, the store of artillery bombardment rockets detonated, and an acre of Caledonian earth heaved up into the sky, overturning guns, smashing munitions tractors and transport crawlers, and mowing down the gunners as they sought frantically to escape.

Pivoting his torso left, Alex zeroed in next on the massed BattleMechs at the maintenance area, loosing another LRM salvo . . . then a third and a fourth as his tubes loaded automatically. As explosions ripped through the facility, shredding the lightweight structures of the gantry towers and the heavier traveling crane mounts, one *Stinger* toppled slowly forward, crashing full-length onto the ground as the magnetic grapples holding it in place gave way. A moment later, a *Hatchetman,* with its rather ludicrous and clumsy hand weapon, was torn open from throat to hip by a succession of internal explosions, and then part of the gantry support behind it came toppling down, smashing the vacant 'Mech to the ground beneath a pile of twisted, smoking wreckage. A fuel tank nearby erupted with crimson and orange savagery, lighting up the darkening plain as the fireball climbed into the evening sky.

By this time, the other 'Mechs of Task Force Skriker had moved well past Alex's position, smashing headlong into the Davion 'Mechs—both manned and unmanned—scattered about the rear area. To Alex's practiced eye, it appeared that Striker had emerged from the Tanglewood squarely behind the Davion right flank, with few of the enemy 'Mechs even facing the woods or otherwise prepared for an attack from that direction. Turning to face the ridge to the south, he triggered the two flare guns mounted outside his *Archer*'s head. With a dull *pop-pop,* two brilliant green stars clawed their way into the sky, a signal to his father that the attack had succeeded as a complete surprise. . . .

The Third Davion Guard 'Mechs were still advancing slowly down the slope from Cemetery Ridge, occasionally stopping to probe the woods in front of them with fire. Receiving no fire in return, they kept moving. Hidden in the woods less than a kilometer away now, Grayson, Major Frye, and the rest of the Third Batt's First Company waited, weapons ready, cross hairs and targeting cursors already laid on their chosen prey.

Abruptly, two greens flares crawled up from behind the ridge, arcing toward the zenith in emerald glory, brilliant against the darkening twilight. "There he is!" Grayson cried over the general tactical chanel. "That's Alex!"

"He did it!" Davis added. "Th' lad did it!"

"Thank *God,*" Caitlin DeVries added with heartfelt intensity.

Someone in the waiting fire team cheered. "Stow it!" Grayson warned. "Stand by! No one fires until I give the word!"

Third Batt's First BattleMech Company, the Firestormers as they called themselves, normally consisted of twelve 'Mechs divided among Command, Fire, and Combat Lances, but losses in their recent campaign on the old Commonwealth border with the Draconis Combine and on the edge of Clan space had not been completely made up, and they now numbered just eight. To reinforce the company, Grayson had added his own supernumerary Command One-one lance, consisting of himself in his *Victor,* Davis McCall's *Highlander,* and Caitlin DeVries's *Griffin.* Also present as supernumerary was Captain Walter Dupré, the warrior who still didn't have a unit to fit his rank but who'd been attached to Grayson's personal staff until a slot opened up. Dupré's ponderous, eighty-ton *Zeus* had taken up position among the trees to Grayson's rear. Irritated, Grayson opened a private channel. "Captain Dupré! What the hell are you doing back there? Move up! I want those people to feel our steel!"

"Uh . . . yes, sir."

"We fight as a lance. No one hangs back!"

"I wasn't hanging back!"

"Just get in line, take your position, and don't move! It'll go down pretty quick, now."

The eight 'Mechs of the Firestormers were mostly on the heavy side, including Lang's *Shadow Hawk,* a *Marauder,* a *JagerMech,* two *Catapults,* a *Guillotine,* a *Vindicator,* and a *Hunchback.* The addition of Command One-one made the unit a motley and mismatched gang ranging from the forty-five-ton *Vindie* to McCall's ninety-ton monster of a *Highlander.* The twelve 'Mechs they were facing were lighter for the most part. The leader appeared to be another *Victor,* but the others included two *Locusts* and a *Mercury* in an advance recon position, three *Centurions,* two *Wolfhounds,* and three *Assassins.* Grayson's combat computer had long since tallied the raw numbers: the twelve Gray Death 'Mechs added up to 790 tons, while the approaching company-strength patrol totalled just 480 tons.

It wasn't at all wise to predict the outcome of a battle solely on the respective total weights of the two sides, but the fact that the hidden Gray Death company so significantly outmassed the other, and that they were attacking from ambush virtually guaranteed an immediate victory. The problem was that when the Legion 'Mechs attacked, they would reveal just how few of them were in place in the woods opposite Cemetery Ridge, a vital bit of combat intelligence that would be immediately relayed back to the Guard headquarters. There was no way Grayson knew of to simultaneously silence all twelve enemy 'Mechs. Some were bound to escape; any could broadcast the critical data in the minutes it would take to destroy them.

Grayson had in fact been considering ordering his line to melt back into the woods, to avoid contact together, but that would have risked the serious danger of the twelve Legion 'Mechs becoming separated in the treacherous labyrinth of the Tanglewood, and the even greater danger being fired on by friendly 'Mechs in that wilderness.

Seeing Alex's signal had decided him, however. With Alex attacking their rear, by now the Guards had other things to worry about than how many 'Mechs were in Grayson's tiny command. The thought was reinforced by a glance toward Cemetery Ridge. A greasy black pall of smoke was rising now against the evening sky, red-lit from beneath, and the sound of multiple explosions could be heard in the distance.

"*Get* 'em, Alex!" he breathed softly.

The Davion 'Mechs were much closer now, less than two hundred meters away. They were picking their way slowly through the torn and ruptured ground in front of the woods, an area plowed by dozens of high-explosive shells and rockets from the Davion artillery base.

The *Locust*s and the lone *Mercury* trod mincingly across the broken ground, now within one hundred meters. The others hung further back, possibly sensing a trap, possibly receiving new orders from their command center. Much longer, and they might be ordered back.

But now they were close enough.

"*Fire!*"

As one, the Gray Death BattleMechs hidden in the woods opened fire on the advancing 'Mech company. Grayson had carefully passed the word to the others to hold their fire, deliberately luring the approaching patrol well into the killing ground of the waiting 'Mechs interlocking fields of fire. One of the *Locust*s went down almost at once, its slender leg shot through by a laser burst from a Legion *Marauder.* An *Assassin* was pinned in the intersecting laser beams from Lang's *Shadow Hawk,* Gonzalez's *Guillotine,* and Sharon Kilroy's *Vindicator.* Thomas Vandermier's *Hunchback* began the steady *slam-slam-slam* of heavy cannon fire from his Kali Yama autocannon. The shells slashed viciously into a *Centurion,* driving it back step by step, shredding armor from its shoulder and side in great chunks that spun smoking through the air.

So devastating was that first volley that there was no immediate response from the ambush victims. Two of their number were down ... then three ... then a fourth, a second *Assassin,* hammered down by rocket fire from the two big *Catapult*s. Finally, the survivors began returning fire, but slowly and with evident confusion, sending rounds and laser beams searing through the trees, but for the most part firing high or between the lurking Legion 'Mechs.

Grayson concentrated his fire on the biggest enemy 'Mech, a *Victor* that might have been an identical twin to Grayson's save that its armor looked newer and less scarred, the paint was brighter, the hull numbers fresher.

No matter. Grayson slammed two Gauss rounds into the other *Victor* at close range one after the other, then followed up with a barrage from both lasers and a salvo of SRMs. The other *Victor,* staggered by the sheer, devastating power of the Gauss rifle onslaught, stumbled and went down. Rising, it brought up its own Gauss rifle, seeking a target, then firing with a shattering thunderclap that felled a tree three meters to Grayson's left.

Grayson fired his Gauss gun again before the enemy *Victor* could recharge, striking the other high in its right shoulder, tearing away a chunk of its heavy pauldron.

The other Davion 'Mechs, those that could still walk, were scattering, running back the way they'd come, their formation broken. Grayson strode from the woods, firing at the retreating Guard 'Mechs. The enemy *Victor,* still holding its ground, fired both lasers, the coherent light washing across Grayson's armored torso in a scintillating burst of reflected light. The other 'Mech seemed to be having trouble with its Gauss rifle, however. Twice, it raised the heavy muzzle of the weapon to aim directly at Grayson's cockpit, then twice lowered it again, as though the pilot had tried to trigger the weapon and failed. Abruptly, the enemy 'Mech turned, flexed its knees, and leaped into the air, jump jets shrieking, leaving a swirl of superheated air and burning grass to mark its passage.

"Forward!" Grayson called. "General advance!"

It was Pickett's Charge at Gettysburg again, with Grayson advancing up Cemetery Ridge with eleven BattleMechs strung out to either side and behind him, the enemy already in complete rout, streaming away and up the slope of the ridge. He could see other 'Mechs atop the ridge, wavering uncertainly. From that vantage point, they must be able to see both Grayson's small line to their front, plus the large number of 'Mechs in Striker coming down on their rear. The explosions flashing and erupting along the crest of the hills ahead indicated that Alex must be hitting them from the far side with everything he had.

An old-fashioned charge, right now, right here, just might break the enemy's will to keep fighting.

A salvo of SRMs streaked across the intervening space from the ridge, angling toward the torso of Grayson's *Victor*. Grayson flexed his 'Mech's knees, then leaped, triggering his jump jets in a fiery burst of superheated steam. He rose into the sky as the missiles howled past. One exploded harmlessly against his side armor; the others missed, passing beneath him. Slowly, majestically, his *Victor* soared across the plain toward the top of the ridge. He would never make it all the way, of course, but his first jump ought to take him about a quarter of the way out from the woods. This, at least, was one advantage the *Victor* had over the *Marauder*. It could jump, though Grayson often thought that the weight and control systems devoted to the jump jets could have been better spent on additional weapons for the *Victor*.

To left and right, others of the company charged forward, those with jump jets using them to vault ahead, those without breaking into a lumbering run up the gentle slope. The company was widely scattered now, the better to avoid making a tempting target for enemy gunners on the ridgetop.

The *Victor* was losing energy, starting to descend. Grayson positioned his legs for a landing, spreading them slightly apart, knees flexed ...

He hit and heard a sharp bang from somewhere below in the same instant. Red lights flared across his console, warning of a critical failure in his right-leg hydraulics. He was losing pressure down there, and fast.

He recovered from his landing, took one step ... and suddenly the ground was rushing toward his 'Mech's cockpit. He crashed into the ground, the impact jarring him, hurling him forward and down against the straps that pinned him in his seat.

Right-leg hydraulics *and* control systems, down. The *Victor*'s knees had been giving it trouble for years, but never anything like this. He must have blown the whole hydraulic pressurization system and shorted out the myomer cyclics. Warning discretes announced catastrophic failure of his right leg. Hell, as near as he could tell, his 'Mech didn't *have* a right leg anymore.

His *Victor,* lying full length on the ground, began bucking and thumping with multiple impacts. There was a devastating slam as something big hit him in the back, and suddenly, miniature lightning bolts were dancing across his console.

Grayson gasped, then screamed as an electric charge surged through his body. The pain was mercifully brief, cut short when the power to his cockpit systems failed, but it left him numb, feeling bruised all over. He couldn't move his legs. Another thump, more violent this time, and fresh lightnings arced past his cockpit window.

A PPC round . . . from behind? Desperately, Grayson tried to engage one of his monitors to get a view in that direction, but nothing was working, nothing! The *Victor*'s cockpit was dark save for the glow of emergency battery-powered lights and the erratic wink of dozens of red warning lights on his console. *"Warning, warning,"* a computer voice said with grating calm. *"Fire in capacitor bank three. . . ."*

Grayson was hanging facedown, dangling from the safety harness of his cockpit seat. Smoke was filling the cockpit, and one of the few operational readouts on his console was the ominous red bar showing 'Mech internal temperature, next to several flashing discretes warning of fire.

Damn! Who had attacked him? All primary systems were out, dead. He couldn't eject, not lying flat like this. He would have to scramble clear through the escape hatch. Would his legs hold him? Feeling was returning, a hot tingling sensation, but he wasn't sure he'd be able to stand up.

"Warning, warning. Fire in the cockpit. Fire in the cockpit . . ."

He would crawl if he had to. The smoke was becoming so thick he could scarcely see his console in the hesitant light, but there was a growing warmth to the smoke, and a hint of a flickering yellow glow. His helmet was not airtight, and he began choking on the acrid fumes. After struggling to disconnect his neurohelmet cables and then unhooking his seat restraints in the close space of the cockpit, Grayson twisted around and yanked on the emergency hatch release. There was a small explosion, and the hatch popped open, admitting a rush of cool, sweet, fresh air. He pushed himself through, his legs dangling uselessly behind him as he hauled himself halfway through the small round hatch.

A 'Mech loomed up out of the rear darkness just thirty meters away. In the gloom, he could still make out its outline easily against the pale twilight sky: a *Zeus*.

Walter Dupré's *Zeus*.

With a harsh whine of servomotors, the fearsome assault 'Mech raised its left arm to aim its massive particle projection cannon directly at him.

28

Meadow Grove
Caledonia, Skye March
Federated Commonwealth
2054 hours, 16 April 3057

The Davion 'Mechs were on the run, streaming away from the point at which Task Force Striker had burst out of the woods in a ragged flight in the general direction of the Round Tops, about three kilometers away. Dozens of 'Mechs were scattered about the maintenance area or close by, slumped dead and vacant on the ground in huge, metallic sprawls, or burning furiously as their internal ammo stores cooked off.

Surprise had been complete, and victory was assured *if* they could keep the pace of battle moving along at its current fast clip. Fully half the Davion force was in all-out retreat. And, best of all, it was retreating in the direction of the other half of the Davion force. A collision would reduce both to a helplessly milling mob. Alex knew that the key to victory was for the Legion forces to keep up the pressure and to maintain coordination as they drove the enemy forward.

He glanced toward the south. His father should have seen the flares, should be on his way now. Once the rest of the Gray Death swept over the ridge, they would have the retreating wing of the Third Davion Guards trapped and funneling toward the Round Tops.

Still, Alex saw no sign of his father's force. Where were they?

Davis McCall landed his *Highlander* in a fiery burst of superheated plasma as the 'Mech's jump jets cushioned his touchdown near the top of Cemetery Ridge. A laser beam stabbed against his center torso, boiling armor, and autocannon shells splashed across his legs and side. Shrugging off the volley, McCall recovered from the landing, strode forward three steps, and swung his 'Mech's right arm in a savage, flat arc, smashing the side of an *Enforcer*'s head.

A Davion *Blackjack* pivoted its torso to face him sixty meters away, and McCall triggered his 'Mech's left-arm Gauss rifle. The hypersonic round struck the lighter 'Mech low in the torso and to the left, punching straight through the armor in an explosion of shrapnel and scattering bits of internal circuitry. The *Blackjack* twisted, as if in pain, and its legs folded beneath it as smoke began spilling from the wound in its side. McCall followed his first shot with another, sending along a salvo of six SRMs as seasoning. Half the missiles struck home, while the Gauss round smashed the lower half of the *Blackjack*'s right arm to metal shards and splinters. As the top of the *Blackjack*'s blocky head disintegrated in a small explosion of smoke and blown-off panels, the pilot's ejection seat rocketed into the sky on a dazzling trail of orange fire.

McCall urged his ponderous mount forward, taking the last twenty strides up the slope and cresting the top of Cemetery Ridge. He was the first one from the Legion to make it to the objective, though Caitlin's *Griffin* and Frye's Pegasus tank were close behind. Now that he'd eliminated the *Blackjack* and the *Enforcer,* the ridge was swept clean of Davion 'Mechs. Most had turned and fled with the survivors of the Davion patrol, which had come bolting up the slope from the south, smashing through their own lines as they kept on going. The 'Mechs in position atop Cemetery Ridge had taken one look at the line of Gray Death mediums and heavies advancing up the hill out of the twilight, loosed a few ineffectual shots, and then turned and followed their fleeing comrades.

More Firestormer 'Mechs joined him, Aleksanyen's *Catapult* and Lang's *Shadow Hawk,* the latter advancing steadily with its big shoulder-mounted autocannon barking steadily as it hurled shell after high-explosive shell after the retreating enemy.

Where was Grayson?

McCall glanced at his tactical display, then turned, searching the darkening slope behind. He saw movement and the orange smear of flame. Shifting his HUD optics to enhanced imagery, he could pick out the broken lines of a fallen *Victor,* the menacing angles of a *Zeus* aiming its PPC at the pilot. . . .

"No! . . ."

There was no time to wriggle free of the *Victor's* escape hatch, no time for anything save throwing both arms above his head as Grayson Carlyle stared into the blackened muzzle of the Defiance 1001 PPC.

"I'm sorry, Colonel," came Dupré's voice, booming from the external speaker of his *Zeus.* "I can't accept your surrender."

Dupré! The assassination attempt on Glengarry . . . The son of a bitch must have been part of that, a plant, a mole in the Gray Death, placed there to feed intelligence to whoever was behind all of this—and to kill its commander at a critical moment.

And I thought I was a good judge of people! Grayson thought with stark bitterness. *Right!*

"Who are you working for?" Grayson shouted at the giant looming above him. *Keep him talking!* "I mean, maybe we could make a deal. . . ."

"No deals, Colonel. I'm afraid I have my or—"

The thunderclap was a shattering explosion of raw noise, the detonation of a lightning bolt striking scant meters away. Grayson's first thought was that the PPC had loosed its artificial lightning, but the *Zeus* staggered back a half step as a portion of its upper torso flared white at the bull's-eye center of an expanding smoke ring.

Instantly, Grayson dropped back down through the narrow mouth of the *Victor's* escape hatch. There would have been no time for him to wiggle all the way out, and with his legs still numb and tingling, he could not have run for cover. The only cover he could reach was to return to the temporary—and burning—shelter of the *Victor's* head.

But as he dropped through the hatch, his left sleeve

snagged on a projecting shard of torn metal. For one horrifying instant, he hung there with his arm still on the rim of the hatch as he struggled to pull it free.

Suddenly the near darkness of the *Victor*'s cockpit exploded with light. Again, Grayson felt the jolt and the numbness of a violent electrical shock as lightning sparked and snapped across the open hatchway. The eerie and frightening part of the assault was that it was all happening in a total, wool-muffled silence. Grayson could see his left sleeve on fire, see the skin underneath blistering, yet he felt no immediate pain or any other sensation at all save the numbing effects of the shock. And the silence lent a dreamlike quality to what was happening, almost as though he were watching it all happen to someone else in a trivid.

Then the burning sleeve tore free and Grayson tumbled back into the cockpit, half his clothing in flames. He was starting to feel the pain now and he could feel himself screaming, but he still could hear nothing save the vibration of his own cries transmitted through the bones of his skull to his ears.

Somehow, thrashing about the close confines of the *Victor*'s cockpit, his right hand closed on a manual fire extinguisher and yanked it free of its mounting bracket on the curving wall. Turning it on himself, Grayson bathed his burning arm and side in a white blast of carbon dioxide vapor, still screaming as the pain seared out of his arm and invaded his chest and head. And all the while he still did not hear a thing even when the extinguisher ran empty and the metal bottle dropped from spasming fingers and bounced off a metal console. Collapsing against the cable and power feed-covered wall next to the display monitors, console, and forward viewport that now formed the cockpit's floor, Grayson stared up at the circle of sky visible through the still-open hatch. The pain was terrible . . . yet distant, as though the nerves of his body had overloaded somehow or simply been seared into total unresponsiveness. He felt as though he'd been wrapped in cotton wool, as if he were floating. The silence that still embraced him together with the awful pain, he decided, must be the result of that final thunderclap.

What, he wondered, his mind starting to drift as his body slid inexoraby into shock, was going on outside? . . .

* * *

Davis McCall fired again, sending a hypersonic round from his *Highlander*'s Gauss rifle slamming into the *Zeus*, striking it in one bulky shoulder and spinning it halfway around.

"This is McCall!" he shouted over the tactical frequency. "Th' Colonel's down!"

The *Zeus* raised its left-arm PPC, loosing a bolt of charged particles that smashed into the *Highlander*'s left leg in a searing burst of man-made lightning. McCall fired the Gauss rifle a third time, striking the *Zeus* in its lower torso. The earlier hits had savaged the other 'Mech's armor, reducing large parts of its torso and shoulder to half-fused areas surrounding gaping craters. As smoke now poured from the hull of the *Zeus,* the pilot was obviously having trouble focussing on McCall's *Highlander*.

Seeing his chance, McCall triggered his jump jets, and the ninety-ton *Highlander* soared clumsily into the air.

"This is McCall! Th' Colonel's down!"

The words, broadcast over the Legion's general tactical frequency, were the first Alex had heard from the 'Mechs he'd left behind south of Cemetery Ridge hours ago, and they burned their way into his brain.

He'd maneuvered his *Archer* into the Davion supply dump while other Legion 'Mechs and dozens of troopers, both Legion commandos and rebels, raced past. Stacks of plastic ammo crates and power cells rose about him, a small, high-tech bonanza—*if* the Legion could hang onto it. His *Archer*'s LRM racks were empty now, and he was hoping to find some missiles stored there, plus enough Legion troops to serve as a working party. McCall's announcement that his father was down struck like lightning, however. Turning swiftly to face south, Alex scanned the top of Cemetery Ridge, immediately picking out the line of Gray Death 'Mechs now reaching the crest. McCall's *Highlander* was airborne, vanishing behind the ridge just as Alex spotted it.

Smashing aside a piled-high mountain of ammo crates, Alex goaded his *Archer* into a flat-out run, racing across Meadow Grove toward Cemetery Ridge.

At the peak of his leap, Davis McCall triggered one more cough from his left-side jump jet, shifting his trajectory a good ten degrees to the right. The course change was enough to confuse the *Zeus,* which was trying to pivot in order to be facing the *Highlander* when it landed. Coming down behind the *Zeus,* McCall also pivoted to face the other 'Mech as he hit the ground, his Gauss rifle already up and aimed squarely at the enemy machine's right-rear quarter.

With a sound like a giant thunderclap, the hypersonic projectile streaked into the center of the *Zeus*'s back, where the protective armor was less than a third the thickness of the slabs of armor plate covering its chest.

The *Zeus* was driven forward a step by the incredible force of the impact, kinetic energy fusing an eight-square-meter patch of armor into a white-hot, molten mass. The projectile plunged through the 'Mech's thin back carapace like a laser beam through butter. Ricocheting off the much thicker armor encasing the power plant, the Gauss slug severed power cables, shredded the endoskeletal framework, and set off the store of long-range missiles stashed in the *Zeus*'s right torso. As secondary explosions erupted from the 'Mech's torso, the right arm tore free, armor plates popped off, access panels blew open, and flame engulfed the machine's lower torso. An instant later, the head split apart as the cockpit canopy hinged open and the 'Mech's pilot inside rocketed clear on his ejection seat.

Cursing bitterly in the fear and urgency of the moment, McCall turned to see to the fallen Grayson Carlyle.

Alex pushed his lumbering 'Mech to full speed, cursing the fact that *Archers* had no jump jets. While the other 'Mechs of Striker continued moving in a long line toward the southeast, driving the shattered remnants of the Third Davion Guard before them, he was moving directly south, climbing the gentle slope of the elevation code-named Cemetery Ridge.

His father was over there, somewhere ... and in trouble. ...

29

Meadow Grove
Caledonia, Skye March
Federated Commonwealth
2056 hours, 16 April 3057

When the Gray Death force came storming through the Third Guard base camp, Marshal Felix Zellner had been faced with one of the thornier problems of BattleMech tactics: how does a MechWarrior *hide* something as huge as an *Atlas*? Nearly fifteen meters tall, massing one hundred tons, the *Atlas* was among the very largest of all 'Mechs in the field, a powerhouse monster that could stand up to incredible punishment without folding. Zellner's *Atlas* was a recent acquisition, too, one of the new AS7-K models sporting a Dragon's Fire Gauss rifle, four lasers of various caliber, and twenty tubes for the Shigunga long-range missile.

He'd eventually found an answer to his dilemma near the center of the temporary 'Mech maintenance area, but it wouldn't work for very long. The gantry structure had collapsed in a spaghetti tangle of girders, struts, and twisted steel, together with the wreckage of several smashed and burned BattleMechs destroyed by the Gray Death forces as they'd first emerged from the forest to the west. Moments after the gantry had collapsed and enemy 'Mechs had begun pouring across the area, Zellner had moved behind the wreckage of the maintenance facility and dropped his *Atlas* prone, using its great hands to pull several tons of broken, heat-warped steel part way across its torso and legs.

He'd played dead, another vacant 'Mech destroyed by the collapse of the gantry structure.

He'd remained there, unmoving, as a Gray Death *Catapult* had stalked past like some huge and improbable flightless bird. He'd waited until the entire Gray Death line had moved on toward the southeast. Then, with a heave of one arm, he'd brushed the tangled steel from his 'Mech's body like straw, then rose—a fully armed and operational *Atlas* squarely in the rear of the enemy force.

Had he stood in place and faced the oncoming line, the Gray Death 'Mechs would have banded together to bring him down. The *Atlas* might have taken out three, perhaps even four of the smaller 'Mechs, but in the end the hundred-ton behemoth would have been torn to pieces. With his simple little ruse, he'd managed to turn the tables on what the Gray Death flanking force had just done to him—place a powerful force at the enemy's rear, and completely by surprise.

Standing next to the fallen gantry, he scanned the backs of the Gray Death 'Mechs, then pivoted slightly to bring the Gauss rifle mounted on his right torso to bear on the rear armor of a *JagerMech*. The thunderclap of his shot echoed across the maintenance yard, the force of the blow picking up the 'Mech and slamming it forward, the thin lightweight armor over the *Jager*'s rear torso shredding like cardboard. Internal explosions followed an instant later as stored autocanno rounds began popping off like firecrackers. Much of the destructive force was vented through the 'Mech's CASE storage cells, but the internal structure was still gutted by the savage, multiple blasts. Zellner triggered his right-arm laser, the beam carving through the *JagerMech*'s damaged left leg like a sword slash. The Gray Death 'Mech collapsed in a burning heap of wreckage. The pilot did not eject.

Pivoting, Zellner brought a second Gray Death 'Mech into his sights, this time a *Vindicator* . . .

Alex heard the scream over the commline as Brian Fox's *JagerMech* exploded. Still moving south, he swung his torso left, picking up the looming shape of the *Atlas* just barely visible near the gantry as it targeted its next victim from behind.

"Strikers!" he shouted over the tactical channel, at the same moment slewing the *Archer* to a stop, raising the 'Mech's arms simultaneously to deliver a deadly left-right blow from both his arm-mounted lasers. "All Strikers, this is Carlyle! *Atlas* on your six!"

On your six was a venerable combat term, one derived from an ancient and forgotten mode of telling time that placed the "six" squarely on a pilot's tail. But though analog timekeeping might be long forgotten, the warning phrase was not. At his shout, most of the Second and Third Company 'Mechs stopped and turned.

Alex's lasers struck the *Atlas* in its side and right arm, the beams flaring in dazzling bursts of reflected light and vaporizing armor. The *Atlas* seemed to hesitate, then turned ponderously to face him. The expression on the round head with its two triangular cockpit windows and the jagged line of ratchet teeth and exhaust vents underneath was the gut-punched shock of a grinning skull.

Now, Alex thought, he was really in for it. The *Atlas* outmassed him by only thirty tons, roughly a third, but his *Archer,* its missiles expended, mounted just four lasers, two facing the rear, one in each arm. A medium laser delivered perhaps a third of the destructive energy carried by a single Gauss round. With both combatants constantly shifting, dodging, and moving, there would be no way for Alex to pile up successive hits on the same spot, save by sheer luck.

And that massive slab armor on the *Atlas*'s breastplate alone was a third thicker than the thickest armor carried by an *Archer.* One-on-one, he didn't stand a chance.

The *Atlas* fired its Gauss rifle. There was no time to duck, no time to react at all. Alex was hit, the slug slamming through his *Archer*'s left shoulder, the force spinning him to the side and nearly knocking him down.

He fired his own lasers again, the beams splashing harmlessly off the armored mountain in front of him. He tried to shift left, but the enemy's right-arm laser sliced into the *Archer*'s side, and an instant later, a cloud of LRMs streaking from the *Atlas*'s chest detonated in a chattering cloud of death and destruction all around him. One missile exploded against the *Archer*'s cockpit armor, and the concussion set Alex's head ringing.

A PPC bolt suddenly struck the *Atlas* from behind, sending it lurching forward a step, lightning sparking off its arms and sides. Several LRMs slammed into the *Atlas* a second later, and the Davion pilot tried to turn to face this new onslaught.

In that instant Alex charged.

A year before, at the Battle of Ryco Pass, he'd charged four pursuing enemy 'Mechs in his *Archer,* an act of desperation—or perhaps of sheer defiance—that he'd regretted ever since.

This time, though, his charge was an act of strategy ... of tactics, for as the *Atlas* turned to face the other Gray Death 'Mechs, it exposed its back. Like all 'Mechs, it had much thinner armor there, less than a third of what it had up front. If he could score just three or so solid hits back there, Alex would be able to punch through that armored hide and reach the tender circuitry and wiring and ammo stores within.

Firing as he ran, he missed the giant's back, the first slug scattering off the giant 'Mech's massive shoulder. His second shot struck home, gouging a crater but doing little real damage.

The *Atlas* paused in mid-turn, hesitated, then swung back to face Alex, pulling the damaged section back around and out of sight. A Gauss round grazed the top of Alex's *Archer,* furrowing armor plate like a plow in soft earth, and carrying away the cowling for his left-side missile tubes.

Like an avenging angel, Maria Delgado's *Catapult* touched ground on shrieking jump jets thirty meters away from the *Atlas* and squarely in its rear. A salvo of Arrow IV missiles burst from her tubes like pellets from a shotgun, slamming into the rear of the *Atlas* in a devastating burst of armor-shredding destruction. She followed that volley with a fusillade of laser fire, striking home again and again and again. Spinning to face her, the *Atlas* turned its torn and smoking back to Alex. From a range of fifty meters, he fired twice more. His left-arm laser, damaged by the earlier hit, failed with that shot, but the other weapon tunneled through twisted, smoking armor to plunge like a hot blade into the *Atlas*'s vitals.

Captain Ann Warfield's *Guillotine* arrived next, slashing

at the *Atlas* from the side with heavy and medium laser fire. Sergeant Terry O'Reilly's *Apollo* added to the destruction with a rain of LRMs. Moments later, still another 'Mech arrived on the scene, this one from the crest of Cemetery Ridge. Becoming vaguely aware of the *Griffin*'s shape in the gathering darkness, Alex realized with a start that Caitlin, from the main body left behind, had just joined Striker.

He kept firing.

The *Atlas* was surrounded now on three sides, the focus of fire from four different heavy 'Mechs and one medium. Each time it turned, it exposed the gaping wound in its back to fire from one or more of its tormentors. A Gauss rifle round caught O'Reilly's *Apollo* squarely in its center torso, but the missiles kept coming until the fire-support 'Mech's tubes were empty. One of the *Atlas*'s arms, the right one, fell away in a shower of armor shards and fragments as an ammo explosion blasted out the rear CASE panels. A fire raged inside that laser-torn hull, and acrid smoke poured through the rents in its armor. A secondary explosion demolished the Gauss rifle, the fire spreading, tongues of flame licking across the huge machine's blackened surface.

The heat inside that *Atlas* must be terrific, Alex thought. His own heat warnings were sounding, threatening power plant shutdown, but he slapped the overrides and moved in closer, firing his single remaining forward-facing laser as fast as he could cycle it.

The explosion was blinding and deafening, an eruption of white flame that tore the *Atlas*'s back and right side to shreds, the hot shrapnel pinging off Alex's armor like spent bullets. What was left of the 'Mech teetered there for a moment, the remnants of its torso wreathed in flame, the left arm still twitching with an eerie life of its own, the skull of the head still grinning at Alex like the Gray Death's own logo.

Then the legs buckled, and the burning wreckage collapsed.

And only then did Alex turn away, his *Archer* limping on up Cemetery Ridge and over the top as he went to find his father.

Grayson Carlyle was aware of Davis McCall pulling him from the burning wreckage of his *Victor,* but he felt very lit-

tle of it. His brain, quickly sinking into the soft and swaddling embrace of systemic shock, was simply refusing to
feel any more pain as his burned and torn body was dragged
through the narrow hatch and out onto the ground.

He could feel the blood caked on his face and trickling
from his ears; he could feel, in a detached and almost disin-
terested way, the burns on his left arm and side—at least the
areas where the burns were only second degree and blistered
instead of charred and blackened. He felt the stab as McCall
slapped his good arm with an autoinjector, firing two hundred milligrams of antidoloric into his bloodstream. Still unable to hear a thing, he wondered if he'd been deafened by
the shock wave of a Gauss slug passing a few meters above
his head.

Reaching up with his right hand, Grayson grasped the
front of Davis McCall's jump suit. "Did . . . they . . ."

He couldn't complete the question. Consciousness was
slipping away like water running through his fingers.

There was so much he wanted to ask, and he couldn't
communicate any of it. Had they won? Was Alex all right?
Had the Davions been pinned or pushed back into a position
advantageous for the Gray Death?

Would the Legion come through this intact?

Davis was saying something, but Grayson couldn't
make out the words. Yet now, far off, in that same distance
that held his pain and much of his awareness, he could
hear a growing, throbbing roar, like surf on an ocean
shore.

McCall hit him with another injection. Other people were
gathering around, but it was hard to make them out. That
darkness . . . was it the deepening twilight, or was he
dying?

He didn't want to die. So many, many questions . . .

Alex. He was there, squeezing in next to McCall, looking
down at him with anguish in his eyes. Alex! He'd come
through it!

Relief washed through Grayson, following on the heels of
the coma drug Davis had just given him.

"How . . . ?"

Alex seemed to understand. Though still looking painfully
worried, he managed a wide grin, then held out his fist, the
thumb pointed up. "We did it," Grayson thought he heard

his son say behind the roaring in his ears. "We won! The Gray Death won!"

That was all he needed to hear. Grayson Carlyle let himself slip away then, into a deep and dreamless sleep.

Epilogue

"How is he?" Caitlin asked. "I mean . . . is he . . ."

They were standing in the public observation lounge of the spaceport at New Edinburgh, overlooking the tarmac and the three *Union* DropShips in their craterlike blast pits. Loading was almost complete. The last few BattleMechs were being taken aboard the *Endeavor* now. Launch was scheduled for 1000 hours, just forty-five minutes from now.

"He looked pretty bad," Alex said, trying to keep his tone neutral, but knowing he failed. He closed his eyes. Every time he thought of that hideously fire-blackened body . . .

"I didn't mean to make it worse."

"You didn't."

"I wonder if you realize what your father really is to the rest of us, Alex? I mean, he's your father. Of course you love him. But we all do, too. Some of us would die for that man, I think."

Alex smiled. "He has that effect on people."

"So, have you heard . . . anything?"

"MedTech Jamison is taking good care of him," Alex told her. "She took off his arm last night."

"Oh . . . Alex . . ."

"They won't be able to fit him with a prosthesis until we

get back to Glengarry, of course, but I'm sure they'll be able to fix him up pretty well. Jamison is good. Real good." He shrugged. "For the rest, I'm told his hearing was damaged, but he won't be deaf. There is a big ... a big question, though, as to whether he'll ever pilot a 'Mech again. A lot depends on, well, on what his condition is when he comes out of the medical coma."

"Damn, *damn!*" Caitlin smacked one small fist into the open palm of her other hand. "They didn't catch the bastard who did it, did they?"

"No. But Dupré'd better hope the Caledonian rebels aren't the ones who catch him. They feel pretty strongly about Grayson Carlyle too."

"Not rebels," Caitlin reminded him. "Not anymore."

The last of the Gray Death Legion's 'Mechs boarded the elevator that would carry it up into the *Endeavor*'s 'Mech bay.

It was only four days since the Battle of Falkirk, but the war—brief as it had been—for all intents and purposes was over and won. The battle had actually sputtered on for some hours following Marshal Zellner's death, but the end had been more or less a foregone conclusion after the destruction of the *Atlas*. It was true the pace of the fighting had been interrupted when so many of the Striker Force 'Mechs had turned to deal with Zellner's attack, and it hadn't helped that Alex had left his 'Mech to tend to his father. No one was blaming him for that, save possibly himself, but his absence from the battlefield for a critical thirty minutes had kept the Legion from achieving a total victory. The Third Davion Guard 'Mechs thrown back from the encampment by Alex's flank attack had routed into the Guard's Second Battalion, still lying in wait behind Big and Little Round Top for the expected Legion march around *that* flank. The collision had resulted in a splendid confusion, but by the time a reunited Legion Third Battalion under the command of Major Frye had resumed the tempo of the advance, the broken forces of the Davion battalion had stopped retreating and, their backs against the Round Tops, had been preparing for a last-ditch defense. They'd lost all their artillery and most of their supplies in Alex's attack, but they still mustered more than a full battalion. A head-on attack by the Legion force would have been worse than futile. It would have been suicidal.

Several 'Mechs on both sides had been lost in the confused fighting that sparked and flashed through the night, with BattleMechs hunting one another with infrared and headlights. In the end, it had been Alex who'd suggested the ceasefire. The Davion commander, Marshal James Seymour, had been only too happy to accept, for by now he'd lost nearly half his force and most of his supplies. Under the terms of the agreement they'd hammered out early on the morning of the seventeenth, the Third Guard's survivors would be permitted to withdraw to their DropShips, then lift offworld, leaving the Gray Death victorious, in possession of the planet. Less than twenty hours ago, they'd rendezvoused with their newly recharged JumpShip at one of the so-called pirate jump points, and, shortly after, vanished into hyperspace.

This still left Caledonia's political future somewhat up in the air. General McBee was now the world's provisional military governor, and he would remain in charge until the general election when the people of Caledonia could vote on a new government, one of their own choosing this time. But the fact remained that the legitimate governor had been deposed by force of arms. Neither Wilmarth nor Folker had been found after the battle, and it was assumed that Seymour had taken both back to Hesperus II. McBee's provisional government had already drawn up a report of their version of events and beamed it by HPG transmission to Tharkad, essentially claiming that Wilmarth's rule had been illegal and that the people had had no other resource but to redress their grievances themselves. No one could guess how Tharkad or New Avalon would react. It might well be the Federated Commonwealth courts on Tharkad that would determine Caledonia's ultimate political fate, and whether or not the revolution had succeeded.

In any case, the Gray Death could do nothing more on Caledonia except, possibly, prejudice those courts against the people. Davis McCall, now in command of the Gray Death with its leader seriously wounded, had given orders to boost as soon as possible, leaving his homeworld to its new government and its uncertain future. The Legion's future, it turned out, was even more uncertain than Caledon's, for an HPG broadcast that morning from Legion HQ on Glengarry had told of FedCom ships arriving in-system in great numbers.

Field Marshal Gareth, in the name of the Federated Commonwealth, was demanding the surrender of Glengarry and of the Gray Death Legion's landhold there.

Alex's mother, Caitlin's parents, everyone else who meant anything to them besides the people here with them now, were in terrible danger back there. It would be weeks, at least, before they could reach Glengarry, and when they did it might well be too late to do anything to help.

But they had to try.

"Come on," Alex told Caitlin. "We'd better board ship. It's a long way back to Glengarry."

Caitlin drew closer to him, and he put an arm around her shoulders. "Alex," she said, her voice tight. "What's going to happen? To the Legion?"

"Happen?" He managed a grin, one with fire behind it. "The Gray Death Legion is a lot bigger and a lot tougher than any one of us," he told her. "The Legion will do what it's always done.

"The Legion will *survive*."

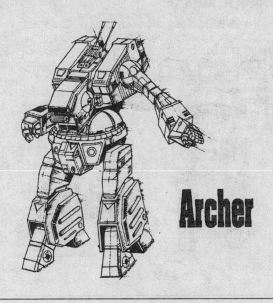

Archer

Atlas

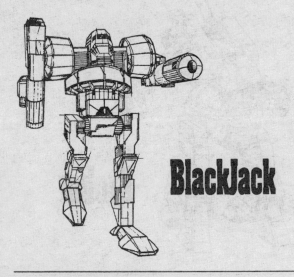

BlackJack

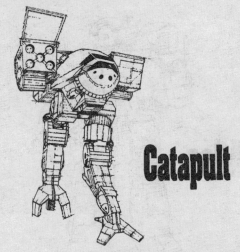

Catapult

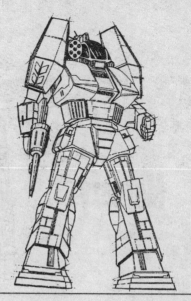

Griffin

Highlander

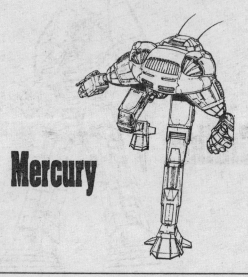

Mercury

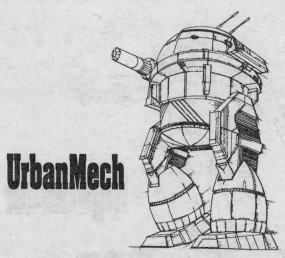

UrbanMech

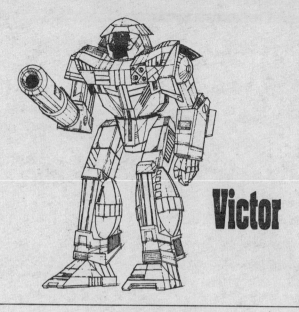

Victor

Zeus

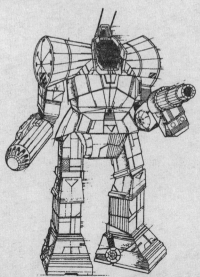

Be sure to catch the next exciting BattleTech novel *Lethal Heritage,* Book One of the *Blood of Kerensky* trilogy by Michael A. Stackpole, coming next month from Roc.

Sector 313 Alpha, Sisyphus's Lament
The Rock System, Oberon Confederation
13 August 3049

"**H**ound Deuce to Hound Leader. I have positive contact." Phelan punched an increase in magnification into the computer of his *Wolfhound.* "Kenny Ryan might think he's a chip off the old block, but we'll put an end to that lie right now."

Lieutenant Jackson Tang answered immediately. "Copy that, Deuce, Is this confirmed?"

"Affirmative, Leader." *Dammit, Jack, I know the amount of iron in this rock has been playing hob with our sensors.* "I have a vislight image at one thousand mag. I mark one *Locust* and one *Griffin* at a klick. Their gold paint scheme and red insignia stand out against the rocks. Want me to count pores on the pilots for you?"

The tone of Tang's reply was apologetic. "Negative, Deuce. Good work. I've got your position. We'll be working our way up."

Phelan glanced at his auxiliary monitor, where the computer displayed a diagram of the star system for a myriameter in radius around his position. Up near the top of the display, Phelan saw the icon representing the JumpShip *Cucamulus,* but it was only shown at half-intensity green. That meant the asteroids between Sisyphus's Lament and the ship prevented communications between it and Tang's lance of four 'Mechs. Likewise, the half-intensity red icon used to mark the last-known position of Captain Wilson and the company's other two lances meant those other 'Mechs were incommunicado.

"Hound Leader, do I sit put until we establish a commlink with the base, or do I move in? I have cover out another five hundred meters." Phelan punched up a data feed and had the computer relay it to Jack Tang's _Blackjack_.

"Hold on, Deuce. The data feed is coming across fuzzy. Let's try to stick together on this. Don't want you jumped like you were back on Gunzburg. I'm one ridge behind you. Trey and Kat are coming up to your left."

The young mercenary frowned. _I guess I deserved that._ "Roger, Leader."

Phelan wiped his sweaty palms against the ballistic cloth covering of his cooling vest. His right hand brushed the cool metal of the belt-buckle Tyra had given him. He smiled and adjusted the Mauser and Gray M-43 needler pistol on his right thigh. He knew that if his cockpit module were breached, this cold rock had just enough of an oxygen atmosphere to rust the rocks and let him freeze to death if no help came. _Even if I could draw the pistol with frozen fingers, it wouldn't do me any good. Somehow, though, it is comforting to wear it. It must be the superstition of routine that makes me feel that way. Strapping the thing on is the only normal piece of this whole operation._

The _Cucamulus_ had arrived in The Rock system at a pirate jump point. Pirate points were jump points a safe distance from the sun, but calculated to be on or near the star's orbital plane. This placed the JumpShip much closer to a system's planets, Janos Vandermeer, Captain of the _Cucamulus_, had brought the _Cu_ in close to the largest asteroid. Known as The Rock, it had given its name to the whole system. It had an atmosphere that made it habitable, and aside from the need to harvest water from the iceballs floating in the asteroid belt, it was supposed to be a pleasant place. Kenny Ryan's pirates had just begun to use it as a base, and the Kell Hounds hoped to catch them by surprise by bringing the _Cu_ in close.

Phelan glanced sourly at his display, then punched up another increase in magnification. "Holy Mother of God, Jack, I mean Hound Leader. Ryan's folks are running from something. I have definite visuals on lasers going in and out and something I mark as long-range missile fire incoming."

Over across the valley, Phelan saw a small, birdlike _Lo-_

cust ducking and dodging between reddish mounds of rock. The awkwardness of its gait was accentuated by the large hops the asteroid's lighter gravity allowed it. Missiles arced up and over the hills behind it, peppering the whole area around the fleeing 'Mech with explosions. Staggered barrages herded the *Locust* diagonally across the hillside, then another 'Mech appeared in a narrow pass between two bluffs.

Phelan frowned heavily as the computer sharpened and tried to label the image of the new 'Mech. Confused, the computer identified the 'Mech first as a *Catapult,* then almost immediately reclassified it as a *Marauder. It's got that hunched-over torso with the bird legs common to both designs, all right. And it's got the* Catapult'*s wing-mounted LRM launchers, but it also has the* Marauder'*s weapon pods. And I've never seen that flat gray color scheme before, either. Who and what the hell is it?*

The unidentified 'Mech jabbed both blocky pods at the *Locust,* sending out twin ruby lasers to skewer the *Locust*'s right flank. The first beam melted the armor from the *Locust*'s torso, making it drip steaming to the asteroid's surface while exposing the 'Mech's skeleton and internal structures.

The second beam stabbed through the hole the first had made. Its fiery touch ignited the machine gun ammo stored in the 'Mech's chest, then destroyed the *Locust*'s gyrostabilizers. As the light 'Mech's right side sagged in on itself, the 'Mech stumbled and rolled down the hillside. Its headlong spill ended with a jarring collision against a huge iron boulder the color of dried blood.

Three more of Ryan's bandit 'Mechs broke from cover and tried to rush across the valley toward Phelan's hidden-watch position. Two of them, the humanoid *Griffin* he'd seen earlier and another humanoid 'Mech, a *Panther,* darted from cover to cover. Both pilots used their 'Mechs' jump jets to quickly cross areas strewn with rocks too small for cover, but large enough to slow their sprint speed. Bringing up the rear came another humanoid 'Mech. Instead of arms, it sprouted twin-barrelled weapon pods. Larger than either the *Griffin* or *Panther,* and without jump jets, it moved more slowly than either of its compatriots. Phelan sensed the pilot's panic as he guided the *Rifleman* down the hillside and discovered he'd boxed himself in.

"Hound Leader, continue your present heading to make the plain. We've got help trapping the rats."

Confusion rang through Jack's voice. "Who . . . what?"

Phelan shrugged and moved from cover. "I can't identify our help, but they're on the ridge a kilometer off, driving Ryan toward us."

Tang laughed lightly. "Enemy of my enemy is my friend?"

Phelan saw Tang's black and red _Blackjack_ appear down on the edge of the plain. Tang's barrel-chested, humanoid 'Mech had arms that ended in the autocannon muzzles, with the muzzle of a medium laser riding piggyback on the outside of the forearm. The scout lance leader wove his 'Mech through the dolmen at the nearest edge of the plain, closing on Ryan's 'Mechs without being seen.

Opposite Tang's position, two more strange-looking 'Mechs entered the battlefield. Phelan's computer again vacillated in assigning a label to the new machines. _It's calling them_ Warhammers _because of the chassis type, but the addition of_ Marauder-_type arms instead of the particle projection cannons is giving it fits._ Both 'Mechs moved in on the trapped _Rifleman_.

Ryan's _Griffin_ turned its attention to Tang's approaching _Blackjack_. Phelan tightbeamed a warning to his Lieutenant, then brought his 'Mech around from behind the outcropping he'd been using for cover. Opening a widebeam broadcast, he snapped a challenge at the pirate captain. "Over here, you excuse for retroactive birth control. We're the ones you said would never get you. Move it. Let's prove natural selection was correct."

The _Griffin_ reoriented itself toward him, then Phelan saw it freeze for a moment. The _Wolfhound_ Phelan piloted had a humanoid form and walked upright, but its unusual silhouette gave most enemy pilots reason to pause. Its right wrist ended in the muzzle of a large laser, and three medium laser ports dotted its scarlet chest in a triangular pattern. Most startling, however, was the 'Mech's head and cockpit assembly whose design accented and heightened the implied threat of the _Wolfhound_'s lean deadliness.

The head had been crafted for both image and function. Its jutting muzzle and twin viewports combined with the upthrust triangular sensor panels on either side to give the _Wolfhound_ a canine appearance. Phelan had taken the image one step further and painted the 'Mech's muzzle to appear that the war machine was baring white fangs in a fierce snarl. Aluminum strips inlaid beneath the paint job outlined the teeth so that the 'Mech's wolfish grin appeared even on magscan and infrared sensor modes.

Phelan started his 'Mech down the hillside as Tang's *Blackjack* broke from cover and raised both its arms. The 'Mech's twin autocannons fired salvos at the pirate *Panther*. Phelan's computer marked the distance between the *Blackjack* and the *Panther* as 800 meters, putting the shot at the extreme edge of Tang's effective range. Despite the difficulty, Tang hit with one of his two shots, pulverizing armor plates over the *Panther*'s heart.

Picking up speed, Phelan worked his way through the debris scattered over the plain's near side. As he saw it, Ryan seemed more intent on running from the 'Mechs pursuing him than evading the Kell Hounds. *It's his funeral* ... With each jump, the *Griffin* came closer and closer to Phelan.

As the range dropped to 600 meters, Phelan brought his 'Mech to a stop and crouched behind the last house-sized boulder between him and the smooth valley floor. *One more jump and you're mine. Five hundred meters may top out my range on this large laser, but if Jack can hit at max, so can I. Come on, Kenny Ryan, let's get it over with.*

Phelan's right hand moved the joystick that dropped the golden crosshairs onto the *Griffin*'s broad chest. A dot in the center of the cross flashed red. Phelan hit the firing stud beneath his right thumb and felt a wave of heat wash through the cockpit as the large laser unleashed its beam of coherent light.

The coruscating beam stabbed into the *Griffin*'s left shoulder, blasting away steaming shards of half-melted ceramic armor. As though unsatisfied with the armor it had destroyed, the beam's terrible energy cut through the myomer muscles on the 'Mech's upper arm, which split like hunks of meat being torn to pieces by some beast. Lastly, the beam heated the ferro-titanium humerus to the point where it glowed white, further melting myomer muscles.

Ryan hit his jump jets at the last second, but it did nothing to mitigate the damage. The abrupt take-off wrenched the damaged arm badly, snapping the metal bone and sending the severed limb flying. Suddenly unbalanced, the *Griffin* reeled like a drunken acrobat and slammed into the ground on its right shoulder. The jump jets pushed the one-armed 'Mech across the plain, leaving sparks and armor plates in its wake until Ryan finally shut them down.

Phelan stared at the *Griffin*'s wreckage. *My large laser shouldn't have done that much damage! Those other guys must really have softened them up.* Phelan shifted his vision to the *Panther* Tang was sparring with. *Yeah, it's been hit all over, but most of the damage has been done to the legs and arms.*

A cold chill ran down his spine as Phelan realized the *Griffin* and the *Rifleman* had been similarly savaged. *Either those other guys are very unlucky, or they're placing shots with greater care than almost any MechWarrior this side of Jaime Wolf or my father.*

As if they had read his thoughts, the three unknown 'Mechs moved in. The one that had brought the *Locust* down came to a stop just over nine hundred meters from the *Panther* and brought both pods up. Twin large-laser beams flashed out and caught the *Panther* in the back of its thighs. What little armor still remained on the pirate 'Mech's legs vanished in a cloud of ceramic steam. Myomer muscles ran like water and boiled away where they touched the titano-magnesium femurs that held the *Panther* upright. The lasers amputated the *Panther*'s legs with surgical precision. Its legs cut out from under it, the *Panther* smashed flat on its back and did not move as the dust stirred up by its fall quickly drifted down to coat it with a red blanket.

"Blake's Blood! Did you see that, Phelan?" A tremble in Jack Tang's normally calm voice betrayed his unease.

Phelan stared at the computer projection of the range and damage done to the *Panther*. *Seven hundred meters for a large laser! That's impossible! They can only hit at 450 max.* He hit a button that opened a tight channel between him and Hound Leader. "I don't like this, Jack. Keep Trey and Kat out of this. Jesus Christ Almighty, look at what they've done to the *Rifleman*!"

The twin 'Mechs moving in on the last operational pirate machine simultaneously let fly with short-range missile barrages and bursts from their dual autocannons. The missiles covered the trapped *Rifleman* with explosions. The blasts staggered the machine and opened cratered wounds in its armor, which oozed melted metal. The pilot, fighting for control, somehow managed to keep the *Rifleman* on its broad, flat feet.

Phelan suddenly found himself hoping for the impossible, that the *Rifleman* could win out.

The gray 'Mechs it faced did not give the pirate a chance. Sparks lanced from the barrels of his guns as one of the pilots walked his autocannon fire along them and into the *Rifleman*'s right shoulder. Armor flew in a blizzard from the damaged limb, then an explosion flipped the arm up and out. It cartwheeled through the air, bouncing off several rocks before it crashed to the ground.

The second mystery 'Mech raked one stream of autocannon shells across the *Rifleman*'s belly. The projectiles ripped jagged scars in the 'Mech's armored flesh while the other autocannon's destructive fire gnawed away at the *Rifleman*'s already-mauled left shoulder. It sliced through the remaining armor and drive mechanisms with the ease of a razor carving flesh. The 'Mech's left arm lurched, then dropped toward the ground, only to be jerked to a halt by useless drive chains and belted links of autocannon ammo. Swinging slowly back and forth, the arm dangled like an ornament, mocking the *Rifleman*'s once-formidable destructive capabilities.

"Hound Deuce, I'm going to hail these guys. I'll offer them the salvage on these 'Mechs. Maybe they'll give us Kenny to take back and collect our pay."

Fear boiled up from Phelan's gut. "Jack, don't. Get the hell out of here." He started running the *Wolfhound* forward. *Move it, Jack! They're up to something!*

"Get back here, Phelan! That's an order!" Anger rippled through Tang's voice. "Dammit, follow my orders just for once!"

"And let you die? No way. Move it, Jack! Jump out of there!"

The two 'Mechs that had dusted the *Rifleman* locked their weapons down on the *Blackjack* in the plain below them. As they triggered their bursts, the *Rifleman* shot at both of them with its torso-mounted medium lasers. At the same time, Tang hit his jump jets, sending his 'Mech into the thin atmosphere on silvery ion jets.

The *Rifleman*'s attacks caught the mystery 'Mechs by surprise, spoiling their aim somewhat. Still, despite the distraction, the range, and Tang's jump, one of the pilots managed to hit with both autocannon shots. The depleted-uranium slugs zipped up the back of the _Blackjack_'s left leg. Its armor peeled off and fell away as if it were diaphanous silk instead of tons of ceramic armor. A silver spray of ions shot out at the back of the _Blackjack_'s thigh, starting the 'Mech into a slow spin.

"Feather the right jet, Jack! This rock's light gravity and thin air mean you can go further. Get clear!" _He'll make it if that other 'Mech doesn't take a shot at him!_ Bursting into the open, Phelan turned toward the first gray 'Mech he had seen. He brought the _Wolfhound_'s large laser up and triggered a shot, but being beyond his maximum effective range, the shot did nothing.

The first gray 'Mech launched two flights of LRMs at the slowly spinning _Blackjack_. Moving at ten times the damaged 'Mech's speed, the lethal rockets slammed into it mercilessly. Explosions wreathed both legs in golden-red flame, then a silver corona ripped the fireball in half. As the brilliant light of uncontrolled jump jets vanished, taking the _Blackjack_'s legs with it, the airborne 'Mech's arms flailed helplessly to counter the backward somersault the missiles had given it.

Jack's 'Mech tumbled to the ground. Armor flew whirling in uneven clumps, then the _Blackjack_'s domed head sheared off. It bounced halfway up the hill as the torso flipped and twisted awkwardly. The _Blackjack_'s body ripped itself apart as the autocannon ammo nestled in its breast detonated.

Hot, salty tears poured down Phelan's cheeks as he cut his 'Mech to the right. The first 'Mech's twin lasers burned parallel tracks through where he had just been, reducing iron ore to glowing slag. _There, dammit, you missed! You're not invincible._

BattleTech 1: WAY OF THE CLANS, Legend of the Jade Phoenix 1

by Robert Thurston

In the 31st century, the BattleMech is the ultimate war machine. Thirty meters tall, and vaguely, menacingly man-shaped it is an unstoppable engine of destruction.

In the 31st century, the Clans are the ultimate warriors. The result of generations of controlled breeding, Clan Warriors pilot their BattleMechs like no others.

In the 31st century, Aidan aspires to be a Warrior of Clan Jade Falcon. To win the right to join his Clan in battle, he must succeed in trials that will forge him into one of the best warriors in the galaxy, or break him completely.

In the 31st century, Aidan discovers that the toughest battle is not in the field, but in his head—where failure will cost him the ultimate price: his humanity.

BattleTech 2: BLOODNAME, Legend of the Jade Phoenix 2
by Robert Thurston

TRUEBIRTH—Born in the laboratory, these genetically engineered soldiers train to be the ultimate warriors. They are the elite pilots of the Clan's fearsome BattleMech war machines.

FREEBIRTH—Born of the natural union of parents, these too are soldiers, but pale imitations of their truebirth superiors. Despised for their imperfections, they fight where and when their Clan commands.

Aidan has failed his Trial of Position, the ranking test all truebirth warriors of the Clan Jade Falcon must pass. He is cast out. Disgraced. His rightful Bloodname denied him.

But with a Bloodname, all past failures are forgiven. With a Bloodname comes respect. With a Bloodname comes honor.

Aidan will do anything to gain that name. Even masquerade as the thing he has been taught to despise.

A freebirth.

BattleTech 3: FALCON GUARD, Legend of the Jade Phoenix 3
by Robert Thurston

A CLASH OF EMPIRES
In 2786, the elite Star League Army fled the Inner Sphere, abandoning the senseless bloodshed ordered by the Successor Lords. Now, almost three hundred years later, the Clans, heirs of the Star League Army, turn their eyes back upon their former home. Nothing will stop them from raising the Star League banner over Earth once again.

A CLASH OF ARMIES
For two years, the Clans BattleMech war machines have overwhelmed the armies of the corrupt Successor Lords. Now, at the gates of Earth the Clans must fight one final battle, a battle that will decide the fate of humanity for all time.

A CLASH OF CULTURES
For Star Colonel Aidan Pryde of Clan Jade Falcon the battle is more than a question of military conquest. It is an affirmation of the superiority of the Clan way, a way of life he has sworn to uphold despite his fear that the noble crusade has fallen prey to the lust and ambition of its commanders.

BattleTech 4: WOLFPACK
by Robert N. Charrette

THE THIRD AND FOURTH SUCCESSION
WARS
THE MARIK CIVIL WAR
THE WAR OF '39
THE CLAN INVASION

WOLF'S DRAGOON WON THEM ALL

Now, in 3005, the Dragoons have arrived in the
Inner Sphere. No one knows where they came
from—no one dares ask. They are five regiments of battle-toughened, hardened MechWarriors and their services are on offer to the highest bidder.

Whoever that might be. . . .

BattleTech 5: NATURAL SELECTION
by *Michael A. Stackpole*

THE CLAN WAR HAS ENDED IN AN
UNEASY PEACE ...

Sporadic Clan incursion into Inner Sphere territory supply mercenaries like the Kell Hounds
with more work than they can handle ... border
raids sharply divide the Federated Commonwealth's political factions, bringing further insta-
bility to the realm standing between Clan's goals
and anarchy.

And while secret ambitions drive plans to rip
the Commonwealth apart, Khan Phelan Ward
and Prince Victor Davion—cousins, rulers, and
enemies—must decide if maintaining the peace
justifies the actions they will take to preserve
it. . . .

BattleTech 6: DECISION AT THUNDER RIFT, The Saga of The Gray Death Legion
by William H. Keith, Jr.

WINNER TAKE EVERYTHING

Thirty years before the Clan invasion, the crumbling empires of the Inner Sphere were locked in the horror of the Third Succession War. The great Houses, whose territories spanned the stars, used BattleMechs to smash each other into rubble.

Grayson Death Carlyle had been training to be a MechWarrior since he was ten years old, but his graduation came sooner than expected. With his friends and family dead and his father's regiment destroyed, young Grayson finds himself stranded on a world turned hostile. And now he must learn the hardest lesson of all: it takes more than a BattleMech to make a MechWarrior.

To claim the title of MechWarrior all he has to do is capture one of those giant killing machines by himself.

If it doesn't kill him first.

BattleTech 7: MERCENARY'S STAR, The Saga of The Gray Death Legion
by William H. Keith, Jr.

AN OPEN BATTLE OF MAN AGAINST MACHINE

The Gray Death Legion. Mercenary warriors born out of treachery and deceit. Now the time has come for their first assignment serving as the training cadre for farmer rebels on the once peaceful agricultural world of Verthandi. And although MechWarrior Grayson Carlyle has the knack for battle strategy and tactics, getting the scattered bands of freedom fighters to unite against their oppressors is not always easy. But the Legion must succeed in their efforts or die— for the only way off the planet is via the capital city, now controlled by the minions of Carlyle's nemesis, who wait for them with murderous schemes. . . .

BattleTech 8: THE PRICE OF GLORY, The Saga of The Gray Death Legion
by William H. Keith, Jr.

THEY RETURNED AS ENEMIES
WHEN THEY SHOULD HAVE BEEN
HEROES

After a year-long campaign in the service of
House Marik, Colonel Grayson Carlyle and the
warriors of the Gray Death Legion are ready for
a rest. But there is no welcome for them at
home base. The soldiers return to find the town
in ruins, their families scattered, and their repu-
tations destroyed. Rumors fueled by lies and
false evidence have branded them as outlaws,
accused of heinous crimes they did not commit.
With a Star League treasure at stake, Carlyle's
need for vengeance against unknown enemies
thrusts him into a suspenseful race against time.
But even if he wins, the 'Mech warrior must
ally himself with old enemies in a savage battle
where both sides will learn. . .

BattleTech 9: IDEAL WAR
by Christopher Kubasik

FIGHTING DIRTY

Captain Paul Masters, knight of the House
Marik, is well versed in the art of BattleMech
combat. A veteran of countless battles, he
personifies the virtues of the Inner Sphere
MechWarrior. But when he is sent to evaluate a
counterinsurgency operation on a backwater
planet, he doesn't find the ideal war he expects.
Instead of valiant patriots fighting villainous
rebels, he discovers a guerrilla war—both sides
have abandoned decency for expediency, ideals
for body counts, and honor for victory. It's a
dirty, dirty war. . . .

BattleTech 10: MAIN EVENT
by James D. Long

BATTLES FOR A BATTLEMECH

Dispossessed in the battle of Tukayyid, former Com Guard soldier Jeremiah Rose wants nothing more than to strike back at the Clans who destroyed his 'Mech and his career. Dreams of swift vengeance turn to nightmares when every effort he makes to rejoin the fight to protect the citizens of the Inner Sphere is rejected.

Forced to win a new BattleMech by fighting on the game world of Solaris VII, Rose recruits other soldiers from the arenas to create a new mercenary unit and take his grudge back to the invaders.

Unfortunately, Rose is long on battle experience and desperately short on business skills. Turning a band of mismatched MechWarriors into an elite fighting unit becomes harder than he imagined when Rose is forced to fight his fellow MechWarriors in order to fight the Clans.

BattleTech 11: BLOOD OF HEROES

by Andrew Keith

HEROES FOR A DAY

Melissa Steiner's assassination ignited fires of civil war, and now secessionist factions clamor for rebellion against the Federated Commonwealth. The rebels plan on gaining control of the Skye March, and thus controlling the crucial Terran Corridor. Throughout the March, civil and military leaders plot to take up arms against Prince Victor Steiner-Davion.

The final piece of the plan requires the secessionist forces to gain access to the planet Glengarry and the mercenary group that calls it home: the Gray Death Legion.

When Prince Davion summons Grayson Death Carlyle and his wife, Lori, to the Federated Commonwealth capital, the rebel forces seize their chances to establish a garrison on Glengarry.

The rebels didn't expect the legion's newest members to take matters into their own hands. . . .

BattleTech 12: ASSUMPTION OF RISK

by Michael A. Stackpole

THE FUTURE OF THE REALM

Solaris VII, the Game World, is the Inner Sphere in microcosm, and Kai Allard-Liao is its Champion. Veteran of the war against the Clans, he daily engages in free-form battles against challengers who wish his crown for their own.

There is no place he would rather be.

Then the political realities of the Federated Commonwealth intrude on Solaris. Ryan Steiner, a man sworn to dethrone Victor Steiner-Davion, comes to Solaris to orchestrate his rebellion. Tormano Liao, Kai's uncle, redoubles efforts to destroy the Capellan Confederation, and Victor Steiner-Davion plots to revenge his mother's assassination.

In one short month, Kai's past, present, and future collapse, forcing him to do things he had come to Solaris to avoid. If he succeeds, no one will ever know, but if he fails, he'll have the blood of billions on his hands.

BattleTech 13: FAR COUNTRY
by Peter Rice

THE DRACONIS COMBINE

claimed the loyalty of regular soldiers and mercenaries alike. But while the soldiers fought for honor, the mercenaries, the MechWarriors, fought for profit, selling their loyalty to the highest bidder. When a freak hyperspace accident stranded both Takudo's crack DEST troopers and Vost's mercenary MechWarriors on a planet for which they had no name, survival seemed the first priority. But that was before they captured one of the birdlike natives of the planet and learned of the other humans who had crashlanded on this world five centuries before. Then suddenly the stakes changed. For Takuda was sworn to offer salvation to the war-torn enclaves of human civilization, while Vost was only too ready to destroy them all—if the price was right!

BattleTech 14: D.R.T.
by *James D. Long*

DEAD RIGHT THERE

Jeremiah Rose and the Black Thorns, flush with success against the Jade Falcons on Borghese, head to Harlech to draw a new assignment. Their only requirement: Their new job must let them face off against the Clans.

They find more than they bargained for. Their assignment: Garrison duty on Wolcott—a Kurita planet deep in the heart of the Clan Smoke Jaguar occupation zone. Wolcott is besieged, but protected from further Clan aggression by the Clan code of honor.

Wolcott makes a useful staging area for Kurita raids on Smoke-Jaguar-occupied territory.

The pay is good. The advance unbelievable.

But they have to live to spend it.

BattleTech 15: CLOSE QUARTERS
by Victor Milan

SHE WAS THE PERFECT SCOUT

Resourceful, ruthless, beautiful, apparently without fear, Scout Lieutenant Cassie Suthorn of Camacho's Caballeros is as consummately lethal as the giant BattleMechs she lives to hunt. Only one other person in the freewheeling mercenary regiment has a hint of the demons which drive her. When the Caballeros sign on to guard Coordinator Theodore Kurita's corporate mogul cousin in the heart of the Draconis Combine, they think they've got the perfect gig: low-risk, and high pay. Cassie alone suspects that danger waits among the looming bronze towers of Hachiman—and when the yakuza and the dread ISF form a devil's alliance to bring down Chandrasekhar Kurita, only Cassie's unique skills can save her regiment.

All she had to do is confront her darkest nightmares.

BattleTech 16: BRED FOR WAR

by Michael A. Stackpole

A PERILOUS LEGACY

Along with the throne of the Federated Commonwealth, Prince Victor Steiner-Davion inherited a number of problems. Foremost among them is the Clans' threat to the peace of the Inner Sphere—and a treacherous sister who wants to supplant him. The expected demise of Joshua Marik, heir to the Free Worlds League, whose very presence maintained peace, also endangers harmony. Victor's idea is to use a double for Joshua, a deception that will prevent war.

But secret duplicity is hard to maintain, and war erupts anyway, splitting the Inner Sphere and leaving the Federated Commonwealth defenseless. And when Victor thinks things can get no worse, word comes that the Clans once again brought war to the Inner Sphere. . . .

BattleTech 17: I AM JADE FALCON
by Robert Thurston

SHAME OR GLORY?

For years, Star Commander Joanna has had to live with the shame of the Jade Falcon defeat at Twycross, and the nightmares of the heroic Aidan Pryde flaunting his bloodname in her face.

Now, with the arrival of the new Star Colonel Ravill Pryde, who will lead them against the Wolf Clan, Joanna must once again fight for her chance to recapture the glory of her victory at Tukkayid. But will her advanced age bring her to defeat again, or will being a Jade Falcon be enough for her to take on the legendary Black Widow in a repeat battle at the Great Gash on Twycross?

BattleTech 18: HIGHLANDER GAMBIT

by Blaine Lee Pardoe

"AUTHORIZED TO SACRIFICE YOUR
PERSONAL HONOR . . ."

With these words Chancellor Sun-Tzu Liao dispatched Death Commando Loren Jaffray to the planet Northwind. His mission: to singlehandedly destroy the elite Northwind Highlanders, the mercenaries who abandoned the Capellans in their hour of need thirty years before. As the grandson of famous Highlander warriors, Jaffray is the perfect instrument to exact Sun-Tzu's revenge. He can win the mercenaries' trust, then divide the Highlanders from within to ignite a war for control of their homeworld.

But Prince Victor Davion is not about to give up this key planet without a struggle. And now, while Northwind and the rest of the Sarna March erupt in war, Loren must wage his own personal battle—one between honor and duty. A battle that can only be fought alone.

ABOUT THE AUTHOR

William H. Keith, Jr., under his own name and several pseudonyms, has written, at this point in the space-time continuum at least, forty-some novels ranging from science fiction to action-adventure to fast-paced military technothrillers. His expertise in military tactics, technology, and the epic theme of men at war has been showcased in several long-running series following modern aircraft carrier combat and the exploits of the U.S. Navy SEALs. *Warstrider,* a military-SF book series, explores the ultimate interface of man, machine, and alien. Bill's first love, however, is hard SF in the tradition of Arthur C. Clarke and Robert Heinlein.

Bill Keith has been writing in the BattleTech universe from the very beginning. His trilogy of novels— *Decision at Thunder Rift, Mercenary's Star, The Price of Glory*—introduced the now infamous Gray Death Legion and kicked off FASA's line of BattleTech novels. With *Tactics of Duty* he returns to BattleTech and the Legion. The Inner Sphere may never be the same again . . .

In 1996, the Legion will return in the sequel to *Tactics of Duty.*

Bill lives in the mountains of western Pennsylvania with his tactical coordinator wife, his combat-ready daughter, and four ninja-assassin cats.

YOUR OPINION CAN MAKE A DIFFERENCE!

LET US KNOW WHAT *YOU* THINK.

**Send this completed survey to us and enter
a weekly drawing to win a special prize!**

1.) Do you play any of the following role-playing games?
Shadowrun ———— Earthdawn ———— BattleTech ————

2.) Did you play any of the games before you read the novels?
Yes ———————— No ————————

3.) How many novels have you read in each of the following series?
Shadowrun ———— Earthdawn ———— BattleTech ————

4.) What other game novel lines do you read?
TSR ———— White Wolf ———— Other (Specify) ————

5.) Who is your favorite FASA author?
————————————————————————————————

6.) Which book did you take this survey from?
————————————————————————————————

7.) Where did you buy this book?
Bookstore ———— Game Store ———— Comic Store ————
FASA Mail Order ———————— Other (Specify) ————

8.) Your opinion of the book (please print)
————————————————————————————————
————————————————————————————————
————————————————————————————————

Name ———————————————— Age ———— Gender ————
Address ————————————————————————————————
City ———————————— State ———— Country ———— Zip ————

Send this page or a photocopy of it to:
FASA Corporation
Editorial/Novels
1100 W. Cermak Suite B-305
Chicago, IL 60608